*To all who strive to build
strong families and strong homes,
and to the Holy Spirit who enables us to.*

Acknowledgements

There are many people who have helped make this book what it is:

My husband, Milton, whose excitement and support have been very contagious.

My son, Joshua, who wants to be an architect.

My older girls, Chantelle and Jewelle, who read my manuscript and inspired Elise.

My younger girls, Danielle and Gabrielle, who had to be patient with me.

I so much appreciated the added knowledge from John Russell and Ben DeBruyn, Donato Gugliotta, and Stephen Farrell for their expertise in building, medicine, and law enforcement, respectively; any irregularities are mine.

Thank you Jerry Jewer for feeding me well on the work of the Holy Spirit, and Susette Gugliotta for handing me the Word Alive flyer.

Thanks to Sherry MacDonald for taking the time to critique parts of my manuscript.

I'm grateful to my dad, Rudolph Russell, for encouraging me to write, and my mom, Linda, who told me about my "special" grade school story, and my seven siblings who had to listen to my childhood "stories."

Thanks to Ricky Earle and Bruk Sinclair for sharing their biracial world.

I cannot fail to mention my friends, Yvonne Harriot, who challenged me to write, and Chris Lewis, who shares my passion for family and home.

Thank you, Holy Spirit, for ALL.

Chapter One

Elise turned off the main street onto a rural road. She felt she had gone this way before, perhaps years ago. It did seem curiously familiar. Three minutes into the pace of endless rows of trees, occasionally broken by private driveways, she slowed her car. She didn't want to miss her destination, and the property markers now seemed even further apart than when she had first started. It could be compared to a wilderness trek, were it not for the obviously affluent waterfront homes mixed in with the more modest, but modern homes along the way. This certainly was no wilderness trek.

She tried to relax her fingers from their clenched position on the steering wheel. Why should she be so nervous? Her right foot slightly touched on the brakes to allow the dark form of a darting squirrel to perhaps survive one more day. All too soon, her mind reverted to its incessant pondering about the real purpose for this trip. Perhaps she had read too much into what had been asked of her.

There, just ahead on the right, were the white numbers on a green 911 marker. She took a deep breath as she slowed her vehicle and pulled onto a rough, dirt driveway with thick walls of trees on either side. After driving a little ways, she entered a wide clearing, also surrounded by mature trees, that stretched about five acres to a large lake beyond. The amount of property that *he* owned went far beyond the clearing, but she wasn't yet privy to that information.

After pulling her keys from the ignition, Elise paused in the warm interior of the car to get her bearings. There were a lot of men working on a huge house in the centre of the property. Most of the structural framing, walls, and roof seemed to be completed, but the house was a long way from being finished.

How did I get myself into this? she asked herself. He had asked her to come and give her opinions of his "dream," and she had come even though she was uncertain about the wisdom of her decision. Certainly, she was doing him a favour as a friend, nothing more. He had shown the architectural plans to only a few people outside his work crew, and she had been one of them. His excitement had been contagious, and she had felt compelled to accept his invitation to provide a woman's view on this dream house of his. After all, he had no sister and his mother had died when he was just a teenager.

Taking a deep breath, she swiftly readjusted the hair band securing her long, curly, dark hair before exiting the car. She paused to zip up her lightweight jacket against the spring's chill, then faced the curious stares of the construction crew. It was painfully obvious why there was a gradual pause of activity on the yard site. As she gingerly stepped around construction debris, Elise scanned the vicinity of the house for a familiar face. Relief filled her when she saw one approaching.

"Mr. Alexander," Elise said, smiling at the sight of a thin, elderly man now a few metres from her. He was wearing a coverall and a white hard hat. As they closed the distance between them, she held out a well-manicured hand to firmly grasp his work-hardened one. Suddenly, she felt at ease.

"Elise Everson," Adam Alexander greeted her warmly. "It's been quite awhile. How are you?"

"Oh, Mr. Alexander, I've been doing well." She now covered his hand with both of hers. "You're right. It has been a long time, but I've been keeping tabs on you through your son."

His dark brown, almost black eyes squinted against the afternoon sun. "Ah, my son," he sighed. "It's really hard to keep up with him these days. As I slow down, his energy seems to increase." He chuckled deeply.

Elise sensed a pride in Adam's declaration. She moved in unison with him as he directed her toward the house. He started to talk again, then suddenly turned and shouted, "Okay, guys, it's not a holiday! You can all get back to work!"

Elise wanted to giggle as the men groaned good-naturedly. Mr. Alexander had definitely not lost the booming voice she remembered from ten years ago when he and his son Josiah had renovated her parents' house. She had been in this man's company occasionally over the years, but that summer held a special memory for her.

As Elise walked with Adam Alexander up the steps of a large front porch, she could hear the resumption of the work site activities. From her earliest blossoming into womanhood, she seemed to effortlessly draw male attention—a fact that had heightened her awareness of her femininity, but with which she had never been quite comfortable. Instinctively, she knew her capacity for great depth of emotions. She had witnessed too many broken hearts from fickle relationships gone awry; that should never have been. Nothing against men. Many of them were her friends, and she had come close to having romantic relationships with some of them, but something in her always seemed to resist. Waiting for… what? She wasn't sure. Perhaps *he* had something to do with it.

"This is huge!" She paused by the front entrance. "I've seen the drawings, but I'm quite amazed at its actual size."

Adam paused with a brown hand on the sturdy doorframe. "Wait until you get inside," he said, back to his usual quiet, deep voice. "It's really something."

The front porch ran the length of the two-storey house and stopped where the upper floor continued over a three-car garage, to the right of the house. It was a lot to take in.

"It's already taking my breath away, and it's not nearly finished." Elise followed the thumping of Adam's work boots through the double doorway into a spacious foyer. She paused to look around. It was impressive, and she could imagine its beauty once it was completed. Adam Alexander was a builder who had passed on his talents to his son. She knew that, at sixty, he was increasingly letting go of his family construction business, as his son took more of the reins.

Elise turned to see Adam conversing with one of the workers who had emerged from one of the doorways off the foyer. They approached her, and she was introduced to a medium-sized man with sandy brown hair. He was slightly covered in dust from his hard hat to his steeled-toed boots.

"Nice to meet you," he greeted her, then nervously wiped his hand along his jeans before taking her proffered hand. He dropped her hand quickly and seemed to have a hard time meeting her eyes.

Adam leaned over and patted him good-naturedly on the back. "This is the Critic," he drawled meaningfully.

4

"Ah, the Critic," came the echo with an ill-hidden chuckle. A nervous chuckle.

Elise eyed one man and then the other. She felt a need to put Jack at ease. "Critic? Mr. Alexander? Jack?" Jack was looking at his boots, so she focused on Adam. "Mr. Alexander, I have a sneaky suspicion you're referring to me."

Before either man could reply, heavy footsteps were heard descending the long, curved staircase adjacent to them. Before she saw him, she knew it was *he*. He practically bounded down the last few steps, stopping on the last one. His dark eyes were intense, yet full of laughter.

"You made it," he declared, his voice deep like his father's, sounding almost surprised. He moved off the last step and stood looking down at her. He was a giant of a man!

Elise looked up at him, suddenly feeling out of her element. "I did say I would come," she joked, wanting to sound lighthearted. Would she never feel totally at ease around him? After all these years... it was ridiculous.

Josiah Alexander's teeth were beautiful against his brown skin. "Well, you know the old saying: it's a woman's prerogative to change her mind." His father had joined him on the last three words.

Elise couldn't help but smile at their obvious camaraderie, even if it was at her expense. She noticed Jack still seemed ill at ease.

"Will you get a hat for her, Jack?" Josiah asked, still grinning. "We wouldn't want our best advisor injured at all."

"It's all right, Jack. You finish what you're doing and I'll get the hat," said Adam as he moved away.

"Thanks, Dad," Josiah called after his father.

"Nice to meet you," Jack said shyly. He glanced at her very briefly, then stared at the floor.

5

"It was nice meeting you, too," Elise replied, somewhat puzzled by his behaviour. Perhaps he was extremely shy. She watched him turn away before facing the remaining man.

Josiah was looking intently at her. She couldn't read his expression and she wasn't sure if she would ever get used to that strong gaze of his. He seemed to look deep into her eyes, into the essence of who she was. It was unnerving.

"Seriously," he began. "I'm really glad you're here. I want a woman's perspective, and I happen to know that you have quite a creative flair."

Before she could respond, Elise had to suddenly reach up and grab at something being placed on her head from behind. It was a hard hat. She turned quickly to see Adam Alexander's mischievous grin.

"Okay, you two, off to work with you," he said with a chuckle. "I'll hang around for about another half-hour."

"Okay, Dad. I'll talk to you later about those plans."

"Nice seeing you again, Elise. Don't be a stranger now," Adam said, in parting.

"I'll try not to be," she replied as he exited through the wide front doorway.

Elise turned back to face Josiah while adjusting the yellow hard hat so it settled snugly on her head. "Creative flair, you were saying. In case you've forgotten, my flair is not interior decorating, but music and languages."

He gave a hearty laugh. "Never mind. It's all creative genius to me." He gently took hold of her arm and directed her to the front of the house. "Let's start at the beginning, shall we?"

*   *   *

Josiah had tried very hard to keep the tour of his unfinished house light-hearted. This had proven to not be an easy feat. He had wanted the serious, thoughtful suggestions of the beautiful, intelligent woman by his side, yet he had also felt the need to curtail the great wonder he had felt growing in him—the wonder he was feeling now that she was here, with him, in this house. His home.

If he were brave enough to face his heart head on, he would acknowledge his hidden desire for it to be their house—their home. The very thought took his breath away. This possessiveness he felt toward her, could it be right? *God*, he thought, *You've got to help me out here.* No, she was just a good friend. He shouldn't feel such ownership of her. He was a believer and she was not. Yet, she was searching and interested in things of eternity—very interested. He and others had seen the hunger in her. He was impatient to have her realize salvation in Christ for her own sake, but he would be lying if he denied it was for his sake also. So he could… what? Declare his intentions, his desires? What if she didn't share his sentiments? What if he had been reading her wrong all along?

They were at the end of the tour, and he was watching her look out a tall, narrow window at the start of the second floor hall. Her slim figure was a perfect silhouette against the pale, orange glow of the late afternoon sun. She had declared that this spot would definitely need to be a sitting area.

"It would be so peaceful to sit here on a rainy afternoon with a good book," Elise remarked, her back to him. When he didn't respond, she turned to face him.

Josiah noticed a dreamy look in her light brown eyes and a slight flush to her honey brown skin as he joined her by the window. "I believe you're right," he said, before gently adding, "Though, I'm a little worried."

She frowned slightly as she looked up at him. "Worried? Why?"

With one hand on the window ledge, he leaned toward her. "I think you're falling in love with my house."

She laughed somewhat nervously. "I do not fall in love with houses. Admire them, perhaps, but not fall in love with them."

"Well even if you haven't yet, I'm sure you will." He leaned away from her. "How could anyone resist it? Just wait until it's finished."

She stepped a few paces away from him and continued to admire her surroundings. "My father asked about you," she told him. "He's pleased to hear that you've settled quite well into your father's company. When I told him it was your company now, he seemed quite impressed. He remembered when you worked with your dad on our house that summer. He said he had seen your passion for design even then."

Josiah perched on the windowsill. He was pleased also. It had taken much soul-searching to decide whether to continue with his father in the family construction business or further his education. He had chosen the latter, earning a degree in architecture. However, it wasn't just designing buildings that was in his blood; he loved to build.

He had to asked the question, "So, what do you think? Give me your honest opinion." He gestured to indicate the house.

Her laughter was like the tinkle of bells to him, and he thought her to be like a rare, delicate flower in the unfinished, rough surroundings. Yet, he knew her true constitution. She was not that delicate.

"I… I am quite impressed with it, if you haven't noticed already."

"Thank you." He let out a rush of air through his lips. "However, the job is not over. You'll have to come back when it's time for the cosmetic touches." There, he had said it. Would she back out now? He could almost see her hesitation.

"Oh." She clasped her hands tightly in front of her and shuffled some sawdust with an elegantly shoed foot. "Okay, if you want me to. Although an interior decorator might be better for you."

Somehow he knew she would go there. "Yes, I have thought about going that route, but I also want a more personal touch." He watched her brush some sawdust from the slender leg of her blue jeans. "Am I asking too much?"

Her eyes widened slightly. She reminded him of a wary doe. Yet he was the one who needed to be cautious. He could easily crawl past those heavy lashes and get lost in those eyes.

"I... No, I'd be happy to help," she managed, then seemed almost relieved at the sudden sound of booted feet on the stairway.

"Jo?" Jack's hard hat appeared, followed by the rest of him. "Sorry to interrupt, but we need you to look at something on the main floor."

Josiah gave his okay to Jack, then turned back to Elise. "Well, I guess we're done here. I really appreciate all of your insights." He gently touched her elbow to direct her toward the stairway. "Tell your parents they can visit any time we're on site."

She smiled up at him as they paused at the top of the stairs. "I'll do that. Though Mom might just relish taking over my role, and she definitely has the knack for decor."

Josiah chuckled as he followed her down. He hated to see her go, even though he would probably get little work done with her around.

Chapter Two

After leaving Josiah's unfinished house, Elise drove to her parents' place in the suburbs of Georgeton. The twenty-minute drive gave her enough time to process some of the unsettling thoughts that plagued her—thoughts that centred on Josiah David Alexander. No one could deny that he was an impressive, honest, and hard-working man. It wasn't him; it was her. She had yet to truly analyze why she felt so peculiar in his presence.

She had felt him to be a kindred spirit, from their first acquaintance, and that feeling had only grown over time. Part of that time she hadn't even been in his life; they had been two ships passing in the night. Yet, upon meeting again, whatever had started… continued. She instinctively knew he was aware of it, but they skirted around the issue.

Josiah's faith in God was deep and abiding. She was still searching. Yet the faith she saw in Josiah and her best friend Alisha pressed her more and more to end her search and acknowledge what she had found. But for the right reasons. She did not see God as someone to be trifled with, but One who wanted her complete loyalty. This was a new way for her to look at God. She had always supposed Him to be a far off being to be summoned for very important and serious matters. Perhaps her search had begun when she had sensed an emerging need for more from the Almighty—the Creator of the universe.

The familiar sight of her parents' circular driveway, against a backdrop of beautifully groomed perennials, created a welcome feeling of normalcy. Their spacious two-storey home, nestled in its garden paradise and situated on a neatly clipped expanse of lawn, also stirred feelings of nostalgia. This was still home to her, even though she had been in her own apartment for a year and a half.

Alisha had laughed when Elise had finally moved out of the nest, a mere fifteen minutes into the city of Georgeton. Elise, however, had determined, at twenty-three, to make a break from her parents' world. How else would she discover what life was really all about? It was becoming an increasingly powerful urge, this drive to discover life's truths about the forces at work around her.

"Let's see. You're a high school teacher of languages, the finest pianist friend I have, and a great cook," Alisha had announced grandly after Elise had revealed her heart. Then she had paused, green eyes intense on a pale face surrounded by glorious, red hair. "What you need is *God!*"

Elise had never unveiled to Alisha how those words had sent chills through her body. She had not understood her reaction herself. After all, she had been raised in church and was a good person. She just needed more time, more … answers.

"Mom," Elise called as she entered the front door of her parents' home. It was unusually quiet for a house which was usually gently filled with jazz or classical music.

"Mom?" She paused at a curved staircase rising to the second floor. Passing by the formal living room, she crossed the spacious hall and knocked gently on the door before her.

"Mom?" She cracked opened the door. Celia Boganda Everson was fast asleep in her favourite armchair. Elise felt a stir of concern; her mother never slept in the middle of the day.

Celia's eyes flickered opened after Elise's gentle tap on her shoulder. She seemed slightly bewildered, then her dark brown eyes focused on her daughter's face.

"Oh my goodness, Lise," she said softly, betraying a French accent. "I can't imagine what happened." Her hands rose to touch her shortly clipped hair. There was slight greying among her tight, dark curls, but no lines on her smooth, brown skin. Celia Boganda Everson was particular about many things, but grey hair was not one of them.

Elise pulled another chair close to her mother's and sat down. "You had me worried there. You rarely nap in the middle of the day. Did you forget I was coming by?"

Celia laughed as she straightened against the back of her chair. "Well, I guess wonders never cease." She gently ran her fingers along her high cheek bones.

"You okay, Mom?" Elise persisted.

"Really, my love, I am fine. I was actually just contemplating on your dad's situation."

Right away, Elise knew the "situation." "You mean that client?"

Her mother appeared somewhat uncomfortable. "Well, yes. I've never known him to be quite so consumed with a case."

"Especially when you're both supposed to be slowing down," Elise chided gently.

"That's true." Her mother smiled. "And I have slowed down, as you know."

Elise folded one slim leg over the other. "Mom, let's not go there. You know as well as I that you've cut back at the college, but you've increased your charity obligations." She leaned to rest her hands on her mother's slender wrists. "Dad talks about slowing down, but it's just that: talk. I don't know what to do with you two."

Celia sighed deeply and stood to her feet. Even at sixty-five, she still carried her tall, bony frame well. Her eyes roamed around the lavender walls of her den. They were lined with shelves filled with books and souvenirs from her many travels throughout the years. Also placed strategically on the shelves and displayed on the walls were many African artefacts from her Central African heritage.

Celia slowly crossed to the only window in the room and looked out. "My darling," she started, then paused uncertainly. She turned to look at her daughter. "Our lives have been busy. Your father and I have always had some sort of wanderlust, even before we met each other. After you came along, and have been our absolute joy, we only slowed down a little." She returned to her seat and sank gracefully into it. "When the time for change does arrive, it's hard to do."

Suddenly it struck Elise that her mother looked very tired; almost worn. Maybe she needed to visit home more often. Perhaps once a week was not enough.

"Now, I don't want you getting that worried look of yours," her mother cut into her thoughts. "Your father and I have never been better. Once we get over this hump of career decisions, we'll find a new niche in life and start all over again."

Spoken like a true Type-A personality, Elise thought. "Where is Dad? I thought he was home today."

Celia nodded. "Yes, he was supposed to be. He was called in for an emergency session with a patient."

"The client?"

"Yes."

"Oh." Elise studied her mother carefully. "Are you concerned, Mom?"

Celia met her daughter's gaze, then looked away.

"Mom?"

"Just a little. I…"

Elise rose from her chair and knelt on the plush rug before her mother. Light brown hands folded over dark brown ones. "What is going on, Mom?"

"Elise, really—"

"Mom."

"There is nothing to worry about. I've asked your father to drop this case and I'm sure he will."

"This client has proven to be dangerous then." It was more a statement than a question.

"Many of his patients have been mentally unstable, Lise. He's a psychiatrist. It's his job."

Elise looked up into her mother's strong, beautiful face. Her father had once revealed to her that it was her mother's face that had first taken his breath away. That she was also strong-willed and feisty under a calm demeanour had been the next thing he noticed. He, a confirmed European bachelor, had fallen for his African Queen. Over the years, he had continued to call her by that title. Elise sighed.

Even an African queen could be vulnerable.

"Dad is sixty-four, Mom. Maybe this guy should be assigned to someone else. You know... Someone younger... stronger."

They both turned at the same time and looked toward the partly closed door.

Elise rose to her feet. "Is that Dad?"

David Richard Everson could feel the tension slowly drain from his body as he entered his home. Unfortunately, his chosen profession didn't always stay at the office. Many times, it stayed with him against his will. The human soul, with its thoughts, emotions, and will, was complex.

He was at a place in his life where he needed to reduce his professional commitments. His family had been a part of this decision-making and, more than anything, he wanted to do it for them. He had come to realize that he really needed time to reflect, to enjoy more freely the life they had been given. God was vague to him, but he did believe He existed and that life was given, not just evolved. There were enough twisted personalities within his line of work to convince him of a "dark side." Philosophically, there had to be an opposite.

He just needed to get through this one case. It was special because he had known this client as a child. This man, who had once suffered horrible abuse at the hands of his parent, had grown up, even after many counselling sessions, to inflict the same abuse. Antisocial Personality Disorder was the diagnosis—a sociopath.

Although there was no cure for the disorder, David felt that somehow he was failing his client. The behaviour modification he earnestly sought for this man was ever elusive. Here was a man who, mostly, could work productively in society, but wounded those closest to him.

However, right now, his thoughts should not be on his failures, but his successes—his daughter being the prime one. He had noticed Elise's car in the driveway, and that had enhanced his sense of well-being.

From long practice, he held out his arms when he saw her head poking around the door of his wife's study.

"I thought I had missed you," he declared as he folded his arms around her slender form. She was twenty-five and was an exceptionally beautiful young woman, but somehow he couldn't really see her as anything more than his little girl, his daughter—the embodiment of Celia's and his love.

Elise didn't need to explain the total sense of security which enveloped her in her father's arms. It had always been this way. She looked up into his light blue eyes. They were the eyes of a man who had experienced a lot, much of it through the lives of those he cared for professionally.

"I'm glad I didn't miss you as well. How are you doing?"

Her father let her go, sighing deeply. "I'm doing quite well, especially with you here."

Elise laughed as her mother joined them in the hall. "Don't tell me you're still smarting over my moving out. It has been over a year," she declared, mimicking his English accent perfectly.

"I don't think I'll ever get over it, my love," he acknowledged. "But I do accept it."

They continued to banter as they moved into the formal living room. Elise sank into a cream-coloured sofa, her feet slightly hanging over its edge. Her father relaxed his long form beside her. *He's much too thin,* she thought. Her mother sat on the edge of a matching love seat, a watchful look in her eyes. It suddenly dawned on Elise that her mother was concerned about their earlier conversation. She sensed that her mother didn't want to broach the subject at this particular time.

"Remember we talked about Adam and Josiah Alexander the other day, Dad?" Elise asked, venturing down a safe path. "Well, I went to see the house that Josiah's building today. It's still in the early stages, but it'll be really beautiful." She could sense her mother's relief.

"Your father has told me that Mr. Alexander has relinquished much of his business responsibilities to his son." Celia smiled, encouraging the direction of the conversation. Mother and daughter understood each other.

"Yes," Elise confirmed. "Josiah now has a degree in architecture, which will probably bring more value to their business. Though Mr. Alexander plans to remain active in the business for a while so Josiah can also complete some sort of architectural internship requirement."

Her father stretched his long legs and loosened his tie. "I've always admired Adam Alexander. He seems like a man who knows just what life's about. One of the reasons I hired him years ago was his reputation for honesty." He glanced at his wife. "Perhaps we could have them over soon, my queen, for dinner. We had Adam over some time ago, didn't we? When was it again?"

Celia smiled at her husband. "Yes, it was after we became reacquainted at a community council meeting." She turned to her daughter. "I think you were in your second year of university, Lise. He had also extended an invitation to us once. I'm not sure why we never fulfilled it."

David ran a steady hand through his thinning grey hair. The dark brown colour had faded over the years. He was still a very handsome man, and Elise sometimes felt excluded when he and her mother would communicate with more than just words.

"We probably went on a trip, as usual, and life continued," Celia supplied. "In retrospect, it must have been lonely for him. I'm sure his son was in his fifth year of university at the time. Isn't that so, Lise?"

"Yes," Elise answered. "I'm sure you meant to include Mr. Alexander. You probably became preoccupied with your work and travels."

David laughed, then glanced at his wife. "Love, I think we're being chastised."

Elise smiled as he winked at her mother. There was that silent communication again. "Well, I, on the other hand," she teased, "have been to the Alexanders' on at least a couple of occasions. Remember their church group? You know, for young singles? They have had some of their meetings at the Alexanders'."

Her parents exchanged glances. "Is that the same church Alisha attends?" Celia asked.

"Yes," Elise responded. "She's the one who actually invited me to the group. She knows Josiah quite well."

"And you've been getting to know him as well." David straightened slightly beside her.

Elise began to feel somewhat uncomfortable. Had she thought this was a safe topic? "What do you mean, Dad?" She failed to conceal the wariness in her voice.

"Now, what is it that I mean?" her father questioned, rubbing his chin. There was a mischievous glint in his eyes. "Let me rephrase that. Have you been getting to know Josiah Alexander better?"

"Dave," Celia cautioned.

Elise suddenly felt as if she were in a shrink's chair. She also discerned in her mother's dark eyes what her father was really asking. She decided to be straightforward. "*Vraiment*, Papa," she said, switching to her mother's native tongue. "Why are you being so serious? Yes, I'm getting to know him better. *Mais, un ami, juste un ami.*" Her father hated French. Served him right.

"I think I get enough French from your mother, Elise." He rose and glared down at her. "Just as a friend, then?" His English accent seemed more pronounced.

"Would you prefer that in Spanish?" she teased, trying to diffuse a potentially revealing moment.

"I'm not one of your students," he growled. He focused on his wife. "Really, Celia, if our daughter is spending her time at a singles club and playing interior decorator to one of its male members, we should know more about it… and him."

"Dad, it's a church—"

Celia interrupted her daughter. "It's a church club, Dave, and Elise is of age. You are, perhaps, overreacting. If it bothers you so much, why don't you get on the phone to Adam Alexander and invite him and his son for dinner?"

"Mom!"

"Are you free for dinner tomorrow, Elise?"

"Dad!"

Celia now stood by her husband, both towering over her. So she also stood.

"Well, yes, but—"

"Okay, my queen, dinner tomorrow at… say… six-thirty. I'll make the call."

Elise's mouth hung opened. What had just happened? She held a hand out. "Wait a minute!" She brushed a stray curl from one eye. "What do you think you're doing? How did inviting the Alexanders suddenly become about me? It was you two who wanted them, because… because you had neglected them."

Her parents remained silent, speaking to each other with their eyes.

"I don't even live here," she finished lamely. *Drat!* She was protesting too much. They would notice that.

Her mother took pity on her. "Lise, we are being a little ridiculous." Celia laughed lightly. "Dave?" she beseeched her husband.

David had resumed sitting, his elbows on his knees. He searched his daughter's face carefully. Finally, he said, "Your mother is right, as always. Sorry, love. Let's start over." He reached out a long arm to pull her down beside him. "May we have dinner with you, Josiah, and his dad soon?"

Elise felt slightly breathless, wanting to escape from this surreal moment. She was also aware of a pair of brown and a pair of blue eyes watching her. Why did her parents have to be so antiquated? And why were they suddenly forcing this issue to the forefront of her life? She pulled her feet up into the softness of the sofa. "I have no problem, really, with you inviting them—and me. I just don't want anyone getting the wrong ideas." She laughed nervously. "We really are just friends."

"Fair enough," her mother said, and bent down to press her lips to her daughter's smooth forehead.

"Great!" her father pronounced. "I'll phone to confirm a date."

Elise grimaced at the choice of his last word.

Chapter Three

Elise's moderate apartment was filled with the sound of voice-mail as she listened to Alisha's message. She pulled the hair band from her ponytail and shook the mass of curly black hair behind her shoulders. All she wanted was a shower, herbal tea, her mother's cheesecake, the couch, and the television remote. She was bushed, and the sound of Alisha's voice lecturing her about unreturned calls was not a welcome one.

"Much as I love you, Ali, you'll just have to wait," Elise flung at the answering machine on her way to the bathroom.

An hour later, Elise's disposition was much improved. She had pampered herself as desired and was stretched out on the living room couch. She lowered the television volume before reaching for the cordless phone.

Without responding to Elise's greeting, Alisha got straight to the point. "Are you coming tomorrow or not? And why was your cell phone not on?" She had a dramatic, take-charge voice.

"I told you that I would," Elise responded mildly, ignoring the second question. Sometimes Alisha needed a balm. She definitely had legendary, red-haired tendencies.

"You said you'd confirm," Alisha reminded.

Elise could almost picture her friend's tight lips and flashing green eyes. She glanced at the room's digital clock. "Okay, Alisha. I only have a few assignments left to mark, so I'll be sure to nest early and meet you in the morning."

Alisha's sigh of relief was audible. "Great!" Then her voice softened, "So we'll meet at ten. I'm very excited you're coming."

"Ali, it's not as if I never go."

"You don't come enough," came the terse but gentle reply. "You haven't been to your parents' church in a while, either."

Elise ran slender fingers across her forehead. "I've been busy. Try being a high school teacher near the end of the term." Alisha didn't need to know her avoidance was purposeful. She wanted to put some space between her and what could be a real "religious" experience. She had been digging into her Bible, as Alisha and Josiah had suggested, for some time now. The increasing urge to pray beyond the usual ritualistic prayers, to allow a place deep within her to be touched by... God? It was somewhat frightening. How much would she have to let go of to let God in? Yet, she wanted—*yearned*—for so much more.

Alisha laughed. "Sorry. I don't mean to lecture. How did it go at Josiah's?"

Due to her earlier experience at her parents' place, Elise wasn't eager to explore this topic, either. She responded carefully. "Oh, it went well. It's an awesome place. I certainly learned a lot more than offered advice." They spoke for a few minutes about Josiah's unfinished house. It was a fairly safe conversation until Alisha's next question.

"So, what did Josiah think of your suggestions?"

Elise rolled onto her stomach. "He seemed quite grateful, actually. I was really surprised at how much he seemed to want from me."

"Really?"

"Yes. I mean, it's not as if it's going to be my home." As soon as the words were out, Elise wished she could revoke them.

True to form, Alisha pounced on the opportunity. "Well, not yet anyway."

Elise sat up. "What is that supposed to mean?" She was sure she heard muffled laughter. "Alisha?" she questioned, a warning in her tone.

"I… I'm sorry," Alisha sputtered. "Honestly, Elise, you're probably the only person unaware of Josiah Alexander's near worship of the very ground you walk on."

Silence.

"Elise?"

Silence.

"Come on, Elise, I've been dying to talk to you about it forever. Surely, you've seen the signs." Alisha paused for a moment. "Are you trying to tell me you haven't seen the signs? Are you trying to tell me you haven't noticed my hints about it?"

Elise could feel herself groan inwardly. "Ali, you're always hinting. If it's not one thing, it's another." She took a deep breath. "I don't really want to be having this conversation. I sort of had it with my parents today already."

"Your parents?"

"Nothing major." How could she down play this conversation? "They were just curious to know why Josiah asked for my input on his house. I assured them we are just friends."

"Wow, even your parents are starting to pick up on it."

Elise drew her knees up to her chest, then glared at the ceiling. "Oh, for Pete's sake, Alisha!"

"Sooner or later, girl, you're gonna have to come to terms with it."

After ending her phone conversation with Alisha, which had not been easily done, Elise retired for the night. She would have to finish marking the assignments tomorrow afternoon. She felt very unfocused and needed a retreat. Her mother sometimes teased her about being somewhat of a recluse despite being the offspring of world traveling social butterflies.

Admittedly, she had to agree with Alisha regarding the "hints." She had known that Alisha wanted to delve into the whole Josiah Alexander mystery, but Elise had simply not cooperated. Her feelings for him were rather confusing, leaving her somewhat off-balance. She had inherited her father's need for harmony and balance. Ironically, his chosen profession challenged him to the maximum to achieve some sense of that in other people's lives.

She had only been slightly acquainted with the Alexanders before they had done some extensive renovations on her parents' home. Josiah had been in his final year of high school, and she in her first. He had been difficult to miss; all six feet plus of him, and his extremely good looks demanded a second glance. With his physical traits and good scholastic and athletic abilities, he could easily have been arrogant and narcissistic. Surprisingly, he had been an all-around good guy, an outstanding example of leadership. His father had been, and still was, well-respected in the community.

She remembered when she had learned that Josiah's mother had died. Apparently he had been in his mid-teens. This knowledge had welled up such compassion toward him. She could not have imagined life without her mother, and she couldn't evoke anything to compare with the change that had occurred in her that summer. The summer of the renovations. To this day, she still found it difficult to fathom what had occurred in her heart.

Josiah David Alexander had touched her soul as no one else had. He had been unlike anyone she had ever met. Yet all he had done was treat her gently and with great consideration as, perhaps, a doting older brother might have.

Her parents had had no reason to suspect that her temporary depression for the rest of the summer had been due to the absence of that "remarkable young man." As youth often did, she had recovered and relegated herself to life without her tall, dark prince. There had been no other princes. None could compare.

Elise snuggled into the softness of her bed, as if to find some buffer for the open box of memories. How did she feel about Josiah? Until her last year in university, they had been like ships passing in the night. She remembered being shocked when, after studying one evening, she had checked her e-mail and had discovered a message from him. Alisha—dear Alisha—had opened Pandora's box when she had passed her e-mail address to Josiah.

What had been dormant in her for almost seven years had awakened to take her completely by surprise. She was still not over that surprise.

Was that her apartment intercom? Elise's thoughts of the past faded as she raised her head off the pillow. *It was.* The digital alarm clock on her bedside table declared it to be 11:15 p.m. No one visited her this late without calling ahead. The sound persisted, so she finally flounced out of the comforts of the warm bed. Someone was going to pay.

"Yes, yes," she answered impatiently once she had bumped her way into the living room. Her heart rate and breathing had quickened slightly at the unexpected interruption. She leaned her head against the wall by the intercom as she waited for a response. There was nothing. She tried again. "Hello, who is it?"

"Elise Everson?"

Elise hesitated, frowning. The voice was male and sounded strange, somewhat distorted. "Who is it?" She held her breath… waiting. "Hello?" Nothing. She stood back, peering at the pad on her wall, then glanced around through the gloom of the room.

When the realization hit her that she was clutching her elbows rather tightly, she took a deep, nervous breath and tried to relax. She couldn't imagine what that had been all about.

I guess he just changed his mind. She waited for any further interruptions, then proceeded to circle her apartment, checking her doors and windows before returning to bed.

Chapter Four

"Hi." Alisha seemed quite docile as she greeted Elise in front of Elise's apartment. The fresh gentleness of the mid-spring morning breeze lent itself to a more conciliatory approach.

"Hi, yourself," Elise greeted, "and yes, you're forgiven." She felt the brush of her friend's soft hair as they embraced briefly. It was hard to hold a grudge against Alisha. They had been friends since childhood. They were like sisters to each other. The only thing that had truly tested their deep friendship was Alisha's pivotal conversion to Christianity a few years earlier. Not Elise's brand of Christianity, but one that invaded one's entire life. One that required her to be a follower of Christ in *everything*. They had never discussed it, but Elise perceived that their friendship remained strong because Alisha would not rest until her best friend also became "saved" and bound for glory. In all honesty, Elise couldn't deny the lasting changes—for the better—that she had witnessed in her friend's life over the past three years.

Their drive to church in Alisha's car started out quietly. Alisha sensed that Elise was somewhat uneasy. This seemed to be a déjà vu occurrence of every church invitation Elise had accepted. She glanced across at her friend's hands clasped tightly in her lap. They were kindred spirits in spite of their differences. Although they were the same height and slender build, there the similarities ended. She envied Elise's honey brown skin that defied sunburns— the curse of the redhead. Elise was more quiet and reflective, while she tended to be more outspoken and, according to Elise, dramatic. The main point was that they clicked wonderfully and Alisha couldn't imagine a more perfect friend. Which was why it hurt so much, the knowledge that her best friend still needed her Best Friend of All Time: *Jesus.*

"I'm glad you're able to make it," Alisha said, breaking the silence as she glanced quickly at Elise. "And I'm sorry for pushing about Josiah." That earned her a piercing look. "Come on, Elise. It's just frustrating that you won't even talk to me about it."

Elise sighed and continued to look straight through the windshield. "What's to talk about, Ali? There's nothing going on between us. There never was."

"Come on, everyone can see the attraction that you two won't admit." It was definitely time to get things out in the open. Enough was enough. "You two have been skirting around each other for the past two years pretending you don't have a thing for each other."

"Ali!"

"It's true. I mean, at first you were just getting to know each other again, and you were really preoccupied with getting through your first year of teaching." She paused as she manoeuvred the vehicle through a difficult traffic spot. "You don't have to admit it to him. I just want us to be able to talk about it. We talk about everything else."

"Like you want to talk about Rick?" Elise threw at her, perfectly deflecting the argument.

Oh, she's good, Alisha thought. "Rick? What's to talk about?"

"Exactly!" Elise declared triumphantly.

Alisha turned her head, and they searched each other's gazes briefly. They had definitely come to a wall. "It's not the same," she countered, somewhat lamely. Elise's grunt confirmed the knowledge that they were probably in exactly the same boat. Rick. The man who drove her to distraction and thought people with "religion" needed it as a crutch.

"Besides, I'm a little worried about my dad right now," Elise said, steering to a different topic.

Alisha didn't miss the slight anxiety in her friend's tone. She willingly shelved the "men" topic. "Why? Is he still struggling with work issues?"

"Not work, per se. Just one client."

Alisha glanced over. "I'll keep it in prayer, okay?"

"Okay. There's something else, too. It's probably nothing, but I had a bit of a scare last night."

Josiah drew in a sharp breath. The church sanctuary, in fact the entire building, was architecturally impressive and was always overflowing with people on Sunday mornings. Yet one sight of her in the throng made him lose sight of it all. He had turned to converse with someone in the seat behind him when he glimpsed her through the glass doors of the sanctuary. Every time she visited, the same thing happened. He felt incredibly delighted and felt that she belonged. Before he knew what he was doing, he had made his excuses and was on his feet to the foyer.

Multiple attempts to shorten friendly greetings from all and sundry finally earned him a place in her vicinity. Alisha was introducing and reintroducing her to their church family. Elise was breathtaking and seemed totally oblivious to it. Her hair was pulled back from her face, but lay on her back just below her shoulder blades. Sometimes her curls were ringlets, but today they fell in waves. At the same moment he sensed her discomfort, she looked over at him. Her big brown eyes said, "Rescue me." At least, that's what he told himself.

"Hey, there," Josiah greeted as he approached her.

"Hi, Josiah," Elise returned. She smiled and moved slightly toward him as Alisha continued conversing with a young couple. "Well, here I am again."

"I can see that," he said, laughing softly as he turned to Alisha. "Alisha, I've got her."

Alisha nodded with a big smile. "Hi, Jo. I'll be with you two in a minute," she responded before returning to her conversation.

Josiah gently took Elise's arm as they stepped aside. "You didn't tell me you'd be here today."

She chewed her bottom lip, then responded brightly. "How could I have remembered when I was so busy taking in 'architectural amazement' at you house?"

He laughed, drinking in the smoothness of her skin, the curve of her lips. "Never mind. I'm just glad you're here. Are you getting used to us yet?"

Elise shifted to allow room for a toddler being chased by another child careening out of control. "Umm. Let me see," she teased.

"Maybe more used to everyone at the home meetings. But I'm kind of okay here, too."

"Really?"

She laughed. "You sound so hopeful."

He glanced around, realizing that he didn't have much time before the service started and Alisha joined them. "Elise, I am hopeful. We've talked about this before. You're seeking and testing the waters, so to speak. Alisha and I are offering what we know to be truth."

She reached out a slender hand to touch his arm. "I know, Josiah, but I have to do this in my own timing, too."

"God's timing," he suggested.

She sighed. "Yes, His timing. I just don't understand this relationship thing the way you guys do, this difference between 'religion' and 'relationship'."

"I know," Josiah assured gently. "It won't always be this way. The main thing is you've admitted your lack. Next you seek, and God will do the rest."

Elise glanced away to see Alisha coming, then looked back at Josiah. "You're a good friend, Josiah. I know you guys pray for me, and I appreciate it."

He desperately wanted to envelope her in his arms. She was becoming way too important to him, and the knowledge left him frequently restless. He had to constantly remind himself that she was not his and could not be his … yet.

After Alisha sat with them, they joined the congregation of Hope Alive Church in vibrant singing. Elise always felt a little lost—perhaps overwhelmed was a more accurate word—during this phase of congregational worship. People here seemed to really have a connection with their beliefs. They didn't seem to just be going through the motions. The contrast to her parents' church, where the Sunday rituals had lost meaning for her, was so evident. It had taken her a while and some honest soul-searching to acknowledge this to herself.

She couldn't help but feel slightly hemmed in with Alisha on one side of her and Josiah on the other. Alisha was a very enthusiastic worshipper and Elise couldn't quite decide whether she wanted her kind of freedom or was afraid of it. Josiah was an entirely different story. She loved the deep richness of his voice as he sang, but his presence beside her was a constant distraction. Occasionally he would smile across at her as if verifying her well-being. Those smiles were costing her that well-being.

Pastor Solomon Sung, the lead pastor, was now reading the announcements, so Elise focused her attention on him. He was a big Korean man who seemed to be filled with an amazing capacity for people. He never failed to have a meaningful word for her when he had opportunity to greet her. He had told her once that God had led her to church for a reason, and to keep returning until she found out what it was. Somehow that had stuck with her.

"Doing all right?" Josiah whispered in her ear. He smelled wonderful.

"Peachy," was the brief reply. He leaned closer, and she wished he hadn't.

"A bunch of us are going out after. Want to come?"

She blinked rapidly, feeling a little flushed. "Umm. I'm not sure. I'll let you know." He nodded and retreated. She sighed in relief.

"You okay?" This came from the other side of her.

She smiled over at Alisha. "Sure," she whispered. "You guys going out later?"

Alisha's green eyes sparkled. "Yes. I forgot to tell you. Want to come?"

Elise managed a nod before they were distracted by a petite blonde woman struggling to strong-arm two little kids down the centre aisle to the back of the sanctuary. She literally held her breath for the obviously distressed mother, as the littlest one, a girl, began to shriek in earnest. All heads once again faced the front of the room as the child's cry was cut off by the sanctuary doors.

"And may the Lord bless *all* mothers," Pastor Solomon joked. The amused hum of the congregation was warming. This was a "family."

Elise shook another stranger's hand for the hundredth time while waiting in the Hope Alive Church foyer. People were so friendly, especially some of the ones she had become acquainted with at the singles home meetings.

Josiah had been accosted by a desperate homeowner and his young adult daughter, who wanted some renovation advice. Elise couldn't help but notice the particular attention the daughter was paying Josiah, but she tried not to gaze in their direction too often. Surely, the unfamiliar feeling stirring within her was not jealousy. She watched Alisha instead, who was positively flitting around after finally accepting that Elise did not wish to flit with her.

She almost shrieked when she felt something warm and wet on the back of one of her legs.

"Oh my," she cooed, looking down into a pair of wide blue eyes. It was the little girl who had been wrestled out of the church service earlier. She had a huge smile on her chubby little face and very wet hands from, perhaps, drool.

"Oh, Mya!" The petite blonde woman was rapidly approaching them. She had another little girl in tow.

"I'm so sorry," the woman apologized in a tired voice.

"Please, no problem," Elise tried to assure her. "We're just having a little visit. She's adorable." She reached down and picked up Mya, who had her little arms raised in silent supplication, defying her mother. "I'm Elise Everson."

"Hi. I'm April Roper," the woman replied hesitantly. "It's so hard to keep up with these two sometimes." She seemed genuinely sorry, and Elise also detected a deep affection for her girls.

"How old are they?" Elise asked, eyeing the older child, who had shifted closer for her share of attention.

"Mya is three and Lily is five." April reached out to take Mya, who was now reaching for her mother. Lily immediately took hold of Elise's hand. They both looked amazingly like their mother.

"Hey, I see you've met the Roper gang." Josiah was leading Alisha and an entourage toward them. Elise hadn't noticed until now that the church foyer was considerably depleted of the earlier crowd.

"Yes, Mya and Lily seem to have become my special friends."

"Mommy's friend, too," piped up Lily. She smiled at Elise for the first time. Those big blue eyes seemed much too serious for such a young one.

April joined everyone's laughter. "Yes, Josiah, we've met your friend, and we think she's very nice. Don't we, girls?" The giggles that followed seemed to be in the affirmative.

Josiah touched April's shoulder gently. "Do you need anything?" The question seemed deep with meaning.

April lowered her eyelids momentarily, then looked up at him. "We're doing okay right now. Really." She was obviously aware of the eyes all around.

Sergeant Danny Rowe, whom Elise had gotten to know fairly well, stepped from the group to face April. "You promised to call one of us if you needed to," he reminded her. He was of medium height with dark curly hair and broad, reliable shoulders. Elise noticed a gentleness in his grey eyes as he spoke to April.

April clutched Mya closer, seeming to gather her strength about her. "Really, Dan, don't worry. I promised I would."

"All right," Dan responded before turning to face the group. "Give me a second and I'll help April strap the girls into the car. I couldn't convince her to come with us, girls and all."

April rolled her eyes. "I told you I couldn't get a sitter and you've never seen these two in a restaurant." They continued to banter as he led them away, his dark hair contrasting sharply with their fairness. Suddenly April turned around and waved. "Nice meeting you, Elise."

"You too. All of you, bye," she responded enthusiastically, returning the wave.

Alisha answered Elise's questioning look with, "It's a long story."

"All right, gang, let's break it up," Josiah said. "I, for one, am a starving man, and I'm sure my little friend here is a starving woman." He draped a big arm possessively around Elise's shoulders.

"When are you never starving?" someone challenged.

"When I'm about to whup someone, that's when." With that, he tore across the foyer after a tall young man. The group of about eight or ten followed much more slowly, as Josiah and his victim barrelled out the front doors.

Amidst the chatter, Alisha spoke for Elise's ears alone. "Now there's a man who's worth *something*." There was a definite mischievous gleam in those green eyes.

Elise wasn't being baited. "Your point being?"

Alisha laughed out loud as she tucked her arm through Elise's and almost dragged her out of Hope Alive Church. "Time will make the point, kiddo. You'll see."

Chapter Five

After an enjoyable lunch with Josiah, Alisha, and the others, Elise found it very difficult to concentrate on the work at hand. She needed to buckle down and be prepared for the school day tomorrow. This was her second year of teaching and summer break couldn't come soon enough. She loved her profession and couldn't imagine doing anything else, but some students, and some parents, needless to say, took more patience than even the biblical Job had. The problem seemed to be an amalgamation of all of life's issues.

She worried about her father and this case that seemed to be haunting him and she worried about its effect on her mother. Josiah was becoming more and more central to her life, and she needed to know *God*. At least, that's what Alisha told her. Would she find satisfaction in Him? How did one know God?

"You talk to Him… you know, pray," Alisha had instructed. "Then you listen to Him by reading the Bible and listening for His voice through your conscience."

Alisha had informed her that God's Spirit, or the Holy Spirit, spoke to people through an inner voice like a conscience. Life was so busy. How did one find the time to figure all that out? Yet something needed figuring out for her.

The phone interrupted her musings and she felt like flinging something at it.

"Hello," she said, unable to help the exasperation in her tone.

"Was it something you ate?" Josiah's laughter sounded through the receiver.

Elise dropped her pen on her desk. She was mortified.

"Oh, Josiah, I didn't know it was you," she said in apology. "Not that I should be this way with anyone," she conceded. He continued to laugh. He had such a nice laugh.

"I just wanted to see if you got home okay and to thank you for being such a good sport with everyone."

"You're welcome, I guess. You were the ones who were really good to me."

"Yes, but it must be difficult to have to meet so many people, especially when they're mostly fanatics about Christ like Alisha and me."

She leaned back in her swivel chair. "Oh, Josiah, you guys are cool. I think you're all great."

"Well, I also wanted to tell you I appreciated you being so nice to April Roper. You know, the woman you met with the two little girls?"

"They are a cute family." Elise finally asked him what had been bothering her: "Where's the dad?"

"That's the problem. They're estranged."

"Oh." She felt a rush of sadness.

"He's been physically and verbally abusive to her. Not to the girls." There was pain in his voice. "To the girls, he was neglectful. Almost like they didn't exist."

"Do you know him?"

"Yes," he sighed. "As far as I know, he's getting professional help, and I'm trying to be there for him. It's otherwise in God's hands."

She felt compelled to ask, "Do you think God becomes involved in situations like that?"

"In any situation, Elise. Nothing is too big or small. If we're willing, He helps us with what we can do, then he does what we can't."

"It says that in the Bible?" She eyed the one sitting on top of the computer printer on her desk.

"Yeah, it does." He made her feel warm—very warm and safe. Josiah, not God. She still needed to know God. "I know you had some work to finish up. I actually have some house plans to go over, so I better get going." Did she detect reluctance?

"Okay," she said. "Thanks for everything." She wished he wouldn't hang up.

"For everything, like what?" He didn't seem to want to.

She played along. "You know. Lunch, the pep talk, being a good example."

"Such as…"

"They look up to you, the guys at your church. I can tell." She wasn't just flattering him. She meant it.

"I've got my struggles, Elise," he said, pausing for a moment. "I constantly need His grace and word in my life each day. I can't stay on the straight and narrow on my own. Sometimes I've taken a detour, but He always, somehow, leads me back. I… I'm actually really struggling with something right now."

She waited for him to elaborate. When he didn't, she said the first thing that came to her mind. "Is it something I can help you with?"

The huge volume of laughter was quite unexpected. Wasn't he being serious?

"Elise … umm … no. *You* can't help me with this one."

She felt somewhat indignant. "Why not? Is it architectural or something like that?"

He was quiet again, then sighed deeply. "I promise I'll tell you about it sometime. I'm hoping you can help me with it one day."

"You do?" she asked. He was being very confusing.

"*Un jour*," he confirmed.

"Nice French," she assured him, laughing. "One day. Okay, I'll accept that for now."

"Good girl."

"Girl! I'll have you know I'm a full grown woman who's been independent for almost two years now." She was standing.

His laughter was quiet this time. "I know, Elise. Believe me, I know that you are a *woman*. My apologies."

"Why did you say *woman* like that?" What was wrong with her? They needed to get off the phone.

"Like what?" he threw back at her.

"You know what I mean," she countered. She felt her adrenaline flowing.

"Okay. We're ending this conversation right now."

"You started it," she chided.

"And what grades do you teach?"

"Watch it, buddy."

"Good night, Elise."

"Josiah …"

"Good night, okay?

For a moment, they were silent. Elise felt breathless. What was happening? "Okay. Good night."

"We'll see you Thursday for singles?"

"I think so." Why did she feel like crying? She wanted him to say "I" instead of "we."

"Take care," he added gently.

"Bye," she responded and hung up.

Josiah collapsed on the edge of his bed. Before his head reached the pillow, he started in on God. "Okay, this is getting way too big for me." He flung his arms across his forehead and groaned. "How do I continue to help this woman to You when all I want to do is help her to myself?"

He jumped out of the bed and crossed to the condo's wide window. He looked out over the city of Georgeton. It wasn't a really big city, but it had been his home for most of his life. Now he was building a house outside of it, where he would still feel connected to it. He had so much.

His church was here. He had a great career. He didn't ache so much about his mother's death anymore, and his father was one of his best friends.

He moved away from the view in frustration. He had his choice of many women. They made it quite clear on a regular basis at his church and in his community. The problem was that not just any woman would do. The house he was building was meant for one particular woman. The only person he wanted more in his dream house than this woman was God. God in his house. That was a given.

The one person who threatened his commitment to his Saviour was this woman. He wanted her, but she could not belong to him. She was not his Lord's… yet.

He sank back down on the edge of the bed, his face raised. "What do I do? How do I walk this path, my God—my King?" Even as he asked, Josiah felt the familiar presence of the Holy Spirit, the soothing balm. It wasn't always this way, but many times it was. He could feel God's assurance in his soul as surely as he knew there was a bed beneath him. Somehow he knew he would be okay. If he walked with his Lord, it would all work out for the good. God's Word had promised. He just didn't know how hard the road was going to be, but he knew enough to rely on God's grace for it.

The night air was chilly, but it was somewhat welcoming to refresh her cluttered mind and soothe her churning emotions. Elise hugged her long, spring coat around her as she leaned against the third-floor balcony wall. A gentle breeze stirred her hair as she gazed below at the park-like landscape at the rear of the building. The city lights glittered around.

"Dear God," she whispered, warily acknowledging her sense of Him. The more she thought of Him and read her Bible, the more she sensed His presence and the more she yearned to connect with Him. To truly know her *eternal* purpose. "I'm not sure what holds me back from surrendering my life to You."

She looked above the city lights to the ones in the dark heavens. It was hard to break the self-sufficient mould her parents had raised her in. Perhaps she doubted God's existence. No, that wasn't it; it was believing He existed, and having to face the awesome question of what that meant for her life—her will. Letting go of one's will, one's own way, was a hard thing.

She thought of the increasing strength of her feelings for Josiah, feelings she was reluctant to face head-on. Would surrendering her life to God also help her with that? Alisha said that God was interested in every facet of human life. Her whole being seemed to gravitate to this notion of such a Creator.

"Help me to know if You are Who the Bible says You are." She closed her eyes, almost oblivious to the faint sounds of petering human and vehicle traffic in the vicinity of her apartment. "Help me surrender my life to You." She opened her eyes.

A movement below, close to the building's rear, narrow driveway, caught her attention. She eased off the brick wall and crossed the concrete floor to the balcony rail. It appeared to be the form of a man separating from a tree, and he was looking up at her. Perhaps she was mistaken. She grabbed hold of the rail and strained to see better. He stayed on the edge of the lawn by the driveway, and he *did* seem to be staring at her, but it was too dark for her to recognize him.

Elise looked at the balconies on either side of her and saw nothing that could have warranted his direct scrutiny. Then she remembered the intercom interruption from the night before. She slowly turned and made her way back through the patio doors to the warmth of her apartment. After closing and locking the doors, she stood there for a moment, contemplating.

She took a deep breath before opening the doors once more and returning to her previous position on the balcony. He was gone. She chided herself for overreacting.

Chapter Six

It was Wednesday, late afternoon, and Elise had remained after school to work while waiting for her mother. She glanced absentmindedly at her watch as she finished arranging some assignment folders. Where was her mother? It wasn't like her to not be punctual. A sound drew her attention to the classroom door window. The low heels of her shoes thumped loudly in the empty room on her way to the door.

It certainly was an unusual sight to see her mother talking to Pastor Solomon Sung. They seemed to be quite engaged in conversation, as Pastor Solomon's adopted twin sons looked on with the bemused expressions typical of teenagers. Elise continued to observe for a moment and was starting to feel as mystified as the two boys. Her mother's pose had its usual elegance, but there was an intense expression on her face as she literally leaned into Pastor Solomon, it seemed, to capture his every word.

Elise was about to open the door, when a form suddenly blocked her view of the little gathering across the hall. She pulled opened the door in frustration.

"Webster," she said, purposefully keeping her voice low, but with a bite. "How many times are you going to scare me by popping up at the door like that?"

Webster Myers, head of the English department, shook his head in mock mourning. "Elise, Elise, why do you constantly barrage me so unfairly?" He reached behind him to close the door, then crossed to the nearest desktop and settled on it. He was immaculately dressed, as usual, in a white shirt, dark tie, dark sweater vest, and shining black shoes. There was hardly ever any variation.

"Your mother and the minister?" His shaggy brown hair, the only part of him not quite put together, flicked in the direction of his nod toward the hall.

Elise sighed and crossed to her desk. She grabbed her handbag and briefcase. "I'm not quite sure what that's all about. My mother and I are supposed to be going out for an early dinner, but I know she still wonders what it is about Hope Alive Church that has pulled me away from our family church." She gave him a pointed look as he adjusted his glasses over his hazel eyes. "However, that is not to detract from the issue of why you keep doing that."

His long face took on the most innocent of expressions. "Doing what?" He raised his lanky frame off the desk. "I should warn you."

She gave him her full attention.

"I know you and Keisha have been discussing many spiritual issues. You've probably been getting a good dose from Solomon Sung as well, but Christianity is not all it's cracked up to be." He seemed so serious.

"Shouldn't I judge that for myself, Webster?"

His gaze shifted. "Well…" He faltered. "I'm not saying it has no merit. I just happen to believe it's a fairytale."

She sighed. "Okay, Webster. Thanks for your input. As for the other issue…" Elise glanced toward the hall. Her mother was looking her way now. Elise smiled and gave a little wave. "…I *have* been out with you, Webster."

"That was with others—for you and Keisha—in celebration of your first year of teaching." He moved slightly toward her, an almost woebegone expression on his face. "It's been almost a year since then, Elise. I'm just asking for one—just one—dinner."

Elise pursed her lips together. She was having a hard time keeping a straight face. It was difficult to know how to deal with Webster, at times. To her colleagues, he was known as "the Walking Dictionary"—to the students, "the Brain." To her, he was a persistent suitor who refused to take no for an answer. She was fairly sure she had given him no encouragement.

Thankfully saved from yet another "pleading" session with Webster, Elise focused her attention on a knock at the classroom door. Solomon Sung poked his head into the room.

"So sorry to interrupt."

Elise moved quickly toward him, noticing her mother now engaged with the twins in conversation. "Oh, no interruption," she said, eyeing Webster.

Webster sidled toward the open door. "Good to see you, Solomon," he greeted.

"Webster," Solomon responded, reaching to shake Webster's hand before he exited the room.

Elise breathed a sigh of relief as she focused on the big man before her. He had a huge smile on his wide face—a very friendly face. She had seen fire in his dark eyes when he preached God's word with intensity. She had also seen great compassion and sadness as he dealt with his sheep— the people in his care.

"Your mother is an amazing woman," he surprised her by saying. "She bluntly asked why, in the past year, you've attended her church maybe a couple of times, but have seen fit to attend mine much more."

Elise glanced into the hall, but couldn't see her mother. She was anxious to know what had transpired between her mother and the pastor.

"She asked you that?"

He chuckled. "That and much more. It was certainly an opportunity to share with her. I wished I'd had more time with her." He raked his big hand through his closely cropped hair. "She instructed me to tell you she's waiting in the parking lot."

"Okay. Thanks."

"I don't want to take up too much of your time. I just want to know how things are going with the boys." He smiled and scratched his neck. "Their mom, you know, she's anxious to know how the last leg of their first year in the public school system is going."

Elise smiled back and shook her head knowingly. "Oh, Pastor Solomon, just keep telling her what I've told you both before. They are wonderful boys. She did a beautiful job home schooling them in their elementary years. I know she was most anxious about French, but they have been doing very well."

Elise remembered when Joshua and Jordan Sung had first come to her classroom. She couldn't have told them apart if she had been offered a million dollars. Now, months later, she knew. She realized the boys weren't sure how well she knew, but she knew. Sometimes Joshua and Jordan used their identical looks to be mischievous in a good-natured way, but they seemed to have settled into the realization that they were no longer able to trip up Mademoiselle Everson. She, in turn, took delight in their fresh and less tarnished outlook on life. Perhaps being home schooled had done that for them.

"I appreciate that," Solomon said. "How about you? How are you doing?"

Instinctively, Elise knew what he was really asking. "I… I'm okay. Josiah and Alisha have been great." She paused, surprised at the welling emotions in her chest. "I've really been drawn to reading my Bible. Sometimes alone. Other times with the help of a devotional." She glanced up at him. His eyes had such a tender look.

"Pastor Solomon, I have to be honest with you. I thought I knew what being a Christian was all about. I believed in being reasonably religious." She ran a finger across her forehead. "Now, I'm not sure. I feel such a hunger for so much more."

"That's what He wants of you, Elise," he counselled gently. "He wants that hunger."

She held his gaze momentarily.

"After talking with Josiah and Alisha, and attending the single's group, do you feel you're ready to meet with me?"

Suddenly she felt an inexplicable sense of purpose—of rightness. Yet she hesitated. "I… I think I need more time to sort through some things. Maybe talk to Alisha and Josiah some more."

He smiled his understanding. "You do that, and Bethany and I will be praying for you."

Elise left the high school building to meet her mother in an almost empty parking lot. The weather had been much milder in the last few days and she felt like a goat kid, ready to be carefree, to run, jump and skip around. She felt ready for something fresh and new.

She could see her mother's silver BMW in the visitor's section, a little way from her own vehicle. Before reaching her mother's car, she happened to look across the city street at one of Georgeton's elementary schools. Perhaps it was the solitary figure of a man outside the fence of the now deserted school property that drew her attention. He was standing very still, gazing into the schoolyard. Something about him seemed familiar, but Elise couldn't be sure at such a distance.

"Sorry. I got held up, Mom," she greeted her mother. She bent toward the car window.

"You do keep busy, don't you?" Her mother's smile was warm, in spite of her words. "Are we good to go?"

"I'll follow you," Elise said, then turned toward her gold-toned Corolla. She threw her handbag and briefcase onto the back seat before sitting in the driver's seat. She grabbed her seatbelt, then looked across at the elementary school again. The man was still there. Something about the whole scene seemed sad to her, almost as if she could feel his aloneness. She gave her head a little shake, then started the vehicle. It wouldn't do to keep her mother waiting any longer.

Celia Boganda Everson carefully watched her daughter as they ate their dinner at one of their favourite mother-daughter restaurants. David was at a working dinner, so she felt this was an opportune time to have some quality "woman" time with her daughter. This precious gem of theirs was who she and her husband had set their hopes and dreams on. They had lived and were still living a full life, but nothing quite compared to a young life full of promise. It, in some way, extended one's own life.

Celia believed in doing well in life. She believed in doing and being "good." For her, belief in a creator, or God, simply made sense. Too much was unexplained without some divine entity.

She had left her Central African home as a curious teenager when her parents had immigrated to Britain. There she had met David, the love of her life, while still a university student. What she had known of Christ was what she had learned from the helper who had kept her family home and cared for her and her now deceased parents and brother. In her and David's newly adopted country, Canada, they had continued to practice a very private, religious Christianity. After their only child was born, they had raised her with high moral expectations and regard for all life.

Yet here was her daughter, with the notion that all that wasn't enough for her. Perhaps it was simply a journey Elise was on, searching for meaning. A parent's way was not always their offspring's choice. However, this minister, Solomon Sung, had made an impact on her, if only from a brief conversation. He had obviously made a greater impact on Elise.

Retrospectively, all of this had started earlier, even before Solomon Sung. Even before Elise's friends' influence. Elise had had a restlessness before this. She had asked a lot of questions they couldn't answer—even her psychiatrist father. Celia had not understood this intense need in her daughter. She remembered discussing with David that maybe it was the result of over-indulgence coming to roost in their daughter. David had vehemently disagreed. He felt they had made every effort to raise their daughter with a good and strong sense of values. He had reminded her how Elise had been required to hold summer jobs once she had turned sixteen, even though it had not been necessary for her to work. She had been strictly raised on the Golden Rule: to treat others as she would want to be treated.

"Mom, it's not that I think anything is wrong with our church," Elise elaborated for, it seemed, the hundredth time. "It's something I needed to do. I just needed a different approach, I guess." She dabbed the corner of her mouth with her napkin. "I'm more aware of spiritual truths than ever before. It's sort of like having my eyes suddenly opened. I mean, really opened."

Celia raised her hands in mock surrender. "Darling, I'm not questioning your decisions or your spiritual needs. I'm just trying to understand."

"Are you really, Mom?" Elise looked deeply into Celia's dark eyes. "We seem to go down this road so many times."

Celia laughed gently before sipping from her glass of water. "We do, don't we? I really don't do it intentionally, at least not most of the time. It just seems to happen." She glanced around the dimly lit restaurant. "So much seems, well, to be changing." She focused on Elise. "Look at Alisha, she is amazingly different. Her character, her lifestyle. Who would have thought that wild child would have turned out to be a Bible-toting church goer?"

Elise had to giggle at the analogy. "Oh, Mom, really. Ali wasn't all that bad."

"Really? She gave your dad and me some cause for concern, especially when you two became like inseparable twins." Celia reached across the table to pat her daughter's hands. "You both turned out great."

"Thanks, Mom."

As her mother released her hands, Elise couldn't help but feel a deep appreciation for the woman her mother was. In spite of her busy schedule, she always took time for her daughter. Elise cared deeply for her parents, and though the natural progression was to build a life outside of them, she believed they would always have a strong connection to her—a strong bond.

"You should both visit some time," Elise suggested.

Celia's eyebrows raised. "Hope Alive Church?"

"Yes. Why not?"

Celia shifted slightly in her chair before responding. "I'll think about it. That Solomon Sung certainly has me thinking. Your father, though, likes certain things to stay traditional."

"I'm not asking you to join the church, Mom. I haven't even joined it. I just like the people and the down-to-earth messages. And the music, well, that's a whole other story."

Her mother seemed to catch on to her light-heartedness. She clasped her long, brown fingers together and smiled. "Perhaps your father might appreciate that part of it. He seems so burdened lately."

"He still doesn't want to let go of this case, does he?" Elise leaned toward her mother. "You know what? I'm going to ask my group to pray about it. They pray about practically everything, and they also like to share the results."

"And do they get results?"

"Well, yes. Though, not always what they expect."

"Well, it certainly can't hurt," Celia conceded with a faint smile. "Let's hope for the best until our cruise."

"Did you change back to the original date?"

"Yes. I decided the sooner we get away, the better. Let someone else worry about the world's ills for a while."

Her mother's words surprised her. Celia Boganda Everson usually wanted to take on the world's challenges. Many of her trips had taken her back to her birth country to contribute in charitable ways. Certainly, this was another sign that her parents were slowing down.

"Shoot." Elise suddenly remembered something. To satisfy her mother's curious look, she said, "I was hoping you would have been around to help me with Josiah's house."

"Josiah's house?" Her mother's expression was doubly curious now.

Elise shifted uneasily in her seat. What had possessed her to bring this up now? "It's nothing much. He just wants my advice on the décor, when it's time. It will probably be mid-August. You'll still be away then."

"Why you? There are interior decorators."

"Yes, I know. He's going to use one, but he also wanted a more personal touch." She nearly gulped her water.

"So he chose you?" Her mother seemed quite incredulous. "Elise Diara Everson, what is going on between you and Josiah Alexander?"

Chapter Seven

Josiah pored over the broad sheets of plans covering the crude work table before him. All seemed to be going well with his house, but sometimes he felt the need to stay awhile after the crew had cleared out. They had broken ground early spring and hoped to be finished by fall. It could have been sooner, but he was borrowing the men strategically, in order not to deplete the numbers needed at the company's major commitments. Alexander Contracting Company was doing well, and he wanted to keep it that way. Soon, he hoped to make it Alexander Contracting and Architectural Design. He felt grateful because the Lord's blessing was evident in all areas of his and his father's company.

He set the plans aside and plopped down on a nearby stool. Hadn't God felt this way after His creation was completed? This house wasn't completed, but it was certainly looking *good*.

Josiah returned to his feet and grabbed his work shirt off the table. Now that the evening was approaching, a bit of late spring chill was in the air. He pulled the checkered shirt over his dark blue t-shirt before heading out the front door. He had heard the sound of a vehicle arriving in the driveway. The front porch lights were functional, but weren't necessary due to the longer daylight hours.

He hadn't realized he was holding his breath until he released it. It was Elise's car. She had parked a fair ways from the house, and he had to restrain himself from racing over to her. He reminded himself that he needed to rein himself in where she was concerned.

Man, but it's hard!

He smiled and waved in greeting as she exited the vehicle. She looked like a teenager with her hair in a low ponytail. She was wearing a white t-shirt under a pale blue cardigan and blue jeans. She was beautiful!

"I'm so glad you're here," she said, meeting him halfway to the house. "I came by on an impulse, thinking you might be." She had a package in her hands, and her lips were curved into a generous smile while her eyes sparkled mischievously.

"What have we here?" He motioned toward the package, when all he wanted to do was feast his eyes on her.

"Supper!" she replied as if it were gold. "That's if you want it." She was playing with him.

He reached for it, but she held it aside. He protested, "I do happen to want it. Matter of fact, before you arrived, my gut was doing some serious conversing."

She laughed, but still held the package captive. "Don't you want to know what it is and who it's from?"

He sighed and played along. Right now, he wasn't hungry anyway. He was getting full from looking at her. "Well, I assume it's from you and I assume that it's food and now I want to eat it." He grabbed for the package again.

Elise quickly turned toward the house, as she tried to balance her burden away from Josiah. "One out of two, right," she breathed, seeming to love every moment of his attempts. "Rick Phillips brought Alisha supper at the hospital. I had stopped in to get some worship music she wanted me to pick up, when she handed me the meal."

Josiah stopped pursuing her. "Rick Phillips? My foreman? He's a rotten cook!"

"She's furious with him. He showed up during her break and made a big scene about making her supper. In front of other staff, too."

Josiah sat down on the top porch step and looked across at her. "So you want me to eat Rick's dinner?"

She stood before him, two steps down. "Alisha's dinner—which she refused to eat in protest. I didn't want it to go to waste, and I was at an early dinner invitation not far from here, so…" She finally handed it to him. He took the package while holding her gaze with his own.

"It was thoughtful of you, I think." He paused and patted the spot beside him. "But I would much rather it was from you." She slowly lowered herself beside him. She was medium height, but to him she seemed so small. Sometimes, small packages held a lot of weight, a lot of power. She had more power over him than maybe even he knew.

"You really feel that way?" Her light brown eyes looked up into his. "I do apologize," she said with a giggle. "My hostess stored it in her fridge, so you'll have to nuke it. I'll try to do better next time. Put it this way, I owe you a meal." She reached out a hand toward him.

Josiah balanced the food on one knee and took hold of the softness of her hand in a shake of agreement. Then the most curious thing happened. He found he couldn't seem to let go, and she didn't pull her hand away. So they sat, gaze on gaze, holding hands in a stalled handshake.

The spell was suddenly broken, when Elise's long, dark eyelashes flickered down onto her cheeks. Her skin was light enough that he could see a faint blush rising for attention. He let her go, set the food on the porch, and stood to his feet.

"It's getting darker," he commented, before daring to reach a hand down to pull her up. It didn't take much of an effort, and he released her quickly.

"Yes," she agreed, using her hands to dust the back of her jeans off before turning to gaze up at the house. "It's so magnificent," she breathed. "It's coming along so well." Suddenly, a puzzled expression crossed her face. "There was a pickup outside your driveway when I got here."

He looked down at her. "Yeah?"

"It seemed odd. I mean, I could see that someone was in it, and it was almost blocking my way for no apparent reason. As soon as I drove partway in and turned to look back, it sped off."

This was getting his attention. "What colour was the truck?"

Elise screwed her face up, trying to remember. "I think it might have been dark green, or grey maybe."

He nudged her along the driveway. "I wonder if it was Rick or Jack. You remember Jack?"

They paused by her car. "Yes. I met him the day I first came here."

"Of course, if it was one of the crew, he would have just driven in. I doubt Rick would have come out here after stirring up our favourite redhead. Maybe it was someone unfamiliar with the area checking their directions."

She leaned against the driver door of the car. He placed his right hand on the roof. "She does have feelings for him, you know," Elise remarked.

"But they're poles apart in their beliefs," Josiah finished for her.

"I know," she acknowledged.

The night sounds of the surrounding woodlands were growing louder with the increasing darkness. It filled their silence.

Elise moved to open the car door, then paused. She looked up at him, studying him. Somehow, he knew what was coming.

"I'm not a believer." It was such a simple statement, but held so much weight.

"You're becoming one," he assured her gently.

She looked down at her feet, then smoothed her hair with one hand. The smile she raised to him was full of meaning. "If I were, you wouldn't be standing here just *talking* to me, would you?"

He took a step back and pushed both hands into his pockets. He didn't answer. He couldn't seem to; she was asking too much.

"Josiah?"

"It's possible." It was the best he could supply. He looked down into her upturned face and felt the intensity of his emotions for her.

She pulled the car door opened. "Don't forget your meal." She got in, and he gently shut the door. The smile she offered him, he felt, was to put him at ease. He knew her to be a very compassionate woman, and it was eating him up to let her go this way.

He put his hands on the frame of the car door and leaned slightly toward her. "Elise," he started. He had to clear his throat. "You're beautiful the way you are. He just wants to make you His."

She fiddled with the car keys. "I actually spoke with Pastor Solomon, about a week ago. I was supposed to talk with Alisha some more about it. You too, I think." She gave him a quick glance.

He touched her shoulder gently. "Elise, talk to Solomon. You don't need Alisha and me as much as you think."

She laughed nervously. "Does it really seem that way?"

"No, that's not what I mean," he backtracked. "You're one of the most independent people I know, but when it comes to spiritual things, you don't trust your own instincts." He bent down so that he could be on eye level with her.

"You've got to trust what you know of God's Word and what you sense of His Spirit."

"But am I sensing His Spirit?" Her voice seemed faint in the recess of the car.

He would not give up. "I think you are."

She slipped the key into the ignition. "Alisha says that, too."

"Well, there you go. She knows just about everything."

Elise laughed. "Yeah, until the next time you two disagree about some stupid thing."

He joined her laughter, then was silent, almost brooding. He straightened and reached down to take one of her hands in both of his. "I've got your back, always. I promise you."

She looked down at their hands and spoke without looking at him. "That's one of the things I really liked about you when I first met you." She looked up at him. "Remember when you and your dad renovated our house that summer?"

He smiled. "How could I forget the scrawny little kid with big brown eyes who followed me everywhere?"

She slapped at his hands with her free one. "Get real! That was your imagination." She pulled her other hand from his and started the car.

He stepped away. "So what did you like about me?"

"Just what you said. You made me feel that you were watching out for me, that you had my back. You made me feel special."

He acknowledged her goodbye with a wave as she drove off his property. He stood trying to mull over what had just occurred. It was hard for him to do because his head and his heart weren't making sense together. He did, however, feel more hopeful about this woman than he ever had.

Josiah tramped toward the house to grab his food and lock up. He wasn't expecting to stop by his dad's for a meal tonight. Then again, maybe he should. He really felt a need for his father's wise counsel now. He hadn't been getting as much of that since moving from the three-storey family home two and a half years ago. He could definitely use some wisdom tonight.

The thirty minute drive from Josiah's unfinished house to Elise's apartment was a quiet one. She had left the radio turned off from the Christian station she found herself listening to more and more. She had much to contemplate, starting with how bold she had been with Josiah tonight. What had gotten into her?

As she hit the lights of Georgeton, she felt she knew what she had to do. She would accept Pastor Solomon's offer of counselling. She needed to fulfill the ever-growing desire within her to know the Divine. She had been told He was knowable. Not only was her procrastination leaving her with what seemed like a hole in her soul, but it was also a wall between her and Josiah. Not that she should make this spiritual decision based on her increasing need for him, but, instinctively, she knew it had to be made regardless of him. This was not only for life now, but *eternity*.

She drove onto her apartment parking lot. Visiting with Josiah after her dinner engagement had been more of an excuse to see him than to deliver a meal to him. She had to admit that she had wanted to see the house as well. He hadn't invited her back since her first visit there. Elise definitely didn't see herself as a man-chaser, but she felt a little hurt that weeks had passed and he hadn't asked for any more of her input on the house. Alisha would tell her she was being juvenile.

She slammed the car door and started toward her apartment building.

"Hi, Elise."

She looked across to see her neighbour, Jake Morris, strolling toward her. He and his wife Margaret were ever watchful of her as a "single gal" living all alone.

"Hello, Jake." She paused under a light post. "How are you?"

"Oh, I'm doing all right. Just thought I'd take in some of this spring night air while it's still good." He squinted at her and scratched his white head. For reasons known only to him, Jake Morris refused to wear his prescription glasses outside of the apartment building. "You had a visitor—two, actually."

Elise waited for the sudden barking of dogs in the adjacent subdivision to decrease. "Two?"

"Yep. Your ma and some other fellow." He hugged his light jacket around his slightly stooped frame.

Elise started to walk, encouraging him toward the building. "Let's go inside out of the chill. You're finished walking, aren't you?"

"I happened to be in the hall when your mother came out of your apartment." They entered the warmth of the lobby. "She let herself in as usual, but I could tell something had upset her."

Jake sat beside her on one of the wooden benches situated strategically around the apartment lobby. "She told me a man had buzzed up looking for you, but wouldn't say who he was when she asked."

Elise felt her curiosity shift to a more serious concern. "Really? I wonder who that could have been. And why wouldn't he have said who he was?" She wondered if it had been the same man who had interrupted her night some weeks ago. "My mother would have been upset. She always worries about that sort of thing happening to me."

"Well, of course, I reminded her how me and Marg watch out for you." He smiled paternally and peered at her more closely. "You don't worry about any strange fellows. There's lots of good people in this building who'd go to bat for you. Plus, it's pretty safe here. Can't let one bad apple spoil the bunch."

Elise relaxed at the humour of his analogy. "Thanks, Jake." She rose to her feet. She had come to appreciate this man and his wife very much. Years ago, when they had retired, they had decided to stick with what they called the regular population instead of a retirement complex. They were both fairly healthy, and perhaps their lack of children was why they felt the need to be connected to the greater population.

He stood beside her. "One more thing. I think what really set your ma off was when the fellow said to her, 'You don't know, do you? You all don't know what it's like living like this.' Direct quote, she told me."

Elise stared steadily at Jake as a feeling of unease crept over her. *What is going on?*

Chapter Eight

It had always seemed hard to imagine the man on the couch before him as anything but gentle. He was, by nature, a quiet man. Personable, even likeable—until one really got to know him. More and more lately, David sensed a significant shift in this man. He had seen this before, but usually in hardened criminals. Rather than this client improving, he seemed to be regressing. It was like someone being taken to a crossroads where they could choose to venture to the other side, turn left or right, or reverse. In this case, his client seemed to be doing even worse than regressing; he seemed to be embracing a **darkness** that David had never been comfortable with or able to reconcile in all his years of psychiatric practice.

Where was he to go from here with this man? He had maintained the sessions with him with a dogged determination that was now waning. These sessions had been instigated by court order, in lieu of jail time, for sporadic violence. And this man had a history of abuse from childhood. The abuser had once been abused, which was so often the case.

Yet he had a unique relationship with this man. He had counselled him as an abused child, when he had practiced pediatric psychiatry, and so the sense that he had somehow failed him was strong.

"If I prescribe anything stronger for sleep, it will be too much with the antidepressants that you're already on." This was a familiar discussion he had with this client.

The man eyed him like an insolent child seeking to have his own way. "I can't sleep at nights, Doc. Nothing seems to be working for me anymore. You don't understand my life. I want my life back—my family."

David tried not to give even a professional sigh. "We've been over this many times. It's not in my power to give you your family back. It's in your power, if you choose."

"I have been stripped of my rights and you have the power to give me back what is rightfully mine." He was becoming increasingly agitated, but it was the malevolent glint in his eyes that caused the hair to rise on the back of David's neck.

"We have a course of treatment—"

"They will listen to your say-so,"—then, the agitation, too suddenly, morphed to pleading, to flattery—"because you're an excellent doctor. Everyone knows it. You're well-known."

David felt his impatience rising. How much more of this could he tolerate, even professionally? He glanced at the wall clock up behind the client's head. He was almost due for dinner with his family, and the Alexanders were finally coming to dine with them. He was truly looking forward to personally observing what he and Celia were becoming convinced was a love interest between Josiah Alexander and their daughter.

He had finally accepted that he was not the one to help this client. It had taken him a lot of soul-searching and acceptance to come to the conclusion that, in spite of his excellent professional record, he could no longer help this man. How was he to convey this to him? This client, seemingly because of their past counselling relationship, had deemed him the one to restore all he had lost.

"That may be so, but we still need to get you where you need to be." David watched the man settle back into his seat. His client was clearly not pleased. He may as well remind him now. "Remember, my office will be closed in two weeks' time with instructions for other contacts for any care needed." This was the opportunity David would also take to make the break from this client. Provisions had already been made with another colleague.

"When can I expect you back?" His visage, his bearing, and his tone were, once again, that of a productive, capable member of society. This was the problem. For the most part, this client was productive and capable until something seemed to take him over, and he would undergo some sort of metamorphosis.

"It will be an extended leave for me." David began to gather the pen and papers on his lap. "But you don't worry about that. Remember, I said there will be other care available to you."

"When can I expect you back?"

David paused, unsure of how he should proceed. "Perhaps, a month." Better to keep it simple. Hopefully, by then, this man would be well on his way in someone else's care. David could then meet with him to discuss the changes. After all, he was supposed to be slowing down, cutting back, to facilitate his impending retirement.

The man remained silent and seemed rather deep in thought. David was fairly certain he did not want to know those thoughts.

*   *   *

"So, Jesus existed before He became… Jesus?" Elise felt such a need to question and question. This was her third session with Pastor Solomon Sung, and she still felt no wane in her thirst for answers. The more he expounded to her, the more she desired. There was so much she had not learned before. What had she been doing all those years in church? Had she been there in body, but not in spirit? Had she not been fed this stuff?

"That's exactly right," Solomon concurred. "According to the Bible, He was referred to as the 'Word' and is part of the Trinity. God, for reasons we do not fully understand, chooses to express himself in three different ways: as Father, Son—or the Word—and the Holy Spirit. Yet, they are one. They are God."

Elise leaned forward from an overstuffed armchair in Solomon's den. "So God, the Word, became Jesus when He took on human form?"

Solomon smiled. "Exactly. You'll be teaching me soon."

Elise returned the smile. She could faintly hear Bethany Sung in the adjacent kitchen with the twins, Joshua and Jordan. Sometimes she could detect their movements through the glass in the den's French doors. All of her visits had revealed a healthy home, even with two very active teenagers and the demands of church and community commitments. She had experienced a really good upbringing, but there had been so many pursuits that, in retrospect, didn't seem that important to her now. She launched her thoughts, once again, to Solomon.

"So you feel there was a lack of real spiritual emphasis in my growing up years? That's the hole, or emptiness, I feel?"

Solomon stretched his sturdy legs out before him from where he sat on a couch facing her. "Yes. In essence, I believe your lack has not been good values or ambitions, but a relationship with Jesus Christ. He became the visible Presence of God to mankind. Religion is the practice of what we do based on what we've been taught, or even what we believe. Relationship is about Who we know." He must have seen her confusion. He leaned forward. "Elise, you can be very religious and not know God."

Elise felt a dryness in her throat as she swallowed. She reached for the glass of ginger ale that Bethany had graciously provided. Even with the wetness of the fluid, she still felt an ache in her throat. There was also a weight in her chest that was harder and harder for her to ignore.

"Pastor Solomon, I'm not sure what to do. What I have known all along has not been enough." Horrors of horrors, tears were forming in her eyes. She blinked rapidly. "I've seen changes in Alisha that I thought, at first, were temporary, but I know now they are not."

"I have shared my own testimony with you, Elise," Solomon encouraged her gently. "The change that Jesus Christ brings to our lives is real and lasting. I've experienced that change. I was not always what you see here today."

She laughed, and the lump in her throat eased a little. "I know. Bethany told me about your seriously rebellious days."

"Would you like me to have her come in now?" he asked.

Elise took a deep breath and nodded. "Yes, please."

In his absence, Elise pondered her condition. She felt no doubt that she had finally reached a crossroads where a choice had to be made. Her Scripture reading had confirmed what Pastor Solomon had preached one Sunday about God and mankind's enemy, Satan, being real. People, in general, didn't like to think about him, yet they were all too aware of the evils in society. They would much rather believe in the goodness of God or blame Him for neglect in not preventing life's calamities.

The door swung open, and the maternal, rounded form of Bethany Sung preceded her husband. She took one look at Elise and came right over to envelope her in a warm, soothing hug.

"Look at all those tears," Bethany cooed, as she pulled Elise from the armchair. They both settled on the couch before Bethany accepted a box of tissue from Solomon. She handed a tissue to Elise.

"I… I'm so sorry." Elise was finding it very hard to contain her emotions. There was so much welling up inside of her.

Solomon looked on helplessly as Bethany smoothed Elise's hair with her hands. "Do you want to accept the Lord Jesus Christ as your Saviour?" Her Scottish accent never sounded more sweet. Her rounded face, framed by bouncy brown hair, lit up in an enchanting smile.

Elise felt a release. "Yes," she whispered. Then a little louder, "Yes."

Bethany turned to her husband and, after receiving his nod, proceeded. She knelt on the carpeted floor before Elise and clasped their hands together before raising her face. "Do you believe that God came as Jesus Christ to take your punishment for sins and reconcile you to God?"

"Yes," Elise responded with confidence. The tears just wouldn't cease. It was like a spring had burst forth in her, and a comforting Presence seemed to be enveloping her.

Solomon was now on his knees, slightly behind his wife. Bethany continued. "Do you accept all that He did for you on the cross?"

"I do."

"Do you acknowledge your sin that separates you from God and your need for forgiveness?"

The Presence felt stronger. "Yes," she breathed.

"Will you make Him Lord of your life?" Bethany's tears were now flowing.

Elise felt a bubble of laughter, and she let it out. "Oh, yes."

Solomon finally spoke. "Let's pray."

Elise slammed her car door and started quickly up the walkway to her parents' front door. She was late! So much had happened at the Sung's, and the passage of time had escaped her. Of all evenings, the one to be spent with Josiah and his father. She had based her timing on her two previous meetings with Pastor Solomon and had anticipated adequate, even generous, timing. She had not known this would be the occasion of her commitment to Jesus Christ. How could she have known?

The door swung open before she could even get the key out of her bag. Her mother stepped out onto the veranda and discretely closed the door behind her.

"They are here," Celia whispered, in French, "and you and your father are both late

Elise turned and noticed a black SUV parked on the road just before the driveway. In her haste, she hadn't noticed Adam Alexander's vehicle.

She turned back to her mother. "Oh, Mom, I'm so sorry."

"Never mind that now." Celia sighed in relief. "Here's your father. You go on in. They're in the family room examining your father's model boats and ships."

Her mother moved off to greet her husband, leaving Elise feeling somewhat panicked. She stepped into the foyer, then slipped into the powder room before going to meet their guests. So much was happening today. She needed a moment to collect herself.

Elise smoothed the flowing skirt of her floral, apricot dress. She took time to brush the curls back from her forehead into a brown clasp before entering the family room adjacent to the kitchen, just as her parents entered the house. Her father would need a little bit of time, she was sure.

She heard the deep timbre of their voices before she saw them— Josiah and Adam Alexander in her parents' home, but not as renovators. They both had their backs turned to her, and no wonder; her father had quite an impressive collection. Josiah towered a head over his father, but they were both slightly bent over a ship model and seemed to be in deep discussion about its parts.

She move toward the baby grand piano in the centre of the room before clearing her throat gently. They both looked up.

"Elise." Josiah's deep voice filled the room as he moved confidently toward her. He looked almost too good in a white polo shirt which contrasted beautifully against his brown skin.

"Hi, Josiah, Mr. Alexander," she greeted. She was feeling a little breathless. Too much had already happened today, with no time yet to sort through it all.

Adam stood beside his son. "Well, hello there, and don't you look awfully pretty." He took both her hands into his work-hardened ones. "We finally have caught up to each other again."

She laughed gently, looking from one to the other. They were similar in some ways. They both had the same soulful eyes and wide foreheads. She could tell by the precision of his hairline that Josiah had had a recent haircut. Her hands itched to run over the tight waves so close to his head. "Yes, we have caught up, and I'm so sorry to be late."

The corners of Adam's eyes crinkled, as he smiled widely. "No bother, child. Your mother saw to it that we were kept entertained by your dad's marvellous model boat and ship collection." He looked at Josiah. "Isn't that so, son?"

"You bet," Josiah agreed, then winked at her.

Elise felt a rush of pleasure as she leaned against the piano for support. Her eyes locked with his before she reluctantly looked away. Could he tell the difference? Could he guess what had happened to her? She hadn't even had time to speak to Alisha because she hadn't had her cell phone. "I'm so glad. Dad's just arrived, so I'm sure we'll be eating soon."

"That's absolutely true," her father's voice materialized in agreement. "Hello, everyone," he greeted enthusiastically. Elise felt energized by the sound of his voice.

"I hear we're both delinquents, Dad," Elise chided as she and her father shared a brief kiss.

David threw back his head and laughed. "I think we're both forgiven now," he said before shaking the men's hands in greeting. "It's great to see you again, Adam. Now, Josiah, I haven't seen you for a while, but I've been hearing great things about you."

"Well, I'm certainly glad to hear that, sir. I wonder where all that information could have come from?" He smiled knowingly down at Elise, who was standing between him and her father.

"Perhaps your father divulged it," she said, deflecting the good-natured accusation.

Adam laughed and spoke directly to David. "Dr. David, if you had a son like I have, you would find it impossible to keep quiet about him, but, in this case, I think your little bird is guilty."

The men chuckled, but Elise was caught up in a nostalgic moment. "Dr. David" was a name evoked from her childhood . That's all she remembered Adam Alexander calling her father the summer of the renovations.

The two older men continued to chatter. It was an interesting contrast, the proper English accent and the more familiar Canadian speech.

Josiah touched her arm gently. "You okay?"

She breathed in the wonderful scent of him. "Yes. Maybe we can talk later." She nodded toward their fathers; one tall and fair, the other medium height and dark, both thin. She was used to differences in this home of racial and cultural diversity and from her travels with her parents to many distant lands. She embraced everyone for who they were, as individuals. "We better feed them," she explained.

It couldn't be helped, and she hoped the two young people didn't notice her persistent observations.

Celia could hardly keep her eyes off her daughter and the handsome young man seated beside her at their formal dining table. After the initial upset of late arrivals, everything had gone beautifully, like clockwork. The atmosphere was most pleasant, and their conversations energetic, witty, and interesting. She couldn't remember the last time she had seen Elise so engaged. She fairly glowed.

She noticed David taking an occasional glance at the pair and knew they would have a lot of notes to compare later. She was relieved to see her husband so relaxed as the conversation circled around the table. She had forgotten Adam's keen sense of humour; it certainly kept David entertained. She had witnessed the strain on his face when she had greeted him in the driveway earlier. Of course, she had set aside her irritation at his tardiness when he expressed frustration over his last session of the day. Even though her husband was bound by confidentiality, she could guess who the source of his stress was. The client.

This client was a source of contention between them in a life where they harmonized on most issues. Even Elise had voiced her concern that her father let go of what she called a "professional hazard." Now he seemed so carefree and light-hearted. Perhaps on their cruise getaway, he would be this way for longer periods of time. It was unnerving to see her usually positive-minded husband experiencing increasing bouts of melancholy.

She sipped her wine slowly and watched as Josiah bowed his head to catch something Elise was saying. Their mannerisms toward each other revealed no tangible sign of romantic connection, yet their interactions supplied every hint of something more than friendship.

All she knew of Josiah accounted for a strong, intelligent, dependable, independent young man. Yet, she could tell, right now, that her daughter held him captive in the palm of her hand. Celia guessed Elise didn't know how much Josiah Alexander was attracted to her.

Celia smiled, remembering the same chemistry between David and herself in the early years. Theirs had deepened to a stronger, mature love. "Josiah," she said, breaking in on their obvious infatuation with each other, "I hear your house is coming along quite well."

Josiah showed beautiful, white teeth as he grinned. "Ah, Mrs. Everson, it's definitely my passion right now. It's something I've dreamed of for a while, and I am feeling a little surreal about its near completion."

Celia warmed to his tone; there was no pretentiousness. "That's wonderful for you, but how will you occupy yourself in such a big house, alone?" she joked.

"That's a good question, my queen," David joined in. "Not to put you on the spot, Josiah."

Josiah laughed. "Not at all. Dad's asked me the same question more than once." He clasped his hands on the table and allowed his excitement to shine through his dark eyes. "It took me a while and much prayer to make the decision, but once it was made, I simply told God that I would build the house if He would supply the family." He raised his thick, dark eyebrows meaningfully. "Starting with the wife, of course."

Celia joined everyone's laughter. Well, almost everyone. Elise was watching them with a slight look of alarm on her face.

"Four bedrooms, is it?" David continued.

"Six, if you count the over-the-garage guest suite," Adam supplied. He seemed almost as excited as his son. "It's just as well I've gotten used to living without him these last couple of years. I'm not even sure how much longer I'll remain in the family home."

"You're planning on selling your home, then?" David asked. He seemed a little tired. After food, fellowship, and earlier events, the day was finally taking its toll.

"Been meaning to for a while, but I hung on to it so Josiah could continue rambling around on the third floor." Adam seemed somewhat wistful. "My wife loved that house."

"She did, Dad," Josiah agreed. He ran his wide hand across his jaw line. "Dad had renovated it, all three storeys from top to bottom, for her."

Adam leaned back in his chair. His dark eyes had a faraway look. "Yes, we did. We found great joy there … and great pain."

Celia was moved. She knew the story of Darlene Alexander's death after losing her battle with cancer. Josiah had only been a teenager. "But you have both done so well," she acknowledged.

Adam's eyes were glistening, but his face was lit with an infectious smile. "We couldn't have done it without the Lord." He looked across the beautifully arranged table at his son. "We look forward to seeing her again."

There was silence.

"In heaven," Elise spoke up.

There was a confidence in Elise's voice that puzzled her mother. Celia was sure she was interpreting the same questioning expression on David's face. Perhaps there was more going on with their daughter than a new romance.

Chapter Nine

Spring was drawing to a close; the increasing warmth of the air testified to that. Elise had her car windows partially down to enjoy the pleasant night air. They were parked outside of Josiah's condominium.

"So, you sent my father on ahead and decided to drop me off because…?"

He was being insufferable, teasing her all the way over about her still owing him dinner. After all, her *mother* had been the cook this time around. It was obvious from his light-hearted bantering that he had enjoyed himself immensely. Maybe too much.

She sat facing him, wanting him to lean forward into the glow of the streetlight coming through the windshield. She wanted to see his expression clearly.

"I'm not going to say a word until you're being serious." She daringly reached across and slapped his knee. "What is wrong with you? You didn't even have any wine."

"Ouch!" He rubbed his knee. "I don't drink," he simply stated. "You know, if I had known I was being abducted to be beaten up, I would have declined."

She glared at him. "You were not abducted."

He reached over and held her chin with his hand. "Then am I free to go?"

As they searched each other's eyes, Elise struggled to breathe. "Don't be ridiculous," she scolded gently.

He sighed and let her go. "I really, really enjoyed dinner with your family. I could tell Dad did, too." He settled back against the passenger door. "I was quite surprised at his moment of nostalgia concerning my mother. I guess the mention of selling the house brought that on. They moved there after getting married."

Leaning toward him, she noticed some sadness in his eyes. "You miss her, don't you?"

He cleared his throat. "It's been easier. It doesn't hurt as much, but yeah, sometimes I miss her. It's been fourteen years, and sometimes it's hard to remember her."

"Where will your dad go? Will he live with you in your house?"

"We're not quite sure yet, but he doesn't want to live in my house." He turned his head to gaze out the windshield. "He says he wants a smaller place. He's tired of wandering around in big houses."

She smiled slowly. "But you want to wander around in a six-bedroom, five-bathroom house by yourself."

He laughed and draped his arm across the back of her seat, almost touching her. "I told you, God will provide."

She looked at him incredulously. "He'll provide the wife?"

"Yes, and she'll provide the kids."

"That's simplistic," she countered, wondering why he was suddenly looking so serious.

The hand on the back of her seat gently pulled on a curly black lock. She felt the small tug and tried to ignore it.

"Sometimes we make things too complicated," he murmured. He let go of her hair, but not her gaze.

She lowered her head, only to have it jerk back up at his sudden change in topic.

"Your mother told me about the incident at your apartment. She was quite upset."

"Yes," she responded, trying to adjust her thoughts. "I'm not sure what to make of it."

"She said your neighbour, Jake Morris, was walking out of the building with her when a pickup came out of nowhere and sped past them."

Elise took a deep breath. "Yes, that was a few days ago, and she's called me every night since." She smoothed a stray curl back from her cheek. "I told her that it was probably a case of mistaken identity. He entered the wrong code."

He leaned toward her, and the streetlight shone on his strong jaw line and furrowed brows. "But she said he asked for you by name."

Her eyes pleaded with him. "I know. I was trying to deflect her anxieties. She wanted to report it to the police."

He remained quiet for a moment. "You have a buddy system with Alisha?"

"Yes, but we don't call each other every night. We know we have other people who we are in contact with on a regular basis. Besides, she's moving back in with her mother soon."

"Oh, yeah, she wants to save money to buy a house."

Elise giggled. "Yes, but if Rick has his way, she'd be moving right into his house."

Josiah chuckled, then reached across to take her hand. "If you have any inkling of unusual happenings like that again, I want you to let me know. Okay?"

She nodded, revelling in the warmth of his hand on hers. He could almost swallow up both of hers in one of his.

"Wasn't there something else you wanted me to know?"

Elise felt her breath catch in her throat. She should have been expecting that question. She felt a dread she couldn't explain, and an excitement at the same time.

"Hey, Earth calling Elise."

She looked across at him. "Josiah… I've become a believer."

"It's crazy, Dad!" Josiah grabbed his temples with both hands in frustration. "The one thing I really wanted—prayed for—has finally happened, and I freeze. I check out, lose my focus, whatever you want to call it." He got up from his dad's kitchen table and began to pace. "I mean, how unbelievably awkward. Man, how do I get past this?"

"Well, son—"

"Good grief! It's not like she's been some woman with unscrupulous values or a history of deception. Why do I feel this way?"

"Jo, I think—"

"How must she feel? It's been a week. She must have noticed."

Josiah felt a hard hand on his shoulder. He jerked around, nearly knocking his father over. "Ah, sorry, Dad."

Adam had a grim look on his face, but his speech was gentle. "Sit down, son."

Josiah sighed deeply and grabbed a wooden chair. He sat back and observed the expression on his father's face. "I'm really acting nutty, aren't I?"

Adam seemed amused. He shook his head in wonder. "Son, that's what happens when a man is head-over-heels in love."

In love? Those words, said out loud, sounded incredible. "In love?"

"What do you think you've been trying to sort out the last year or so? You didn't expect to stay just her friend forever, did you?"

Josiah shifted uneasily in his chair. "Yeah, but..."

Adam shoved a cup of coffee across the wooden table. "Here, finish your coffee before it gets cold." He stood up and made his way to the fridge and opened the door. "Jo," he began, his voice somewhat muffled with his head inside the fridge, "for an intelligent fellow," he straightened up to make his point, "you sure are dumb."

Josiah stared at his dad and suddenly felt overwhelmed. "We talked about *my* feelings for her," he said lamely.

Adam sat down with a tangerine and began to peel it. "And what do you think those feelings are? How is it that you've been struggling with them for what seems like forever? It's time to acknowledge them for what they are and get on with life."

His father was a fairly calm, steadfast sort of guy, but he sure could be blunt.

"You don't have to propose to her tomorrow, but you've got to face the reality of this love you have for her head-on." Adam was enjoying his fruit as if the world was all right, as if it didn't seem to be shifting out of control.

Josiah was a disciplined man. He had been raised that way. He usually knew what he wanted out of life. He worked hard and he liked to have control. He didn't like what was happening now.

"You don't know whether she embraced the faith because of you, or in spite of you." His dad's eyes were full of wisdom. When he didn't respond, his dad continued. "You feel like you need to test the waters, so to speak."

Josiah nodded slowly. He crossed one leg on top of the other and laughed uncomfortably. "Dad, you've pretty much summed it up, perfectly." Leaning toward his father, he asked, "How did you figure it out?"

Adam chuckled deeply. "Son, when you're sixty-odd years old, you must have learned a few things along the way. Don't worry too much about it. Keep praying and take it one step at a time. I think it's good for you to want to see the authenticity of her faith, but you have to balance that with her real need for support in this new walk."

"Maybe he just has to adjust to the idea of a 'believing' Elise," Alisha puffed as she did battle with the treadmill. There weren't many customers enjoying a morning workout at the fitness centre, so it wasn't difficult for her and Elise to converse while they exercised.

Elise dabbed at the layer of perspiration on her forehead. "You think so? Why would he have to do that? I thought he'd be ecstatic." Her legs were really burning as she jogged beside Alisha. With school almost out, she wouldn't have any excuse for a sedentary life. She needed to workout more regularly during the school year. That, however, was not her focus of concern presently. Josiah's behaviour toward her had left her puzzled; actually, more than puzzled. He had left her feeling downright hurt. It was as if he had accepted her with reservations as an unbeliever, but rejected her as a believer. At least, that's how she felt. Not that he had done anything in particular to solidify that suspicion. It was just a strong impression she had. He seemed more distant, almost as if he were keeping himself under some sort of restraint.

Alisha stopped and stepped off the treadmill. She used a towel to dab at the back of her neck where her red hair was swept up in a thick ponytail. "Who completely understands the male psyche? My guess is that he may feel he needs to give you time to, you know, have Christ as your focus without him interfering." She paused, and a twinkle appeared in her green eyes. "You know, Elise, for a girl who was allergic to the notion of romantic commitment not so long ago, you're certainly singing a different tune."

Elise had been resting by her treadmill, and now she swung her towel at Alisha. "Ali, don't get smart. You know that… well, that—"

"You have feelings for Jo, but it's been hard to admit it," Alisha finished smugly.

Elise sat on a nearby stool and raised her arms above her head in a stretch. She sighed and lowered them. "I guess, I'm not sure what to think. You're right, of course." She looked up at her best friend and saw compassion in her eyes. "I do have strong feelings for him, but I certainly don't want it to get in the way of my growth in Christ." She looked down at the rubberized floor. "Perhaps he's right to do what he's doing." She felt Alisha's hands on her shoulders.

"Come on, Lise, don't let it get you down. It will work out. The Lord has a way of taking care of these things when we commit them to him." She stepped back and threw her arms into the air. "Besides, I didn't wait all these years for your salvation so we could have a pity party. Let's go shower. Lunch is on me."

Elise managed a smile, then looked over Alisha's shoulder. "I don't know, Ali. I may not be the only one with man troubles today."

Alisha turned around to see Rick Phillips' tall, well-built form approaching.

"Alisha Adair," he said, stressing her name as he stopped before her. His brown eyes were alight and his dark hair a little rumpled. "I came into town for some supplies and guess who's car I spotted?"

Elise couldn't help the smile that curved her lips. She liked Rick. He was a happy-go-lucky type of guy, but his constant teasing and attention drove Alisha crazy.

"I can't imagine whose car you saw, Rick." Alisha's arms were now on her hips. "But it seems like Josiah doesn't have enough work for you to do or you wouldn't be driving around checking out people's cars."

An adorable grin appeared on Rick's perpetually baby face. "Actually, not people's cars—just Elise's." With that, he slipped around Alisha's rigid form and stooped before Elise. "How are you doing, sweetheart?"

Elise eyed him uncertainly. "Fine." She looked over his head at Alisha's very curious expression. "Umm... thank you for asking. How are you?"

"Oh, pretty good... pretty good," he assured her, all the while nodding repeatedly. "I heard that you got bitten by Josiah and Alisha's bug."

"Bug?" Elise giggled nervously. "What are you talking about?"

He straightened up, ignoring Alisha. "You know, the religious bug."

"Rick—" Alisha started in on him.

He held a hand up to silence her. "Don't get me wrong, I'm not making fun."

"For a change," Alisha remarked sarcastically, coming closer.

He continued to ignore her. He actually had a serious look on his face. "If you don't mind, I'd like to talk to you about it. Soon."

Elise stood to her feet. The noise in the fitness centre was increasing with recent arrivals. Even so, in the quietness of her heart, she felt a desire stir. "Sure, I'll talk to you, Rick. I'd love to."

He nodded to her. "Great! Thanks. I know Josiah tries with me, but, I don't know, I think it might be different coming from you."

She smiled at him, then watched him turn swiftly. Before Alisha could react, he grabbed her by the waist and kissed her soundly on one cheek. Elise saw his dark pickup pass by the centre's large front windows before Alisha uttered a word.

Chapter Ten

Elise and Keisha Rogers were slow in finishing their lunches in the staff room. One more day, and they would once again experience the novelty of "the end of school." They would also have two years of teaching under their belts.

"You know, Keisha, it's times like this when I know that I love to teach. When I've almost finished a year, and I know I've done well, it feels good."

Keisha nodded her head in agreement. "You hit it right on the head, girl. Though I definitely stress the 'I've finished' part. I really need a vacation."

They both had their feet up on the room's worn-out coffee table. It was a pleasant enough room. Last year, a group of them had painted it a pale blue to match the fairly decent overstuffed couch and armchair. It served well as a getaway, but they were the only two "getting away" presently.

"So, what are your plans for the summer?" Elise asked Keisha. They had become closer over the last year, even meeting sometimes outside of work. The fact that Keisha had a personal relationship with the Lord Jesus as well was a bonus. Now they could strengthen each other at work.

"Actually, I plan to visit my folks in Jamaica." Keisha's parents had recently retired to their country of birth after raising Keisha and her six siblings in Canada. Elise got the impression that the move had left Keisha and her siblings with mixed feelings. They respected their parents' right to autonomy, but also wanted them close. "They're supposed to come back for Christmas, but I can't wait that long to see them. What about you?"

"Oh, I'm not sure. Maybe I'll spend it getting braids like yours." Keisha had long, natural braids down to her waist. She looked like a full-figured African goddess with her dark skin and high cheekbones.

Keisha laughed. "I don't know if you'd be able to sit still that long."

Elise lowered her legs to the floor and smoothed at the bun on top of her head. "Actually, my mother tried it once when I was thirteen. It was the first and last time. She offered to have a hairdresser do it, but I stubbornly declined."

Keisha laughed. "You may have to spend your summer incognito because of Webster Myers."

Elise groaned. "Please, don't remind me. He's already decided to increase his efforts in cracking the Elise code."

"You know, Elise," Keisha said, leaning forwards, "I would be totally freaked if someone kept at me like that. It's really strange."

Elise thought for a moment. "I don't know, he seems harmless enough."

"Maybe, but I just feel really uncomfortable about it all. You know, the flowers, little notes, and that huge helium balloon on your birthday. All from a guy who you keep saying no to." Keisha raised her dark eyebrows for effect, then got up to lounge against the staff room's low windowsill.

Elise had to admit that Keisha had a point. Perhaps she needed to put the issue to rest once and for all before the next school term. Webster was a very capable teacher and a very friendly person, though somewhat oversensitive, but she was getting weary of it all and it was becoming a bit embarrassing; even the students had now caught on. They were being dubbed "Beauty and the Brain."

"Well, speak of the devil," Keisha moaned, looking out the window.

Elise joined her. They both looked out to see Webster Myers exit a dark pickup.

"I thought he drove a car," Elise remarked absentmindedly.

"He does," Keisha said. "That's his uncle's truck. His uncle runs a farm and sometimes Webster brings his truck in to get supplies." She looked at Elise and grinned. "Webster definitely doesn't strike me as the farming type."

"I think he's coming in," Elise said with a sigh. She dutifully returned the wave he directed to them after spotting them at the window. She turned her back to the outdoor scene and noticed Keisha's pained expression. "What?" she asked.

"He's probably coming in here," Keisha declared pointedly. "What are you going to do about it? Today is a good day to start."

Elise braced herself against the windowsill. "Easy for you to say," she started, then whispered as she heard sounds outside the staff room door. "Don't you dare leave me alone."

The door swung opened. "Well, hello, ladies," Webster greeted as he breezed into the room.

"One more day, and it's time to celebrate." After acknowledging them both, he focused on Elise. He crossed the room to stand before her. "I thought we all, if you like, could make some plans."

"Plans?" she queried uncertainly, looking over his shoulder at Keisha who had a "do it now" expression on her face. She decided to skirt around it. "How was your appointment, Webster?"

He seemed puzzled for a moment, then his hazel eyes cleared. "Oh, that. Nothing major. Just a dental thing." He turned so he could include Keisha. "What do you say, Keisha?"

"To what exactly, Webster?" Keisha had her arms folded.

Elise was certain she was being purposefully difficult.

"Come on, girls," he said enthusiastically. He threw his arms up dramatically. "The end of year celebration! I didn't come back here after being under Frankenstein dentist's hand for nothing. I could have retired to the comforts of home."

Keisha was not budging an inch. "Webster, there's such a thing as the telephone or e-mail."

Webster stared at her for a moment. "Do I detect some opposition in this room?"

"Guys, I really have to get going," Elise interrupted, eager to dispel the increasing tension in the room. She brushed past Webster and touched Keisha's shoulder. "We can discuss this later, okay?"

"Sure," Keisha said with a trace of defiance.

Webster stood still, mouth slightly opened, scratching his head. Impatiently, he smoothed his wayward brown hair. "Fine."

Keisha flicked her braids over onto her back and grabbed her handbag from the nearby armchair. She was halfway to the door before turning around. "Coming, Elise?"

Elise took a deep breath. "Give me a second, okay?"

Keisha stared at them both uncertainly, then nodded before leaving the room.

"What is up with her?" Webster asked even before the door had closed.

Mindful that another teacher could walk in at any moment, Elise got straight to the point. "Webster, I need to say something to you."

"Uh-oh. Why don't I like the sound of that, and why do I think I won't have time to psyche myself up for it?" He fidgeted with his glasses nervously.

Elise felt sorry for him, but Keisha was right. It was time to do something. "I do like you, Webster, as a person. I think you're a wonderful teacher, but—" She could see his eyes twitching, and she almost aborted her train of thought—"I think you need to know that there can never be anything between us." There, she had done it. She was, however, unprepared for what happened next. Webster quickly strode over to her and shoved his face close to hers.

"No worthy battle, Elise, was ever won without a fight. And even if there is no victory, the hero always goes down fighting."

Before she could move back or respond, the staff door started to open, and at that moment, Webster stormed from the room.

"Everything okay?" One of the math teachers had entered the room. He had a worried expression on his face. "Keisha is standing outside the door. She asked me to come in."

Elise felt her heart slowing. She forced a smile on her face. "It's okay, I think."

"Was Webster bothering you? I mean everyone and their dog knows he has a thing for you."

She decided to reach out for a little help. "I don't think he knows how to take no for an answer."

He nodded understandingly. "Look, guys like Webster are good with academics and such, but when it comes to relationships, they might be ill-equipped. If he were your average Joe, you probably would take it more seriously. I say take it seriously. Keep it straight with him until he gets the picture. Okay?"

She nodded. "Thanks. I appreciate it."

Outside in the hall, Keisha accosted her. "I heard his outburst. Do you want it reported?"

Elise shook her head wearily. "No, Keisha, let's just leave it alone for now. If things get worse, I will, but I really don't think that's the best route right now." The last thing she wanted to do was get the principal involved. Surely it wouldn't come to that.

"Okay," Keisha said, "if you're sure. Trust me, I wouldn't waste my sympathy on him. He's not the one who's being harassed."

"I know, Keisha," she groaned, "but hopefully, after all that, he'll settle down."

"I don't know," Keisha said shaking her head repeatedly.

The students' exit from Elise's French class was truly sporadic. Some kids were eager to be on their way, while others trickled out, talking to their classmates or making little comments to their teacher. The room was finally empty except for two.

"What's up guys?" Elise questioned the Sung twins, who had lingered. They started nudging each other, and Elise couldn't help smiling as she waited patiently for them to sort out who would speak first. They finally came forward with their eyes looking anywhere but at her. They were pleasant looking boys, with dark bangs almost over their eyes, of Korean ancestry like their adopted father.

"Madamoiselle Everson, Mom wanted us to give you this." This was from Joshua, the firstborn, who then looked meaningfully at his brother.

"W–we wanted to thank you for all of your hard work." Jordan looked up and handed her a small package.

Elise accepted it. "Oh, thank you, boys. That's so thoughtful." She searched their faces. "Should I open it now?"

"Sure," they answered simultaneously, chuckling. They were more relaxed.

"Okay," she said, and with big fanfare tore the beautiful wrapping off a small jewellery box. She paused to note them watching her intently. "Ohhh," she breathed, "what have we here?" She lifted the lid. It was a silver cross pendant.

"Look at the back," Joshua commanded eagerly.

She did. It had her initials engraved on it. She felt her eyes tear up and blinked rapidly.

"Mom said it's to remind you that your name is written in God's book, the Book of Life," Jordan explained.

"It's really lovely, guys." She reached out to touch them both on one shoulder each, her gift clutched in one hand. "Thank you so much and thank your mother for me. I have just the right silver chain to wear it on."

They were grinning and seemed quite pleased with themselves, then Jordan sobered. "Mademoiselle Everson, you help remind us to be good examples when it's hard, so t–thanks."

This time she couldn't help it. She reached out and squished them together in a brief hug. "You guys have been awesome, and you have inspired me with your Christ-like examples."

They smiled awkwardly. "No problem," Joshua responded, then they gathered their belongings. "Well, we gotta go. See you tomorrow and… *au revoir*."

She saw them out the door, then closed it behind her. The empty classroom with its wide windows, walls of charts, and colourful assignments didn't seem the same without the bodies. She thanked God for such an opportunity to affect so many lives. Yet how was she to affect her colleagues, even one like Webster Myers who tested her newfound faith? Without a question, she needed to deal with the situation between them. She had probably let it go for too long, but she wasn't sure that Keisha's belligerent attitude was the answer either.

"You know, Elise, I've been meaning to clarify something."

Elise looked up from her meal with Keisha. They were at Elise's apartment, after school, sharing the dinner they had both thrown together.

"I'm actually not proud of my attitude toward Webster today, and it's a good thing God knows why I may have reacted as I did."

Elise breathed a sigh of relief. She had wanted to bring up this very subject, but was reluctant to spoil their evening. She watched her friend struggle to find the words.

Keisha leaned both elbows on top of the medium-sized glass table. "I especially was concerned about my example in front of a new believer." Her eyes were dark with feelings. She gently chewed on her bottom lip. "I wanted to ask you to forgive me."

Elise was awestruck. She had not expected this. "Sure, Keisha, but there's nothing to forgive.

Keisha eyed her pointedly. "Yes, there is. I wasn't taught to be that way, especially as a believer. My middle sister was the victim of a stalker, and no one took it seriously enough until she was raped."

"Oh, my goodness!" Elise felt terrible. Now she understood Keisha's dilemma with Webster's behaviour. "I'm so sorry, Keisha. I had no idea."

"I don't share it with a lot of people, but I've become quite sensitive about women's issues." There was a determination in her voice mixed with pain

"Was your sister okay?"

"Eventually, but she was afraid of her shadow and wary of practically every male between eighteen and, I don't know, fifty-five, for a long time."

The clatter of the dishes stemmed the conversation as Keisha stacked them and the cutlery to take to the kitchen sink. "Fortunately, she's met a great guy and is happily married. My niece and nephew are gorgeous, and one more is on the way. This was seven years ago, but it made quite an impact on me."

Elise rose and gathered the glasses, then they both moved from the dining area into the kitchen. "I'm so glad to hear that. There is a woman in our church who is separated from her husband because of domestic abuse." She bent to open the dishwasher. "It must be even harder to accept that the one who should love you would hurt you."

"Oh, yeah." Keisha leaned against the kitchen counter. "I actually volunteered at a woman's crises centre once. Many of them tend to blame themselves for their partner's behaviours. It's like having to un-brainwash them of their own self-brainwashing."

Leaning against the counter as well, Elise asked, "So how old are your sister's kids?"

"Four and two. She's going to be pretty busy, but her husband is pretty good at helping out. They're having a bit of struggle with the racial questions their four-year old is starting to raise."

Elise raised her brows, puzzled. "What do you mean?"

Keisha chuckled. "Oh, I didn't tell you; her husband is white. Maybe you can help me, Elise. Let's forget women's issues for a moment. How do you deal with being biracial?"

Elise folded her arms and thought for a moment. "Well, I don't know, I think probably my issues with racial identity were more prominent in my pre-teen and teen years. I guess I struggled with which race to identify with. My parents stressed that I am both, but I basically had to work it out for myself."

Keisha pulled her long braids over one shoulder. "Most people who are black-white mix tend to identify as black. Why is that?"

"I think it's because that's the dominant skin colour seen." She moistened her lips. "Eventually, I decided people could see me however they wanted to see me, as long as I and my family and friends knew it was *me*."

"That's beauuu–ti–ful, Elise," Keisha pronounced and reached over to give her a hug. She stepped back and smiled. "I've noticed that about you. People are just people, no matter their race."

Both ladies jumped at the sound of the apartment intercom. "I better get that," Elise said and rushed out of the room. After her "hello" into the speaker, she waited. She tried again. "Hello?" She turned to look at Keisha, who had followed her. She tried a third time with no response. She shrugged. "That's strange. I wonder if someone is pranking me? This has happened before."

Keisha laughed. "Do you have a secret admirer, Elise? Stalkers, I can do without. Secret admirers ... well that's another story."

Elise aimed a fake slap at her. "Oh, for Pete's sake, Keisha. You're going to need more than a secret admirer to handle you. You're going to need a psychology major for the philosophical paces you're going to put him through." They both started laughing, all seriousness aside.

Josiah had just pulled into Elise's apartment complex parking lot when a dark pickup drove past him at an alarming speed. He braked and turned quickly, trying to notice anything familiar about it. He was remembering Elise's mother's reference to a pickup scare the day of the strange message through Elise's apartment intercom. It screeched away from the complex before the fir trees along the property's lawn hid it from his view. He focused again on parking his vehicle. He should ask Elise if she'd had any problems since her mother's incident, but he hadn't exactly been as involved with her of late.

He sat, his right thumb tapping impatiently on the steering wheel. His cell phone rang, and he fumbled for it. "Yes?"

It was Rick Phillips. "You've got Jack working with us at the end of the week?"

"Yeah, thought I'd give him a change."

"You mean you need a break," Rick said with hidden meaning.

Josiah laughed. Rick was a good guy, likeable and absolutely dependable as a foreman, but bluntness was one of his potential irritants. "We all need a break from life's little trials every now and then." A movement caught Josiah's eyes, and he looked through the windshield to see Elise and one of her teacher friends, Keisha somebody. They were laughing and talking as they walked across the parking lot, thankfully away from his vehicle.

"Just checking." Rick brought him back to the reality of the phone in his hand.

"Ah, no problem, Rick. I'll talk to you later." He dropped the phone on the passenger seat.

Keisha had gotten into a car as Elise continued talking. A gentle, warm breeze was teasing Elise's long curls around her face. It was not often that she left her hair completely loose, at least not in public. He could hardly take his eyes off her and was both peeved and relieved that he was at least twenty feet from them.

He watched her wave as Keisha's car started out of the parking lot, then she lightly jogged back to the building. As she disappeared into the building, he suddenly felt deflated. He had been on his way home after checking on one of the work sites in town when he followed the urge to turn into her place. He wasn't sure why. He had only visited her apartment as her chauffeur or during a singles group meeting. Now here he was like a pathetic, love-struck adolescent. It certainly wasn't his style. He needed to get past this.

Josiah started his vehicle and drove out to the street. Sooner or later, he would have to meet this thing head-on. Sooner seemed to be fighting hard for first place.

Chapter Eleven

The work at the site for a new corner store was coming along well. It wasn't a very busy section in the city of Georgeton, but the residents were glad to have it near them. They were especially content that it would save them inconvenient trips into the more commercial areas, so there had been no residential opposition toward the building permit. Josiah was always satisfied when the paperwork and legal wrangling were put aside and the "real" work of building began. This was not a big job for his company. Certainly, not compared to the new senior's centre another of his crew was working on two cities away.

The licensed architect he had apprenticed under had been very cooperative in working with them in Alexander's Contracting's best interest. Of course, the architectural firm had also profited.

"Great day for building, isn't it?" Rick announced from behind him. Rick's white hard hat never seemed to be on quite right, and he usually had a smudge or two on his face, but he knew his job.

Josiah grinned and continued to look over the scene. "Couldn't be better. I wish I were back at the house right now, but I left that in Dad's hands. I gotta check on the Wellington project after this." He noticed one of the site supervisors talking to Jack, who seemed to be getting frustrated. "What's up with Jack?"

Rick's hat was slightly knocked aside as he reached up to scratch his head. "Ah, you know Jack. There's always something with him. Who knows what it is this time?"

"Mmm. Maybe I'll have him back at the house after a day or two. He's usually pretty good there."

"Any response yet on the license?"

Josiah moved his head back in a roll to dislodge the kinks from his neck. He seemed to have too much on his plate lately, but that would change. "Not yet. But I try not to think about it too much. I felt pretty confident about the exam."

A slow whistle eased its way out of Rick's mouth. "Imagine that. Soon you'll be a fully licensed architect, but the real kicker is, you already have your own company. I'm proud of you." His brown eyes shone with genuine pride and good wishes.

Josiah turned his back to the sun's glare. "Thanks, man. I really appreciate the sentiment."

"No problem." They stood silently for a moment, taking in the sound of the work site. It was a good sound.

"So, how have your sessions been going?"

Rick was slow in answering, but his tone was confident. "Good. It's been like a lifeline, you know?" He seemed a little embarrassed.

"Some days are better than others. Soon, hopefully, my family can accept me back and I can make up for all I've caused them."

Josiah knew it had taken much for him to share. He nodded in understanding and support. "All in God's timing, man. All in His timing."

Rick snickered. "Who knows? One day I may actually believe it like you do, especially with Elise on the case." He shook his head in wonder. "Man, she has a way of going on about her beliefs that makes you want to just believe—if nothing else, for her sake."

Josiah shifted to look at his face. "What do you mean? She's been talking to you?" He wasn't sure he wanted to acknowledge the jealous feeling that had began to seep into him.

"Oh yeah. I mentioned it once to her, and it's like she's made it her life's mission." He shook his head in wonder. "She was always a pretty decent girl, but there's definitely something different about her of late."

Before Josiah could comment, they were interrupted by a sudden explosion of men's voices.

"*Fight! Fight!*"

Josiah and Rick stood rooted in place for the moment it took to notice the work crew all running in one direction. They both took off at the same time.

"I still can't get over him kissing me like that, in public too." Alisha spread her hands in frustration, and Elise was sure she knew what was coming next. "I mean, it was like he thought he owned me or something. The nerve."

"Ali, I think you liked it," Elise stated as she concentrated on driving through the more narrow streets in this part of the city.

"Elise, if you say that one more time, I won't be responsible for what happens," Alisha fumed, then proceeded to freshen her lip gloss. It was a little difficult with the car enjoying every rut in the road.

"It's true, and you know it," Elise said, refusing to back down. She slowed down for a cyclist. "Come on Ali, it's me. If you want me to be honest about Josiah, you need to do the same when it comes to Rick." Elise turned her head to look at her when she didn't answer. "Alisha?"

An extreme sigh filled the car, followed by a groan. "Lise, you have no idea. How can I acknowledge to myself what I feel for him when there can't be any us?"

"I don't understand? Run that by me again?"

Alisha relented. "Oh, Elise, I'm sorry. Of course you know. You were on the other side of the coin."

"I'm still on the other side, it seems, if Mr. Josiah David Alexander has anything to do with it."

"Whoa—who's having the pity party? You or me?" They both started laughing at the absurdity of it all.

Elise wiped her eyes with one hand. "What a pair we are. Anyway, why do you think I've been working so hard on Rick?"

"For me?"

"Partially, but there's something else. From the moment he asked me to share my experience with him, I've had what you would call a 'burden' for him."

She had Alisha's complete attention. "That's the Holy Spirit. Oh, Elise, do think it's possible he'll come to the Lord?"

Elise concentrated on slowing down to turn the car into a parking lot beside their destination before she answered. "'With God, all things are possible.' You were the first to teach me that."

"Now the teachee is teaching the teacher," Alisha said with humour, but there was also sincerity in her voice. They smiled at each other, then moved to exit the car. "Well, let's go find Rick."

Elise paused to remote-lock her doors and nearly dropped her keys at Alisha's voice of alarm.

"Oh, my goodness, Elise! What is going on?"

Both women stood, eyes wide and mouths opened. There appeared to be a brawl at the work site where they were heading. They instinctively grabbed each other's hand and moved quickly toward the increasingly loud disturbance. On their way over, they noticed house doors in the vicinity opening to let people out as the noise filtered in through their opened windows.

When Elise and Alisha reached the scene, they stood far enough away to escape any jostling from the brawl, but close enough to observe two men fighting.

Elise recognized Jack from Josiah's house site—at least, it looked like him. He was grappling with a taller, but thinner man. Both their safety hats had been knocked off their heads, and she could detect a red, wet trail down one side of the thin man's face. As the group of men looked on— some disturbed, others apparently enjoying the change in action—another man kept trying to get hold of Jack from behind. Every time he tried, Jack would flail and struggle madly to slip from his grip like an eel. There was rage on his face as he swung his left fist to connect with the thin man's upper abdomen. The man bowed over, and Jack grabbed him by the neck and twisted viciously to flip him to the ground. The man hit the ground with a thud, and still Jack went after him.

"Hey! Break it up!" It was Josiah, with Rick alongside him, racing to the scene. They were both big men, so they easily barrelled through the peripheral group. Josiah threw his arms around Jack from behind to save the man on the ground from further injury. Jack struggled wildly, his eyes wide and his teeth bared almost like a rabid dog, but there was no getting out of Josiah's hard grip.

Elise shivered, then focused on Rick attending to the man on the ground. Now that Jack was apprehended, there was an incredible silence as the men realized the difference about this fight.

"Man, he was like a maniac," someone commented.

"That guy is nuts!" Some of the men seemed to be ashamed of their earlier celebratory attitude toward the fight.

"He's okay," Rick finally pronounced.

The men cheered and moved closer to see their fellow worker.

Elise finally unclenched her hand from Alisha's. "Josiah's never talked about this sort of thing happening before. Well, maybe a little fight once in a blue moon, but nothing this vicious." She glanced at Alisha. "Are you going to examine him?" She nodded in the direction of the injured man.

"Yes, I should. Come on." Alisha grabbed her arm and they made their way to the now smaller cluster of men. Many of them had noticed the women by now, so their attentions were further diverted. Both women ignored the appreciative looks and went straight to Rick who had his back to them.

"Let me have a look at him, Rick," Alisha said gently.

Rick jerked around, clearly surprised to see them. "What in the blazes are you two doing here?" He kept one hand on the shoulder of the injured man who was now sitting up on a plastic lawn chair. There was a first aid box on the ground beside them.

"We were passing by, and I thought it would be a good time to remind you of the group meeting at my place." Elise felt slightly silly as she witnessed the confused look in his eyes. His attention was clearly on more important matters. He was the foreman. But his response surprised her.

"Oh. No, don't worry. I haven't forgotten." His eyes had softened, and his baby face held a slight grin. He focused on Alisha in a way that caused the red from her hair to seem to seep into her skin. "Okay, Nurse Adair, do your thing."

Elise watched Rick introduce Alisha to the injured man, then she turned to search for Josiah and Jack. She couldn't see them. Most of the men had resumed their duties, though a few still lingered at the scene of the incident. She heard Rick order them back to work at the same time she saw Josiah, with a cell phone to his ear, exit a vehicle a little further away. There was another man sitting in the vehicle, and she presumed it was Jack. She took a deep breath and decided to go that way. She wasn't sure who made her more nervous, Jack or the big boss himself.

His dark eyes narrowed as she walked toward him. He flipped his phone shut and shoved it into his jeans pocket, then turned to look in the direction of the vehicle he had just left before facing her.

"I didn't expect to see you here today," he stated. The deepness of his voice was like music to her ears, but his expression was unreadable.

"I didn't expect to see you here either," she responded carefully, maybe defiantly. She stopped three feet from him. He studied her for a moment, then his lips lifted at the corners.

"It's my company. What's your excuse?"

She couldn't help but return the smile. He was being obstinate. "Well, I'm not chasing you down, if that's what you're insinuating." She glanced back to the scene she had just left. "Alisha and I came to see Rick. I didn't know you'd be here." There. Let him chew on that for a while.

The smile left his face, and his eyes narrowed. "Yes, Rick's been telling me about your efforts." He seemed to struggle, then took a moment to check behind him again. Satisfied, he turned back to her. "I think it's great. God will use those efforts."

"I'm glad you think so." She looked toward Jack. "Will he be okay?"

"He's settled for now." He sighed. "He's a bit of a complicated issue."

She looked down at the ground, then saw his dusty work boots edge closer. She looked up into his eyes. "You promised to have my back." Her voice shook slightly, but she held her own, determined.

He swallowed and rubbed the back of his neck.

"I hope you'll come tomorrow. It would be a great encouragement for Rick." She didn't give him time to answer before turning and walking away. She felt like crying, but she wouldn't give him the satisfaction. She knew he wouldn't come after her with Jack there waiting on a "time out."

Elise paced nervously around her apartment, making sure everything was just so. Why was she so nervous? It's not like she had never hosted a singles meeting. She had opened her door for two meetings before, and there had been no problems.

She paused and checked the snack tray. It was probably the combination of Josiah and Rick both coming. *If* Josiah bothered to show up, after she had acted like a complete baby. So what if he had backed off? It was a free country, and he was an adult. It's not as if they had made any type of commitment. At least, not officially. Had she imagined it all?

The intercom activated, and her heart thudded. What if he was the first to come? She wished Alisha had not been scheduled to work this evening.

She answered the intercom.

"Hey, kiddo. It's your one and only, Ricky."

Elise laughed. "Come on up, Rick. You're the first to arrive." She clapped her hands in glee. "Thank you, Lord Jesus. Rick's come!"

It had been a hard day, and Josiah felt like he had been running all over the place. Of course, the situation with Jack the day before hadn't helped. Fortunately for Jack, charges hadn't been pressed, but Josiah had insisted that he meet with Danny Rowe for a good dressing down. Jack had a lot at stake if he kept messing up. For once, Josiah had been very hard on him. He had stressed to him that he couldn't flip out on the other workers every time he didn't agree with them.

He approached the entrance of Elise's apartment building. He was late, but he had to come. She had practically dared him, and her big brown eyes had haunted him all through the night and much of the day. Maybe seeing her tonight would earn him a good night's sleep. Or not. Besides, he had also felt the Holy Spirit's convicting power that all was not well. Basically, he needed to take up this challenge, not hide from it.

As he entered the first set of doors, he saw someone approaching his direction from the lobby. It was April Roper, and she let him in through the second doors.

"Hey, April, what are you doing down here?" he asked, as he followed her to a bench where she had left her belongings. He lowered himself to sit beside her.

She sighed and tucked her chin-length blond hair behind one ear. "I saw you coming and decided to wait and go up with you." She had dark shadows under her eyes.

Josiah smiled and joked. "Well thanks, ma'am. I definitely think I need an escort to this function." His smile turned to a grin when she started giggling.

"Josiah, have you ever felt that you just can't take even one more blow life has to offer?" She was sombre again.

He stroked his chin thoughtfully. She seemed so frail, this single working mother of two. Life had not been good to her in the last two years. "He's caused problems again?"

She looked down, then nodded wearily. "He called and ranted for a couple of minutes, then got eerily quiet before he started pleading for me to let him come home." A pathetic sob escaped her. "I should report him each time, but I just can't bring myself to. It would set him back so far."

"It's okay, April." It was hard for him to know how to comfort her. The very one who should comfort her only brought her pain.

She angrily wiped at a trail of tears and looked desperately around the building's ground floor. "I pray to God constantly, but you want to know the honest truth, Josiah?" She turned her blue eyes to him. "I don't know that he wants to be helped."

"Ah, don't say that, April."

"It's true," she stated emphatically. "How does even God help someone who doesn't want to be helped?"

When Elise's apartment door opened to admit April and him, Josiah noticed her eyes widened in surprise. April had buzzed in and not informed her of his arrival.

"Oh, April, I'm so glad you could make it," she whispered before giving her a brief embrace.

"Sorry we're late," April whispered back. She seemed to have recovered from her earlier meltdown.

"It's okay," Elise shushed her. "I'm glad your sitter was available." As April moved from the front hall into the living room, Elise faced Josiah.

"Hi," she said, finally acknowledging him, brown eyes intent on his. He could see the gang piled on the living room couch, loveseat, and the various chairs positioned around the room. Pastor Solomon was leading the group for a change. As much as he wanted some time alone with her, this wasn't a good time. They were being a distraction. "Hi. Sorry for the lateness." If he was hoping to get April's treatment repeated on him, he was sadly mistaken.

"Thanks for coming," she whispered before turning to lead him where he could sit. To add insult to injury, she left him and sat on the area rug almost on the opposite side of the room. He reluctantly tore his eyes away from her as he acknowledged the nonverbal greetings from those nearest him.

"Josiah and April, we're basically talking about the need to build the type of house God desires," Solomon said before continuing. He was sitting on a chair where he could be seen by all.

Among those in the room were Rick Phillips and Danny Rowe. Josiah noticed Danny watching April. It wasn't the first time he had seen Danny's particular attention to the young mom. He was concerned about what appeared to be the young sergeant's interest in her. The complication was that, although April's estranged husband had been abusive, she was still legally married to him. Danny was playing with fire. He tried to focus on Solomon's words.

"I know you're, for the most part, single. But now is the time to know this." Solomon glanced around the room. He was never one to rush a message. "I know that most of you are eager to join the other group." He smiled broadly. "I tend to forget what they call that group. As you know, my wife heads it, and she always chastises me for going blank on its name. Whether it's the young couple's group or the newly married's group, I can't remember."

"The young couple's," someone piped up. "I know because dating, as well as married, couples go."

Solomon chuckled. "Thanks. So, whether you want to be a part of that group or not, what I'm going to say is important to know." He waited for all of their attention. "God uses the marital relationship to help us understand His, Christ's, relationship with the church. Now, I'm not talking about how a lot of marriages are, but how they are meant to be. As a man and woman commit to each other, they also commit to building a house together. The house they build is physical, figurative, and spiritual. Physical, so they can have a place to live and raise their children. Figurative, because it's more than a house; it's a home. Spiritual, because of God's place in it."

Elise's gaze was glued to Solomon, and Josiah thought she seemed to be listening intently. Alisha's words had hit him where it hurt when she had told him that Elise was soaking up Scriptural truths from anyone who would oblige her. He had, to his shame, excluded himself from that list.

"When a person commits to Jesus, they build a house together. However, the house that's built is you. He dwells in us by way of the Holy Spirit's presence in us, and builds us up into what he created us to be. In other words, it's literally having God in your body, or house, if you want to put it that way."

*   *   *

As much as she had enjoyed her time with the group, Elise found it hard to wait for some time alone with Josiah. At least, she had hoped for some time alone with him, but that also depended on whether he would accommodate her. She felt both relief and trepidation when he lingered until everyone else had left. She had never had him alone in her apartment before. She was breaking her and Alisha's golden rule about not being alone with guys in their apartments. Now that he was here, what was she to do with him?

"Do you want this here?" Josiah held up a white snack tray and nodded toward one of the kitchen cupboards.

"Yes, thanks," she directed quietly. She could tell he was trying really hard to be helpful, and he was. All dishes and trays had been handed back to those who had brought goodies, and her apartment was back in tip-top shape.

"Josiah, really, you don't have to do any more." She laughed nervously when he started wiping down the counters.

"Are you sure there's nothing else?" he asked. He looked so big in her home.

"I'm sure," she assured him.

He leaned back against the kitchen counter and studied her. "I'm sorry," he said simply.

She blinked rapidly. "Can you explain?" she asked.

He moved toward her. "Come here," he said, reaching for her hand. "Let's sit down."

She allowed him to lead her back to the living room where they sat, one seat apart, on the couch. He moved closer, and she felt her heart start to race.

"I haven't been a very good friend lately," he started. "This is a lousy excuse, but it's like finding it hard to believe in something too good to be true." He looked deeply into her eyes, then reached across to take both her hands in his. He seemed to struggle for a moment, and when he spoke next, his voice held a hint of that struggle. "I–I've been really happy that you belong to Him. It's more than I can put into words, but I'm so glad."

Elise saw the truth in his eyes and felt a weight lift off her chest. "It means a lot to me that you feel this way, Josiah. Everyone seemed so happy for me, but you… well, you became distant."

He threw his head back and let out a great sigh, then returned his gaze to her.

"I don't think everyone else has the same interest invested in you choosing to follow Christ as I do."

His playing with her fingers was distracting her. "What do you mean?"

His hands stilled. "It's about my 'struggle' that I mentioned to you before."

She was puzzled, and she definitely found it even more difficult to think with his thumbs stroking her palms. Her confusion must have shown.

"Never mind. You'll understand later. Just tell me: am I forgiven?"

She smiled and teased, "Are you asking me to?"

He squeezed her hands slightly. "You know I am." He leaned his head to one side and waited.

She looked down at their joined hands and felt a strange wave of emotion rise from within her.

She looked up at him. "I do. I do forgive you, and I really want us to be even better friends."

His weight shifted on the couch as he leaned toward her. "Define 'better friends,'" he demanded gently.

The nearness of him was intoxicating, but she tried. "You know— better than before we were, ah… both believers." She bowed her head to escape his gaze.

He let go of one hand, then tipped her chin with his free hand. "So, better could mean a lot of things?"

What was he doing? He had her chin locked in his hand. "I… guess…yes." He stared at her and she felt the heat rise in her face. She grew breathless as he let go of her chin and slowly lowered his head to hers.

"So, it could mean this," he stated softly, then gently touched his lips to hers.

She felt a tremor within her as she waited for him to deepen the kiss, but he didn't. He moved back and than reached to touch her lips with his fingers, tracing them slowly and gently.

"Is it okay for it to mean that?" He continued to hold one hand, while gently smoothing her hair.

Elise was sure she had never felt so mesmerized. Did he feel the same way? She wanted him to kiss her again. "Yes," she breathed.

After her answer, he slowly rose to his feet, pulling her up with him. He locked fingers with hers. "But not again tonight, cause I'm here alone with you, and I want to be responsible."

They continued to stand facing each other, staring at each other. They had crossed a bridge, and there was no way back.

Suddenly, he started toward the entrance, pulling her with him. "If we keep standing here with you looking at me like that with those big brown eyes, I might not be responsible for what happens next."

She jerked at his hand as he readied himself to go. She didn't know for sure what she wanted to say, but she needed to say something. "Josiah..."

He paused by the door and looked down at her. When she didn't say anything else, he smiled. "Elise, I've never known you to be so speechless."

That did it. "Well, it's not every day that I have a guy up in my apartment kissing me and then walking out, just like that."

"Do you want me to leave now, or stay the night?" he countered.

She dropped her gaze. He was right, of course.

He lifted her chin. "We'll do it right. It means we'll start to date, or court, or go steady—whatever you want to call it."

"Josiah!" she exclaimed, but felt her lips answering the smile on his.

He reached down and brushed his lips across her cheek. "Then we'll see where it all leads." He waited, expecting an answer.

She nodded slowly. "Okay."

After the door closed, Elise stood staring at it. Suddenly, she rushed toward it and flung it opened. He was gone, and he had taken part of her with him.

Chapter Twelve

Celia turned quickly when she heard an ill-hidden chuckle behind her. She glared at her husband as he entered their spacious bedroom Saturday afternoon. "It would be nice of you to share what you think is so funny."

He squeezed her shoulders and gestured toward the mounting pile of clothes on their king-size bed. "I knew you would start packing early, and I bet nothing in that pile belongs to me."

She brushed him off and proceeded to fold the piece of clothing in her hand. "Never mind. It's always interesting to note who's asking for this and that when it's time to go."

The side of the bed sank as he sat down. He ran his hands over his thinning hair, then gazed up at her. "I'm really looking forward to this."

She smiled, wondering at the deepening lines around his eyes and mouth. "Yes, I am, too. I think we really need it. We're becoming more city and country bound in our old age."

He chuckled. "Elise doesn't mind. As much as she likes her independence, she doesn't like us being away." He rose and moved over to the window, looking out into the tree-filled backyard. "For some reason, she still has no plans for this summer. I suppose she may just want to coast for a change."

Celia sat where her husband had vacated. "Or maybe she's waiting around to see what Josiah might have for her to do in regards to that house of his."

David faced her, a funny expression on his face. "Why do you say it like that?"

"Dear, haven't you noticed that her whole focus seems to be him lately?"

He drew closer to her. "I wouldn't say that. It seems to me her focus has been more on that church."

"Yes, but he's part of that church also."

He paused to ponder her point before speaking. "Really though, Celia, there is something different about her." His brows wrinkled. "I also get the feeling she's been trying to tell us about it."

Celia threw up her hands and stood up. "Men! *Mon dieu.* She's in love, Dave."

He sighed and lowered himself onto one of the room's two armchairs. "Yes, I believe you're right."

Celia crossed the room to sit on the second chair. They both stared off into space. "What do you think? It all feels so strange. I–I'm just a little afraid for her. I don't want her to be hurt."

He reached across the side table between them and took her hand. "He's a great guy, Celia. I mean, if you didn't see him as a prospective husband for our daughter, you would find no fault with him."

"Have I said that I've found any fault?"

He gazed across at her. "No, but your tone indicates it, my African queen."

She sighed. "She waits on him too much." When he didn't respond, she looked over to see his head bowed and eyes closed. "Dear, are you all right?" He was so dear to her, and she worried about him. Outside of her distant relatives in Africa, he and Elise were her only family. He had one brother living back in England, but they had never been close. Unfortunately, Elise had not grown up with the expected family around, so the roots developed in this community were important. Perhaps her being married should be in the near-future after all. If Celia were being honest, she would admit that Josiah wasn't the problem. She just didn't want to lose her only child. Yet, she would actually be gaining a son—and grandchildren. Her heart lightened considerably at the thought.

"Dave?" She shook his hand, getting his attention.

His head jerked up. "Umm? Yes, I was going to say, if she's going to make a life with someone, then I think he's the man for her." He leaned toward her. "You know, my darling, it's usually the father who has difficulty letting go of his daughter."

Before she could form a rebuttal, she was interrupted by the phone on the table between them. David let go of her hand and reached for it.

"Hello? Oh, hello, Adam." He winked at Celia. "Funny, we were just talking about a particular member of your family."

*   *   *

David settled back into the sofa as his wife placed a tray with two cups of tea and one of coffee on the coffee table in the living room. He always felt relaxed in Adam's presence, which seemed just as it should be. Perhaps they would be family in the future.

"Are you certain you won't have a bit of snack, Adam?" Celia asked, ever the gracious hostess.

Adam waved a hand. "Oh, no, no, Celia. This will do fine." He was seated in the armchair opposite the sofa. The slight sprinkle of grey in his tight curls served to project a distinguished look.

David waited until his wife was seated. She had lost the earlier tenseness that had been brought on, he was sure, by their conversation about Elise's life. Perhaps they should have had more children so they wouldn't be so focused on the one they had. Grandchildren would definitely share their focus. His eyes lingered on the still beautiful, strong form of his wife. She would make a wonderful grandmother. He decided to focus his attention on the matter at hand.

"You wanted to share something of importance with us, Adam?"

Adam folded his fingers together and leaned forward slightly. He did seem rather purposeful. "Yes, Dr. David, Celia. I haven't been asked to do this, but I felt I could be instrumental. So I asked permission to share a little something."

David and Celia looked at each other, then nodded in unison.

"Okay," David agreed. "Go ahead, Adam."

Adam nodded, but then reached for his cup of coffee and took a satisfying sip before starting. He set his cup down and looked them, one before the other, in the eyes. "There was a pilgrim who had been traveling on a long journey. This journey started out beautifully and simply. The pilgrim basked in the glow of the world and the privilege of growing up with all needs and desires satisfied. Now, this pilgrim

116

also had enough to do and contribute to the world so that there would be no bloom of disenchantment to mar their beautiful life."

He paused to take another sip of coffee. "Bear with me," he said, then continued. "As much as the pilgrim was given and had to offer, after a time it was hard not to notice the things that did mar the beautiful world. Things that no one seemed to be able to do anything about, no matter how many different approaches and tactics were tried. The pilgrim became increasingly more disenchanted with the world and began to seek for an answer. The familiar things no longer satisfied, and each new thing did not seem to, either."

David mentally shook his head. All his years of psychiatry were not helping him to figure out where Adam was going with this story—for that's what it seemed to be. Judging from Celia's expression, this was not what she had expected, either. He was, however, very intrigued.

Adam was steadfast. "Eventually, the pilgrim began to hear tidbits about a road that would lead one to the answer for all the world's ills."

Now David was sure he knew what Adam was up to.

"The journey to the road was difficult, confusing, and trying at times, but there were others to help. When the pilgrim got to the road, a huge gate reading 'The Way' barred it. The pilgrim was told to ask for entrance, to look for a way through and, finally, to knock. At first, the pilgrim was reluctant because no one was seen on the other side of the gate. However, the road already traveled had been long, and the road ahead seemed different somehow. More promising. The pilgrim's desire overcame all else. After doing all three things, nothing happened."

David shifted uneasily in his seat. He really hoped he wasn't going to have to be a psychiatrist to his friend.

Adam continued, unperturbed. "Finally, after three days of asking, looking and knocking, the pilgrim felt discouraged, but the others kept encouraging. Sometimes other strange ones would come with suggestions and enticements to lure the pilgrim away from the gate. Sometimes the pilgrim felt there was really nothing more beyond the gate, and the way back should be accepted as being all there was. Yet somehow, as if by an unseen force, the pilgrim felt compelled to stay and ask, look, and knock.

"Finally, the gate slowly opened, and what was hidden before was seen. The One who stood on the other side was real and had been waiting. With opened arms, He welcomed the pilgrim to the road—The Way."

After his third sip, Adam addressed the two people in the room directly. "Listen carefully to what I'm going to say. From then on, the pilgrim's life changed because it now belonged to the Opener of the gate. All else remained the same in the world, yet the pilgrim had changed, so nothing seemed the same anymore. The One of the new road remained with the pilgrim always with promises that one day all would be made right. All. In the meantime, the pilgrim was to continue on the road and help others also to find The Way. Dr. David and Celia, your daughter Elise is the pilgrim."

David stirred quietly and slowly in his bed. He didn't want to wake Celia, but he was finding it increasingly difficult to sleep. He checked the glow of the alarm clock. It was after two o'clock. It was useless. He got up and went to the adjoining bathroom. After closing the door so the light wouldn't disturb his wife, he peered at himself in the mirror.

"Old man, you must be getting older than you think to be thinking the way you are." Adam Alexander had gotten to him. He wasn't sure why. Probably because what he had to say had struck closer to home than anything else had in recent memory. It had involved his daughter. So, that was the difference he had been noticing. His daughter, a religious fanatic. No, according to Adam, she had gone through a transformation of the heart-spirit-soul, whatever he had called it.

He turned a faucet on and gently rinsed his face with cool water. He pulled a towel roll from a fancy basket on the counter and dabbed at his face. If he were being honest, he would admit that he didn't know God. At least, not like Adam had explained. He knew of God, but he didn't know Him, and neither was he challenged to know Him where he went to church.

He lay the towel down and turned to lean back against the counter. He wondered what his wife really thought. She had been surprisingly quiet about Adam's quaint visit and even quainter message. The most significant thing she had said was: "Obviously, he felt that he needed to share that with us because Elise is our daughter. But, I think, he's asking us to think about it for ourselves, too."

David switched the light off and crossed the dark bedroom out to the hall. He used the moonlight filtering in to judge his way down the curved flight of stairs. He lay down on the living room sofa and sighed out loud. It was going to be a long night. He was getting too old for this.

It was the ringing of the phone that informed David that he had actually fallen asleep, because how could one be wakened by such a rude noise if one had not fallen asleep? He grappled for the phone on the sofa table, hoping it had not wakened Celia.

"H–Hello." He noticed the approaching dawn. It was still quite early. "Yes, this is he." David attempted to straighten up, then froze. "Who is this?"

"I know what you're trying to do, but it's not going to work." The voice on the line was low, but tight. "You of all people should know what it's like for me, but even you have turned against me."

"What do you want? Tell me who you are." Could it be he? Surely not. He wouldn't know anything until he and Celia returned from their trip.

"I will die a fallen hero, fighting for what is rightfully mine." The line went dead.

"Hello, hello?"

"David, what's going on? Why are you in the living room?" Celia was coming down the stairs, clutching her housecoat around her. She saw his face. "David?"

Chapter Thirteen

She opened her apartment door, and he was waiting–all glorious six feet plus of him. She smiled and reached out to hold him, but he disappeared, and somewhere she could hear a phone ringing.

Elise opened her eyes to the warm morning glow of early summer through her window shade. She rolled to one side and reached for the phone.

"Hello," she managed to mumble. Her voice was still asleep.

"Hey, sleepyhead."

"Josiah?" Her dream had come true—sort of.

"The one and only," he declared. He sounded wide awake, but then he still had to get up for work, while she lazed around.

"Hi, how are you?" She suddenly felt alive! She struggled with the bed sheets to sit up.

"Great, especially for certain reasons."

"Which would be…?" She pulled the ponytail holder from her hair with one hand.

"Umm. I'm not sure I should discuss this on the phone. I'm down in your parking lot."

The hand that had been fluffing her hair froze. "M–my parking lot?"

"Yeah," he confirmed, laughing at her obvious disconcertment.

She threw the covers off, wishing that her apartment windows viewed the parking lot side of the building instead of the beautiful park landscape she usually preferred to see.

"W–why are you there?"

His voice was dangerously soft. "Why do you think?" When she didn't respond, he laughed at her silence.

She was getting a little perturbed. "All right, mister, what do you want? I was asleep when you called. I haven't showered, dressed, or breakfasted, so get to the point."

He laughed even louder, then became conciliatory. "Okay. Would you like to have breakfast with me? I'll take you out."

"You could have called last night and given me the head's up." She wasn't about to give him an easy yes.

"I know. You're right. I apologize, but it was an impulsive thing, which usually isn't really my style."

He sounded so good. "Really? Well, I guess I'll accept then." She moved around the apartment with the cordless in her hand. "So, do you want to come up and wait?"

"No. You buzz me in, and I'll meet you in the lobby."

He was real all right, sitting there talking away to Jake Morris as if he had nowhere else to be. She saw his eyes light up when he noticed her. She hoped she hadn't taken too long, but it wasn't every day that a girl got a call to meet her boyfriend for breakfast at the crack of dawn. Boyfriend. The word was awfully new to her—only three days old. It sent shivers through her. Jake also caught sight of her and grinned as he squinted at her. Somehow she would have to convince that man to wear his glasses. Today, however, that was not a priority.

"Look who I found waiting for you, Elise?" Jake blurted out, as if he had invited Josiah.

"Good morning, Jake. Thanks for keeping him for me." They had both stood up. She looked up at Josiah and suddenly felt shy. "Hi," she almost whispered.

"Hi, yourself." His dark eyes held hers captive, and she found it hard to look away.

Jake cleared his throat. He was standing almost directly between them. "Well, I guess I better let you two young ones go."

Elise blinked and focused on her neighbour. "Say hi to Margaret for me, will you Jake? And thank her for the goodies she sent over."

He nodded, smiling as he looked from her to Josiah. "I will, I will."

"Nice talking to you, Jake," Josiah said as they turned to go. He reached for her hand.

She looked up at him as he held the door open for her. On the other side of the door, he lowered his head and kissed her. His lips lingered.

"Good morning, beautiful," he breathed against her lips.

She pulled back a bit to answer. "Good morning."

He touched his lips briefly to hers again, then asked, "Ready to go?"

She felt like she was floating on air. "Sure."

He usually had a big appetite, so Josiah assumed it was sitting across from Elise that made him feel less need for sustenance. She was having a light breakfast, but he assumed that was usual for her, judging by her slender figure. Her honey brown skin glowed with good health, and her rose-tinted lips and bright eyes held him captive. He knew without a doubt that he wanted to be with her each and every morning. Every night, too. Now his head was going where it shouldn't. He focused on her words.

"So, I haven't spoken to my parents since your dad talked to them. I really didn't want him to have to do it, but he insisted on paving the way." She grimaced slightly, using her fork to toy with a piece of fruit on her plate.

"He really wanted to do it, though," he assured her. He heard her sigh—beautifully.

"I know, but on top of that, I now have to tell them about us."

He took a sip of coffee. "What about us?"

Her eyes widened, then she lowered her gaze. "You know, that— that we're together." She looked across the table at him.

He wanted to go across to her, but instead he reached for the busy hand with the fork. After laying the fork on her plate, he pushed it aside and locked his fingers with hers. "Are we together?"

"Josiah, don't tease," she pleaded with a slight pout. "You've probably had a lot more experience than I have."

"Experience? What experience?"

Her face was slightly flushed. "You know what I mean," she explained.

He was serious. "What do you mean, Elise? I've never been serious about anyone, until now." He noticed she kept her eyes down. "Not that I haven't had lots of opportunities, but I wanted to wait for the right one."

"Me too," she whispered.

He chuckled deeply. "Are we getting too serious?" He released her fingers.

She smiled, her head to one side, examining him. "Maybe."

Laughing, he said, "Do you want to come to the office? I need to go there for a little while."

Following her "Okay," he paid for their meal, and they left the pleasant little restaurant. In the restaurant parking lot, he opened the door of his white SUV and helped her in. After clearing the way from the flow of her white ankle-length skirt, he closed the door. Once inside the vehicle, he looked across at her.

"I really appreciate you being such a good trooper with all of this unexpectedness."

"Well, thank you for treating me," she responded, smiling widely.

"Keep that up and you'll have another kiss coming," he warned.

She smiled even more widely, then shrieked and held her hands up in front of her when he reached over to grab her. He held firmly to her wrists and gently pulled her closer to him.

"I did warn you," he declared and claimed his kiss.

Not long after, they pulled up to Alexander's Contracting Company's office building and parked in one of the reserved parking spots. It was a fairly new building, built a few years ago after the company had significantly outgrown its former storage yard.

"So, have you been playing hooky this morning?" Elise asked as Josiah held the passenger door open for her. He certainly hadn't rushed at breakfast, and now he was having her intrude on his day at the office.

Josiah laughed as his fingers gently touched her waist to direct her to the building's entrance. "One of the good things about owning a business is that no one will ask me that question." His brown skin looked rich and clear in the midmorning sunlight, and even the best shave couldn't hide the slight shadow along his strong chin and jaw line.

Elise paused on a wide concrete platform before double glass doors. "Josiah, I just asked you that very question."

"Elise," he said, stressing the syllables in her name, "you don't count. You don't work for me." He opened one door. "Come on. It's been a while since you've been here."

The air was cool inside. Josiah greeted the receptionist by name, then added, "Got my message?"

"Yes, I did." She eyed Elise uncertainly. Josiah's hand was still resting lightly on her waist. "Your father is in."

"Great," he said, then looked from the receptionist to Elise before adding, "Do you remember Elise Everson?"

There was a definite curiosity in her eyes as she directed a smile at Elise. "Oh, sure. Nice to see you again, Miss Everson."

"Elise, please. It's nice to see you, too." Elise smiled, noticing the gradual appearance of heads through different doors just past the reception area.

"I think you're going to be causing a stir," Josiah whispered for her ears only, as he moved with her across the room to Adam's office. "I think I'll sit you in with Dad for a while."

"Morning, Dad," Josiah greeted his father enthusiastically. "Look who I brought with me."

Adam looked up from some papers on the desk before him. He smiled widely, his eyes twinkling. "Ah, my morning has been considerably lit up, and not by my son."

Elise laughed. "Oh, Mr. Alexander, you certainly know how to charm a girl." She sat in a black leather armchair, offered by Josiah after he closed the door behind him.

Josiah perched on one side of his father's desk. "I figured I better land her in here before I have to start satisfying some intense curiosity."

Adam leaned back in his chair, hands folded on his lap. "Well, son, it's not every day that you walk in here with a beautiful woman by your side. Besides, the world and its neighbours can notice your change in attitude toward her. There are bound to be questions."

"I want to spend the day with her. I don't have time for questions. I just came in for some stuff I needed to make a few calls. I've taken the day off."

"There's nothing wrong with that. You hardly take any time as it is."

Josiah rubbed a hand across his jaw and glanced Elise's way, then back to his father. "I'm glad you think so."

Adam chuckled. "Elise, one thing you may be better at teaching my son than I is how to take time. He's a true workaholic. Mind you, he comes by it honestly."

"From you?" she asked.

"From me," he admitted. His arms indicated the office around him. "All this cost me a lot of wasted years with my wife. Years I never realized I would never have opportunity to recapture. So I'm glad to see there's something about you that's made him put his work aside, so to speak." He seemed quite pleased as he looked at them. "No other woman has ever been able to do that before."

Elise emotions were mixed. "Other women?" she questioned. "I thought you said there had been no other women."

Josiah gave a longsuffering sigh and got up off the desk. "Dad, you're going to get me in trouble." He directed his gaze at Elise. "I never said that. I said I had never been serious about anyone else before."

She searched Adam's face for confirmation. He nodded slightly.

"To the best of my knowledge, my dear, you're it."

She caught Josiah's eyes and declared boldly, "I think I'm going to enjoy staying in here with your father. There's a lot I need to know."

Elise was thoroughly enjoying herself with Adam Alexander in his office. He had, just as she desired, shared further about Josiah's life, the founding of the business, and, surprisingly, about his deceased wife. She felt she gave as much as he just by listening to him ramble on. His ramblings, however, were truly entertaining and full of information, and he seemed to earnestly want to share with her. Then he said something that sobered her.

"Your parents, Elise, I think have felt God's call."

She set aside the refreshments he had brought her. "How can you tell?"

He smiled encouragingly. "God's call to a person doesn't just happen overnight, but over time. When I was sharing about your conversion, I strongly sensed it for both of them."

Elise desperately wanted to believe. "So, I keep praying and…"

"Yes, keep praying and living. A living example for Christ is one of the best testimonies to the lost."

Before Elise could speak again, a soft knock sounded. They looked up to see a woman through the glass portion of the door. It was April Roper. The door cracked opened.

"Sorry to interrupt. Josiah was busy with a call. I didn't know you were visiting, Elise."

Elise rose at the same time Adam did and went over to her. She seemed tired and frail. "Hi, April. It's okay. I'm sort of an unexpected guest. What are you doing here?"

"She works here," was Adam's gentle reply.

Elise's eyes widened. "You do? I didn't know that."

April glanced at Adam before responding. "Not a lot of people do. I work mainly from home, courtesy of Josiah. It really helps me be more available for my girls and also keeps me away from here."

Elise frowned. "What do you mean?"

April glanced at Adam, helplessly.

Elise shifted her attention to him.

"Her husband is Jack—Jack Roper, and he works for us, too."

Elise's mouth fell opened, and she reached out to take hold of April's upper arms. "April, you mean Jack is the abusive husband and neglectful father of your children?"

"The one and only," she sighed wearily. "I'm sorry. I didn't realize you didn't know."

"Please, April, sit down." Elise directed her to the chair she had vacated. "Josiah never mentioned his name to me. I just assumed I had never met him."

"Good old Josiah," April said, smoothing her hair away from her face. "He probably kept confidence for Jack's sake. As he's helped me, he's tried to help Jack. There weren't many people who wanted to employ him." She smiled wryly. "He hired him as a favour to me."

Adam gently cleared his throat and headed for the door. "I'm going to leave you ladies to visit." Before they could protest, he was out the door.

April giggled. It was refreshing to hear it coming from her.

"Imagine us kicking the founder of the company out of his own office," she remarked.

Elise smiled. "They're great."

"They are," April agreed. "I don't know how I would have made it without them and the church. Pastor Solomon and Bethany have been very supportive. I just don't know how much longer I can do this. You're probably wondering why I attend the singles group." Her blue eyes were sad. "It's because I feel single. The man I married seems to no longer exist, and the only record I have of the man who once was is two girls. I don't know. I seem to find a lot of solace in that group."

"It's probably more about the people than what the group has to offer," Elise suggested.

April's eyes teared up, then spilled over. Elise grabbed some tissue from a box on Adam's desk. "Oh, April, I'm so sorry."

That's how Josiah found them—Elise comforting, while April blubbered out her problems. He decided against going in, and was gently closing the door when he heard an unexpected voice behind him.

"Hi, Jo," Danny Rowe greeted. He was in uniform and his grey eyes seemed troubled.

"Hey, Sergeant." He indicated with his head that they move away from the door. "April's in there with Elise."

Danny turned to go with him, asking as they went, "What's going on? I couldn't get her at home or on her cell."

Josiah opened the door to his office further down the hall. His office staff was really lucking out on entertainment value today. "Let's put it this way: she's in better hands than we can offer her right now."

"Drat!" Danny ignored Josiah's offer of a seat. Fortunately, the office was spacious enough to allow for the pacing that followed his entrance into the room.

Josiah had to smile. Here was a police officer, armed and in full uniform, walking around like a caged tiger about to be interrogated.

"He doesn't deserve her!" Danny's dark brows were furrowed and his hands were clenched at his sides.

"Dan, sit down, will you?" Josiah was feeling a little frustrated. He had left his condo this morning to spend time with the woman of his dreams, only to have it partially derailed by company calls, a weeping woman, and a pacing policeman.

"If I had the authority, I'd lock him up now and throw away the key," Dan growled.

Josiah decided *he* would sit down. "You want to talk about it?"

Danny whipped his hat off, causing his short, dark curls to spring slightly. He finally sat down. His eyes were pleading. "I want so badly to help her, Jo. I–I know she's not mine to help, and that's killing me. I have to talk to God about this everyday to keep my wits about me. Sworn to uphold the law, I'd like to break it for her sake. Am I crazy?"

Josiah pondered on his friend's words for a moment. He could understand Danny's passion because of his own feelings for Elise. Yet Elise was free; April was not. "How did you get so emotionally involved with her, Dan?"

"I–I don't know. It just kind of happened. Probably from the first report of abuse, I felt a connection to her—and the girls. Who knows what she suffered before she actually started reporting." Suddenly, he looked suspicious. "Look, I haven't touched her or anything…"

"I know, man. You don't have to touch someone to become attached to them. You were, and have been, there for them."

"It's more than hero syndrome, though."

"What are you going to do about it?" Josiah could see the desperation in his eyes.

He shook his head back and forth. "I don't know, and I think she's been distancing herself, lately."

Josiah got up and went over to him. "She's right to do that, though. It's probably better for you both in the end."

"You're right. I know you're right." His shoulders were slumped and his head bowed.

Josiah felt immense compassion stir within him. He felt the Spirit's call. "Man, let me pray with you. Later, I think you should book some time with Solomon."

Danny looked up at him, his eyes thoughtful. "Yeah, you're right. You want to pray with me now?"

"Yeah. Right here, right now."

Chapter Fourteen

Elise was immediately folded into Celia's arms upon entering the house. After the embrace, she stepped back to examine her mother. "Mom, is everything all right?"

Celia put her arm through her daughter's as they moved through the foyer of the Everson home. "Can't a mother hold her child—even a grown one—without being questioned anymore?" There was an emotional quality to her voice.

Elise slipped in front of her, forcing a halt. "We have a lot to talk about, but I want to wait for Dad."

Celia stroked her daughter's cheek and smiled. "I know, darling. It wouldn't do for you to go over it twice."

Elise still couldn't shake the feeling that something wasn't right. She kept searching for more signs as they moved into the kitchen where they would finish preparing the evening meal.

"Okay, let's see," Celia said as she started moving about the kitchen in a business-like manner. "I'll leave the salad to you—it's shrimp—and I'll finish up the pasta." She began gathering supplies, bringing them to a large work island in the centre of the room. "I wonder if we should try this new sauce or stick with alfredo."

"Mom, do you want to talk now?"

"You know, I think we'll stick with the alfredo. Your dad's been having a bit of stomach trouble lately, so I don't want to try anything new."

"Mom, please." Elise touched her mother's upper arm, claiming her attention. "I know Mr. Alexander's been to see you both, and we haven't really spoken since then. It's not because I've been wanting to keep things from you or alienate you." She had been feeling somewhat cut off from her parents and felt a desperate need to connect again. "It's just that a lot has been happening all at once, and not just with me. I have a new friend who's going through a really hard time. She's estranged from her husband and has to raise two girls on—"

"Elise Everson! I do not need to hear second hand that my daughter has found a new path and a new love." Her mother was looking at her strangely. "I expect to hear such life-altering news from my own offspring's mouth."

Elise froze. Her mother was really upset. It was evident in her eyes and in the tightness of her lips, speaking French. Those same lips began to tremble. Elise threw her arms around her mother's lean frame, then lay her head on her shoulder.

"*Vraiment, je suis désolée,*" she whispered. And she truly was sorry. She had never seen her mother so vulnerable. Was she the sole cause?

A shudder passed through Celia's body as they stood holding each other for a long moment. Finally, Celia disengaged herself partially and gazed into Elise's eyes.

"I feel like we're losing you," her mother admitted.

"No, Mom," she assured her. "That could never happen. I love you too much."

Celia smoothed a hand down one side of her daughter's head. "I know I'll sober shortly and apologize for overreacting, but you mean the world to us, and as much as it's right for you to be independent, we like to think you still need us, even if just a little."

Elise felt her heart break. "Oh, Mom. How can you say that? I still need you. I'll always need you."

"What's going on with my two girls? And, please, in English."

Both women turned to see David enter the kitchen, briefcase still in hand. His hair was slightly mussed, and his eyes and bearing weary. Elise left her mother's side to go to him.

"Dad, you look terrible!"

"Thanks." He smiled down at her before placing a kiss on her forehead. His eyes held a question for his wife.

"I'm afraid I didn't hold out too well," Celia admitted to him.

He sighed. "Well, how would life be if I didn't have my two girls to keep the drama alive?"

"Here's to all of life's dramas," Alisha declared that evening, at Hope Alive Church, as she raised her bottled water. "May they never cease to keep us on our toes."

"And that's not the worst of it," Elise whined as she thumbed through sheets of worship music. "Now they want to have Josiah over again, ASAP, so they can third degree him… as if they don't know all there is to know about him already."

Alisha left her position, leaning against the grand piano on the church sanctuary platform, and scooted onto the piano bench beside

Elise. "Don't worry about Josiah; he can take care of himself. Besides, next week I move back home with my mother. Be thankful you're not me."

Elise faced her, and Alisha could see the worry and frustration on her countenance.

"I feel badly for them—mostly Mom. She's the one that seems more affected by all this. Dad takes most things in stride, though he hasn't seemed himself lately. I've been meaning to talk to him about his problems at work, but I've sort of left it. Probably because I know they're going on their trip soon and will get the recoup time they need." She slapped the binder of music down on her lap in frustration.

"Don't they have anything but chords here? I play better by notes."

Alisha grinned. "Yes, little Miss Classical, but you're going to have to learn to chord or hardly anyone here will be able to play with you."

"Whose idea was this for me to join the worship team anyway?" Her brown eyes narrowed.

"I'll let that pass because I don't remember if it was Josiah or I who did the damage." Alisha reached down and picked up another good-sized binder from the pile by her feet. "Here, why don't you try learning the songs by notes first and then you can try the chords?"

Elise took hold of this new material like a lifeline and opened the pages. Seconds later, the large, beautiful sanctuary was filled with glorious music of praise.

Alisha slowly rose from her perch on the stool to give Elise more room, then she paced some feet away to enjoy the sound coming from the instrument. Elise was definitely an artist, but most of their musicians were amateurs and wouldn't be able to keep up with her. She would have to settle for chords, whether she liked it or not.

Moving even further away, Alisha watched her get lost in the music. Her arms, shoulders, head—all involved in the swell and dip of the piece. Alisha began to sing.

Alisha wasn't sure how long they had carried on before she noticed they were not alone. Josiah was walking slowly down the aisle on her side, and she could tell he was awestruck. He stopped a few feet away from her and nodded, not wanting to interrupt the wondrous flow of melody. If there was ever a time when she had witnessed the look of pure, passionate love in a man's face and bearing, it was now. She was, all at once, elated and deflated to be privy to such rapture that totally excluded her.

"We'll get you working with our music director. He's got a music degree, but knows how to play with the least of them," Pastor Solomon assured Elise. He had come up from a board meeting in Hope Alive's basement boardroom, and, along with most of the board members, had stopped to enjoy the music.

Josiah noticed that Elise seemed a little overwhelmed by all of the attention. Granted, almost everyone had dispersed after the last swell of music died, after Elise had discovered she had an audience of more than one. Now she kept looking in his direction from where she was sitting trapped by Solomon's wide frame. As much as she seemed to want his attention, he was sure he wanted hers more. Would she never cease to amaze him? He tore his gaze away from her and looked a row behind where Alisha had draped her arms over the back of the chair next to his. Her red hair hung loosely down one side of her face, which had an amused expression.

"You've got it bad, don't you?" she teased. Without waiting for his answer, she pronounced sentence. "Serves you right."

He swivelled his body in her direction. "Alisha…" he started, then searched her face carefully. "Alisha, your turn will come. He's coming around."

Her eyes widened. "What do you mean, Jo?"

The hope in her eyes made him ache for her. "He's been asking a lot of questions and started coming out to some men's stuff. He won't do Sunday yet, but he's been coming."

Alisha closed her eyes and sighed. She looked at him. "Tell her I had to go," she said, nodding toward Elise. She stood up and smiled down at him. "Thanks, Josiah," she whispered. "I'll talk to you later."

After Alisha left, Josiah sat for a while. He glanced at his watch and was about to get up when he heard someone approaching from behind. It was Alisha rushing back in. She had a puzzled expression on her face, and he stood as she came directly to him.

"There's a guy here who's looking for Elise. I think he's one of the teachers from her school. He claims to know Pastor Solomon, too."

Josiah glanced back at Elise and Solomon at the piano, still going through pages of music. Elise seemed more relaxed now, but then, that was Solomon's way. He said to Alisha, "I'll come see what he wants."

Alisha grinned, her green eyes flashing, as they made their way out of the sanctuary. "Ever the protector."

"You're never going to let me live this down, are you?"

"What, your statement that no woman would ever have you eating out of her hand?"

He could see someone waiting inside the entrance of the church doors. "That was eons ago, Alisha. Eons ago. Is that him?"

She nodded. "That's him all right."

As they approached the man, he seemed uneasy in Josiah's presence. He was slender and tall in build, dressed in a white, short-sleeved shirt and dark pants.

"Hi," Josiah greeted, while Alisha looked on. "I'm Josiah, a friend of Elise's. She's a bit tied up right now. Could I take her a message?" He wondered if this was Elise's "trial" from school that she had told him about.

The man's eyes were intelligent behind his glasses. "Ah, I'm Webster Myers. I was really hoping to get in touch with her personally. I was told she would be here."

Josiah felt uncomfortable. He easily outsized this man, but there was something about him that bothered Josiah. He began a third degree. "You're a teacher at Elise's school?"

"Yes," he responded hesitantly. "Look, could I just have a few words with her?"

Okay, "intelligent eyes" was getting on his nerves, and he had to remember he was in the house of God. "Sure, but you'll have to wait a bit."

"Fine," Webster responded, not backing down, but he glanced Alisha's way as if for assurance.

She smiled, then waved to Josiah. "Well, I really should be going. I have a nightshift at the hospital. Nice meeting you, Webster. See you later, Josiah."

Both men acknowledged her, then resumed their study of each other.

Elise was playing again, and the strains of music could be heard sufficiently through the closed sanctuary doors.

"Is that her?" Webster asked as he sat down on a wall bench by the front doors.

Josiah remained standing. "Yes, that's her. You might want to try her another time." He looked down at Webster.

Webster looked up at him. "I'd prefer to talk to her now, person to person."

Josiah didn't have a chance to respond. Elise and Solomon could be heard chattering loudly and happily as they made their way out of the sanctuary.

Josiah could tell she was looking for him when she and Solomon came through the doors. He also interpreted the stunned look on her face when her eyes found Mr. Webster Myers. It was Solomon who spoke first.

"Well, Webster, how are you doing? I don't think I've had the pleasure of a visit from you here before." Solomon seemed clearly puzzled, but his natural friendliness broke through.

Webster was already on his feet, after catching sight of Elise. Her face was aglow with the excitement of her newfound music commitment, and Josiah read the desperate look on Webster's face. Elise hadn't been joking; this man did have a "thing" for his woman!

"Hello, Solomon. Actually, I came to see Elise." He looked directly at her. Josiah moved closer to her.

"Hi, Webster," she finally spoke up.

Eying the two men guardedly, he responded, "Hi. Is there somewhere we can speak privately?"

What Josiah was feeling, he hadn't quite experienced before. It was similar to the fire that burned in him whenever he witnessed someone disadvantaged at the hand of someone stronger. What was now rising up in him was much greater.

"Whatever you want to say—"

Elise cut him off. "It's okay, Josiah. I'll talk with him." She turned to Solomon expectantly.

"Well, yes… Josiah, let's go to my office," Solomon said, and placed a big hand on Josiah's shoulder.

"Elise—"

"Please, Josiah, just for a moment," she pleaded. She seemed confident and smiled when he gave in.

"Okay. We'll be close by," he agreed reluctantly, then turned to go with Solomon after a dangerous glance at Webster.

Elise could see Webster breathe a sigh of relief. They were alone in the cavernous church foyer. She began to feel some sympathy for Webster; Josiah could be an intimidating figure, and with Solomon as a back-up… well… poor man.

"I thought you were away, Webster."

He cleared his throat and appeared more confident. "Yes, but I decided to cut my trip short. It didn't seem to have the same draw as before." He ran a thin hand through his brown hair. Even what looked like a recent haircut hadn't improved its appearance. "My research just wasn't going well at all."

She sat on the bench he had vacated earlier, and he followed suit. "How will you write your book then?" Webster had been working on a non-fiction piece for some time.

He faced her, his hazel eyes earnest. "Elise, my life is just not how I had envisioned it. What I had planned, what I had wanted, has suddenly become obsolete." He seemed to struggle for the words, and perhaps the courage. "I think it's because of you."

Elise was feeling very uncomfortable, but she was determined to shine through for her Lord, even in this. She felt no fear of the man seated beside her, but she needed a release from him. "Webster, I don't know what to say. What I told you earlier still stands. I don't think it's helpful for us to revisit it. You must respect my right to know what I want."

He reached over hesitantly and lifted her hands from her lap. He held them gently. "Perhaps, if we tried…"

She shook her head firmly and withdrew her hands. "No, Webster. Whatever you need, I don't have to give. I can't fulfill your needs. Only one Person can do that, and you want nothing to do with Him."

He remained silent, his eyes downcast. He sighed deeply and ran a finger across his upper lip, then looked into her eyes. "I'm in love with you and have been for a long time. I gave you all the signs I could think of. I've never been good with the dating scene; books are more my passion. You, however, changed that, and now you won't give me a chance."

Elise glanced at the hall off the foyer where the men had gone, then back at Webster. "Webster, I tried not to encourage you. You just wouldn't accept *my* signs. If we had tried, then you would have been left worse off with a broken heart, and I would have been, well, responsible and very wrong."

He threw his head back and laughed dully. "So, what do I do? Go back to life as it was? Nothing is the same anymore." He stood and walked a few paces away with his head bowed, hands in his pocket, and his shoulders slumped. Suddenly he faced her and came back.

"This wouldn't have anything to do with my rejection of religion, would it?"

"No, Webster. We're just not—"

He cut her off. "I know, I know."

She stood beside him and said gently, "Webster, I don't know what to do for you. I can't pretend what isn't, and it wouldn't be right for you, either."

He looked solemnly at her, then reached out to touch her cheek. "I would take anything from you, Elise. Even a pretence."

She kept her eyes on his and stated firmly, "No, Webster. That would not satisfy you for long, and I would be ashamed to use you that way."

His hand dropped. "There's someone else." He searched her eyes diligently.

"This has nothing to do with anyone else."

"But there is someone else."

She looked down and sighed. "Yes," she said simply.

He contemplated for a moment. "It's that guy—Josiah." After her nod, he asked, "Why have you never told me?"

"It's recent, Webster. We've known each other for years, but we're together only recently."

He moved closer to her. "You live with him?"

She blushed, and exclaimed, "No! We're not married."

He chuckled mirthlessly. "No, of course not. Your religious convictions would never allow for that."

She clutched her handbag closer, wanting to end their meeting. "I hope not. I hope my relationship with Jesus would keep me from making mistakes like that."

He shook his head and sneered, "You're bound by a fairytale." When she didn't answer, he looked at the exit. "When I was a kid, the jocks always got the girls while the girls used the geeks for marks. It's the same when you're an adult. Brawns versus brains… brains always loses."

Elise was tired of the conversation. She was no longer wanting to be the sounding board for a grown man's whining. She hiked her handbag further up her shoulder and said, "I'm sorry, Webster, I should get going now. If you ever want to consider all that I've shared about my relationship with Christ, you know Pastor Solomon. He would be more than happy to help you. I remember what it was like to feel emptiness before Christ filled me. One more thing, Webster. Josiah, the brawns, happens to have a degree in architecture."

As soon as Elise walked away from Webster, Josiah appeared. He walked quickly toward her, and before she could wonder at his conveniently-timed, sudden appearance, he folded his arms around her, nearly smothering her with his embrace.

"You okay?" he asked. When she didn't answer, he held her away to see her face.

She smiled, looking up at him. "I couldn't speak."

He grinned. "Oh, sorry." He loosened his hold on her.

She leaned back against the circle of his arms. "Yes, I'm fine now. But just how far away were you?"

His grin widened. "Put it this way, only Solomon went to his office. There was no way I was gonna leave you with that guy."

Elise revelled in the warmth of his care. "I didn't think so. I thought you were going to pick him up bodily and throw him out."

"I almost did." He touched his forehead to hers. "Thanks for defending my intelligence, by the way."

She was having trouble thinking with his face so close to hers. "You heard that?"

"I heard everything, baby." He let her go, only to take her hand. "Come on, let's tell Solomon we're leaving."

Chapter Fifteen

After leaving Hope Alive Church, they decided to take a stroll through a nearby community park. They needed time alone, and Elise really appreciated being with Josiah to wash away the unwanted remains of her meeting with Webster. The park was nearly empty of people, and the lights there created some appealing contrasts with the evening shadows. They were sitting on top of a picnic table, breathing in the warm summer air, when Elise blurted out, "Keisha wants me to come to Jamaica for a week." She felt his shoulder move where her head rested in the circle of his arms.

"Are you going?" His voice was quiet, deep.

She raised her chin and turned her head slightly to see his face. "I don't know. I'm thinking about it, but I don't want to be gone when the decorators come to the house."

He sighed. "I've been meaning to tell you about that. There's going to be a delay."

"Really? What's happened?"

"We've fallen behind schedule on the senior's centre in Wellington, so I've had to redistribute the men."

"Oh, I'm sorry," she remarked, turning the side of her shoulder into his upper chest.

He squeezed her gently to himself. "Are you?" he asked, his eyes on her mouth.

"Of course I am. You want it finished, don't you?" She loved the feel of his strong arms holding her, protecting her.

He changed the subject. "So, when would you go?"

"Umm. Probably the week before my parents come back from their cruise. I promised I would look after the house. They're back the third week of August, so I would get someone else to check on things for me the week I'm gone."

"So, you'd go the second week. I'll check on the house."

She laughed, and it caught the attention of a couple walking their dog. She piped down to a quiet giggle.

Josiah frowned. "And the humour in that is … ?"

She pulled slightly away from him. "I was just thinking how proud Webster would be of you figuring the week out." She placed her slender fingers over his one arm, just below the elbow, and squeezed. "Though, I can see why he insisted on labelling you 'brawns.'"

Josiah shook his head and pulled her back to him. "That guy's crazy. While you were talking to him, Solomon updated me a bit. He knew him from—you'd never guess where."

"I'm too tired to guess. Where?" She stifled a yawn. She was so comfortable. Maybe she wouldn't go to Jamaica, but she didn't want to spend her days waiting for her evenings with Josiah. Maybe she should do some volunteering, learn something new… or go to Jamaica.

"Bible college," he said, laughing.

"No way. Webster? Are we talking the same Webster who thinks Christ was a good man, but has been in the tomb for over two thousand years?"

"That's right." He shifted her weight slightly.

"What happened to him?"

"I don't know, but apparently Solomon has reached out to him, to no avail." He moved his head back in a stretch. "I don't want you to go, but you should go."

She stroked the large knuckles of his hand. "You're trying to get rid of me?" The rumble of his laughter vibrated against her back, then the warmth of his lips pressed on the side of her neck.

"As if. Even in my dreams, you're with me. If I could, I'd go with you, but things are too busy."

"That's sweet," she whispered.

"You're much, much sweeter," he declared.

After Josiah dropped her off at her apartment, Elise researched flights to Jamaica on the internet. Her parents would be leaving for their trip in a few days, so she wanted to make sure to book a flight that worked with their plans for housesitting.

After finishing with the computer, she picked up the phone. Keisha had told her to call her parents' Jamaican home late, when she was guaranteed to be home, or just e-mail her. Having e-mailed her multiple times before, Elise thought a call would be nice.

"Hello, may I speak with Keisha?" The connection to Keisha's family's cell phone was good.

According to Keisha, most people in Jamaica tended to use cell phones rather than depend on land lines, which were easily piggy-backed, leaving homes with bills from unfamiliar calls.

"Hi, Keisha, how are you?"

"Elise. Girl, it's nice to hear your voice. I actually tried calling you earlier."

Elise settled on the length of her living room couch. "I was out with Josiah."

"Of course," came the pert reply.

Elise laughed, then asked, "So how is sunny Jamaica?"

"Just as sunny and hot as ever. A little too hot. I've been keeping pretty cool at the beach, though, and it's great being around my family. I have two other sisters here, plus…"

"Plus?" Elise prompted.

"Plus, there's someone I'd like you to meet."

Elise screamed. "No. You've met someone in Jamaica? Why doesn't that surprise me? Now, tell me. What's his name?"

"Gavin, and he's very fine. So now you've gotta come," she pleaded.

"Actually, that's why I called. I've decided Jamaica is calling my name this year."

After updating Keisha, she shared a little about Webster's meeting with her.

Keisha exhaled into the phone. "So he's finally met Josiah. That's good. That could be just the thing to end this whole mess. How did he take it?"

"Which one, Josiah or Webster?"

"Well, now that you mention it, both."

"Webster did not take it well, but you're right, meeting Josiah may have solved this. As for Josiah, he was marvellous not to break the 'thou shalt not kill' commandment in church."

The women eventually disconnected, and Elise prepared to retire for the night. When the phone rang, she assumed it was Josiah saying good night, as had become his habit. She had just finished brushing her teeth and had to rush to answer it. It was not, however, the nice, deep voice of her beloved that greeted her.

"Hello?" She could hear someone breathing heavily, but there was no answer. "Who is this?" She quickly looked to see if her call display recorded a name and number. It was unknown. She almost dropped the phone when a raspy voice finally spoke.

"What I have lost, you will one day lose. You all don't know what it's like living like this." It was said slowly and deliberately.

Then the line went dead, and Elise finally breathed. She realized how hard she had been gripping the phone when her knuckles began to ache. She set it down and stared dumbly at it. She could hear her heart palpitating, and her mouth felt dry.

"Jesus, what was that?" She looked around the room, then back at the phone. She grabbed it and pressed a button. This time, she was taking things seriously!

Before he could finish his "hello," she was talking. "Josiah, are you home?"

"Just on my way. I stopped at the office for a bit. You sound upset."

"Can you come back, please?" It had just occurred to her why the call sounded familiar. The caller had used the same words as the intercom message her mother had described.

"Are you okay?" he asked, worry evident in his voice.

"Yes. I mean, I'm okay right now, but I had a scare." She didn't want him to panic, but she needed him.

"Elise, was someone there?"

"No, nothing like that. It was a call." She had systematically started moving around her apartment, looking out all the windows.

"Okay. I want you to call the Morris' and see if you can go over there. When you get there, call me back. I'll be right there."

Minutes later, she was across the hall at Jake and Margaret Morris' apartment being coddled. She literally felt rescued when Josiah came and took over from them.

Jake walked with them over to Elise's apartment. His white hair was mussed and his robe hung carelessly over his stooped frame. "You might better get the police involved, Josiah. That's the second time this has happened. Even Margaret is getting a little spooked, and it has nothing to do with her."

They paused outside Elise's door. "Oh, Jake, I'm sorry. I don't want Margaret to be afraid," Elise said, hugging her light, calf-length robe over her shorts pyjamas. She smoothed at her hair, which she knew was wild around her head. She didn't dare correct Jake on how often *she* had really been spooked.

"Ah, she'll probably forget about it by next week. It's you we gotta worry about." He seemed ready to defend her at a moment's notice.

Josiah smiled. He had his arm wrapped protectively around Elise. "Thanks, Jake. I really appreciate your kindness and feel better knowing you're here for her."

Jake took Josiah's hand and shook, man to man.

As soon as he entered her apartment, Josiah pulled her tightly to him. "You scared the life out of me," he murmured against her curls. She responded by standing on tiptoes and throwing her arms around his neck.

"I'm sorry. I panicked, I guess." She gasped when he put one arm behind her knees and swung her up into his arms. He easily carried her from the front hall to her living room couch and sat with her gathered on his lap.

"Is there anything else you want to tell me? Do you think you recognized the voice at all?" he asked, his eyes intent on hers.

"No, no. I only know that it was a male voice and scary sounding," she said, trying to pull one part of her robe over her bare legs. "It wasn't a distorted voice…"

"As in distortion caused by using a device?"

She nodded. "Right. It wasn't like that. It was just very unpleasant." She shuddered.

He pulled her head to his shoulder. "Jake was right. Because of its similarity to your mother's incident, I put a call in to Danny on my way here. He wants to talk to you in the morning and file an official report. I told him you'd probably be at your parents'. That's where I want you to sleep tonight."

Her head jerked up. "Will he have to speak with my mother, too?"

"Most likely, he'll want to compare the two."

She pushed against his arms, and he reluctantly released her. She stood looking down at him and stated firmly, "Then no. He can take my statement tomorrow, but I'm not going to my parents', and I don't want him talking to my mother."

Josiah leaned forward, knees apart, and reached to take hold of her hands. "Now, I know you're going to explain all that to me."

She knelt before him, hands still in his and face raised. "Do you know what that would do to them? My mother would freak. The first time, she called me every night for days. Also, they would absolutely not go on their trip."

Josiah sighed heavily. He studied the face before him. Her eyes were wide, her lips incredibly inviting, and her hair fell crazily around her shoulders and upper arms. She was gorgeous. Apart from all of this craziness, he wouldn't be here, with her, being tempted by curves partially hidden under her night attire. He closed his eyes tightly, then looked over her head and around the room.

"What then? I don't want to leave you here and… I certainly can't stay with you." He looked down at her again. "What about Alisha's?"

She pulled her hands from his and tried to bring some order to her hair—to no avail. "She's working tonight."

Suddenly, he knew. He stood and reached down to help her up. "Pack a few things. We're going to Dad's."

Elise woke to the low sound of male voices. For a moment, confusion washed over her, and then she remembered where she was, and why. The "why" brought its own sense of anxiety, but just as quickly, remembering where she was, dispelled it. Her prince charming was down beneath this room where he and Adam had secured her late last night. She was smack dab on the middle floor of the three-storey family home.

She raised her head to look around the dim room. It was the master bedroom, still with its century-old original trimming and moulding. The Alexanders had renovated the entire house to maintain its classic look. This room had been used as a guest room after Darlene Alexander's death, and Adam occupied one of two other rooms on the same floor.

She sat up in the softness of the bed and hugged her knees to her chest. Josiah had mentioned something about being in his old haunts for the night—the third floor. She had been up there before with some of his other friends, and they had marvelled at the most creative bachelor pad they had ever seen. She had never been in this room.

For some reason, she felt sad about the For Sale sign she remembered seeing out front. Josiah had been a part of this house for years. Yet there was the new house to look forward to, and that was something. Of course, she felt a little shy at entertaining thoughts about her having a certain ownership of the new house, too. Josiah had been right. She was falling in love with his new house, but she had fallen in love with him first. Even before plans for the house were conceived.

She closed her eyes. "Dear Father, thank you ever so much for your care. Thank you for Josiah and Mr. Alexander—even Jake and Margaret. I know I can hope in You and trust in You. Please help me to continue to do that, through Jesus. Amen." She kept her eyes closed for a moment, then quickly opened them and gathered the linen around her after hearing a slight knock on the bedroom door.

Josiah poked his head around the door before fully emerging. The room suddenly seemed smaller with him in it. The strength of his form was evident through the white t-shirt and dark jeans he was wearing.

"Morning," he whispered, leaving the door slightly ajar. His bare feet padded softly on the wooden floor as he crossed the room to sit on the edge of the bed.

"Good morning," she whispered back. She could see he hadn't shaved yet, and she longed to run her fingers across the stubble along his strong jaw line, but she kept them clutched around the sheets.

He had a slight frown as he studied her, then his lips turned up at the corners. "You look about sixteen."

She smiled back. "Well, I feel like about that, after having been grounded from my own place." She smoothed at her hair self-consciously. His hair lay snugly in tight waves on his scalp, never messy. Her fingers ached to change that.

He placed his fingers along her cheek. "Are you okay? Did you sleep well?"

She nodded, disoriented by the warmth of his hand.

"We'll go to the station this morning. We'll worry about you going back to your apartment later."

Again she nodded. If he moved his hand, maybe she could think for herself, but he didn't. Instead, he added the other hand to her other cheek, shifting closer to her as he did so. He began kissing her gently and deliberately, not like anything he had done before. She felt it was more than their lips connecting; it was their souls. She grabbed hold of his wrists, feeling the need to hang on to something before she was totally swept away. Then he pulled his mouth away, and she felt his hands shaking against her face.

"Josiah," she breathed, her gaze swallowed up in his.

He let her go and got up, then stepped back a few steps. "I gotta go," he said in a strange, hushed voice. Then he turned and left the room, closing the door firmly after him.

Elise sat in a daze. What had just happened?

After a quick shower, Elise dressed and then brought some order to the room. She felt more herself, no thanks to the incident with Josiah. Obviously, he was having as much difficulty as she containing their desires for each other. Normally, they were rarely alone—usually meeting in public places. Last night had created havoc in greater ways than probably intended. A message meant to intimidate had also caused a greater need and opportunity for intimacy.

"Well, good morning there," Adam greeted warmly when Elise appeared downstairs in the kitchen. He set his newspaper down on the kitchen table where he was sitting with his morning coffee.

"Good morning, Mr. Alexander," she responded. He seemed so cheerful, normal, and … safe.

She joined him at the table. "Thanks so much for putting up with me."

"You'll just have to believe me when I say it's been absolutely no problem." His eyes crinkled at the corners as he smiled. He was dressed and seemed ready to take on the day. Somehow, when the time came, she couldn't imagine him retiring. "Would you like some coffee?"

"She drinks tea, Dad." Josiah walked into the kitchen. He had exchanged his white t-shirt for a blue-grey, short-sleeved shirt. He looked at her without really looking at her. "How are pancakes for you?" he asked.

His sudden appearance had thrown her off. "S–sure. Thank you." She kept her eyes on him as he busied himself around the kitchen. Something was amiss.

Somehow they made it through breakfast. Josiah was sure even his father had felt the tension in the kitchen, and he had felt like a heel every time he caught Elise's eye and saw the confusion registered on her face. Wisely, his father had not commented and sent them on their way after declaring he would set the kitchen in order.

As soon as he reached his side of the vehicle and sat down beside her, he let it out. "Elise, I'm sorry." He looked at her. Her light brown eyes were wide. "You were vulnerable, and I took advantage."

"Josiah—"

"I should have known better. I should have done better."

"Please, Jose," she pleaded.

He stopped. "What did you just call me?" He was facing her fully. "Say it again," he commanded.

"Jose," she repeated uncertainly.

He grinned widely. "My mother used to call me that." He felt a sense of release, of peace. He leaned toward her. "Why did you call me that?"

"I–I don't know. It just came out. I'm sorry if it was your mother's name—"

"No, no," he assured her. "I want you to use it. Say it again." After she obliged him, he asked. "Am I forgiven?"

She shook her head. "There's nothing to forgive."

"You wouldn't say that if you knew what I was feeling at the time, what I wanted to do—almost did." He held her gaze steadfastly with his.

Elise was quiet for a moment, then said, "You wouldn't feel so badly if *you* knew what *I* wanted to do." She shifted closer, reached up, and ran her fingers over his hair down to his jaw. She loved the soft, slight ripples of his hair. She pulled his face to hers and kissed him lightly, sweetly. "Now, let's call it even." She let him go.

Chapter Sixteen

The afternoon sun beat down on their heads once they were outside of the cool interior of Elise's car. Two little hands clasped hers as they trumped, like the three musketeers, up the walkway to her parents' front door. Lily and Mya Roper were helping her in her housesitting duties, and they were taking it very seriously.

"Now that we have the mail, we'll go in and water the plants," Elise instructed brightly.

"That's because they're thirsty," Lily piped up. "What are they gonna eat?"

Elise smiled down at their chubby faces, slightly tanned from everyday romps in their backyard. "They like stuff from the dirt they're in. Don't you worry, they get lots out of the dirt."

"Lost and lost," Mya chimed in. The three year-old rubbed her button nose, then pointed to the perennial blooms all along the front of the house. "I wan de fower—pitty fower for Mommy."

Elise laughed as she opened the front door. "Okay, but let's go inside first, and when we come back out, you can pick a pretty flower just for Mommy."

"Me too, me too!" five-year old Lily hollered, jumping up and down.

"Okay, you too," she consented. She hoped she wasn't spoiling them for their mother. April tried fairly hard to balance the disciplining of her children with words of affirmation and spending quality time with them. It was a lot for a woman raising two little girls on her own and holding down a job. The summer break afforded Elise time to pitch in and lend a hand, which she was more than willing to do. April's girls had grown on her, and she felt real affection for them.

At first, the girls stuck by her side inside her parents' home, but then their natural curiosity caused them to venture further ahead. She allowed them to have free roam on the main floor and "explore."

Fairly certain about Lily's promise to make sure Mya didn't "hurt" anything, she moved throughout the main floor, making sure all was in order. While she collected water for the indoor plants, she kept an eye and ear out for the girls. April had been grateful for Elise's help after her childcare option had cancelled last minute. Elise still carried a weight in her heart for April, especially after finding out about Jack. She knew that Josiah was becoming increasingly frustrated with Jack, and would have already fired him if April hadn't begged for another chance. It was amazing how much April chose to uphold this man who had wronged her so. Knowing that there was a restraining order, and that Jack had relocated a city away, gave Elise a sense of relief for April's sake. April had been the victim of verbal and physical injuries from her husband, time and time again. It had been hard to imagine until Elise saw the drastic shift in Jack's personality at the work site brawl.

"Lily! Mya!" she called. "Do you girls want to come upstairs with me?"

They came rushing from the family room where they had been held captive by the sight of her father's boat and ship showcase. Mya trailed behind her sister, her chunky little legs trying to keep up.

"Walk, girls, walk," Elise admonished.

"Up, up, up," Mya sang. They clambered around Elise's legs on the stairs.

"Be careful," she managed to say as she held the watering pot in one hand and tried to keep her capri pants up against the weight of Mya's security grip. "Here, let go of Elise's pants, Mya, and take my hand."

They made it to the second floor in one piece, where Elise showed them her old room. The girls squealed in delight as Elise pulled out some of her toys from their storage totes. She wondered if her parents would ever get rid of her things.

She hoped they were truly being prudent to rest well on their trip. She had received every indication from their communications that all was well and enjoyable.

Once again, she congratulated herself for not sharing her frightful incident with them. Danny Rowe, however, had been thorough in questioning her, and Josiah had been understandably upset when the other "incidences" were revealed. Danny had also been puzzled about the intercom message received by her mother. Once the person had ascertained that Elise wasn't home, why still leave such a message with her mother? Next, Danny had questioned motive, and Josiah had promptly pointed out that she couldn't possibly have any enemies, but that Webster Myers was a victim of unrequited love. Elise had found humour and disbelief in that suggestion. Danny had taken his cue from Josiah; both had been dead serious.

"Oh, can we keep some? Pretty please?" Lily whined after Elise instructed them to pack up the toys.

"Want tum, pease," Mya echoed.

Elise looked down into their blue eyes. They looked so much like their mother. How did a mother explain such a father to them? If all failed, how would April find the answers to give them in their later years?

"Okay, you dumplings, but only one each."

They giggled at her name for them. "Dumplings! Dumplings!" Lily yelled as she hopped around the room. Mya sat down to play, forgetting to pick a toy and clean up.

"I'm going downstairs for a moment, girls. Lily, help your sister choose one toy, then please clean up. Okay?" After Lily's exuberant promise, Elise raced lightly down the stairs to the main floor laundry room. She dumped the remaining water from the watering pot before replacing it on an upper shelf. She turned to go and shrieked, her hands jerking up over her mouth.

There had been a face at the laundry room window! She was sure of it!

For a moment she was frozen, then, with her heart thudding from fright, she rushed to the window and looked out into the backyard. Nothing. She twirled around and quickly rushed through the hall to her mother's den. She pulled the door open and rushed to the window. Just as she looked out, she saw the figure of a man race around the corner to the left of the driveway. Seconds later, a dark-coloured pickup careened away.

Her breath was coming in gasps, but suddenly remembering Lily and Mya, she raced up the stairs. She heard their lively chatter, so normal sounding. She slowed her pace and tried to slow her breathing, then walked into the room.

"Look, Lise." Lily came toward her with a princess doll in her hand. "I want this one."

Elise knelt before her, breathing more easily. "May I have this one," she corrected.

"May I?" Lily repeated, her eyes wide with hope.

Before she could answer, Mya joined them. "Me too! Me too!" She held out a fat, wooden hippo her mother had brought from Africa.

"Sweetheart, maybe there is something else you could choose. I don't think my mommy wants me to give this one away." She waited for the protest.

"Otay," the dumpling child said, before eagerly returning to the pile of toys.

"Yes, you may keep yours," Elise whispered to Lily. She patted her blond hair before rising to glance out the window. She could see her car in the driveway and some movement from one of the neighbours' houses across the road. All seemed well in the suburbs, but all was not well.

As soon as Mya had made her decision, they returned downstairs where Elise gave them a snack to eat at the kitchen table. She allowed them to keep their new toys at the table, then she moved across to the dining room.

"Danny?" she said into her cell phone. "It's Elise."

The tangy aroma from the sauce being added to the chicken on the grill was causing Elise's mouth to water. She hadn't eaten since breakfast and, in her busy day with April's girls, hadn't thought to eat. The episode at her parents' house certainly hadn't helped her appetite, but that had been hours ago. After dropping the girls off at home, she had gone to Georgeton's police station to talk with Danny before showing up for her scheduled visit with the Sungs. They had invited her and Josiah to a backyard barbeque, but Josiah had been held up on the job and would be late.

She sat curled up on a lawn lounge chair waiting as Bethany checked her husband's status with the barbeque. The twins, Joshua and Jordan, were out front on the driveway, trying to outdo each other shooting hoops. Her earlier attempts with them had left her breathless and a little sore. They had seemed a little disappointed when she had begged to quit.

The Sung's backyard patio, wide and inviting, took up about half of their backyard. The rest was a carpet of soft grass and a decent-sized vegetable garden. The fencing wasn't high enough to completely ensure privacy, but it gave the sense of it.

Bethany strode back Elise's way and plopped down on a lawn chair beside her. "Well, at least the mosquitoes seem to be busy elsewhere tonight," she remarked. Her Scottish accent was soft and inviting. "Depending on the humidity or whether there's a breeze or not determines their activities."

Elise loosened her arms from their tight embrace around her middle, then pulled her thick, single braid around to her chest. Even in this peaceful sunset setting, she was feeling some tension. She glanced at Bethany's beautiful, round face. "I guess that's kind of like us. We base our activities on what's happening in our lives at the time… the pressures and so forth."

Bethany nodded thoughtfully, her shoulder-length hair bouncing. "Yes, I guess you could say that. I never really thought of the mosquito comparison before. But, you know, I believe everything happens for a reason."

Elise switched to her side, facing Bethany. "Everything? You mean, of significance?"

"Certainly. But what we may think is significant or not may not be God's spin on it. He uses different situations in our lives to shape and direct us. He's in the big things, the little, and the in between."

"So, we don't ask Him about the little things because we think He doesn't care, or we shouldn't bother Him about them. Then we worry that we'll need Him in the big things, but He may not be there."

Bethany smiled. "You've hit the nail on the head. Which is why in the Bible, Jesus specifically told us not to worry. The birds and the flowers don't, and He looks after them..."

"And we are much more important," Elise finished. She paused in thought, then spoke her heart. "How do I not worry in all of this?"

Bethany twisted in her chair and reached over to pat her hand. "Oh, honey, of course you're worried. The key is you bring that worry to the Lord. You tell Him about it and then trust Him to take care of it. If you don't have that trust, you ask Him for it."

Elise threw her head back and laughed. "It's a lot of asking, isn't it?"

"It is, but that's the way, the only way, we'll realize and accept our dependence on Him. He lives in us, and the more we give ourselves, our will to Him, the more the trusting becomes a part of us."

Elise sighed and moved her hands up and down her bare arms. "I do believe all of that. I guess I'm still just new at it." She noticed Solomon venturing around to the front of the house. "I'm not sure when to tell Josiah about this latest incident. Now *there's* a worrier."

Bethany laughed heartily. "Oh, darling, I don't think worrying about you is something he's going to give up easily. I've known Josiah for many years, and I have never seen him so besotted by a woman. But even he has to put his trust in the Lord. He can't be with you 24/7."

The twins burst into the backyard, followed much more slowly by their father. He came over to the women. "Well, I think they're definitely ready to eat. It's a pity we'll have to start without Josiah." His broad face was slightly reddened from the heat of the barbeque.

Elise waved his worries aside. "Please don't be overly concerned, Solomon. He's the one who insisted we go ahead without him. Besides, Bethany and I were just talking about not worrying. Right, Bethany?"

Solomon glanced at his wife to see a satisfied smile on her face, then spoke to Elise. "Well, I'm finally glad you've decided to call me just Solomon. I was worried about that." He stressed "worried." "We count you and Josiah as dear friends."

Elise was touched. "Thank you so much. That means a lot." Then, she acted on a thought that came to her. "I know the boys want to eat—yesterday, by the looks of it—but will you pray with me quickly, first? I'm not sure what's really going on, but it's all a bit disconcerting. Pray for Josiah also. I'll have to tell him. He'll find out from Danny, anyway."

Bethany chuckled. "I'm sure if he could, Josiah would have you under surveillance by the entire police force."

As Solomon prayed, Elise could feel the lingering tension drain from her body.

"I'm gonna miss you," Josiah whispered in Elise's ear. He was keeping a constant rhythm of the patio swing with his legs, while Elise sat with her feet up, curled beside him.

She snuggled closer to him, her head on his shoulder. "I'll miss you, too," she sighed. "It's nice of the Sungs to let us finish our evening in their yard."

Josiah chuckled. "I don't know about those boys, though. They're probably hanging out some window as we speak, trying to eavesdrop."

Elise glanced around the dimness of the yard, then up above them. "No, part of the roof hangs over us, so they can't see us, and… we're whispering."

He stopped the motion of the swing. "Elise, you don't know boys like I do."

Josiah had arrived halfway through dinner, but that hadn't stopped him from consuming more than his share. He had been working on his house when he was called to another site. Apparently, the engineer and one of the site supervisors had locked horns due to a rigid difference of opinion. His day had been the pits, until he got to the Sung's backyard and saw Elise holding the twins' attention rapt, while she did a pretty good version of their favourite Christian rap. He knew puppy love when he saw it.

Somewhere deep inside, Josiah felt a growing need to make a significant gesture to this woman by his side. He struggled with the realization that he was having difficulty sharing her with so many people. His time at work was a must and, even with her break from teaching, he felt he couldn't get enough time with her. What did a man do when he consistently felt that way about a woman? He had even gone as far as asking Solomon for advice.

The idea of marrying Elise had always been in the back of Josiah's mind. How could it not be? She was everything he wanted, and more. He had a great career and was building a house. Most importantly, she was now a fellow believer. They hadn't been dating for very long, but he had known her for years. Solomon had suggested that he consider a lengthy engagement with marriage counselling. Josiah wanted to marry her now—tomorrow, if she would—but Solomon was right.

He turned her head to face him. "Hey, I have something for you." He could see her smile in the dim glow of the patio lights.

"Is it a present? I love presents." Her voice was girl-like, but certainly not the way she was looking at him, nor the way she smelled, nor the way she fit perfectly by his side.

"I know you like wearing that," he said, gently lifting the Sung's cross pendant from her chest above the "v" of her light, summer blouse. "I didn't want to compete with it quite yet, so…" He pulled a small box from his back pocket and handed it to her.

She took it and he watched her open it. She pulled a delicate gold chain with a heart locket from the box and held it up to the light. "It's beautiful, Josiah." She looked at him lovingly. "It doesn't compete?" she asked in good humour.

He reached beneath the heavy braid at the back of her neck to unhook the silver chain. "Well, one is silver and one is gold." He ignored her puff of disbelief and handed her the silver chain and cross. His hands felt unsteady as he fastened his gift. He kissed the top of her head, her forehead, and just before he kissed her lips, he said, "Our initials are engraved on the back. When you leave tomorrow, will you wear it?"

She nodded slowly, her eyes partially closed, as she waited for his kiss. He kissed her fiercely, possessively, and then he couldn't help himself:

"Marry me." He uttered the words, it seemed, against his own intention.

She was still and silent. She opened her eyes to look at him. He could hardly breathe, while she studied him intently. She pulled away from him.

"You asked me to marry you?" she whispered.

He didn't answer. It was too soon. He would scare her off.

"Josiah?" There was a lot of question in the sound of his name on her lips.

He sat back, freeing her, and took a deep breath. "I rushed into that, didn't I?" Suddenly, he felt a determination that refused to take the coward man's way. He faced her as she sat waiting. He couldn't read her expression, but he knew, with everything in him, that he wanted her to be his.

"Elise, I'm totally and completely in love with you. I want you for now and always in my life. I want to give you everything I have." Three sentences. Only three sentences to change his entire life.

Her eyelids fluttered, and her hands fidgeted with the gold heart on her chest. Finally, she looked at him and seemed to weigh her words. "Josiah, please, will you ask me again when I get back from Jamaica? Please?"

His heart clenched at the emotions he read in her face, her posture. He had made it difficult for her. Then, she put his mind at ease. She reached out to take his hands in hers.

"It's just that I can't imagine saying yes to you and then boarding a plane tomorrow to go away."

He pulled his hands from hers and wrapped his arms around her, pulling her close and causing the swing to wobble. This woman had his heart, and he knew it was absolutely safe with her.

Chapter Seventeen

The pick-up area of the Jamaican airport was teeming with people. The noise level served to match the riotous mass of carts, taxis, and people. Unlike the Canadian airport, the airport in Kingston was open to the outdoors of the island paradise.

The blast of heat that had hit her immediately upon emerging from the plane reminded Elise of a trip she had once taken with her mother to Africa . It was an intense, unexpected heat. The scenery, however, made up for it—breathtaking. Even from the airplane, she had begun to appreciate the country's tropical beauty.

She also found herself the object of constant attention. Either someone wanted to help her with her luggage or flatter her with comments about her looks, usually, "Hi, pretty lady." It seemed a lot of Jamaican men were very free with their words and eyes. It probably didn't help that she most likely had that "wide-eyed" tourist look all over her face. Nevertheless, she held her ground and refused to give up her luggage or venture from the airport where Keisha had made her promise to wait until she came to claim her. Among the heavy Jamaican accents, she suddenly heard a familiar one.

"Elise! Over here!" Keisha was walking rapidly toward her through the jungle of people.

"Keisha, it's so good to see you," Elise said, laughing in relief and returning her friend's embrace. Keisha looked very happy and healthy. Her long black braids were twisted on top of her head, and her full figure looked dashing in a colourful, calf-length sundress.

"It's so good to see you, too," Keisha replied. "You look great as usual. Any trouble with the fellows?"

Elise laughed. "How did you know?" She was already starting to feel more relaxed. Perhaps the combination of a different culture and missing Josiah wouldn't be as challenging as she thought.

Keisha nodded her head knowingly. "Trust me, I've traveled back and forth enough to have gotten the full treatment." She reached for one of Elise's luggage. "Come on. Let's go meet my family and see Jamaica."

The lateness of the hour was finally taking its toll on Elise. She had spent the afternoon and most of the evening meeting Keisha's parents, sisters, nieces and nephews, aunts and uncles, cousins, and various friends. It had been a party-like atmosphere with eating, laughing, and storytelling, each one trying to outdo the other's tale. Her level of concentration had also been seriously tested as she tried to weed through the thick Jamaican accent of some of those around her.

Finally, Keisha must have noticed her wilted condition and made excuses for her. The party continued full swing without her.

"Sorry. You must be so tired, and I hadn't notice the time." Keisha sat on the edge of the bed in the room they would share. "My family are mostly night hawks, and Jamaicans, well, they like to congregate."

Elise pulled some night attire from her luggage, then brought them up to her face to smother a yawn. "Yes, I noticed. People seem a lot more friendly here. Not as closed off."

"You're right about that. Here, in the city, you walk down the street and basically hear what people are saying or smell what they're cooking."

Elise looked at her quizzically.

"The windows are always open, and people are always out and about. In Canada, we tend to be more closed away, especially in the colder months."

Elise nodded. "I see. Maybe tomorrow I'll take a walk and smell the cooking, but right now I just want a bed, Keisha."

Elise had fallen into a deep sleep, then wakened some time after three in the morning. Fortunately, there had been no time difference between the two countries this time of year. She listened to Keisha's soft breathing beside her, the mixed sounds of insects, and the hush of a gentle breeze coming through the open window shutters. According to Keisha, no one closed their windows—with single thin "blades" of glass—except in bad weather, or when they were away from home for a time. One of Keisha's uncles had teased her about lizards coming through those open windows. That thought, and the fact that she wasn't used to sleeping with someone else, kept her awake. The house was a fairly big one built of cement blocks, as were most Jamaican homes. However, with the visiting families present, having a room to herself was not an option.

It wasn't hard for her mind to drift back to her most recent conversation with Josiah. They had talked by phone, and once he had established knowledge about her safe arrival, he had lambasted her.

"You left without telling me that some maniac was spying on you while you were with April's children at your parents' place," he accused her. "Why wouldn't you have told me something like that?"

She had defended herself. "I don't know I was being spied on. It could be that the house was being spied on. He could have been someone who knew my parents were away and wanted to, I don't know, look for an opportunity to commit a crime."

He had pounced on that. "Elise, with your track record of recent events, I'm pretty sold on the you-were-the-target scenario." Then he had added, for good measure, "I didn't like finding out from Danny. You should have told me."

She sighed and stuck one hand behind her head. She should have told him. She had meant to.

Josiah scratched his head while he and Danny went over his collection of facts and suppositions. Impatient with the slow pace of police wheels, Josiah had roped Danny into going over all the possibilities regarding Elise's harassment.

"So you're saying we can get the telephone company to put a 'trap' on her phone to determine where the calls are coming from?" They were at Josiah's condo, where he had treated Danny to dinner in return for the favour of picking his police brain.

"Yes, but she'd have to keep a log with the time and dates of all telephone calls so the origin of each call could be pinpointed." He took a last swig from his glass of soft drink, while Josiah wrote on the sheet of paper. "And we don't know if she'll even have a repeat call." He winced at Josiah's glare. "All I'm saying is, it's a lot of trouble to go through for only one reported call."

Josiah leaned back in his chair. The kitchen table had been cleared of most of the evening's meal. "Look, Dan, her mother received a strange intercom message that was probably meant for her, she's had those "silent" buzzes, she's had a threatening call, now she's got a peeping Tom."

"Yes, but only one of those calls was actually threatening," Danny insisted. "We need to have a threat of harm."

Josiah dropped his pen impatiently on the table. "Are you telling me that all these incidents are coincidences?"

Danny shook his head convincingly. "No, Jo. I personally don't believe they are, but the system likes to see more concrete evidence."

"You mean, the kind where the person ends up abducted or dead before it's taken seriously?"

Danny was silent. He ran a tanned hand through his springy hair, then looked Josiah in the eye. "Look, man, I'm on your side. I'll do all I can and work with you. I'm concerned for her, too."

Josiah flexed his arms behind his head, trying to calm down. He believed Danny truly did care and wanted to help. He realized that he was still peeved at Elise for leaving without informing him of the incident at her parents' place. He also realized that he was worried about her, and that, after three days, he missed her incredibly. Still, he shouldn't take it out on Dan.

"I know you care, Dan. Sorry."

Danny brushed it off. "Hey, no big deal. Like I said, if you can get from Elise the exact day of the intercom message, we can look back on the apartment surveillance tapes to see what we find. I'll ask the Everson's neighbours if they noticed anything odd the day of the spying."

Josiah pushed back his chair and glanced around the open-concept kitchen of his temporary home. He got up and exhaled loudly, his back to Danny.

"Want to pray about it?"

Josiah turned to look at him. After a moment, he spoke, "Seems we did this not so long ago regarding a totally different woman. Seems easier to understand your frustration now."

Danny glanced down at the table. He pushed his drinking glass aside and rested both elbows on the spot before him. "Yeah. It's a nasty feeling, isn't it?"

Josiah chuckled and rested his hands on his hips. "Yeah. The kind where you know there's only so much you can do, and the rest you gotta put in His hands."

"Keeps us humble, I guess."

"Sure does. Hey, Danny."

"Yeah?"

"Don't forget. Pray with me, man."

Elise lazed under a huge beach umbrella while Keisha's family frolicked in the warm, salty Jamaican ocean. She and Keisha had decided that today was a good day for laying on a beach mat and doing absolutely nothing.

"I think I'll take him home with me."

Elise turned her head to face Keisha who was also lying on her stomach. They both had beach wraps on the lower half of their bodies that were sticking out from under the umbrella's shade.

"Who?" she asked. The heat made her feel incredibly drowsy.

Keisha rolled over and sat up. Her braids ran down her back. "Gavin, of course. I don't know that I'd want to make this my permanent home, but maybe he'll consider moving."

Elise craned her neck slightly and wished Keisha would lie back down. "What do you mean? Are you guys that serious?" Elise had finally met Keisha's Gavin the day before. The medium-built Jamaican with light-brown skin certainly seemed to be all that Keisha had espoused him to be. He also had a gentle, thoughtful manner that had easily impressed Elise.

"I don't really know how serious we are," Keisha admitted. "Once I leave, I don't know how we'll find out. Things are hard here for a lot of people. The dollar value is very poor, but Gavin has a great architectural job which keeps him upper-middle class. I don't know if he'll want to leave, or immigrate to the United States where he went to university."

"So you wouldn't consider relocating, but you want him to?"

Keisha squinted down at her, then looked out toward the hot white sands and rolling waves in the distance. "You certainly have a way of getting straight to the point."

Elise laughed and sat up. Her skin, which was slightly darkened from the Canadian summer, had darkened even more from the Jamaican sun. Keisha's mother had said it created a startlingly beautiful blend with her light brown eyes and the bleached brown hints now running through her long, black curls.

"If Josiah lived elsewhere, would you relocate?" Keisha challenged.

Elise reached for her bottled water, hoping it was still cool. "The way I miss him now, I would follow him to Timbuktu."

"Seriously, Elise," she insisted.

Elise grimaced at the warmth of the water before answering. "Yes, Keisha, I would. Of course, right now, he's mad at me, so he may not want me to go anywhere with him." She reached down and created trails in the warm, fine sand at the edge of her mat, while her thoughts focused on one man across the ocean.

Josiah rushed to the basket and let the ball go up, smooth and fluid, then down into its target. The twins groaned, then Joshua grabbed the rebound and passed it to his brother who shot a three-pointer.

"Great shot, Jordan," Josiah said, breathing hard. Working at construction and playing basketball definitely didn't require the same sets of muscles, nor the same lung capacity for that matter.

"You beat us, though, Mr. Alex—two against one." This from Joshua, who didn't like to lose. Both boys were sweating, but not breathing nearly as hard as he.

"Yeah, but I've had more experience. Just keep working at it. You're both doing great." They had been at it for an hour in the Sung's driveway since after supper. With Elise in the Caribbean, Josiah was glad to find ways to fill his evenings.

"Hey, isn't that the 'Brains,' Joshua?"

Both Joshua and Josiah looked out to the residential street to see a dark pickup driving slowly in their direction. The long daylight of summer allowed them to see Webster Myers in the driver's seat. He waved in response to the boys' call and nodded with a surprised look at Josiah as he drove by.

"I didn't know he drove one of those," Joshua declared.

Josiah asked casually, "What does he usually drive?" Something other than the discomfort of his sweaty t-shirt was niggling at the back of his mind.

"Ah, just a regular four-door, kinda boring. At least we don't have to watch him ogle Mademoiselle for another couple of weeks."

Before Joshua had finished his sentences, a flood light shone in Josiah's mind. He needed to get in touch with Danny Rowe, and soon!

*   *   *

"Hey, calm down, Josiah," Danny repeated. "Why don't we go back inside to the office?"

Josiah felt guilty. He knew Danny had been on his way out of the police station when he had shown up with barely contained excitement.

"I'm really sorry, Dan, but this just can't wait," he justified, as he followed Danny into the building. He noticed the curious stares of the other evening personnel around. Most of them knew him and their friendly greetings slowed him from his reason for being there. Finally, they were behind closed doors.

"Jo, I know we're really good friends and brothers in the Lord and all that, but I've just had a headache of a meeting, so this had better be good." He sighed and sat down behind his desk. Josiah remained standing.

"The pickup, Dan. We haven't considered the pickup." His eagerness was difficult to hold in.

Danny's brow furrowed in confusion. "What are you talking about? What pickup?"

Josiah placed his hands palm down on the desk, forcing the seated man to look up at him. "Celia Everson reported being scared by a dark pickup at Elise's apartment. Elise saw one parked inexplicably outside my house site. I saw one racing from her apartment complex driveway the same evening she and Keisha had the 'silent' intercom interruption. And, most recently, the peeping Tom drove off in one."

Danny blinked, then lowered his gaze in concentration. "Sit down, Josiah," he said before placing a pad of paper on the desk.

Josiah pulled a vinyl covered chair close to the desk. He turned it backwards and sat on it, his arms hanging over its back with his fingers bunched. He could feel the tension in his muscles, but he willed himself to let Danny jot whatever he needed to get down on paper. Danny scribbled for a while, then looked across at him, his grey eyes serious.

"Bear with me while I tell you what I have. Elise's apartment superintendent and I did view the surveillance tapes. There was one suspicious incident of a man who seemed to purposefully keep his face down. He also had a hat on, the kind with the full brim worn when fishing. There were a couple of views of what seemed to be the same person in the entrance of the building, who would come in and go out without going any further inside. Also, more than one of the Everson's neighbours have reported seeing a dark green or black pickup parked, at different times, on their street in the vicinity of the Everson's home."

Josiah never once took his eyes off Danny as he recited the collection of data. He waited.

"Who do we know with a dark green or black pickup who knows Elise?"

Josiah was ready with the answer. "Webster Myers." He wasn't prepared for the next question.

"Who else?" When Josiah didn't answer, Danny looked at him. "Jo?"

"What do you mean?"

Danny sighed in frustration. "Well, you can't just name the first person who comes to your head, and we're done."

Josiah frowned. "I know a few more people," he admitted.

"Who know the Eversons, particularly Elise?" Danny pressed.

Josiah's frown deepened. "Well, yes, but…" Suddenly, he felt a weight on him. He shook his head and ran his fingers across his brows.

"Josiah," Danny urged. He was leaning expectantly across his desk.

"Jack Roper has a dark grey pickup that could be mistaken for black, but…" He hesitated. "I don't see what grievance he would have against Elise or her family."

Danny wrote. "Who else?" He was dogged. Now Josiah knew why he was sergeant.

"Rick Phillips has a black pickup." Then he quickly added, "But, as you know, he's one of my foremen and a good friend."

Danny looked up from his pad of paper. "Is that it?"

Josiah nodded slowly. "Yes. At least the ones who know Elise. I don't think any of them know her parents, though. Maybe they only know of them, I don't know." Now that all he had held in was out of his system, he ached to talk with Elise.

Elise counted it a pleasure getting to know Keisha's sister Miranda, who had suffered from a stalker attack seven years ago. The expectant and content mom of two didn't resemble anything of a traumatized victim now. In her shy way and with her beautiful smile, she recounted how many sessions of counselling and support group therapy had helped her to put the worst of her nightmare behind her. She admitted that she tended at times to be overprotective of her kids, but she felt that God had created a miracle of healing in her heart. It was as if the attack had happened to someone else.

Elise had also enjoyed getting to know Miranda's two children, especially her four-year-old daughter who reminded Elise of herself as a young child, the offspring of a white father and black mother. Elise had felt very useful sharing some of her early struggles with Miranda so that, perhaps, she could help her children with their own struggles, both now and later. In turn, Miranda's life story filled Elise with renewed hope for April.

With Keisha out with Gavin, Elise was having a rare moment alone in the bedroom when Miranda, with a knowing smile, brought her the house's cell phone. Alone once more, she greeted the caller, knowing who he was.

"Hi, Josiah." She got comfortable in a cushioned wicker chair.

"Hi, yourself," his deep voice responded. "What are you up to?"

She hugged the phone to her face, as much as a cell phone could be hugged. "Not much…taking a break. We went shopping with Gavin. After that, he took us boating."

"Umm. How did it go?"

"The boating was great. The shopping—too hot. Gavin said we should probably have shopped later in the day. He had some other good suggestions for tomorrow, though. I'll have to see if I'm up for them." She waited for his next question, but he was silent. She pulled her ponytail to one side.

"How are you?" she questioned carefully.

"Probably not as up to speed as Gavin, or whatever his name is. Who exactly did you say this guy was again?" His tone wasn't harsh, but it was provoking.

"Keisha's boyfriend," she answered. She didn't like where this was going.

"You sure?"

"Josiah—"

"Because if you're not sure…"

"If you continue, I *will* hang up!" She was furious, and her eyes were smarting from the tears that were threatening to come. "H–how dare you make insinuations like that. You're being absolutely mean." She missed him so much, and yet he was being very unlike himself. Where was her caring, thoughtful prince?

"Elise, baby, I'm sorry," he breathed into the phone.

"You better be. You're being horrible, and… and I miss you terribly." The tears rolled down her cheeks and she wiped at them angrily.

He continued to plead with her. "Please believe me, I didn't mean any of those things. I'm an idiot…"

"And an arrogant, falsely accusing jerk," she helped him out.

"All of the above," he agreed.

She took a deep breath, then giggled. "I'm sorry."

"Am I forgiven?" His voice was soft and inviting.

"What got into you, Jose?"

"Ahhh… there's that name," he said, chuckling. "I don't know. Stressed, tired maybe… I miss you like crazy!"

"I miss you, too."

"I told Alisha I'd pick you up at the airport."

"Are you sure? It'll cut into your day." The two days left couldn't go quickly enough.

"I don't care. I'm supposed to be in the office drawing up some plans. I don't think I'll be able to draw a straight line with my mind tracing your every move from the airport."

She laughed. His words were a balm soothing her heart. She touched the gold locket at her breast. "I look forward to my escort, and, Josiah, I absolutely forgive you."

Chapter Eighteen

The entire morning and afternoon seemed surreal during the transition from one country to another, one culture to another. She felt somewhat nostalgic at leaving new friends and a palm tree-ridden land behind, yet longed for the familiar. Keisha and her family had prayed with her, especially regarding the difficult unknown which lay ahead. She didn't like being nervous and conscious of the need to look over her shoulder, now that she was back where she had left all the drama. She would, however, put up with the drama if it meant she would be with Josiah.

She had just cleared customs when she sensed him, even before she saw him, coming her way. The human traffic and buzz around her seemed to fade increasingly as she straightened from her luggage and saw him approaching her with his eager stride. He had a wide smile on his face, enhancing his dark good looks, and his tall, well-formed build challenged her senses crazily. She felt her smile widening to answer his. He didn't even speak; he just gathered her into his arms and held her closely and tightly as if he would never let her go. The crowd parted around them as if they were dry ground in the midst of the Red Sea.

She felt wonderful in his arms, she smelled great, and he never wanted to move his face from the cloud of hair pulled back to surround her shoulders. His memories hadn't compared to this, and she had only been gone seven days. Finally he released her, and they gathered her belongings.

"How was your flight?" he asked, glancing at her sideways as they made their way out of the building to the underground parking. He had taken the bulk of her luggage, leaving her with a handbag and small overnight case.

She raised her voice above the noise of the traffic. "It was just fine. I slept most of the way."

He noticed she kept stealing glances at him, and whenever he caught her, she would smile and quickly look away. He laughed. "I haven't grown horns since you left."

She frowned, walking quickly to keep up with him. "If you're referring to our heated phone conversation, you're wrong. I have other things on my mind."

He slowed his pace for her sake. "Want to share them?" He stopped by his white SUV and pulled his keys and remote from the pocket of his tan, knee-length shorts.

"Not yet," she said smugly. She moved away from his side of the vehicle to avoid a turning car. She spoke over the hood. "I have plans."

He straightened from heaving her things onto the back seat. "The last time you had plans, you ended up where you're just coming from." He joined her inside the vehicle, filling his hungry eyes with the sight of her.

She shook her head. "Not travel plans, silly. You'll see."

It was hot, so he started the engine and cranked the air conditioner, then he faced her. He wanted to touch her, but the strength of his emotions frightened him. It was crazy and downright scary to feel this way about someone. They sat and drank in the sight of each other, then she asked the obvious question.

"Aren't you going to kiss me?" Her voice was soft, almost a whisper above the air conditioner.

And so, he did.

It had to be perfect, this dinner. She had planned it well and carefully. Her glass table was draped with a wine-coloured table cloth. The centrepiece was a beautiful water lily arrangement, and there were tapered candles on either side.

After the appropriate cutlery, dishes and glasses, she checked the contents of the oven for, it seemed, the hundredth time.

"Mmm. You smell good," she whispered. "Too bad I hardly have an appetite." It was lamb, which she knew he loved. She looked about her. All was in order. She hurried to the floor-length mirror in her bedroom. Was she in order?

Elise checked her reflection with a critical eye. Her hair had been piled high on top of her head with trails of ringlets hanging just so—courtesy of Alisha Adair. Her makeup was flawless, blending with the darker, tanned tone of her skin. She loved the flow of the pale green sundress over her hips, and the dainty gold sandals on her feet. She twirled elegantly away from the mirror and headed back to the kitchen.

Her parents were due back tomorrow, so she needed to do this today. Josiah would have her undivided attention for one evening. After being back for only twenty-four hours, she had found herself catering to an awful lot of people. She had always had numerous friends, and belonging to a new church had definitely increased that number, but her focus would be captivated by one particular person tonight. In about two weeks, she would need to focus on twenty-plus hormone-laced bodies, four periods a day for five days a week. Now was the time.

After his brief intercom message, she waited for him to come up. Her nervousness surprised her, but she was determined to play her role well.

"You look nice," she said as Josiah stepped into the apartment. He was dressed up in a white short-sleeved shirt and black pants. His hand was adorned with red roses.

"You… are gorgeous," he returned the compliment. He handed her the roses and kissed her cheek.

"Thank you, Josiah." She inhaled the beautiful, light fragrance of the flowers, needing to divert her attention from the heady sensations his presence was evoking.

"Something smells really good," Josiah remarked as Elise found a vase. "I finally get the meal you owe me after all this time."

"Don't tease," she scolded, placing the roses in a vase, partly filled with water, on the kitchen counter. "It's better late than never."

He joined her at the counter. "Is there anything I can help you with?"

She shook her head quickly, and the tendrils of hair moved gently. She raised a hand to sweep them from her eyes, but he beat her to it.

He gently smoothed the curls away from her face, then allowed his hand to linger. He moved his hand to the back of her head, careful to maintain the beautiful form of her upswept hair, and gently pulled her forward until their lips met.

Background music filled the apartment as they lounged on the couch after a light dessert.

"We're doing well behaving ourselves, aren't we?" she asked.

"Yes, we are," he agreed. "It's worth the effort to respect the woman I love. Just don't make it hard for me, okay?"

She sighed. "I'll try not to, but I'm glad we're able to be totally alone for a change."

"Guess what?" he asked.

"What?" she questioned. Her back lay against his chest, and her legs were stretched out upon the couch while his were stretched out before him to meet the rug on the wooden floor.

"My architectural license came through."

She arched her neck to see him. "Oh, Josiah, that's great! I'm so pleased for you."

"I'm pleased for myself, too," he joked. He kept running his fingers through the hair at the top of her head. "Now I have everything I want, except for two things."

"What are those?" she asked, her neck still arched.

He lowered his head to kiss her briefly, before saying against her lips, "A completed house and—you."

She straightened her head, remained still for a moment, then struggled to leave his arms. "Josiah, let go for a minute."

"Where are you going?" he asked playfully, keeping her imprisoned.

"Just give me a second. I promise, I'll be right back," she maintained.

He let her go reluctantly. Her bare feet were light on the floor as she left the room without a backward glance. But true to her word, she returned momentarily. She knelt on one side of his legs and placed a small, flat box on his lap. Then, suddenly, she grabbed it back.

"Oops! I forgot something," she explained, then disappeared into the kitchen. She returned with one of the roses he had given her, then resumed her kneeling position before him. She looked up at him with her big, brown eyes. Her hair had lost some of its order, and her lipstick was practically gone, but she looked adorable.

She took a deep breath. "Josiah David Alexander, will you marry me?"

Marry her? *She* was asking *him* to marry her? He was speechless. Whatever he had thought she was doing, it hadn't been this.

"Josiah?" Her voice was quiet, uncertain. His delay in answering was costing her.

"Yes," he said simply. He smiled and took the rose and box she offered him, his heart thudding in his chest.

"Open it," she commanded.

He did. Laying against a white, satin background was a man's gold bracelet. Its linked chains were attractively arranged and interrupted in one spot by a name plaque bearing their initials.

"It's awesome, Elise," he remarked, examining the piece of jewellery.

She returned to the couch beside him. "Do you like it?" she asked, sounding breathless.

"Love it." He fumbled to clasp it onto his wrist, then gave up when she reached over to help him. It glittered attractively under the room's light.

"It looks nice on you," she said, and seemed to be quite satisfied.

He shifted on the couch to face her. "Thank you, but you sure know how to steal a man's thunder." Before she could react, he pulled a much smaller case from his pants pocket and held it in front of him, not offering it to her.

"What do you think is in here?" he whispered, his voice slightly hoarse.

Her gaze was glued to the box as she chewed on her bottom lip. She raised her eyes to his. They shimmered with gathering tears. She held her left hand out expectantly. It trembled slightly.

Her vulnerability caused him to delay no longer. He opened the jewellery box to reveal the beautiful diamond solitaire hidden beneath. He heard her gasp, and knew he had chosen well.

"Oh, Josiah." The tears now ran down from her eyes, sparkling almost like the diamond being placed on her finger.

He kept hold of her hand. "Elise Diara Everson, will *you* marry me?"

"Yes, yes," she declared and fell into his arms.

David felt like he had been shaking his head in disbelief all evening. He had gone away for a few weeks only to come home and find his daughter engaged to be married. Even Celia, surprisingly, seemed to take it more in stride than he. Usually it was the other way around, and he wasn't sure how to account for this change. To him, it had seemed like something in the distant future; now it was in the present. All Celia wanted to talk about was an engagement party. Why? The deed was already done. Being a psychiatrist didn't mean he understood women.

"That's what happens when we old folk turn our backs for a moment," Adam said, chuckling. "Our kids fall in love, get married, have babies…"

"Whoa, now, Adam. Let's just take this one step at a time," David interrupted, stalling him. "I'm still trying to get past the part they're at now." Adam, Josiah, and Elise had dined with them for the evening, the meal courtesy of Elise. Celia was in the family room with the young couple, getting all sentimental over their wedding album, while he and Adam hashed out the why's and wherefore's of youthful decisions.

"They're perfect for each other, though."

David regarded Adam where he sat across from him on the loveseat. He had a satisfied look on his face. "Yes, you're right. I can't imagine a more likely couple." He ran a hand across his thinning grey hair. "To think they met as teenagers, and all these years later…"

"Yet God had already seen it," Adam stated simply. "Though, I must admit, I've seen it long before now."

"Adam, I think you just have a grandfather-want-to-be mentality."

Adam laughed, his eyes crinkling at the corners. "Nothing wrong with that. Nothing wrong with that at all." He eyed David thoughtfully. "Think about it, we both only have one opportunity, one offspring each."

David hadn't really thought of it that way, but Adam was right. Unfortunately, it wasn't one of the many life issues he had tried to sort through on his trip.

"So, David," Adam started, his eyes holding a speculative gleam that indicated a dual meaning to whatever was coming. "Did you get all that you needed on that cruise of yours?"

David's body tensed up for a moment. It was uncanny how Adam's question had connected with his thoughts. He shook his head.

"You know, I would say yes and no. The pace was definitely slower, and the sights intriguing, but I had some difficulty resting my thoughts." His hands were clasped tightly on his lap. "There is a difficult situation possibly looming in my practice, and I've been doing some soul-searching."

"Soul-searching is good," Adam acknowledged. "I'm not sure about the other issue. Could I, perhaps, be your sounding board for a moment, as you have been for so many others?"

David was deeply moved by the sincerity he saw in his friend's dark eyes. Suddenly he truly felt the need for this role reversal. He leaned toward Adam.

"I think I will take you up on that. You're right, it's not often that I share my burdens, and since you're a praying man…"

Adam held his gaze expectantly. "Fire away."

So David shared what he had been holding in for so long, things he had not shared fully with his wife for fear of alarming her. He spoke of his feelings of inadequacy, at times, to meet the needs of his clientele and to come to terms with the basest, most degrading of human conditions. He believed there was a fine line between sanity and insanity, and that mankind, with all of its achievements, did not have all the answers. He vaguely shared about the difficult client situation that reminded him time and time again just how limited he was. Then, without really meaning to, he shared about the threatening phone call he had received, and two subsequent ones. He almost regretted it when he saw the look of alarm on Adam's face.

"Are you able to share the nature of the calls?" Adam probed. He seemed overly interested.

"Well, I didn't really understand what the man wanted, but I definitely felt the intent of his call was to intimidate me. I toy with the idea that he may be a client of mine, so I've kept it to myself. I even made up some excuse about it to Celia."

Adam moved forward to the edge of his seat and peered cautiously out into the hall before speaking. "David, I need to share something with you, and then you can determine how you will broach it with your daughter. You are aware of the strange intercom message your wife received at Elise's apartment? Well, there's more."

Celia was laughing until her eyes watered. Whether her tears were a result of Josiah's humour, or a mixture of joy and slight delirium, she wasn't sure. He had insisted on interpreting the thoughts of many of the guests featured in her wedding album. She hadn't quite seen this side of him before. No wonder her daughter was captivated by such a charming young man. Even Elise couldn't keep from childish outbursts of mirth.

"Last, but not least, this woman here, in the purple, she's thinking about the moment when she can go home and loosen her skirt after eating so much." Josiah was sitting between the two women on the family room couch. His upper body was hanging over the album on the coffee table.

"No," Celia declared, laughter bubbling under the surface. "I don't believe that for a minute. If I recall correctly, she was a co-worker of mine who suffered from a back injury."

"You sure?" Josiah challenged. "Because the way she's holding herself…"

"Josiah, give it up. Your imagination is way too active." Elise gave him a light swat on the shoulder before rising from her seat. He grabbed the offending hand before she could move away.

"Hey, that's not what I expected for providing the evening's entertainment." He held onto Elise while she tried to pull away, then, with his back to Celia, pulled her down for a brief kiss.

Celia noticed her daughter's face was slightly flushed as she glanced at her mother. Elise was obviously not comfortable being intimate with her fiancé in front of her; perhaps that, and also the effect he had on her. Celia smiled reassuringly.

"He does have a point, sweetheart. I can't remember the last time I laughed tears." She glanced at Josiah fondly. "I believe he's a keeper."

"Ah, now there's a woman after my own heart," he declared warmly. With that, he threw an arm around his future mother-in-law and kissed her soundly on the cheek.

Celia smoothed self-consciously at her blouse. "Well, you do have a way with women, don't you?" She stood and reached for Josiah and Elise's hands. She studied both their faces, then spoke sincerely. "I know I've said this before once I got over the shock of your wonderful news, but I want to say it again. I am so very happy and satisfied with your decision." As her emotions swelled, she felt her words wanting to come in her mother tongue, but for Josiah's sake she pressed on in English. "In the past, I felt marriage would take my daughter away, but now I know I will have gained a son and … " she paused with a bubble of laughter, "and future grandchildren."

"Mom," Elise protested, looking embarrassed.

"Yes, dearest," Celia insisted, squeezing her daughter's hand. "You may as well know. I want lots of them."

Josiah's deep voice broke through. "Mrs. Everson—"

"Celia."

"Celia, we'll be more than happy to oblige." He looked down at Elise, smiling smugly.

She ignored him, focusing instead on her mother. "Mom, thanks for being so understanding about our engagement. It was something I had wanted to talk over with you after you returned, but the timing seemed so right and—"

"No ands. It's perfect." Celia alternatively took their faces in her hands and sealed her words with kisses. "Now, let me go see what those two are up to and give you two some time alone."

As soon as they were alone, Josiah pulled her to him and drew her arms up around his neck. After wrapping his arms around her waist, he kissed her eagerly, tenderly.

"Now, we're really official," he joked, then said in reminder, "and so are the grandchildren."

Elise pushed against his chest, feeling overwhelmed. "It seems you two are too quick to plan the future."

"What? An engagement party? Babies?" He held her unwaveringly, his eyes intent on hers.

She gave up her struggles. "There's a lot we haven't discussed," she admitted. Although her mother had surprisingly and wholeheartedly accepted their engagement, she suspected that her father was having some trouble with it. Not her choice of fiancé per se—she knew he thought much of Josiah—but the timing.

Josiah loosened his hold on her, his expression now serious, thoughtful. "That's where Solomon comes in. We'll talk about setting up some time with him for counselling, okay?"

She sighed. "Okay." The word was hardly out of her mouth when Celia came into the room, a troubled expression on her face.

"I'm sorry, Josiah, Alisha is on the phone. She says it's urgent."

Josiah went to her and took the cordless phone she held out to him. "Thanks, Celia," he said before speaking into the phone. "Alisha?"

Elise drew closely to him, noticing the worry on his face. Alisha knew about their evening and would not have interrupted unless it was very important.

"Where is he now?" Josiah was asking. "Okay. Tell Danny I'll come now. Will you stay there until I come? Okay, I'll see you soon." He handed the phone back to Celia, who had stayed in the room, and turned to Elise. "Rick had a relapse."

"A relapse?" Celia questioned.

"He's one of my foremen, Celia. He's a recovering alcoholic and he's accountable to me. He's at the police station in town. Apparently he's being uncooperative and belligerent."

Chapter Nineteen

Alisha sat impatiently in the waiting area for Josiah to arrive. The police station wasn't exactly in her comfort zone, and she was upset and worried about Rick. She knew he was a recovering alcoholic, but she had never witnessed him drunk. He was not a nice drunk. Fortunately, Danny had been the one on duty when Rick had been brought in, and he had called her after being unable to get a hold of Josiah. Josiah had probably turned off his cell so he wouldn't be interrupted at the Everson's. Who could blame him? It wasn't every day that one had an engagement dinner.

"Coffee?"

Alisha looked up to see a styrofoam cup in front of her. She accepted it gratefully. "Thanks, Danny." She took a sip and looked at him as he lowered himself on the chair beside her. "Is he still carrying on?" she asked.

Danny rubbed the back of his neck with his hand. "I didn't think he had it in him. He's been sober for eons, Alisha. I don't know what could have triggered this." He glanced at her, his grey eyes compassionate. "He said some pretty mean things to you."

She kept one hand wrapped around her cup and used the other to swipe at a loose red strand from her upswept ponytail. "Yes, he did, but I can't really blame him. He's not himself. He keeps asking for Josiah. I think he really needs to see him." She hadn't even changed from her shift at the hospital. She looked down at her pale green uniform and white shoes and wished she could go shower and change. Yet she felt such a need to stay. Until Josiah arrived, she felt she was all Rick had. No matter how this man had caused her grief with his incessant teasing and innuendos, she still held deep emotions for him.

"Here he is now," Danny announced, getting to his feet.

Alisha felt relieved when she saw Josiah's tall figure marching into the station with Elise in tow. He stopped to talk with Danny, but Elise kept coming toward her.

"Oh, Ali, are you okay?" Elise asked, reaching down to put her arms around her.

Alisha returned the hug, feeling somewhat comforted that they were here to help her cope. "Rick is not okay. It's like he's absolutely gone off the deep end, Lise. I couldn't reason with Him. It's like he'd forgotten who I was."

Elise took the chair Danny had left. The waiting area was empty except for them. "Drunkenness does that, though, Alisha. He probably won't even remember anything that happened tonight. Do you know what set him off?"

She shook her head. "I don't know, but he kept going on about life being unfair, and some people having it all. Also, he said some hurtful things to me."

Elise held her and stroked her back. "Oh, Ali, what did he say?"

She took a deep breath and aimed her cup at a garbage bin close by. "He said things like I was an 'ice queen,' too stuck in my ways to see all that he had to offer. He said I needed to grow up and let him show me how to be a real woman. Stuff like that. I don't feel like going on about it."

When Danny brought him where Rick was, in a cell, Josiah was even more sobered. Rick, foreman extraordinaire, was on the bare cell floor weeping like a baby. "Let me in, Danny," he demanded softly.

"Are you sure? He was pretty reckless before."

"Danny, is he under arrest?"

"No. I just put him there until he sobers up."

"Then just let me in."

After Danny unsecured the lock, Rick looked up to see what the commotion was about. His eyes and hair were wild looking and his face was wet with tears. He had an ugly bruise starting on the right side of his forehead just below the hairline. When he saw Josiah, he staggered to his feet and stumbled backwards.

"Now you know—now you know what I'm really like." He stumbled around the small cell. "Won't want to put your company in my hands now–nooo way hosea."

Josiah stood still, aching for his employee and friend. "Rick, you're the best foreman I've ever had, hands down." He noticed Danny moving away. He crossed by Rick to sit on the cell's single bunk.

"You sure you want to s–sit with the likes a me? T–too good for me." He suddenly grabbed his temples and bellowed. "Alisha won't have me, and you've got a screw-up working for you."

Josiah worked at keeping calm. Even though he and Rick were pretty evenly matched in strength, he felt a little nervous. Rick's eyes were red and he reeked of alcohol, but it was the crazed look in his eyes that unnerved Josiah. Compassion, however, won over.

"Rick, look at me."

Rick tried to look but couldn't seem to focus. He shook his head like a rabid dog, then peered again at Josiah.

"No one is better than you, and you know that Alisha is crazy for you. We joke about it all the time. What happened, man?"

Rick pulled at his rumpled clothes in confusion, looking suspiciously around him. "What do I have to give?" he blabbered. "I have nothing. What do I have to offer her? Everything I gain, I lose. Why can't you understand?"

Josiah leaned toward him. Rick was leaning against the far wall, but now he slid along it until he hit the floor.

"You have something, Rick. You have a job with Alexander's Contracting that you're perfect for, friends who'd go to bat for you, and God, who loves you immeasurably, is looking out for you. Talk to me. Tell me what happened."

"I don't know, I don't know." He swore and tilted his chin up so his head rubbed hard against the wall. "I screwed up."

Josiah got up slowly and went over to stoop by him. "Come on Rick, it can't be that bad. You know I got your back. Let me help you, man."

Rick slowly opened his eyes, which had been squeezed shut, and looked with some clarity at Josiah. "I messed up, Josiah." He reached up to grab the front of Josiah's shirt. "I messed up big time, and for what?" Deep groans erupted from him and he sobbed uncontrollably.

Josiah grabbed him around the shoulders, giving support. It really hurt to witness a grown man cry with such abandon. He wanted to say something that counted, that would make a difference.

"God's good with messes, Rick. I've told you, Jesus is all about cleaning up messes."

"God, God. It's all you talk about," Rick accused hoarsely. "What's He gonna do for me? How's He gonna set me free?"

"You have to ask, Rick. Ask Him to help you believe." Then he said, more to himself than to Rick, as a prayer, "Lord, help his unbelief."

Josiah held on to Rick for a time and felt his frame begin to relax as his anguish diminished. He then gently but firmly nudged him to get on his feet. "Come on, Rick, let's get you lying down. Sleep it off, then I promise we'll talk some more."

Rick mumbled his consent and, with Josiah's support, dragged himself over to the cell's bunk. Once he had slumped down heavily, Josiah pulled a light grey blanket up over him. Josiah stood by him, watching the heavy breathing of exhaustion that made his whole body seem to rise and fall. He would sleep for a while. Before he left the cell, Josiah reached out a hand over Rick and prayed.

Elise and Alisha were watching him expectantly when he returned to them. They both looked tired, especially Alisha, who had dark circles beginning around her eyes. They stood as he approached.

"I hope you don't have to work for a few days, Alisha." Josiah put a comforting hand on her shoulder while reaching for Elise's hand with his other. He relished the softness and warmth of her fingers wrapped around his.

"Has he calmed down?" Alisha asked anxiously.

"Sleeping like an exhausted baby."

Alisha heaved a sigh of relief and sank back onto her seat. Elise let go of Josiah's hand to be right there beside her.

"Danny's going to let him sleep it off. I'll get him in the morning," Josiah reassured her.

Alisha shook her head, kneading her brow with her fingers. "I don't know what happened. Danny couldn't get it out of him, either. I only know that yesterday, on his day off, he went out of town. I don't know if he went to visit his family or not, but something must have happened while he was gone. He was at a bar when the owner called the police. He wouldn't stop drinking and was becoming disruptive. The owner was also afraid he would try to drive home."

Josiah grabbed a chair and placed it near the women before sitting down. "Don't worry, Ali, I'll get to the bottom of it. I know he's been attending AA regularly, so I'm not sure what triggered this. I mean, as far as I know, he hasn't been inside a bar in years, and he doesn't keep the stuff in his house. So something pretty serious must have precipitated this."

Alisha seemed less tense, but still had a worried look on her face as she succumbed to Elise's intermittent back rubbing. Suddenly, Elise paused with her mouth opened and her eyes widening by the second. Josiah turned to look behind him, toward the station entrance, just as the doors swung opened. Two police officers entered with a handcuffed man accompanying them.

"Oh, my goodness. What is Webster Myers doing here?" Elise asked, amazed.

Elise could hardly believe her eyes. Would this day's surprises never end? Studious, mild Webster in handcuffs. His head was down, his hair dishevelled, and his polo shirt slightly askew. As he was escorted past them, he glanced up. His gaze moved quickly over them, then rested on Elise before he was directed away by the officers. She couldn't help but notice his split, bloody lip.

"That's the teacher from your school, the guy who came looking for you at church," Alisha noted.

Elise nodded dumbly, seeking Josiah's eyes.

"You know," Alisha continued, "Rick was the one who told him where you were that evening. He remembered because he knew that I'd be with you. He's developed this habit of keeping tabs on me."

"How did Webster come to be asking Rick where Elise was?" Josiah questioned. He had captured Elise's hand again in both of his and was rubbing his thumb along her engagement ring absentmindedly.

Alisha shrugged. "He's probably seen Rick around town with us."

"He does know Rick," Elise confirmed. "Remember when you gave Rick some worship music to drop off to me? Well, he came to school with it and Webster was present at the time. I introduced them."

Josiah sighed heavily. "Listen, Alisha, Elise and I should walk you out. You look pretty wiped."

"You're right," she said, struggling to her feet. Her face was pale and her green eyes had lost their usually sparkle. "To answer your earlier point, Jo, I do have the next three days off, thank God. Please let me know tomorrow when you're coming back to get Rick. I'll bring some breakfast by his house for him."

After seeing Alisha off, Josiah and Elise hung around on the lawn adjacent to the police station parking lot. Various light posts served to illuminate the area fairly well. Georgeton seemed peaceful tonight, perhaps deceptively so.

Josiah studied her for a moment, then he pulled her head against his chest and enclosed her in his arms. He rested his chin on top of her head.

"I suppose we should call our folks. They're probably wondering what happened."

"Mmm," she mumbled, leaning most of her weight against his solid frame.

"I should also call Solomon to get him and the prayer chain praying."

Elise moved her head from under his chin and looked up at him. "What do you think happened with Webster?"

Josiah took his time answering, his face dark above hers. "It looks like he was in a fight. The strange thing is, he doesn't seem like the fighting type."

"No, he doesn't. When he looked at me, I couldn't help but feel, I don't know, somewhat responsible."

Josiah frowned down at her, holding her slightly away from him so he could see her better. "Responsible, even though you don't know what he's in for?"

She nodded slowly. "I know it sounds silly, and I can't explain it. I just do."

"Well, I don't want you to feel that way," he stated firmly.

She laughed. "I can't help how I feel—at least, not right now. You can't control everything, Josiah."

He pulled her back to him. "Don't I know it. If I didn't know it before, this night has certainly shown me that."

"You're wonderful, though," she said. "What would we all do without you?"

It was his turn to laugh, then he tipped her head back with one hand. "You keep making me feel needed like that, and I'll be sure to grow a few more feet."

"Jose, you're past the growing stage," she reminded him, smiling up at him.

"I love you," was his response.

"I love you, too." She knew he had meant to kiss her, but the night air was suddenly filled with the sounds of booted feet, slamming car doors, and the piercing cry of police sirens. They turned and watched as two police cars sped off onto the city streets.

"Come on," Josiah said, pulling Elise along. "There's Danny."

They walked quickly over to Danny, who had stepped out onto the parking lot to get into his car. He paused when he saw them and spoke before they could ask.

"It's April and Jack. He broke the restraining order." His voice was strained.

"Where are they?" Josiah asked intently.

"He's at the house! He went to the house, Jo!" He banged his fist on the roof of the squad car, swearing mildly. "That guy's going to be the death of her."

"Let me go with you, Danny." He turned to Elise. "Take my vehicle to your place, and I'll get dropped off there."

"No!" Danny exclaimed, getting into the car.

"Josiah!" Elise protested the same time as Danny.

"Come on, Dan, you're in no condition to go over there. I can help with Jack. Better yet, let Elise come, too. She'd be good for April and the girls." He had positioned his large frame between the car door and Danny so Danny couldn't close the door.

"You're interfering with police business, Jo," Danny ground out, then looked at Elise for a moment. "Okay, but I want you to stay out of it, Josiah. I'm only doing it for April and the girls. I don't give a heck what happens to Jack. Follow me in your vehicle." Josiah moved and Danny slammed the car door shut.

As they raced after Danny, Elise used her cell phone to dial her parents. She updated them quickly, and her mother reassured her that she would notify Adam. Elise promised to call later and then hung on for dear life.

By the time Josiah had pulled over along the cul-de-sac where April's little bungalow was, police statements were already being taken. Danny had paused in the front yard to get an official update from two officers on the scene. From what Elise could overhear, April's neighbours were about for different reasons. Apparently Jack's loudness had stirred them from their abodes, and the police cars had further thickened the drama. Some were available out of curiosity, while most wanted to help. April was spoken of fondly as the little mother who worked hard to raise her children. Jack was given no such respect, and had also fled the scene.

Afterwards, Elise and Josiah hurried to follow Danny into the house, away from the various neighbours' curious looks. Once inside, Elise could see April standing in her living room, clutching her girls to her side, while reporting to a female and male officer. At first glance, everything seemed normal, but for the dazed, wide-eyed looks of the children. As soon as April saw Danny, her rigid, stoic posture changed to one of vigour and purpose.

"Please, Danny, I don't want to press charges. He didn't hurt me, I just got scared." She had pulled Lily and Mya with her past the two officers and headed toward Danny in the front hall.

Danny held up both hands, his back toward Josiah and Elise. "April, please don't ask me to do that again." His voice was filled with emotions held in check. "You can't keep living this way. It's no way for you, it's no way for the children."

Elise moved around Danny and reached down to get hold of Mya, who grabbed her fiercely around the neck. She held her warm little body securely, feeling the rigidity there.

"Please, Danny, he needs help. He's getting help," she insisted.

"He's been getting help forever, April. When are you going to wake up?" Danny was now barely containing his anger.

Elise couldn't remain quiet any longer. "Dan, please, the girls."

Danny looked from one child to the next and pushed his hand through his springy curls in frustration. His expression was grim as he was approached by the male officer.

"Sergeant, the perpetrator has fled the scene."

"I got that already," he snapped. "Are you finished taking Mrs. Roper's statement?"

"Yes, sir," was the pained replied. He was a young officer and seemed mildly embarrassed.

"Well, she's refusing to press charges, so I guess we just wasted our time here."

April stood holding Lily's hand and looking dejected. She glanced around her as if she didn't know what to do.

"Round up the guys outside," Danny directed the officer. "I'll see you all back at the station."

Josiah, who had remained quiet so far, laid a hand on Danny's shoulder. "Dan, let's go into the kitchen." His directive was in a tone not easily ignored even by the discontented, uniformed officer before him.

Danny looked at April, who refused to meet his eyes, then said to Elise. "See to her and the girls." His voice was burdened.

"I will," she promised, then she and April watched the two men disappear into the kitchen.

They stood in the front hall for a moment, listening to the murmur of the men's voices inside the kitchen.

"Mommy, I don't want to see Daddy again." Lily's plaintive, child's voice stirred them back to the moment.

Elise reached out to touch April after hearing a strangled sob escape from her. April was looking back and forth at her girls, and her face was filled with despair.

"April?" Elise questioned, sensing her pain and confusion.

Her eyes pleaded with Elise. "I tried so hard to help him. I wanted him to see the Light in me and be drawn to it. I know about some of what he suffered at the hand of his own mother. I wanted to make it better for him, but I can't. The One who can help him, he won't acknowledge."

Elise stroked the top of Lily's head while holding Mya with one arm. "It's not your fault, April, but I think Danny is right. You can't protect Jack forever. Eventually, the consequences of his choices will catch up with him."

For the next hour, Elise helped April bathe the girls. When their clean-smelling bodies were tucked in under the covers in April's bed, Elise offered to stay with them while April ordered herself and the house.

Danny had already left after promising to regularly patrol her street. They weren't sure where Jack was, or if he would return. Danny had been a lot calmer after his interlude in the kitchen with Josiah, but had been pointedly firm. "If I so much as hear he's set foot on this street, I'll personally throw his rear end in jail, with or without your permission."

April had not uttered one word in defence.

When Elise left April's bedroom, after making sure Lily and Mya had fallen asleep, she found Josiah sitting in the living room, talking to Solomon on his cell phone. As she passed by him, she paused to run a hand along his back before heading for the kitchen. He squeezed her fingers and smiled in acknowledgement before letting her go.

"They're off to dreamland," she announced, entering the kitchen. April was moving back and forth, emptying the dishwasher. She seemed robotic in her movements, but Elise knew there must be some therapy in doing the everyday things. April looked at her and smiled wryly.

"Oh, to sleep like a baby now."

"Will you be okay, April?" Elise asked gently.

April left her work and sat on one of two stools in the small kitchen. "I always bounce back, Elise. Don't worry about me. Pray for me, pray for Jack. He's so messed up. His mother used to beat him with a rubber strap and lock him in a dark, unfinished basement for hours. By age ten, he was rescued by social services only to be tossed around from one foster home to another. He never knew his father. He found out later that his mother had a mental disorder and should never have been left to care for a child." She sighed, as if the words poured out of her had lightened her load.

Elise moved closer to her and leaned against the dishwasher. "I'm so sorry. I didn't know all of his story."

April threw her head back and brushed her blond hair back with one hand. Weariness was evident on her face. "I don't think anyone knows his whole story. I thought I knew him, but I don't. I love him only by my actions. I have no affection for him, not after the second time he put me in the hospital."

"Oh, April." Elise felt her heart tug.

"I'm just glad he never hurt the girls, at least not physically. They've never really had a daddy, because he treated them like they didn't exist. It was Lily who dialled 911. I had taught her to, in case I was ever in trouble and couldn't do it myself. I'm so proud of her."

"Wow, that's amazing—especially for her to stay focused enough to do it in a scary situation."

April seemed to struggle for a moment, bunching the hem of her pale blue skirt in her hands. "Do you know, Mya has called Danny 'daddy' before? At first, I thought she had mistaken 'Danny' for 'daddy,' but Lily, who always seems to interpret what she says, repeated it."

"Have you ever considered divorce?"

Her answer was immediate and sure. "No. I took my vows seriously, for better or worse. He's never, to my knowledge, committed adultery. I don't have to live with the abuse, but I have no biblical grounds for divorce."

"Wouldn't God understand, April?"

April smoothed at her clothes. She smiled sadly. "Then we would all have different barometers of acceptable reasons for divorce. Where would we draw the line?"

Elise sighed. "I never thought of it that way. Josiah and I are supposed to schedule some time with Solomon for premarital counselling. I guess issues like this would be addressed."

"Jack and I never had counselling. We actually should never have married. I was a believer; he was not. I don't know, though, if anything can prepare you for this kind of thing. I guess just knowing not to fall into the trap of blaming yourself for someone's abuse of you, and knowing to get out before it's too late, are good starts."

Elise touched her on the arm. "Will you let me pray with you?"

April's eyes were moist and she was blinking rapidly. "Please do. You've both done so much tonight. I'm so grateful for God sending you my way."

They prayed while in an embrace, and Elise ended her prayer by saying, "Please, Heavenly Father, bring release for April. Please bring your protection and your peace."

Chapter Twenty

Elise could smell the cleanness of the gentle breeze. She could feel its warmth, too, on her face, where the blindfold wasn't. The ground felt uneven under her sandals, but Josiah held her securely around the waist. He had insisted on ensuring her surprise by temporarily robbing her of her sight. She was not impressed.

"Josiah, aren't we there yet? You could be taking me out to the lake for all I know."

"It would be a lot more windy out there," he assured her, humour evident in his tone. "Come on, just a few more feet."

The end-of-summer days were slipping by too quickly, and she wanted to hang on to them. She almost felt like another break before school started in a week's time. There had been too much drama the last few weeks, but life did have to go on.

"Okay, right here," he finally announced. She felt his fingers fumble at the cloth tied at the back of her head just under her ponytail.

Before her sight was restored, she felt his lips press against hers, and she couldn't help but respond.

"Voila!" he declared, moving away with the blindfold waving in his hand.

The sight of the house drew her eyes away from his huge smile. According to Josiah, the house was finished minus the décor, which she would oversee. She consciously rubbed her fingers together to feel the ring that reminded her that this was her future as well.

"Oh, Jose, it's beautiful!" And it was. She was standing at the bottom of the wide porch steps. Josiah had blindfolded her before driving in on the long, curved driveway. Now she noticed that the wide front yard and circular part of the driveway had been graded and readied for shrubs, grass, and pavement. The woods surrounding the yard had been cut back an attractive distance, creating a mysterious wall of privacy. It was twelve acres in all. The house itself had a luxury farmhouse appeal, as Josiah had designed it to have.

She took hold of the hand he offered and went up the wooden steps onto the very wide, covered front porch, but not before she was able to appreciate the contrast of the dark shingles of the roof with the pale stucco outer walls. The white of the upper storey's multi-pane, gabled windows tied into the white of the huge columns supporting the overhanging roof. She listened to him chatter on, some architectural phrases she didn't understand, but was only too happy to have him enjoy his role.

Through the double front doors, the now familiar, vaulted foyer spread wide before her. The floors and walls were still void of colour, but were poised ready, begging to have their cosmetics applied. On her left were the wide, arched doorways of the living and dining rooms respectively. To her right was a generous closet area and powder room. Following the powder room, past the curved rails leading upstairs, was a French door leading to the study. Straight ahead, down a wide hall, were double French doors leading to the kitchen.

"Here, talk to me for a second." Josiah grabbed her around the waist and hoisted her onto the kitchen's marble-top island before she could protest. Her legs, bare below her knee-length shorts, felt the coolness of the marble beneath her. She purposefully swung her legs back and forth, barely missing Josiah. He pushed his body against her legs to still them and placed his arms on either side of her.

"What do you think so far?" he asked eagerly.

She put on a dramatic, thoughtful pose. "Well, I love the bayed breakfast nook over there and the abundant cabinetry and counter space in here. This house, the property, is helping me forget the other troubles of life."

He grinned. "Coming out here does that, especially when you go by the water."

"Will we have a boat?" she asked, interested.

"A boat, yes, and the boathouse I plan to build next year."

They peeked out the nook doors into the yard, then continued to the right of the kitchen, entering a generous family room with a second staircase leading upstairs. Elise absolutely loved the second staircase idea. Double patio doors opened to a future patio area in the large, park-like backyard. A smaller hallway, with rooms on one side, led from the family room. These rooms were the laundry and sewing rooms. Across the hall, one door led to the three-car garage, above which, Elise knew, were two guest rooms and a shared bathroom.

"We'll design the basement to include a music room, in time," Josiah said, pointing to another door just before the one leading into the garage. His eyes had not lost their first sparkle; this was very exciting for him.

"We?" Elise teased, then screeched when he suddenly caught her up in his arms and spun around the family room with her.

"Why do you ask like that? It is our house—our home." His eyes were fixed on her boldly, and she felt weak at the power of his gaze and strength of his arms.

They eventually made it upstairs, their footsteps echoing loudly in the empty house. At Elise's favourite spot, the landing by the window, they paused. The glow of the sunshine bathed the area beautifully.

"Your sitting area, mademoiselle," Josiah declared, then his voice lowered and became serious. "When you were here for the first time, this is where I felt an overwhelming sense that I didn't want to live in this house without you."

"I remember," she said quietly. "This is where I felt really intuitive about our possible future together."

They finished their tour of the guest suite, three family bedrooms, and two bathrooms before moving on to the master suite. Elise entered it almost reverently, then started waltzing across the floor.

"I think," she said, catching her breath, "I will take this whole room to myself. It will be my escape." She laughed loudly as his dark brows lowered in a frown.

"Escape from what. From whom?" He was approaching her.

Elise kept twirling around, her gathered hair bouncing off her back, trying to evade him. She flitted past two tall multi-pane windows which showcased the beauty of the woods beyond. On one side of the grandiose room were two doors leading to his and hers walk-in closets. Other doors from the closets opened up to a massive five-piece bathroom with double sinks.

Elise danced her way into the bathroom from one of the closets and got lost in the wonder of it. She turned to exit and bumped squarely into Josiah. Naturally, he grabbed hold of her.

"There is absolutely no way you'd be occupying these rooms by yourself," he said.

She laughed playfully. "Don't be silly, Josiah. I'm joking."

"Not about that," he emphasized, then pulled her fiercely to him. He kissed her breathless, then released her suddenly. "Now tell me again how you want to be here alone."

Her gaze locked with his, and she found she couldn't answer. He reached for her again, and they became lost in each other's embrace— tasting, telling, promising. When she could hardly take it anymore, and just before she lost all reason, he pulled away.

"This is not a good place for us right now," he uttered, breathing unevenly. She took his cue and shakily preceded him until they got safely to the main floor. By the time they hit the front foyer, she felt more herself. She glanced at Josiah, but wasn't so sure about him. He had his eyes focused on her. She smiled.

He scowled. "Don't even go there," he warned.

She stopped at the front doors. "I'm not the one with self-control issues."

His brows matched his scowl. "And what exactly would you have done if I didn't have self-control?"

She thought for a moment. When she looked at him, she knew he could see the truth in her eyes.

"Just as I thought. Little Miss Prim and Proper on the outside, but molten lava on the inside. A man could get burned by a woman like you."

Elise pulled opened one door, then glanced back at him. She wasn't sure if she should be insulted or complimented by his last statement. "What exactly does that mean?"

He shoved firmly on her lower back to boost her out the door. "It means, like the Bible says, let every man have his own wife so he doesn't get burned."

She protested. "It doesn't say it like that, Josiah." She stood hands on her hips, facing him on the porch. "It says, rather than burn with passion, every man should have his own wife."

He laughed, showing strong white teeth. "When did you get so biblically entrenched? I can't even pull one over on you anymore?"

Elise swatted at him, and he evaded her, laughing even more loudly. He rushed to hold her from behind.

"Be still for a moment," he commanded. "Take a look at all of this."

She looked at the house, at the view, but was more interested in the secure feel of being encased in his strong arms.

"All of this would mean nothing without Jesus Christ. My heart and soul belong to Him first, and then to you. The awful pain I felt at my mother's death, the pain that wanted me to lash out and run away from Him, was the beginning of what He took to draw me to Him."

He turned her to face him, and she saw the depth of emotions in his eyes.

"God... Jesus means everything to me. The Bible says, what does it profit if I gain everything the world has to offer, but lose my soul, lose eternity with God? Do you understand?"

She nodded, afraid to speak and break the solemnity of the moment.

"Baby, you've become my life, so I need you to understand the depth of my commitment to Him, and I need to remember that I had a head start. So if I'm impatient with you, at times, please tell me where to get off."

She smiled, holding back her laughter. "I'll try to do it. Nicely."

He hauled her back into his arms, pressing her head against his heart. "You're a gem."

Chapter Twenty-One

"I don't understand. Why do they keep calling you about this client when he hasn't been in your care for weeks now?" Celia was standing in the doorway of David's home office. Her mind was mostly entrenched with planning the engagement party for Josiah and Elise, but her husband's preoccupation with work was making inroads on her attention.

David looked up, surprised. He had been hunched over some papers on his desk.

"Yes, David. These walls are not soundproof. I overhear enough phone conversations to know what's going on."

He sighed. "Celia, it's a simple consult because he was in my care for years. That's all." She stood, waiting.

"There have just been some unexpected developments. That's all. I'm just giving my advice. That's not unusual in an emergency."

"Emergency?"

"Well, yes. I mean, there was an emergency a couple of weeks ago, but that's over now. Consulting me is just an offshoot of that."

Celia frowned. "If you use 'just' and 'that's all' one more time, I don't know…"

He chuckled softly and got up to go over to her. He gently brushed her still smooth skin, the paleness of his hand contrasting against its dark brown colour.

"I know you're worried, my darling, but it'll be all right. The first step is over, and time will take care of the rest."

She raised her hand to place it on his. "I thought you would be free of him once the decision to refer him was made."

"I know, I know." He sighed again. "I guess things are never as simple as they seem. Nevertheless, let's focus on the beautiful things of life, like Elise and her ambitious fiancé. Weren't you going to help give her advice on that house of theirs?"

"David, don't use psychiatry on me. I may have retired now, but I'm not dead." With that, she left him standing in the doorway.

David shook his head and mumbled to himself, "That woman was always too smart for me." However, she was right. It was just as well that she didn't know the full nature of the problem. The police had issued a report to the clinic regarding a recent incident with his former client. The writing was on the wall and David was not sure if there would be any escape from it. He gazed upwards.

"God, I've not been much of a praying man, but I pray this has nothing to do with what's been happening to my daughter. Please do not let the failures of a father visit his daughter."

*   *   *

"He's pretty depressed, Jo," Alisha stated. "That usually crazy, bubbly man is depressed."

"I've noticed," Josiah commented. "I hate seeing him like that, but I don't know what else to do for him except continue to encourage him and pray."

Alisha had some time off and was helping him sort through stuff at his father's house. Adam was moving to a nice new bungalow built by the company. He relished the thought of having everything at his fingertips on one floor. He had declared that his old bones didn't like the stairs anymore, and he wouldn't have to continue putting up with real estate house showings at all odd hours. As far as he was concerned, their three-storey home could stand empty for as long as it took for the right buyer. He was ready to move on.

Josiah was happy for his dad, and he couldn't help but wonder why he himself no longer felt some connection to his old home. It was as if he had lived another life here, and now, with his dad moving out, that life had been left behind. He had no doubt that Elise and the new house had a lot to do with it. He had also been praying for a complete release from any bondage of the past. Would Rick ever get past his demons?

"Do you think your dad will want to keep these old magazines?" Alisha asked.

Josiah grimaced. "I don't know. Just put them on top in that box and leave it opened for him to see. People can get worked up about the most unlikely things."

Alisha heaved a partially filled cardboard box unto the coffee table in the living room. "At least he's talking to me now. Those first few days, after he relapsed, were the quietest I'd ever seen him."

Josiah collapsed on the living room couch. "Yeah. He can't seem to get past the shame of it. He feels like he's let us all down. The best I can get from him is that he went to see his parents and his sister, and they'd still have nothing to do with him."

"Even with him having been sober for three years? I don't understand. What kind of people are they?"

Josiah gazed through the bay window of the living room. The days were getting shorter again. He'd have to get home soon to finish up some plans he had taken from the office. He knew Elise was more busy now because of school preparations, but he wished he could interrupt her. However, he couldn't break his promise to give her some space this evening.

"I don't know, Alisha. We can't be too quick to judge. We only have an inkling of what he may have put them through over the years."

"What about forgiveness? Will they never forgive him?"

He looked her in the eye. "Will he ever forgive himself? I don't know what all he's done, but that's the question. Forgiveness is such a big thing, yet it's a simple concept. Look at April. She forgives Jack time and time again, but he finds no forgiveness for himself or his mother. I found out through the grape vine that that Webster guy got into it with some kid's father because Webster called the kid a 'buffoon' for calling him a 'nerd'."

"Wow," Alisha said, shaking her head in disbelief. "Elise was talking to Keisha, and apparently Webster has not returned to Georgeton High."

"Well, no matter what that boy said to him, he had no business returning like for like, especially being a teacher. Someone called the police, and the boy and his father accused Webster of trying to beat up the kid. The charges were dropped after it was found out to be false. They had it in for Webster for failing the boy in English the year before."

"Turn the other cheek?"

"That's right, Ali. Easier said than done, but preach it like it is."

They left off their conversation when they heard Adam's footsteps on the stairs. He had probably left his work on the second floor to come down and inspect theirs.

After Alisha left, Josiah stayed for a while with his father. They had just finished eating supper when Adam asked a cautious question.

"So, you're letting Jack go?"

Josiah swiped at his mouth with a paper napkin before answering. "I've got to, Dad. He hasn't shown up to work since he broke into April's house. She didn't tell the police that, though."

"What?"

"That Jack had broken into the house. They came because he had broken the restraining order. It was the little girl, Lily, who dialled 911. They could have charged him with breaking and entering. Danny would have loved that. He knows now, and he's as mad as a hornet."

Adam chuckled and scratched his greying head. "Poor child. It must have been hard for her to do."

"Sure, but with enough love and care, little kids can be resilient."

"Spoken like a man ready for commitment."

"And you know I'm ready, Dad."

Adam smiled and reached across the kitchen table to pat his son's big hands. "I'm proud of you, son, for all the decisions you've made and all you've done. But, marriage, that's one of the biggest. You've chosen very well. Your mother would have been pleased."

It felt good to hear that. "Thanks, Dad. If it weren't for you, I might not have met her."

"Yes, the skinny little girl who trailed us while we worked."

"She wasn't so little back then, Dad, and she's sure got enough curves to make up for any skinniness now," Josiah declared proudly.

Adam laughed, then sobered. "Is it the right decision about Jack? Won't that set him back?"

Josiah stared up at the ceiling and rubbed his chin, then looked at Adam. "Dad, Jack is behaving in ways I just can't fathom. You know, you've heard the talks when the guys are working. He's bad for the team, no matter which team he's on. He hasn't shown up or called work, but I've heard he's around. He hasn't returned my calls, so as soon as I see his face, he's fired. I hope he's been seeing his shrink, because I've had it with him."

Josiah took his time getting out of his vehicle. He felt tired and he wanted badly to hold a certain young woman. Their session with Solomon tomorrow couldn't come soon enough. The only problem was that Solomon, possibly, would have to sit between them if he wanted their reasonable attention. Josiah chuckled to himself at the thought. His work boots echoed loudly on the pavement leading to his building. He tapped the uncovered plans against his thigh in rhythm with his steps. A warm shower and soft bed was definitely in his vision. Maybe a short phone call to Elise would be okay. No, she had specifically asked him not to call. That phone call would turn out to be long, and he knew it. As he walked, he whistled, and wasn't prepared for the shadow of a man rushing out to him from the side of the building. He automatically tensed up until he could make out the medium build of Jack Roper.

"Jack," he pronounced. Jack stood staring at him for a moment, as if trying to gauge his reaction.

"I need to talk to you, Josiah."

Josiah stood with legs apart and hands tense at his side. "Talk away."

Jack stepped closer, the lights from the building picked out his drawn features. He looked unhealthy, like he hadn't been eating or sleeping well.

"I need you to help me, Josiah, to get my family back. A man shouldn't have to live without his family. It isn't humane. They took me from my mother—"

"Your mother wasn't good for you, Jack." He glanced about him. People were coming and going intermittently. "Come up to my place, and we'll talk there."

"I don't want—" Jack was talking to empty air. Josiah had already moved off with a purposeful stride.

In the elevator, the silence was ominous, and the smell wasn't much better. It was obvious to Josiah that Jack had ceased to care for himself in more ways than one. However, he wasn't feeling very compassionate; he was tired, cranky, and fed up. This man continued to put his family through hell, and no matter how much help he had received, nothing changed.

Once inside the apartment, Josiah tossed the plans on his kitchen table and faced Jack, who was looking desperate and wary at the same time.

"Sit down, Jack," he said gesturing to the chairs at the table. "Would you like some coffee?"

Jack shook his head impatiently and ran his hand through his sandy hair. It looked greasy and unkempt. "I–I haven't been doing well. I need my family back." He slowly sank onto one of the chairs, his eyes on Josiah.

"Why, Jack? Why do you need your family back?" Josiah had remained standing.

Jack seemed almost taken aback by the direct question. He frowned. "They're m–mine, and I've lived without them for long enough."

Josiah sat across from him and studied him quietly, then he asked gently, "Why was it that you had to live without them, Jack?"

With a lowered gaze, Jack rubbed the black veneer of the table anxiously. He didn't answer.

Josiah answered for him. "You hurt your family, Jack, again and again. You agreed with the court to complete a period of treatment, which you haven't yet completed, and you've broken a court order to stay away from your family for a period of time."

The rubbing on the table was increasing, causing it to vibrate slightly. Josiah sighed heavily. "What do you want me to do, Jack? I've given you a job, which you haven't shown up to for days now. I've tried to befriend you—"

"I've changed." The sound coming from Jack was almost animal-istic. He raised his eyes and the emptiness there shook Josiah. "No one wants to believe I've changed." His fists were balled and his posture rigid.

Josiah held his ground. He wasn't sure what he was witnessing, but it felt evil. "Then abide by the wishes of the court and your wife, and finish what you have started—"

Jack was on his feet, his hands splayed on the table. "It is enough! I've been in their power long enough! What do you, who has the world at your feet, know of it?" He started a string of vulgarity that caused the hair to rise on Josiah's neck.

"That's enough, Jack!" he almost shouted. He stood, feeling the strength of the Spirit in him. "We can't control everything that happens to us, but we have the power of choice as to how we deal with it."

"Choice? I had no choice when my mother…" He continued on again cursing belligerently. "I had no choice when they shipped me from home to home—dirty, filthy people."

"You have the choice now, Jack. You're not a helpless child anymore."

Jack's eyes became glazed, and he shook his head sorrowfully. "It's too late." His arms were trembling, and he threw them around his middle, rocking back and forth, agitated.

Josiah saw the change in him and used the opportunity. "I've told you before, Jack, it's never too late with Jesus. The systems of the world may fail, but God will never fail you. Will you give it over to Him?"

Jack's arms flung out before him, palms facing out as if to ward off the words. He became hostile again. "No! No! I don't want your Jesus!" He spat out the Name vehemently and turned forcefully.

"Jack!" Josiah called, going after him. By the time he got to the front door, Jack was already out into the hall, nearly knocking over two teenaged girls in the process. They stared wide-eyed after the disappearing form of Jack, then looked at Josiah.

"It's okay, girls. My friend's just had some bad news."

They nodded uncertainly before one of them spoke up with the optimism of youth. "Oh, well, hopefully he'll be okay."

Josiah smiled wearily. "I hope so, too."

Elise stopped in her tracks, unsure of what to do. Webster was standing by her car, apparently waiting for her. The school parking lot was almost empty, because it was well past school hours, but she had decided to work late instead of bringing any work home. She wanted her first evening of premarital counselling to end with a night free of school responsibilities.

She took a deep breath and held tightly to her bags. The sound of her heels on the paved surface echoed her heartbeat.

"Hi, Webster." She kept her tone light and impersonal.

He ran a hand through his hair, which actually looked decent for a change. He adjusted his glasses nervously. "Hi," he returned. "I hope you don't mind. I tried calling you last night, but there was no answer."

"I got your message. I wasn't answering my phone last night."

"Oh." He was dressed, unusual for him, in jeans and a lightweight hoodie.

"I had a lot of work," she explained. What was he up to? She fidgeted with her load.

"Oh, sorry," he said, standing away from her car door.

She opened the door and tossed her things across to the passenger side. She straightened. "Did you want me for something specific, Webster?"

She noticed he was staring at her left hand, his lips slack. He looked at her.

"You're engaged?" he asked incredulously. He blinked rapidly, seeming to struggle with his discovery.

Elise held her hands together self-consciously.

Without waiting for her answer, he asked, "When?"

Elise felt irritated and annoyed. "Webster, it's not really any of your business."

He stumbled backwards slightly and held his hands up. "Not my business. Of course not," he mumbled. Suddenly his eyes became intense. "Were you engaged that night you saw me at the police station?"

"Webster, I really don't want to get into this. I was told you had moved on."

"I was falsely accused, you know. I was cleared of any wrongdoing," he continued as if he hadn't heard her.

"I understand, Webster—"

"People need to teach their children to respect others."

Elise jerked her hands up, and with her head flung back, she let loose. "Look! Webster, you don't need to explain to me. I don't wish you any ill. I hope you're doing fine elsewhere, but please stop trying to meet with me."

He was silent for a moment, his hazel eyes wounded. "I–I didn't mean to upset you. I thought we were, at least, friends. I didn't know you were en–engaged."

"Webster, please, let's just be good fellow citizens. Please don't try to contact me again. If we see each other in public, we'll smile and greet, but that's all."

"We can't be friends?" His voice was almost childlike.

She shook her head firmly. "No. You and I both know it wouldn't work."

He reached out and grabbed her upper arm. "Elise, please—" She jerked away from him, feeling the intimidation of her space being invaded, then she shoved on his chest with both hands. He floundered, trying to keep his balance.

"No!" she said forcefully.

"Is there a problem?"

Elise turned to see one of the school's custodians marching purposefully toward them. She noticed the pained look on Webster's face as she looked at him expectantly.

"No, no problem. I was just leaving." He gave Elise a long look, then turned and walked away.

"You sure you're okay?"

She looked at the sturdy-looking man and smiled. "Yes. Thanks for coming out."

"No problem," he said sincerely. "But you seemed to have it pretty well under control, I tell you."

She thanked the custodian again and got into her car, as he walked back to the school building. She drove to the edge of the parking lot and, just before she turned onto the street, she paused until her pulse slowed.

For some inexplicable reason, her eyes were drawn across the road to the elementary school. It was déjà vu. She was sure it was the same man she had seen back in the spring, gazing into the schoolyard. He had the same look of loneliness in his bearing. Perhaps that was why he seemed familiar this time; she had seen him before. She flicked her turning signal on, then paused. He was looking her way. She peered through the windshield. It was Jack Roper. Why was he there?

"Of course," she whispered to herself. "That's where Lily goes to school every other day."

As she drove past, she didn't look at him again until she could do so in her rear-view mirror. His aloneness seemed so evident, yet he was a monster to his family.

"Dear Jesus," she breathed in prayer, "please help this crazy world."

"Hey, you're late," Josiah said as he vacated his vehicle and went over to Elise's. She had just parked beside his SUV after coming from the school. They had planned to meet here, at one of their favourite restaurants, for dinner, and then go on to their meeting with Solomon. He rested his arms along her open car window and searched her eyes.

What he saw there caused him to hurry over to the passenger side and pull the door opened.

"What happened?" he asked after he was seated beside her.

"Will you just hold me for a second?"

He studied her for a moment, then drew her into his arms, her smallness heightening his protective instincts. He kissed her on the forehead and stroked her arm repeatedly.

"Webster showed up at the school."

"He what?!"

"He didn't do anything, but was being quite persistent about knowing all my business. Fortunately, after I shoved him—"

"You what?" He moved his shoulder from beneath her, causing her to flop back on the seat where he could see her face. "Why did you need to do that? Did he get physical with you?"

She ran her hands over her pulled-back hair, then drew the long curls over to lay on one side of her chest. Her long dark lashes hid her eyes, so he watched her lips carefully.

"He just grabbed my arm, that's all—"

"Good grief, Elise, will that guy never quit?"

He listened carefully as she reiterated the whole story. She kept darting glances at him as if afraid he would erupt, so he tried to remain calm, but he was feeling anything but that. He could feel the tension in his jaw.

"Listen, I want you to get on your cell and call me if he comes near you again. It doesn't matter when or where, just call me. I'm dead serious, Elise."

She nodded, looking up at him.

He took hold of her chin. "And next time, kick him where it counts, okay?"

She giggled, then bit at her bottom lip with even, white teeth. "Are we ready to eat?"

"Are you feeling better?" he asked, letting go of her.

"Much better," she assured him. She reached up and stroked the side of his face with her hand. Her palm felt cool and smooth on his skin. He placed his hand over hers, then lowered his mouth to hers. He kissed her with a confidence and calm assurance that she was his and would remain his.

Afterwards, they looked deeply into each others eyes, and he revelled in the wonder of what they had and all that was to come.

"Okay, let's go eat so we can be ready for Solomon and all his wisdom."

She giggled again, and he loved the sound of it.

Chapter Twenty-Two

Sitting at her table, Celia felt proud and weepy at the same time. If she felt this way now, how would she manage the wedding? The engagement party was going fabulously. The hall they had rented was spacious enough, without being overly so, to maintain an intimate atmosphere of family and friends.

The combination of Elise's new church friends with the old had certainly jacked up the numbers. Those from Celia's church had long ago accepted that her daughter had moved on, as many of them seemed to have expected of their own children. One of her oldest friends had reminded her, "Well, they do have to make their own way. Just be thankful she allows you in her life. Mine seem to conveniently remember me only during the holidays."

There were also some of Elise's colleagues from the high school and others from Alexander's Contracting and Design. Josiah's employees had been a hard number to whittle down. And, of course, the

Alexander extended family—consisting of Josiah's aunts, uncles, cousins, and two great-aunts from both his parents' family—more than made up for the lack on her and David's side. David's only brother did promise he would make it for the wedding. That remained to be seen. It was possible she would have two of her cousins visit from her homeland, if she paid their way. Gladly, she and David would do so. Nothing would be too much for their only child.

"Mrs. Everson, is there anything else you need me to do?"

Celia's thoughts were dispelled as her attention turned to the attractive red-haired woman bent over her. She had known Alisha for what seemed like forever. There was a time she had been worried about Alisha's wild influence on Elise, but now she was grateful for such a lifelong friend for her daughter. Having left her country of birth so many years ago, she knew what it was like to have that lack.

"No, my dear. You have been like a right hand in all of this already. We can't depend on those men to see these sorts of things through," she said, indicating David and Adam.

Alisha smoothed at her beautiful light green dress. "No, I guess we can't," she agreed, laughing a little. David and Adam seemed to be having the time of their lives circling around the beautifully dressed tables, talking to the guests.

"And when will your turn be, my dear?"

Alisha pursed her lips, glancing uneasily at the others around the table. "I don't know. It's in God's hands," she admitted in a low voice.

Celia smiled and ceased the questions, realizing she was perhaps embarrassing the young woman.

Josiah found it very hard to keep his eyes off Elise. She was absolutely breathtaking in a simple but elegant slightly off the shoulder dress that emphasized his heart locket on her chest beautifully. The dress's deep apricot colour brought out the honey tone of her skin and seemed to set her light brown eyes on fire. The skirt of the dress draped smoothly over her hips and flowed loosely down past her slender calves. Every time she stirred beside him, a tantalizing fragrance teased him. He longed to pull her hair down from its coiled place on her head and bury his face in it. She was stunningly aglow.

"You keep looking at her like that and everyone will think you're going to eat the bride-to-be instead of the food before you," Danny whispered in his ear. Alisha had been sitting on that side of him, but she must have gotten up without him being aware.

He chuckled and whispered back. "Is it that obvious?"

"Do fish swim?" Danny looked smart, out of uniform in a dark dress shirt and tie. His springy curls were fairly tame.

"Hi, Danny," Elise called. "Is April doing okay?"

He waved nonchalantly in April's direction, two tables away. "Yeah, she's fine. She's starting to worry now about the kids. I told her to stop bellyaching. They'd be perfectly fine with my folks."

Her eyes widened. "You didn't say that to her?"

He grinned. "I said it nicer, Elise. You look smashing, by the way."

"Thanks," she said. "Don't stay away from her too long. She looks a little lost."

"Well, here comes Alisha back for her seat. Talk to you two later."

While Danny and Alisha exchanged pleasantries, Josiah reached under the table for Elise's hand. His fingers played the same message to her hand that his eyes were telling hers. He loved her; he couldn't wait for her to be completely his.

Solomon returned to his seat beside Elise. He observed them for a moment, then counselled, "Next time you two come for a session with me, this is exactly how you're not going to sit."

"Solomon," Bethany cautioned from beside him.

"Beth," he started, looking at her, "I could hardly keep their attention. It was like the newlywed game instead of premarital counselling."

Elise's face was slightly red; Josiah was sure it had nothing to do with the warmth of the room.

"Jo, Rick still hasn't come," Alisha said, distracting him. "I don't think he's going to come." He had noticed Rick's absence by the untouched table setting on the other side of Alisha.

"Did you try calling him?" He could see the upset and worry in her green eyes.

"Yes, but he's not answering. Same thing with the house phone. I don't want to bother you, but I thought you should know."

Elise struggled under the load of gifts in her arms, then laughed out loud when Keisha mischievously stacked another on top. All of the guests had departed, and her parents and Adam had also left to secure the out-of-town guests for the night.

"Keisha, for Pete's sake," Elise groaned. Alisha reached, just in time, to help prevent the packages from tumbling to the floor.

Keisha helped Alisha, all the while bubbling with laughter. "I'm simply trying to get you used to the weight of marriage that comes after this. It'll be a lot heavier than this, I tell you."

"As if you would know," Elise shot back.

Keisha threw her head back, her unbraided, newly straightened hair flung down her back. "I plan on knowing in the near future, my dears."

Elise and Alisha looked at each other.

"Keisha, what are you telling us?" Elise asked.

"Did Gavin propose?" Alisha followed.

Keisha took her time answering. "Well…"

"Keisha!" the other two urged at once.

"Okay, okay," Keisha gave in. "He hasn't asked me yet, but I know he will… in the near future."

"Oh Keisha," Elise groaned, then her eyes brightened. "I think we should take those locks of hers, Alisha, and tie her to one of the posts over there," she declared, pointing to one of the majestic columns in the room.

Keisha smiled smugly until Elise moved intentionally toward her, then turned and raced across the room. Elise continued after her with Alisha not far behind. Their high heels clattered noisily on the tiled floor and their girlish squeals drew the attention of the staff working to clean up from the party.

"No, no!" Keisha yelled, her laughter and gasps filling the room.

"Corner her, Alisha!" Elise yelled, then turned to go the opposite way. She ran full force into Josiah. He grabbed her, keeping her pinned to himself.

"My, my. You do seem to make a habit of this." he declared, looking down at her. His tie was loosened and his pale gold shirt was opened at the neck.

"Josiah, let me go. Alisha and I are on a mission." She could see Alisha had given up the chase, and Keisha was laughing at the top of her lungs.

"And what if I don't want to?" he asked, his voice warm and deep.

"Josiah." She smacked his chest with an opened palm. "You're spoiling our fun."

"Spoil away, Josiah!" Keisha taunted. She had plopped down on a chair and was removing her shoes from her feet. Alisha joined her, breathing hard. They seemed content to watch the little drama unfolding before them. Elise noticed the staff pretending not to notice.

"Josiah, you are embarrassing me," she remonstrated, still locked in his arms.

"Oh, am I?" Suddenly he released her, only to bend slightly to easily lift her. He walked with long strides out of the hall to a coat room on the far side. She could hear the women whooping it up loudly at her expense. Josiah didn't even set her down. He just lowered his head and kissed her like there was no tomorrow.

When he was finally finished, he eased her down, but still held her close. Even with her heels, she stood on tiptoes with her arms around his neck.

"I've been wanting to do that all evening," he explained, his eyes dark with hidden passion. She lowered her arms from his neck and encircled his waist, then lay her head sideways against his chest.

"I love you," she breathed. The strength and depth of her feelings for Josiah frightened her, yet she submitted willingly to them.

"I love you first," he joked, then sobered. "How much do you love me?"

"More than all the pretty dresses in the world."

He laughed loudly. "You mean like the one you're wearing to take a man's breath away?"

"You're still breathing, aren't you?" she asked, looking up at him.

He laughed again, more softly. "It was a great night."

"Yes, it was," she agreed, losing herself in the pleasure of his gaze. He touched her lips gently with his, their breaths mingling, their minds not quite knowing what their souls could tell. Their kiss deepened, and for a moment all else was forgotten.

On her way home from the engagement party, to her mother's place where she now lived, Alisha stopped by Rick's small, two-storey house. As far as she knew, he had lived there since moving to Georgeton some years ago, but now it was up for sale. She hadn't even known he was selling it, until seeing the sign a few days ago. It was on a fairly quiet street, but she wasn't sure she would want to live in the house. Of course, any house could be made into a home. Now, Adam Alexander's house was a different story. She had always loved that house, from the first time she'd entered it with Josiah and a bunch of friends from church.

She parked on the short driveway. His pickup wasn't there. The house had no garage, and she didn't see his pickup in the vicinity along the street. She stared at the darkness of the house. No lights at all. Granted, it was late, but Rick was usually a night hawk.

She got out of her car and walked up the few steps to the front stoop. She knocked, then rang the door bell. She waited for a while, then repeated her actions several more times. She was pretty convinced he wasn't home.

It was Monday morning, and Josiah was getting a little frustrated. Rick's work crew had called every thirty minutes, since the start of the day, to report that he hadn't shown up for work. It was now several calls later, and Josiah had finally told the crew to continue on, and he'd come out by midday. He was staring at some plans before him when his desk phone rang. His receptionist announced a call from Alisha.

"What's up, Alisha?"

"Josiah, has Rick shown up for work?" She sounded really worried.

"Actually, no. He's very late."

"Jo, I don't think he's been home."

That got his attention. "What do you mean?"

"You know how I tried to reach him Saturday? Well, I tried all day Sunday, and went by his house for a second time. His pickup wasn't in the driveway either days and he hasn't answered the door."

He thought for a moment. "That is strange. None of the guys who work with him seem to know why he hasn't come to work. Did he mention anything to you?"

"No," she said. "What do you think we should do?"

Josiah sighed. "I don't know. I have to think about this. You don't think he went back to the bar?"

Her answer was immediate. "I called them all over the last two nights."

"All of them, Alisha?"

"All," she confirmed.

"Danny, he's been missing for four days now," Josiah reiterated, a day later.

"He's a grown man, Josiah."

"He's missed work for two with no explanation."

Danny stopped writing on the form before him. "You've got a point there. He's always been pretty diligent about work, hasn't he?" They were at the police station where Josiah had asked to see Danny personally.

"You bet. That and AA have been his lifelines," Josiah confirmed. Alisha had wanted to file a missing person's report, but they decided it would be more legitimate if he, as Rick's employer, filed it.

It was midday, and already he felt pressed for time. It seemed like a collage of things had been taking over his life, and he had no say over which ones to allow in. Jack kept leaving him the odd message, rambling on about how he was changing his life. One particular message made him wonder if he shouldn't inform Danny. Jack had said he was back in treatment, and something about setting things right, that everything would be okay because he would set things right. Of course, he always phoned when he knew Josiah would be out, and he never answered the return calls. It was obvious he didn't want to be talked out of whatever he was up to.

Elise had also received a few messages from Webster by e-mail. In them, he wrote about being sorry for everything, and that he was moving on with life. His following two messages seemed to belie the first, by their very existence. Elise felt he had written them to give her a chance to change her mind about him. She had ignored all three and wondered about changing her e-mail address. He, on the other hand, felt very restless about the whole thing and was checking on her more frequently.

Rick, the one person he wanted a call from, wasn't calling or answering his phone. No one seemed to have seen hide or hair of him.

After Danny and he were finished, he went out and sat in his vehicle for a breather, but his mind refused to quit. His father's move was only days away, and he was contemplating whether to rent or sell his own condo. Elise had been meeting with an interior decorator in her spare time, and plans were moving full steam ahead. He had said yes to practically everything she had recommended to him regarding the home decor, but her suggestion that he move in once it was completed gave rise to an unexpected decision. He supposed somebody should live there once it was finished, and tradition warranted that he be the one, but for some reason he had pictured Elise there instead. She and Celia had protested, as if he had suggested Elise move to Siberia.

"It's the man who waits at the home for the woman, *mon cher*," Celia had emphasized. Her corrective tone had not made him feel like her "dear."

Of course, Elise's protest had made more practical sense. "Josiah, I wouldn't want to be in that big house by myself for months."

His weariness had caused him to say the dumbest thing, and in front of her mother, too. "Well, why don't we just elope and kill two birds with one stone?" It had not gone over well.

Chapter Twenty-Three

David was sitting on a garden bench in his picturesque backyard. His long legs were stretched out in front of him, and he gazed absentmindedly somewhere beyond them. He still had his jacket and tie on from his day at the practice, but he had needed to sit in the silence and clear his mind.

He had been asked to reconsider and accept his former client back. In all his years of psychiatry, he had never purposefully given a client away; therefore, he had never been asked to accept one back. He had been told the progress of his former client was at stalemate because the client stubbornly and consistently insisted on returning to his care. It was not a solution, they had agreed, but it was a last resort attempt at what his colleagues thought was a hopeless case. David had steadfastly refused, reminding them that he had already met with the client and sorted through the referral issue. His client had not wanted to be referred, but David had ascertained that he had reached an impasse with this client, and with his impending retirement, it was an appropriate decision.

It was obvious then that, at some point, the client would most likely do something that would have him committed. David had been suspicious that this client was his crank caller, but he was no longer sure. It did, however, seem too much of a coincidence that Elise had also had similar happenings, though neither he nor she had had any more disturbances for a while now. She still did not know about his situation, even though he had questioned her about hers.

"That's not something you should have kept from us, sweetheart," he had told her, feeling a little hypocritical about his own secret. Of course, he couldn't helped but be touched by her thoughtful reason of not wanting to ruin their trip. They had both agreed to keep it from Celia.

He stood and reached up in a stretch. The shortening days and changing colour of the leaves seemed to affect his mood more easily this year. He was being too sensitive these days. He would be retired just after Elise's wedding, planned for next spring. It would be a new life for her and a new life for him. He felt optimistic about the future, and he certainly didn't want to take any footsteps backwards, especially not with this client. As Adam had once said to him, "New life in Christ is like putting your hand to a plough and not looking back." He wasn't sure about the new life in Christ, but Adam's influence in his life was making it look more appealing as time went by.

Before going into the house, he paused by the laundry room door and examined it, as he had been doing since learning about the peeping Tom incident. Their house had always had an alarm system in place, so he wasn't worried about a surprise break-in. It must have been unnerving, though, to have someone intrude on your privacy, uninvited.

He looked across at the yard gate. Perhaps he should get a lock for it. He entered the house through the family room patio doors, thinking about another thing to put on his to-do list.

The house was silent, and he remembered that Celia was supposed to be at a hospital charity fundraiser with a big donation from Josiah's company. He turned into the kitchen and started to wash his hands at the sink. He hurriedly dried them when the phone rang.

"Hello, Everson's," he answered, cradling the kitchen phone between his shoulder and cheek while he finished drying his hands. At first he heard heavy breathing, and he felt a familiar dread creeping up his spine, then a grating voice spoke.

"I will die a fallen hero, but how will you die? You who have abandoned me and betrayed me."

"Who is this?" David said forcefully into the phone. "The police are on to you." That's what Sergeant Rowe had told him to say.

"It doesn't matter," came the chilling reply. "Nothing matters anymore."

David spoke his ex-client's name into the phone. "Is it you?"

Suddenly, the line went dead. His hands shook as he replaced the phone on its base.

Alisha finished charting on her ICU patient. She cast an experienced and critical eye over the still form on the hospital bed before her. She then moved around the room and did one last check on the monitors and tubings that were her patient's link to life. Satisfied, she got ready to report to her replacement for the day shift.

Her link to Georgeton's only hospital was all that seemed to keep her sane these days. She felt numb with worry over Rick's disappearance. She knew Danny was following all leads, including contacting his estranged parents and sister, and she knew that the Hope Alive Church prayer chain had been activated, but she still felt lost.

After leaving the hospital, she started the short walk to her mother's house. One good thing about moving back home was the savings on gas and rent. Her mother was really a good soul, but rather absentminded. She had accepted Alisha's conversion years ago and even visited the church occasionally, but didn't see that she needed to make any changes in her own life. She had worked hard as a single mom, and, as long as her pension cheques, weekly bingo, and favourite TV shows continued, she was set. Alisha prayed regularly for her that somehow she would, even at sixty-nine, find God's ultimate purpose for her life. She was grateful, though, for the ability to save for her own home, and her mother seemed pleased to accommodate her in this way.

The morning air was a little cool as the fall days crept in. She hugged her sweater around her and kept up a brisk pace along the sidewalk. Her mother's house was in a well-kept, older subdivision with very mature trees. The trees reminded her of the ones along the street where the Alexanders' old house was situated. It was empty now, and she wondered if she should talk to Mr. Alexander about it. She knew he was in no rush to sell, but she wondered if Rick would like it. As soon as the thought hit her mind, she was horrified. Where had that come from?

It took her a moment to realize she had actually paused on the sidewalk. She smoothed at her flyaway hair and resumed her pace. It was no use denying that she was in love with Rick Phillips, big goon that he was. She had loved him for a while, which probably explained her sometimes antagonistic behaviour toward him. She didn't want to be in love with him. He was not a believer, and even though Josiah felt he was close, Rick's recent drunkenness and even more recent disappearance left a lot to be desired.

She couldn't help the worry she felt for him. Even her absentminded mother was noticing the trouble she was having eating and sleeping. He had been gone for six days now.

Alisha had almost reached the walkway to her destination when she saw a small blond woman with two children walking toward her from the opposite direction. It was April Roper with Lily walking beside her and Mya in a small stroller.

She waited until they were close enough before greeting them. "Hi, April. You're out early today."

April took a deep breath and smiled. "Hi, Alisha. I'm helping at Lily's school today, but I've got to get Mya to daycare first, and my car is in the shop."

Alisha chuckled. "Good grief, April. Why didn't you call somebody?" She reached over to playfully squeeze Mya's dimpled hand. Mya chortled, moving her hands from off the stroller bar.

"Oh, I didn't want to bother anyone," April said, looking uncomfortable.

Alisha frowned. "I thought Danny's mother was looking after Mya now."

April pursed her lips for a moment, then glanced at Lily, who stood with her backpack balanced precariously on her back, staring up at the tree above her.

"I don't think it's a good idea for me to stay so dependent on Danny," April finally admitted softly, but firmly.

"Oh," Alisha said meaningfully with her arms folded across her chest. "So that's how the cookie crumbles."

April had a pained expression on her face. "Alisha, I'm still married to Jack. Danny and I—well, it can come to no good."

"You do have a point," Alisha conceded. April seemed relieved, but Alisha wasn't finished. "What if you were free, April?"

April's blue eyes widened. "Alisha," she protested.

"Well, what if you were?" Alisha insisted. "Would you mind being dependent on him?"

"I don't want to be dependent on anyone again," she said fiercely, her blue eyes clouding up.

"You know what I mean," Alisha said, showing no mercy. "Would you let someone into your heart again?"

April seemed to freeze for a moment, then she looked Alisha straight in the eye and declared with a sob, "I already have. God help me, I already have." She grabbed Lily's hand and jerked the stroller with the other.

Alisha let her go, wanting to call her back or go to her, but knowing instinctively that she should wait for another opportunity. She was not the only one with troubles.

Elise surrounded Alisha with a full hug. She had asked Alisha to join her at the newly finished house to help get her mind off Rick's situation.

"Come on, Ali, what do you think?"

Alisha stood looking around at the newly tiled foyer and smiled. "Boy, does it ever look good in here. It's a good thing I absolutely love older homes or I might be tempted by envy."

Elise laughed, then eased herself down on the floor to sit cross-legged beside some over-sized pattern swatches. She patted a spot for Alisha, who also lowered herself to the floor.

"I'm sorry, the only table and chairs are in the kitchen nook," she apologized. She fingered the swatches absentmindedly, keeping her eyes on her friend. "I guess there's still no news on Rick."

Alisha shook her head dejectedly. "No. Danny is trying to figure out the next plan of action."

Elise bent waist over and took Alisha's hands. "Oh Alisha, I don't like to see my future maid-of-honour this way. I wish I could do something."

Alisha wrapped her fingers around Elise's. "You are. You're praying and you've been keeping tabs on me. This is supposed to be a happy time for you and Josiah, yet you're both there for me and April at every turn."

They both looked up when they heard a rattle at the front door. Seconds later, Josiah opened one door and came through. His expression was thunderous.

"You would not believe who I saw sitting in a pickup just outside the gate!"

The two women looked at each other.

"Webster Myers!"

Elise and Alisha's mouths fell opened.

Josiah stood looking down at them like a mountain gone bad. "That little weasel is still up to his old tricks! I swear if I catch him—"

Elise scrambled to her feet. "Josiah, please." Knowing that Webster had been out there, so close, sent her anxiety level up. Josiah's tirade was only adding to it.

He ignored her and glared at Alisha. "How long have you been here?"

Alisha was also on her feet, looking alarmed. "Not long, maybe ten minutes." She looked at Elise for confirmation.

"That's right," Elise agreed, "but you're upsetting Alisha, and she has enough on her plate already."

Josiah's eyes softened slightly as he looked at the women. "Sorry," he said.

Elise moved closer to him and laid a hand on his arm. "What did he do when he saw you?"

He puffed through his lips. "What do you think? He drove off like the weasel and coward he is, preying on helpless women."

"We're not helpless, Josiah," Elise disagreed.

"From where I'm standing, you are," he argued. The foyer was silent. Alisha looked tired and uncomfortable, then she giggled unexpectedly.

"Am I witnessing your first lover's spat?"

Elise looked at Josiah, and he looked back, his dark eyes assessing.

"We're not helpless," she insisted, and turned to walk down the hall toward the kitchen.

"Excuse me, Alisha," Elise heard Josiah mutter, before she felt him directly behind her. She turned to see him, just as he grabbed her arm above the elbow and pulled her along with him through the kitchen and into the family room.

"You're not taking this seriously," he accused, glaring down at her. "You were here alone before Alisha came. Who knows if he had been close by before she arrived, possibly thwarting his plans—and you want to fight with me?"

She jerked her arm from his hold. "I don't want to fight with you, but you're treating Alisha and me like we're responsible for him being there."

"What—" He looked toward the kitchen and lowered his voice. "What are you talking about? I'm not upset at you two. It's the fact that some guy who's been harassing my woman was waylaying her to do heaven knows what."

All reason called for Elise to understand the truth in his statement, but she felt so on edge that she couldn't seem to stop. "I don't need you to babysit my every move and to make Alisha feel bad w– when she's missing Rick so much. I'm tired of Webster and missing people. I've got this house to get done, marriage counselling, and work, so I don't need you flipping out on me."

Josiah stood still, watching her try to blink away threatening tears. His eyes softened and he reached out a hand to touch her. She batted it away. He reached out and pulled her to him, holding her close. They were silent for a moment, and she could feel the strong thud of his heart under her face.

He pushed his fingers into her hair and held her head back. "I'm sorry, I didn't see it that way. Please forgive me."

She closed her eyes and sighed. "Okay, I forgive you. I'm sorry for being so mad at you. I know you overreacted out of concern." She felt him stiffen.

"Overreacted? How would you feel if I hadn't reacted at all? If I calmly entered the house and said, with just a little upset, did you know that Webster the weasel was waiting outside the gate? I wonder what he wanted?" His tone was mild, but the look in his eyes was not.

She looked at him, then lowered her eyes. "Okay, you have a point," she conceded, then wondered if she'd said the right thing when he suddenly moved her away from him.

"Oh, shoot!" he exclaimed, then grabbed her hand and, once again, pulled her through the kitchen back into the foyer. They almost missed Alisha, who was sitting on the second step of the stairs.

"Alisha, in all the commotion, I forgot to tell you." He went to her and pulled her up from the step. "Danny's heard from Rick's parents. Rick's been to see them."

Elise could see the shock registering in Alisha's green eyes. She moved quickly to put a supportive hand around her shoulders.

"Are you sure?" Alisha asked incredulously.

Josiah's smile was wide, and he nodded. "Yes. We still don't know why he left, but a couple of days after Danny phoned his family, he showed up there. He asked his family to phone, but didn't want to talk to anyone yet. He's spending a couple of days with them and then he'll come home. Apparently he has a lot to tell us."

The relief in Alisha was so evident, then her posture straightened. "He has a lot to tell us? When I see him, I'll have a lot to tell him!"

Elise and Josiah looked at each other and smiled. Another lover's spat was imminent.

Further conversation was delayed when Josiah answered his ringing phone. It was April. He stepped away from the women and did more listening than speaking, then he flipped his phone shut and came back toward them.

"April is trying to find Danny. She wants him to know that she had a registered gun in the house that's gone missing."

Chapter Twenty-Four

Pouring over her Bible, since her conversion, had come easily for Elise. Lately, however, she seemed to be having difficulty. She was still very much enjoying the Sunday services and the marriage counselling sessions she and Josiah had started after quitting the singles group. Her understanding of God's Presence in her had become increasingly real as she experienced Him more.

Sitting up in her bed, Saturday morning, she read, *"Or do you not know that your body is the temple of the Holy Spirit who is in you, whom you have from God, and you are not your own?"* It was as Solomon had explained about marriage; it was about two people in relationship, no longer about one. God was in her. He had chosen to be part of her. It was a fantastic, amazing thought! So when she lived, she had to bear in mind that He was in her. Solomon had explained that it wasn't that she should suddenly stop being herself; but that, as she allowed, Jesus would make her more of what He wanted her to be. More like Him.

Perhaps she was on some sort of plateau, after her initial step to know Christ personally. She sighed and closed her Bible. She had a lot of errands to run today, but not before she spent some time in earnest prayer. Lately she had been feeling more burdened than usual.

Josiah had come into the office early to finish some work. The office was usually closed on a Saturday, so it was very quiet, and he liked it that way. He could think, draw, pray. For some reason, he had been feeling a real urgency in his time of prayer. He didn't always understand the ways of the Spirit in him, but he recognized the call. He hoped it wasn't anything to do with Elise, though he habitually prayed for her.

He stood up and walked out of his office after hearing movement in the hall beyond. He peered toward the reception area, where it was dim. He had only turned on a few lights, and the morning sun didn't quite hit the front hall this time of day.

He smiled. It was his father.

"Dad, what are you doing here? I thought you'd still be sorting through your new house."

Adam stopped just outside Josiah's office door. "Oh, I will, I will. I just thought I'd drop by on my way to meet David for breakfast." He looked comfortable in a dark blue sweater over his shirt.

"You still okay about the move?" Josiah still wasn't sure if his father was going to have a delayed, negative reaction from moving out of their old home.

Adam smiled at him, confidence and quiet peace in his dark eyes. "You know, son, if you'd asked me that five years ago, I would have had a different answer, but the time for the move was ripe and right."

Josiah leaned against the door jamb. "Okay, Dad. Where is Celia? How come you're going out with David for breakfast?"

Adam wrinkled his brows. "He actually asked me. I'm not sure what he wants, but I do believe God is mightily at work in his life. I think he's been having struggles that need a bigger hand, if you know what I mean."

Josiah laughed and threw an arm around his dad. It had been just the two of them for years. After his mother had died, they had stuck together through thick and thin. He couldn't imagine his life without his dad. It was good that his dad's new home was on the side of Georgeton closer to his newly built house.

"I won't stay long," Adam continued, saying, "but there was something I wanted to tell you. I spoke with Webster Myers."

Of all the subjects his dad could have brought up, this was not one he had foreseen.

"You spoke with Webster?"

Adam nodded nonchalantly. "Yes, and I think we have an understanding."

Josiah studied his father closely. One thing Adam Alexander was known for was an incredible ability to remain calm in storms. That calm, great instinct, and sheer hard work had built their company.

"Do we need to sit down for this, Dad?"

Adam waved him off. "No, just listen. This morning, I decided to have a quick stroll before starting the day. It's also a good way to canvas a new neighbourhood. Anyway, I noticed Webster, who I recognized because of the Sung twins' school performance—the one you couldn't make—"

"Yes, Dad," Josiah said, trying to speed him along.

"He was coming out of one of the houses with a For Sale sign, so I went over to introduce myself."

"Just like that."

Adam patted him on the shoulder. "Just like that. He seemed a little surprised, at first, then he settled down once he realized I wasn't going to bite. I explained about you and Elise, so he would understand, coming from a future father-in-law, that there is absolutely no hope for him and Elise. I couldn't help but mention that there *is* hope for him in Christ. Funny enough, we talked about that for a while, and probably would have continued longer, but I told him I had a breakfast engagement with the other future father-in-law."

Josiah shifted impatiently. "That's it?"

"More or less. He politely thanked me for confirming that a recent decision he had made was a good one."

"Come on, Dad." He could swear that his father was enjoying stringing him along. He'd been told he had inherited his mother's impatience.

Adam smiled paternally. "He is moving, hence the sale sign. He felt he needed a new start, so he would be tying up some loose ends and moving on, even before his house sold. Basically, I helped solidify his decision by declaring your concrete commitment as a couple and the incredible support of your families behind you. Webster really does need our prayer, though, Josiah. I sensed a confusing darkness about him."

After Adam left, Josiah dedicated some serious time to his work. His father had indicated, that they should perhaps think about hiring an architectural assistant to help ease his load.

"I don't think you're going to get away with the hours you put in once you're married," Adam had counselled. "You'll have someone to answer to then, and when children come…"

He knew his father was looking ahead, not wanting his son to make the same mistakes of misplaced priorities as he had. In one of the premarital sessions, Solomon had indicated that the husband's role as "head" of the home was better translated "leader." It was not a role of dominance, but rather a role of guidance and care, and most importantly, a role of leading by example.

Solomon had joked about how his sons often referred to him as the head, but said their mother was the neck that turned the head. Elise had taken issue with Solomon's counsel that a deadlocked decision meant the family should go the husband's direction; the house would not prosper with two generals in the same camp. Solomon had put it into perspective by mentioning that the husband had a solemn duty to love and cherish his wife; so she, in turn, could set a good tone for the home.

The husband should strive to put the needs of his family first. Too many men saw the "headship" role as the right to have their way, but the biblical way was contrary to that: as Christ loved the church and lay down His life for her, so a husband had to be willing to lay down his life for his wife. Consequently, the wife's role of submission and respect would come more easily.

Josiah yawned loudly and looked at his watch. He wanted to call Elise, but figured she'd be out shopping or something. He manipulated his neck and shoulders where the muscles were tight, then started straightening the work on his desk. He was about to vacate his chair when the entrance bell rang.

He hurried down the hall to reception and saw Elise outside the door. He felt a smile tug at his lips and warmth fill him just from the sight of her. Solomon must have been joking. How was he ever going to maintain a headship role when the very sight of the woman concerned made him want to walk on the moon for her?

He pulled the door open, and she came in with a glorious smile and a sweet fragrance. Before she could utter a word, he had her in his arms with his lips on hers. He vaguely heard something thud to the floor, then felt her arms circle his neck. After a while, he broke the kiss by burying his face into her hair and the side of her neck.

"Ahhh," he groaned, pulling away. "This gets harder every time."

"What?" she asked innocently, her eyes pulling at him.

"Never mind," he murmured, then noticed the package she had dropped on the floor.

"I did some shopping," she explained. "And I wanted you to see this."

He picked up the shopping bag and proceeded to open it, then stopped. "May I?" After her nod, he pulled a broad, tissue-wrapped object out. He handed the bag to Elise and unravelled the wrappings.

"It's a good thing it's not breakable," he said, chuckling. It was a beautifully finished wooden plaque with *"Ma Maison"* carved into the wood.

"My House," he read, in translation.

"Yes, I saw it and fell in love with it. I thought it would remind us of what we talked about. You stressed wanting God in our lives, in our home, and I've been learning so much about God in us, I thought it would be a good name."

"For our house?"

"Yes," she said uncertainly. "But, if you don't think it's appropriate, I can return it. It's not like I had it made."

His heart constricted at the forlorn look on her face. He smiled and brought her hand up to his lips. He kissed the soft, warm skin of her palm.

"It's beautiful like you, and it's very appropriate."

"Oh, Josiah," she gushed, relieved. "I'm so glad because I really love it." She continued on in a flood of words, and he never would have imagined someone could describe the purchase of one item in such detail. He managed to direct her over to a small couch in their lounge area. She looked sophisticated and adorable at the same time, in a cream turtleneck, brown slacks, and heels. Her hair was loose and held back by a brown hair band. He sat across from her, elbows on his knees, until she was finished.

"What?" she asked, noticing his gaze and his silence.

He lifted his hands slightly. "Nothing. I just love listening to you, watching you. No biggy."

She looked at him curiously, then laughed softly. "You're such a flirt."

"As long as I'm flirting with the one wearing my ring."

She held out her left hand to display its impressive piece of jewellery, then, just like a woman, said, "I would love to see one of these on Alisha."

He sprawled back into his cushioned seat, arms on his lap, legs spread. "Well, that would not be my job. Already been there, done that." He easily caught the cushion she hurled his way.

"I mean Rick, silly," she chided, then reached down to slide her heels off. She lounged to one side, her hand supporting her head. "Ali actually got a call from him. She was so excited, she called me screaming. She said he sounded funny, like he was holding something back, but he assured her he would be home today. He said there were some things he needed to set right."

He tried hard to focus on her words because anything about Rick was important right now, but her lazing in front of him was making it difficult. Her next words served to throw cold water on him.

"Will you pray with me?" she asked, straightening up. "I don't know what it is, but I've been having a real strong sense of something being wrong. I don't know, maybe an omen. I know the Bible says we're to pray instead of worrying. I have been praying, but I can't seem to shake it."

Josiah mentally prepared himself, expecting his heart to follow suit. "Sure, I most certainly will." He got up and went to sit beside her. He took her hand in his, and bowed his head.

"You start out, and then I'll pray in agreement," he instructed. And she did. She spoke to God with simplicity and earnestness. Her thoughtful, faith-filled conversation with her Heavenly Father warmed his heart and soul. He was seeing more and more that she was not just a woman to complete him, but his best friend and a wonderful spiritual partner. When she was finished, he had no hesitation in praying a prayer agreeing with hers.

David had gotten up early Saturday morning for his appointment with Adam. He had kept his anxieties about the latest crank call to himself long enough. He needed to talk to someone else—a friend. Celia was noticing his changing state of mind. Fear was not an attractive thing, especially when it was unknown. He wondered about reporting again to the police, but knew they would revisit putting a trap on his phone. He wasn't sure he had time for that, but Adam was a level-headed man, and he needed a sounding board.

He had told Celia that he was having breakfast with Adam in town, and then he would come back to pick her up on the way to the new house. They were to join Elise and Josiah there to meet with a landscaper. Since he and Celia had such good experience with their garden paradise, the couple had wanted them on board. Nothing could have done their hearts more good as being needed by their daughter and her fiancé.

He left Celia, still wrapped up in bed, with a quick kiss, then made his way downstairs to his office to pick up his cell phone. If plans changed, he would need to call Celia.

He accessed the garage from the house, and got into his convertible. He used the rear-view mirror to watch the garage door open slowly. He looked backwards as he reversed out of the garage and noticed a large object laying across his path on the driveway. He reversed the car fully out and decided to see what was blocking his way before shutting the garage door. Perhaps it was something he needed to put in the garage. It wasn't. He exited the car.

A huge tree limb lay across the driveway. It was from a white birch and full of yellow leaves. It looked like it had been cut at one end, not broken. He looked around, puzzled. It didn't resemble any trees close enough for it to have fallen from one of them. He sighed. Maybe some kids had played a prank. He bent down and grabbed a sturdy branch, then heaved it off the driveway to one side of the lawn.

He dusted off his hands, then made his way back to the car. He had just eased himself onto the seat and pulled the door shut when he saw a movement behind him. The rear door on his side was pulled opened, and a man quickly entered the vehicle.

Before David could turn, the door slammed shut, and he felt something pressed hard to the back of his head.

"Not a sound. Drive." The words were short and clipped, immediately filling the heart of the driver with dread. He recognized the voice.

Celia made her routine morning tour of the house, straightening this and that. She paused at different windows to admire the fall scene. The Canadian seasons still mystified her, but she had come to appreciate what each had to offer. She had long decided, however, that winter was her least favourite.

She noticed a large tree limb on the side of the lawn while looking out her den window. She wondered about it for a moment. It hadn't been windy last night. She left the room and went to the front door. Once outside, she examined the limb and glanced around. She frowned, noticing the open garage door on David's side. She could not remember him ever leaving it opened before, especially not with her car sitting there. She shook her head at her husband's neglect and rectified it before returning to the house. She made her way to the kitchen to start her breakfast. She wanted to be at her best for this task at the new house. As she aged, she realized she needed to take care of herself to be at her best.

She had just plugged in the kettle when the phone rang. She reached for it. It was Adam.

"Well, good morning, Adam. How are you?"

"I'm doing all right. How about you, Celia?"

"Fairly well, thank you. I take it you two are having a good breakfast."

He cleared his throat. "Well, that's the thing. I'm sure it's this morning your husband was to meet with me, but… he hasn't shown up."

Celia's hand stilled from opening cupboard doors. "Well, he should be. He told me so, and he left about an hour ago to meet with you."

"I've been waiting for about forty-five minutes. It only takes fifteen minutes from your place to town, right?"

"Yes, about that." She rubbed her hand across her forehead. "That's strange. Why don't I try his cell. Hopefully he remembered to take it with him."

*   *   *

David was forced to drive about twenty minutes out of town until they came to a deeply rutted, isolated road. The whole time, his abductor had barely said two words to him, even though he had repeatedly asked questions. Finally, he had been directed down this old farm road, which he had passed many times, but had never had a reason to turn onto. He felt an overpowering sense of fear, but he fought to keep calm, hoping reason would win out in the end.

An object tapped him on his shoulder. He hadn't seen it, but he knew it was a gun.

"Stop here, and don't turn around. Give me the keys."

David complied, his hands shaking. He felt his chest tightening. Everything felt surreal. He noticed the trees, close by, and they drew his eyes and mind to reality. They were white birch. The limb, he now knew, had been purposefully put on his driveway.

His abductor spoke with a voice that no longer sounded in command. It was shaky and weepy.

"Why? Why does everyone always give up on me? Why is there no real life for me?"

"I'm sorry—"

"You're not sorry! But you will be if you don't make sure I get what I want." He was weeping, his raspy voice angry and mournful at the same time.

David tried to see him through the rear-view mirror. He needed to reason with him, be a psychiatrist to him. "What is it that you want? I'll try to help you get what you want."

"Do you even care about what I want, what I desire in my life? Everyone throws me off like a dirty rag. No one knows what I've been going through."

"I know what you've been going through. Let me help you."

"Words!" he roared. "You only speak words."

David could now see his face enough to make out the disturbing expressions imprinted there. He was literally dealing with madness, and he had no help, no needles, and no lock and key.

"I bet you'd care if something precious was lost to you, wouldn't you? Like your daughter?"

David suddenly felt a rage welling up in him. "It was you who scared my daughter."

"More than once. Many times I could have taken her, until I got what should be mine." His laughter was eerie and desperate. The car was filled with his agitation.

"What do you want from her? What has she to do with you?" David agonized. He needed to get out of this situation. How could he with a gun pointed at him? He nervously felt for his cell phone in the pocket of his lightweight jacket.

"I never hurt her, never treated her like everyone treats me. I only want what is mine." He was weeping in earnest, his voice almost like a child's.

"You never hurt her, but you scared her—"

He pounded on the back of the seat by David's head. "Don't tell me what I did! I know what I did!"

In desperation, David said, "Tell me what you want. How do I help you? Tell me, and I will." He was beginning to feel light-headed and clammy.

There was an uneasy silence for a moment, then his abductor spoke. "Will you?"

"Yes, yes," David lied. "I'll try my best to help you."

"I don't believe you," he whispered, than started laughing crazily. "You think I would believe you? No, what I want you may not be willing to give. First, promise me."

"I'll do my best to help you, I promise."

"Get out of the car."

David hesitated.

"Now!"

He gingerly opened the door and got out, not wanting to do anything to set him off. The man followed suit, then grabbed him by the arm. He could feel the pressure of the gun in his side. Refusing to answer where they were going, his abductor force-guided him across a shallow, bush-filled ditch, then deep into the woods.

David wasn't sure how long he stumbled ahead of his captor, barely aware of the twigs and branches slapping at his body. His mind was focused on survival.

When they stumbled into a clearing, the peacefulness of it eluded him. His abductor sat on a stump at the edge of the clearing and indicated with his gun for him to do the same. For the next twenty to twenty-five minutes, David was forced to listen to the misfortunes and accusations of his captor. He verbally pummelled David with questions and became belligerent when he didn't like the answers. Then he would accuse him of not sorting through his dilemmas properly.

"You are a psychiatrist! Why can't you help me?" He seemed to struggle with an inner war, then he glared at David. "You promised to help me," he reiterated.

"Y–yes," David confirmed. He was feeling weary from lack of food and stressed from the tirade forced upon him.

"Good," he acknowledged, sounding almost normal. His free hand reached into the pocket of his torn jeans. He paused, then swore and fixed his glare on David.

"Do you have a cell phone?"

David, hesitated. Suddenly, his captor was on his feet charging toward him.

"I–it's in the car! I left it in the car!" David cried out quickly.

The man stopped in his tracks, then smiled slowly. "That's fine, that's fine. We'll have to meet her there anyway."

David tensed up. The relief he had felt that his phone had been programmed to vibrate rather than ring was short-lived.

"Let's go back to the car," came the command. So they trudged back the way they had come. After resuming their previous positions in the car, David covertly looked around, hoping against all hope that someone would come along.

"Now, phone your daughter and tell her to meet us here."

David remained still, his heart in his throat.

"Do it! I've been kept from what is mine long enough!

David turned rapidly in his seat, as he felt his control slipping.

"No! You'll have to kill me to get to my daughter."

The maniac jerked the car door opened and rushed out of the car. Before David could push the lock down, his door was yanked opened. The sickening presence of the man overwhelmed him as he bent over him, gun shoved to his chest. David instinctively grabbed hold of the barrel and struggled. The man was younger, stronger, but he didn't care. He had his daughter to think of.

The gun went off!

Chapter Twenty-Five

Elise stood at *Ma Maison*'s doorway watching Alisha and Rick get out of Rick's pickup. Josiah joined her.

"Hurry up, you guys!" she prompted, excited to see Rick, excited to see them together.

"Hold your horses there, kiddo," Rick drawled, laughing.

Elise laughed. Rick was himself again, hale and hearty. His baby face was a little thinner than usual, but his expression was light and clear. Alisha clung to his arm, joy spread across her face.

When they reached the porch, Elise met them and gathered them both in a firm embrace. She let go of Alisha to focus her grip on Rick. He gently squeezed her, then remarked, "Elise, darling, you need to back up now. I don't like the way that big fellow behind you is watching."

Elise tapped him hard for good measure, then Josiah spoke up.

"That big fellow would like to join the procession." With that, Josiah threw his arms around Rick and they embraced each other tightly.

Elise was amazed when she heard a manly sob from Rick. His words were muffled by his and Josiah's hold on each other. She turned to Alisha, who winked and tilted her head toward the opened door. They entered the house, leaving the two men to catch up.

"I'm so glad to see him," Elise said, standing in the foyer. "He looks good."

Alisha's smile was wide and infectious. Her red hair was loose on her shoulders and her green eyes sparkled. "He does, doesn't he? He came by the house early this morning, causing my poor mother to drag herself out of bed. I was in a heavy sleep after tossing and turning for most of the night, so Mom had to get the door. Then she had to entertain him while I showered and dressed."

Elise put her hand up to her mouth, smiling. "Your poor mom."

Alisha threw her head back and laughed. "Are you kidding?" she asked, then lowered her voice. "Before we left, she cornered me and told me to make sure I didn't let this one go."

His mind felt fuzzy, and he couldn't remember where he was or what he had been doing. Something was hard and uncomfortable under him. Why did he feel so weak? His eyes blinked open, then shuttered against the clear morning sky. They opened again quickly, because of what he had seen at the edge of the sky. White birch trees. He remembered. He raised his head to get up and immediately fell back, gasping in pain. His chest heaved, and he tried to calm it to ease the radiating pain. He slowly moved his right hand to touch his chest. It was wet and sticky there, on the left of his sternum. He pulled his hand away up to his face. It was red, and the smell of blood filled his nostrils. He was bleeding to death.

"Dear God, no. Please, no."

He felt panic setting in, but he fought against it. As hard as it was, He eased himself to one side. The gravel from the side of the road poked at him through his light jacket, and white hot pain was ripping through him, but he managed to sit up. Without taking hardly any time to rest, he cried out loudly as he eased out of his jacket. Almost sobbing, he let the cell phone slide from the pocket, and then he bunched the jacket together and pressed it to his chest.

David nearly passed out, but he couldn't afford to. He didn't know how much blood he had lost, nor how long he had been laying there, but he needed help fast. With one hand firmly at his chest, he used the thumb of his other hand to dial.

Elise could hear Rick's loud voice throughout the house as Josiah finished touring with him. It was a welcome sound. Everything would be perfect, except for the fact that her parents were late. She had wanted to go over some ideas with them before the landscaper arrived.

Her mother had called to say that her dad was delayed, and that she would call as soon as she knew what was going on. Elise could tell she had been trying to keep some anxiety out of her voice.

Josiah and Rick came toward the table in the kitchen nook where she and Alisha were going over a gardening book for appropriate autumn planting. The two men, practically the same size— one dark, one fair—seemed totally at ease with each other. Josiah stood back as Rick approached the women.

"Ladies, I have an announcement." He held his palms together and cleared his throat. "I have three things to say that are very important." He paused and ran his hand over his brown hair, then looked at Alisha.

"One, I plan to buy Josiah's old house…"

Alisha gasped, her eyes wide with disbelief.

"Two, I need to say before three. I'm now a Jesus fanatic…"

This time both women gasped, but couldn't utter a word before Rick went on.

"And three, I want Alisha to know I'm mad for her, and when the time's right, I want to marry her."

Dead silence. Elise looked from Rick to Alisha. Rick's look was fastened on Alisha, whose face seemed paler than usual. While Rick waited, Alisha's facial colour slowly changed, trying to match her hair.

Elise finally noticed Josiah beckoning to her, so she quietly moved past Rick to take hold of Josiah's hand. They moved quickly out of the house to a new bench Celia had purchased for the porch after accusing them of being sluggish in getting furniture for the place.

Josiah drew Elise onto his lap, and she felt her jeans slightly catch on his as she drew her legs up to snuggle against him. He kissed her forehead and stroked her hair lightly.

"Well, I'd say that's a lot of drama for one day."

Elise laughed, then sobered. "What happened to him, Josiah?"

He rested his chin on top of her head. "Well, to give you the abridged version, he had reached a crossroads where he knew whatever choice he made would either make or break him. He went away to his cabin where he basically told God if He allowed him to reconcile with his parents and sister, he would give his life over to Him."

"Oh, Josiah," she breathed.

"Yeah. So, apparently, he spent some time in prayer and Bible reading—things he had learned from the men's meetings—then went to his family and tried again. He begged them to put the past behind them and give him another chance."

Elise looked up at him. "What happened in the past? Are you allowed to say?"

"Hey, he can't wait to give his testimony in church." He took a deep breath. "About six years ago, Rick decided to drive home drunk from a friend's party. His sister was with him, but couldn't persuade him not to drive, so she got in the vehicle with him, rather than leave him alone. They got into an accident. Funny enough, their vehicle was hit by another drunk driver, but Rick's parents still blamed him. His sister lost the use of both her legs that night."

Elise straightened on his lap. "Oh, my goodness. No wonder he's been so hard on himself. So, his family has finally forgiven him?"

"Yes," Josiah said, smiling. "Don't you just love a story with a good ending?"

She curled her arms around his neck. "Yes, and I wish this one with my parents would end well today. Maybe I should phone Mom back."

"Never mind," Josiah said, looking out to the circular driveway. "Here she is now. Strike that... here she is with my dad. What's going on?"

Elise and Josiah went down to meet their parents, wondering at their sombre expressions. Celia came directly to Elise, her hands outstretched, until they fastened to her daughter's upper arms.

"Lise, your father is missing. We don't know where he is, and he's not answering his phone."

"We thought we'd better come talk to you both. We're thinking of calling the police," Adam added. Even he seemed ill at ease.

Elise raised her hands to hold her mother just below the elbow. Celia's dark eyes were filled with anxiety and she had a pinched look to her face. "What do you mean, he's missing? What are you talking about?"

"Dad, didn't you breakfast with him this morning?" Josiah asked calmly.

"No," Adam answered, shaking his head. "He never showed up, and I waited for about an hour. I phoned Celia, and she said he had already left to meet me. We haven't been able to contact him, and he hasn't called."

"And he left the garage door open," Celia remarked. "He never does that."

"So, let me get this straight," Josiah said with emphasis. "He missed his appointment with you, Dad, and, contrary to his usual habit, left the garage door open."

"He's never done that," Celia insisted again. She had loosened her grip on Elise and was squeezing her hands together in rotation.

"And he hasn't phoned?"

"No," both Celia and Adam answered.

Elise looked at Josiah, not sure what to think. "Josiah, what do you think?"

Josiah shook his head, frowning. "That means he's been unaccounted for, for about how long?"

Celia looked at Adam. He scratched at his greying, tight curls.

"I'd say almost two hours, counting the twenty minutes it would have taken him to drive into town. We were scheduled to meet at nine."

"Should we call Danny, Josiah? Remember, Dad's had those crank calls," Elise reminded him.

"What crank calls? Elise, what are you talking about?" Celia cried.

Elise's hands rushed to cover her mouth. In her growing anxiety, she had forgotten that her mother was in the dark about the calls.

269

Celia groaned. "*Mon dieu*, what have you been keeping from me?" She looked at Adam, then at Josiah. She searched his face. "Tell me, now, what has been going on."

Before Josiah could answer the challenge, Rick and Alisha came out of the house, and Josiah's cell started ringing.

"Did someone die?" Rick asked innocently. He and Alisha were holding hands and looking very happy, until they saw everyone's expressions.

"Elise?" Alisha questioned, leaving Rick to join Elise and the others. She never got a response; everyone suddenly became aware of Josiah's phone conversation.

"What are you saying, Danny?" he asked seriously, holding his hand up for everyone's silence. "Will he be okay? He's on the way now?"

They waited in silence for him to finish, and when he did, they were not prepared for it.

His dark eyes were bleak. He moved in front of Celia and placed his big hands on her bony shoulders. His voice was strained. "Celia, David was found a short while ago. He's being taken to the hospital with a gunshot injury."

How many times had she visited this hospital for routine things without anticipating a visit like this? She felt as if she had slipped into another world, another existence where the things that only happened to other people were now happening to her and her family. Elise maintained connection with her mother through the gripping of their hands.

Josiah had driven them to Georgeton General Hospital as quickly as he could. He had paved the way through Emergency until they were met by a police officer and given a further update.

Her father had been found on the side of an old farm road, shot in the chest. Apparently he had been able to dial 911 to report his whereabouts before passing out. The police had arrived on the scene only seconds before the paramedics and found him unconscious and in shock due to blood loss. The paramedics had stabilized the bleeding and taken him to the hospital where David was undergoing emergency surgery. His prognosis was uncertain.

After their questions had been answered, Celia asked her daughter to pray and to keep praying, then she remained silent.

Elise glanced up when she felt a hand on her shoulder. Josiah was looking down at her and Celia where they sat in the waiting room.

"Can I get you something, tea... juice?"

Elise glanced over at her mother. Celia seemed to be wrapped in a cocoon of despondency. "Mom, Josiah wants to get us something to drink. What do you want?" Elise asked.

At first, Celia appeared as if she wouldn't answer, but then she raised a hand absentmindedly . "A drink? Perhaps, some tea." She looked at Josiah. "When will they let us speak to the doctor?"

Josiah stooped down before her and placed his hands over her and Elise's clutched ones. "The surgeon is with David, Celia. I'm sure as soon as the surgery is finished we'll be informed about his condition."

Celia, beautiful and poised, even in her senior years, looked helpless and uncertain. There was an ashy tone to her dark skin, and her gaze clung to Josiah as if drawing from his energy.

"He's everything to me. I don't know what I'd do without him. What if I don't get to say goodbye?" Her question was barely a whisper.

Josiah squeezed their hands gently. "Celia, I've asked Solomon Sung to bring this to our church's attention. They will be in earnest prayer. Would you like me to pray with you?"

She glanced briefly at Elise, then nodded.

"Would you like to go to the chapel?"

"No," she answered, her voice breaking a little. "Right here is fine."

Elise felt, with all her being, the fervency of Josiah's prayer as, in a lowered voice, he beseeched God for David and all involved. Her heart, though filled with anxiety, reached for the hope that was only found outside of human strength. Right there, in a partially filled waiting room, she placed her hope and confidence in Almighty God—the one who was Jesus, who was full of compassion.

When Josiah finished, she felt Adam, seated beside her, pat her arm reassuringly.

She smiled over at him, then turned to see her mother embracing Josiah. Celia patted his cheeks, then wiped at the tears trailing down her own.

"Thanks, son. Thank you for your faith."

About an hour and a half had passed, and Elise still felt weary. Not weary from the wait, but from the burden of waiting for the unknown. She had just returned from the restroom. Josiah and Adam were sitting with her mother, who had a spaced out expression on her face. She noticed Josiah rising to his feet and looked in the direction of his gaze. Finally, the surgeon.

Elise moved toward them as they went to meet the doctor, who was still in her surgery garb. She was a petite Native woman with a no-nonsense look about her.

"Mrs. Everson?" the surgeon questioned, looking at Celia. After Celia's nod, she eyed everyone else with a measured look. "I'm Dr. Brant. This is your family?"

Celia nodded, her eyes steadfast on the surgeon. "Yes. This is my daughter, Elise, and her fiancé. Adam is his father."

Dr. Brant nodded, satisfied. "Mrs. Everson, your husband is critical, but stable."

Celia's sigh of relief was audible, as if she had been holding her breath the whole time.

"He suffered extensive trauma from a bullet wound to the chest. He was very fortunate it missed his heart, but there was profuse bleeding which required multiple blood transfusions."

"Will he be okay?" Elise asked. She felt as if the doctor was holding something back. Josiah placed his arm along her arm around Celia's waist.

Dr. Brant's dark brown eyes lowered as she seemed to search for the right words. "The surgery was successful. The bullet lodged very close the heart, but he was very fortunate, it did not penetrate the heart. He does have a rib fracture, which suggests the bullet lost energy by hitting the rib first, another very fortunate thing. We removed the bullet, and repaired all damaged tissue. However, due to Dr. Everson's age and the massive blood loss, he will need to be carefully monitored."

Dr. Brant explained further about David's care, really taking the time to assure the family that everything possible was being done for him.

"Once he regains consciousness in ICU, the police will want to interview him."

"Thanks, Doctor, we appreciate all you've done," Josiah said for them all.

After their time with Dr. Brant, Elise felt out of sorts. Her father was under good care, but he still had a ways to go. She wanted so much to see him and talk to him. What had it been like for him? Who had taken him? Was it the client? The crank caller? Were they one and the same? She was in the hospital corridor with the others, looking at each other.

"Elise, we should take your mother home—"

"No," Celia said, cutting off Josiah. "I need him to be awake before I go."

"It's just so you can rest, Celia. We'll come back later," Josiah insisted.

Elise stroked her mother's arms. "Josiah, please, let her be. If it were me, would you go home?"

Adam chuckled, the first real sound of release any of them had made in the past two hours.

"She's got you there, son," he said.

Josiah sighed heavily and circled both women in a gentle hug. "All right, but he better wake up soon." He looked up. "Hey, it's Solomon."

Pastor Solomon had been unable to come earlier because he had been officiating a funeral. After he was updated on David's condition, he assured them that the church was praying and wanted to know what they could do for the family.

Celia looked at him oddly. "What do you mean?"

"They want to know if they can bring meals, help out with anything your husband would normally do, and so on."

"They would do that for me, a stranger?"

Solomon chuckled. "Well, Elise, Josiah, and Adam are not strangers, and you are God's precious child. Of course, they would do it for you." The conversation took on a spiritual tone until Danny showed up with the officer who had met them earlier.

After directing them to a quieter area of the hospital, he got right to the point. "We are looking for Webster Myers on charges relating to suspicion of abduction and attempted murder."

Elise heard his words, saw his lips move, but couldn't quite process the message. Josiah moved from the other side of her mother and put his arm around Elise's shoulder protectively.

"Are you sure, Danny?" he asked.

"David Everson was found off County Road 9, on an old farm road belonging to Myers Farms, owned by John Myers."

"Webster's uncle?" Elise asked, finally finding her voice.

"Webster Myers from your school, Elise?" Celia questioned. "Why would he want to hurt David?"

Danny's grey eyes were speculative. "Mrs. Everson, when your husband called for help, he was able to pass on minimal information before he went unconscious. He mentioned the words 'Myers Farms' to indicate his location, then he told the operator something very strange. He begged them not to let 'him' get your daughter. We believe your husband's abduction was possibly a means of getting to Elise."

"He had been obsessed with Elise, but I thought that was all over," Celia remarked, confusion written all over her face. It seemed too much for her; first her husband, now her daughter.

"But would all that make him capable of abduction and murder?" Solomon questioned.

"His intention may not have been murder, but something may have gone wrong," Danny explained, then fixed his gaze back on Celia.

"Mrs. Everson, I need you to tell me about any unusual occurrences this morning before and after your husband left the house."

Chapter Twenty-Six

"The branch Mrs. Everson found on her front lawn came from a tree on John Myers' property," Danny explained to Josiah. "We found evidence supporting this at the tree line close to where Dr. Everson was found. John Myers also reported his chainsaw missing from his barn about a week ago. As for Webster Myers, his uncle said he hasn't had contact with him for a couple of weeks. Apparently, they had a falling out over Webster's decision to pull up stakes and move out of the area."

They were sitting inside Solomon's church office, after the church service. Josiah had come at the end of the service to thank everyone for their support and prayers, and to give an update on David's condition.

"So where is Webster?" Josiah asked. He was feeling a little antsy. He didn't like the idea of Elise being outside of his presence with a maniac roaming around.

"Don't know," Danny said, shaking his head. "I'm working with the investigator in charge."

"Yeah, but what are *we* going to do, Dan?" Josiah asked, tipping his chair back. In spite of the long day yesterday, he felt high energy, like he needed to go out and conquer the world.

Danny ran a hand through his springy hair and sighed. "Jo, it's being handled. You don't need to get involved."

Josiah snorted and leaned toward Danny. "Now, does that sound like me? Just pray and hope for the best?"

"Your name means 'God hears,' Josiah," Danny reminded him, grinning. He glanced through the windows of the office, then raised his legs to place them on the broad wooden desk before him.

"Very funny," Josiah responded, eying Danny's legs. "I wouldn't let Solomon come in here and see that, if I were you. He's very particular about the state of his desk, next to his obsession with the state of people's souls."

Danny kept his legs up. "Look, I'm keeping an eye on things. We're talking about our girl, Elise. It's personal."

"*My girl*, Dan," Josiah emphasized. "And I don't like the idea that she may still be a target. She's got enough problems worrying about her father."

Danny reached out and touched Josiah's shoulder. "He's still not awake?"

Josiah shook his head and rubbed the day's growth on his chin. "No. They're not sure why. They're running more tests, including a CT scan. Dr. Brant will be consulting with some other specialists as well. I don't know much else, except that his blood sugar was fairly low before he was shot."

"Well, from the scene of the crime, his abductor had him take quite a jaunt into the woods before the incident on the road, and all before breakfast, too."

"Yeah, well, I hope he pulls through soon. Celia… I've never seen her so withdrawn. Elise is worried about both of them now. I don't like what she's going through."

"You can't protect her from everything, bud, but you can support her through it."

Josiah smiled slowly. "I think the sergeant has learned something from his experience with a certain blond?"

Danny shook his head wearily and smiled. "She's barely talking to me. I know she's keeping me at a distance. Every time the girls say 'boo' to me, she finds an excuse to redirect them."

"It's probably best, though, Dan. I mean, with Jack and all… speaking of which, have you seen him lately?"

Danny scratched his head. "Now that I think of it, no. How's he living? I mean, he's not working for you. What's he been doing?"

"Dan," Josiah warned.

"What?"

"Solomon." The legs came off the desk with lightning speed.

"No, Alisha, I'll be fine," Elise said into the phone for the second time. She pushed the heavy hair off her face and lay back against a pillow. She felt in such disarray.

"I believe you will be, Lise. I'm just worried about you. Rick is, too."

"You couldn't stay with me anyway. I'll be at Mom's. After we finally persuaded her to go home last night, I stayed with her. I just came here to get some things."

"What about work?" Alisha asked. Elise could tell she was really feeling badly for her.

"I've taken a leave of absence. I need to go in tomorrow with some prepared work. I'll have a week to concentrate on Mom and Dad. I really hope that's all I'll need."

"Are you scared?"

She squeezed her eyes shut and sighed deeply. "I don't have time to be."

"You're not just trying to be brave?" Alisha probed.

Elise raised up on the rumpled bed. There were clothes strewn across it. "No, I just can't focus on me right now, when my parents need me so much."

They spoke for a while longer, and Alisha promised to keep praying. "Dr. Gaho Brant is a good cardiologist," she assured Elise before hanging up.

Elise felt somewhat relieved after hanging up the phone. Alisha's concern was touching, but also exhausting. She was feeling very tired, and she had not slept well at her parents' place. Maybe a hot bath and a change of clothes would do her a world of good.

She managed to drum up the energy to quickly pack a small suitcase and gather her school supplies together. While she worked, her mind wandered back to her time with Josiah after he had taken them to her parents' place.

He had checked the house and seemed ill at ease about leaving them, until Celia reminded him of the house security. He had seemed more accepting of that, but had still pushed them to reconsider staying in town at his father's place. Even though Adam's place would be closer to the hospital, Celia insisted she wanted to be at the hospital or in her own home. Elise couldn't fault her. Her mother wanted to be with her beloved or in her own familiar surroundings.

Saying goodbye to Josiah that night had been very hard. She had relished the security of his presence, his arms, and his common sense approach. No doubt, he was also worried about her father, but he had never once wavered in his care and attention for them. She felt proud that he was to be her husband, and when he had held her close to kiss her goodnight, she had wished that he was.

Now she needed to rely on the One who would never leave her. He was around her and in her. He knew no limitations and He needed no words to know her fears. She clung to that for all she was worth.

Instead of heading for the longed for bath, Elise found herself on her knees, her upper body draped over her bed, sobbing. She poured out to her Saviour her uncertainties, her worries, and her needs. She wept out the strain and the pressures, then she petitioned for her hopes. Without intending to, she found herself praying for His will and way, His wonder in it all, and she thanked Him. After all of that, she felt a calm assurance she couldn't explain, but she accepted it. She clung to it.

After finally getting herself together, Elise stepped outside her apartment with her belongings. She had turned to lock the door, when she heard the one across from her opening. She looked around quickly, realizing she was on edge, then smiled in relief when she saw Jake Morris coming across to her.

"Hi, Jake," she said, her smile widened. "You're wearing your glasses!"

"Yep," he said proudly, nodding his head repeatedly. "Margaret always nags me that I should, but what you said to me makes perfect sense. You said one day I might miss something worth seeing because of a little pride."

Elise laughed. She felt like hugging him as he stood before her with his wide-framed glasses perched on his nose. "Jake, seeing you with those glasses is a sight for sore eyes. You've made my day."

He smiled proudly, teetering back and forth on his heels. "I figured you could do with some cheering up. I've been hearing the disturbing news about your folks. Even though I'm not much of a believer in God, I've been sending some hearty pleas upwards."

This time she did hug him. "Thanks, Jake. I could use all the prayers." She quickly updated him on her situation. "But please don't tell Margaret too much. I don't want her getting upset."

"No, I protect the little woman at all costs. If you need anything, let us know. I'm glad you'll be staying with your mother for a while."

After saying goodbye to Jake, Elise headed to the elevator. She found herself constantly praying for her father. It truly was an analgesic for her worry. She hummed a reassuring tune on her way down in the elevator. Outside, she waved to some other tenants who would, no doubt, hear or read about her unfortunate circumstances by midday tomorrow.

As she walked toward her car, dragging her wheeled luggage behind her, in her periphery she noticed someone coming toward her. She tried not to stare, but suddenly felt nervous. She reached her car, then turned her head slightly so she could see who was approaching her. It was Jack Roper. She felt only a little relieved. She didn't feel like dealing with Jack right now.

"Hi, Jack," she said brightly, trying to put the best foot forward. She waited for his approach. At least he was clean. Josiah had described him as being a mess the last time he had seen him. She also noticed something else. His facial expression seemed very strange, and he had one hand stuck to his side in a funny way.

He didn't answer her greeting, but stopped right in front of her. His eyes were making her feel like an insect pinned to a board.

"I didn't mean to do it," he said in a strained voice. "You've got to believe I didn't mean to do it."

She felt the car against her back. "What are you talking about, Jack?"

"Get in the car," he said. "I gotta take you."

Elise clutched the handle of her luggage, frowning. "Jack?" Then suddenly, before he showed her the gun, she felt the icy fingers of fear spreading across her back.

"Webster Myers has been arrested," Danny announced to the unsuspecting group.

Josiah, Adam, Alisha, Rick, and Solomon were congregated around a table in the church fellowship hall in the basement. Some of the church ladies had provided a meal for them. Afterwards, they would spend some time in prayer regarding the Everson family situation. Josiah was grateful. He needed to be distracted until Elise met him, then they would return to the hospital together.

Earlier, he and Elise had been to see her father in the hospital. They had left her mother there so Elise could get some belongings from her apartment. He had wanted to escort her, but she had insisted that he make an appearance at the church, then wait for her there. Danny's sudden news made him feel better about her being by herself.

Danny pulled up a chair and started helping himself to some food. "I just got off the phone. He was picked up just outside the city. He claimed he was returning for some items left at his house."

Josiah leaned over his plate of food toward Danny, who had sat down across from him.

"So what else happened? Did he admit to anything?"

"As if," Danny said, stuffing his mouth with creamy mashed potatoes. The tangy smell of mayonnaise and herbs floated around. "When have you ever known a criminal to admit to anything? Apparently, he emphatically denied any wrongdoing. He swears he was out of town the whole time of the abduction. We'll have to check any alibis, of course."

"Is it possible he's telling the truth?" Alisha asked. She was sitting beside Rick, partially leaning on him, on Josiah's side of the table.

"That's a good question," Solomon confirmed.

Danny wiped his mouth with a napkin, then took a quick drink of water. "There's always that possibility, but I highly doubt it."

"Why?" Josiah pressed. "What if his alibi checks out?"

Danny took his time answering. He was obviously enjoying the drama. "Remember the peeping Tom?"

Josiah frowned, his impatience getting the better of him. "Come on, Dan. Spit it out."

"Webster admitted to following Elise to her parents' house that day and sneaking peeks at her while she was in the house."

"That creepy, no good—"

"Son," Adam admonished. Josiah looked across at his father, who was between Danny and Solomon. His father had an understanding but stern look on his face. Josiah held his peace. He faced Danny again.

"What else?"

Danny seemed more sobered. "He swore that was all he did. He admitted to his obsession with her, but insisted he would never resort to something so desperate as committing a crime."

"So, Dan, what if he's telling the truth? Are there any other suspects?" Rick asked. He had his arm around Alisha and seemed to be taking the whole report seriously.

Dan thought for a moment, then he winced. "Actually, you could have been a suspect at one time."

Rick drew back. "Me?"

Alisha jumped to his defence. "Danny Rowe, don't be ridiculous!" she exclaimed, her green eyes flashing.

"Whoa, whoa," Danny said, chuckling. "It was just based on the fact that the peeping Tom drove a dark pickup, and was most likely the crank caller as well. Probably someone who knew Elise's and her parents' names, phone numbers, and addresses."

"All of us here probably have that information," Alisha supplied.

"Ahh, but not everyone has a dark pickup or a motive," Danny stated.

"What if the crank caller isn't the same as the peeping Tom?" Rick asked. The answer to his question was delayed by Josiah's abrupt statement.

"Jack Roper has a dark pickup."

Everyone looked at him, then Rick asked another question.

"Jack? He's a little crazy at times, but could you see Jack kidnapping and trying to kill someone?"

No one responded, but Josiah could tell he had them thinking. Something was niggling at the back of his mind.

"Has anyone seen Jack lately?" Danny asked. His gaze was intense and searching.

Everyone shook their heads, and Alisha said, "He certainly hasn't bothered April since he broke into her house."

"So, where's he been?" Josiah asked, not expecting a response. He looked at Danny. "Have we been barking up the wrong tree? Didn't

April report a gun missing? And wasn't that after Jack broke into the house?"

Danny seemed more alert, his grey eyes speculative. "Yes, it was Jack's old club handgun. She had even forgotten it was in the house, until she decided to clean the closet it was in. She found the empty case."

"Did they run a check on the bullet from Dr. Everson yet?" Solomon asked. His broad forehead was riddled with concentration lines, and his heavy frame was hunched over the table. All thought of eating was forgotten.

"They're working on it," Danny responded, then added, "We did find Dr. Everson's car at the edge of town, though. We'll see what fingerprints they come up with."

Suddenly Josiah got up from the table. "Excuse me," he said, as he walked a little ways from the group. He got his cell phone out and dialled. After getting Elise's voice mail, he disconnected and tried again with the same result. He nearly jumped when he felt a hand on his shoulder. It was his dad.

"I can't get her, Dad."

"Maybe she has her phone off, Josiah," his dad said calmly.

Josiah stared at him directly, wanting him to understand. "But I made her promise to leave it on, so I could reach her at any time."

Adam pursed his lips. "Why don't you try her apartment phone?"

He did, but there was no answer there, either. He looked at his dad, then looked across at the others, noticing their curious stares. He felt slightly off-balance. He didn't want to panic, but his imagination was getting the better of him.

"Josiah," his father began, then paused when they heard footsteps echoing outside the fellowship hall

Josiah nearly breathed a sigh of relief when he heard a female voice just as one of the doors opened. His relief was short-lived. It was April Roper.

"Hi, everyone. I made it back." An easy smile lit up her face, then faded momentarily. Danny got up to greet her.

"April, we're glad you made it back. Are the kids okay?" he asked.

She eyed Danny uncertainly, but no one else was talking to her, so she gave him her attention. "Y–yes, the girls are great." She paused and swept a curtain of blond hair behind one ear. "Is something wrong, Danny?"

"April, did you get a chance to talk with Elise today?" Josiah interrupted as he made his way over to her.

April turned her gaze to him, curiosity written all over her face. "Actually, I did try her a couple of times. Once, about an hour ago, and just before I came."

"Well…?" Josiah prompted.

"Oh, I didn't get her either time. Is she not here yet?"

That did it for Josiah. "Danny?"

Danny didn't need to be asked twice. He turned to the rest of the group. "Okay, guys, we're just going to do a little drive around. Jo's getting a little worked up about not being able to contact Elise. So I'm going out with him for a bit."

Solomon and Rick started getting up. Danny put both hands up.

"Why don't the rest of you stay here and pray like we were supposed to be doing? Somebody's got to mind that post."

"He's right," Solomon said. He looked at Josiah. "We'll be praying up a storm. You guys let us know as soon as you hear from her, okay?"

"We will," Josiah promised, then checked with his father. "Dad, will you go see Celia? But don't—"

"I know, son," Adam said, gently. "I won't cause her to worry."

*   *   *

"I don't want to hurt you, but you must cooperate," Jack instructed in the same monotone voice he had been using since he initially accosted her. He firmly wrapped her wrists behind her with duct tape before cutting it with a pocket knife.

"Put your knees up," he told her. He rolled her pant legs up and pulled her socks down before duct taping her ankles together. He had beads of sweat on his forehead, and his breathing was slightly laboured.

He stood back and looked down where she sat propped up against a wall. He raised the hand holding the duct tape. "I won't tape your mouth, so long as you keep quiet."

"Thanks, Jack," Elise said quietly. She watched him walk to the opposite side of the room and slump down on the floor. Suddenly, he jumped up and walked back over to her.

"I'm sorry, I do have to cover your mouth. I have to get rid of your car." He taped her mouth, then said, "When I come back, maybe I'll take it off." Before he left, he checked the window for a second time and left the blinds closed. He didn't even glance at her as he pulled the door shut. She heard the rattle of the door handle and knew it was being locked from the outside with an old-fashioned key. As he descended, the sounds became quieter until there was silence. She was alone.

Her breath started coming in a rush, as if she had not been breathing before. She looked around the room. It was bare except for the carpeting and the window blinds. On one side of the door, there was a wide window looking out of the room toward an open-concept area. This area included a lounge, studio, and refreshment booth. The other door in the room led through a huge bathroom to a walk-in closet.

She tried to roll to one side to get her footing, but ended up shoving herself up against the wall behind her until she was standing. Her elbows and the back of her head felt bruised. Ignoring her discomfort, she hopped toward the exit.

When she reached the door, she paused, her nostrils flaring above the duct tape as she breathed heavily. She eyed the door knob, knowing it was locked, but she had to try. Hopping around, she grabbed hold of the knob from behind and tried to turn it, but she couldn't get the door open, and her hands were starting to ache.

She didn't know what to do. *Please help me, Lord.*

She glanced to her right, then started hopping toward the bathroom door. She struggled with the awkwardness of opening it from behind with bound hands, but she accomplished her goal. Turning around, she looked through the dimness of the bathroom to the closet beyond. She couldn't remember if it had a window. It seemed a long distance for her bound feet..

Lord Jesus, help me. Please help me get through this okay. From the beginning, she had been in constant prayer. She hung on to her faith like a lifeline. If God allowed this to happen, there must be a purpose in it, for His will. She couldn't explain why the first tentacles of fear hadn't remained with her. She simple chose to cling to her faith and the knowledge that He was with her—in Her. She prayed about her situation, and she prayed for Jack.

The journey across the bathroom tiles to the closet was shorter, but it didn't matter. The absence of clothes made it easy for her to see that there were no windows. She felt like crying.

Chapter Twenty-Seven

Alisha stood beside Celia Everson, gazing at the man in the hospital bed. David Everson appeared to be sleeping, but it was a sleep he should have roused from hours ago. Celia was seated beside the bed with her hands wrapped around one of her husband's. She spent most of her waking moments here by his side. He was most likely unaware, but who knew what the soul of a person could sense?

He seemed normal, except for his slightly sunken cheeks, the ventilator in his mouth, and other myriad of tubing going to and from him. His thinning grey hair fell back from his narrow forehead, and his eyes remained shut against the world. He had given no response to any stimuli. His comatose condition had finally been diagnosed to have resulted from a cerebral aneurysm, a totally separate problem from the bullet wound to his chest. He had received adequate treatment to reduce the pressure on his brain, and now it was a waiting game. His age and the grade of aneurysm didn't leave a good prognosis.

Alisha watched a colleague check the intravenous lines and vital signs monitor. She knew all the ins and outs of life in the ICU, but it was different when it was personal. She didn't quite look at it with the same efficiency and detachment as usual.

She patted Celia's shoulder gently, conveying her care and concern. The older woman looked up at her. Her dark eyes were weary, but she smiled.

"You are all still praying?"

"We have never stopped, Mrs. Everson," she assured her.

"Celia."

"Celia," Alisha said.

He didn't know where he was. It was unlike any place he had ever been. There was no description for it, because it was like no other place. Literally. It was *no* place. He felt no sense of time, space, or distance. Yet instinctively he knew he was in between two places, literal places. There was no sense of how long he had been there before the realization of each place, on either side of him, dawned on him. Without knowing how, he knew the in between place was vast, even though he had no sense of space or distance.

The longer he was there, for there must have been some passage of time, the more he could sense the difference between the places on either side. He felt a quiver run through him as he became aware of sensations from left of him. He felt an aching loneliness greater than anything he had ever experienced. It left him with a yawning emptiness, until he felt a brush of wind. Was that wind at his right? Perhaps not, but there was something there. He tried to see—he desperately wanted to see because where he was, there was nothing.

It was a faint glow. He could see it! But more than that, he could hear a whisper of wind. He felt warmth, and it was very cosy. He felt his taste and smell being tantalized. His body ached for the touch of the light. How he wanted the light to come closer. Instead, it receded slightly.

Again he felt a great yawning emptiness. The fear came unexpectedly! He wanted to cry out! Great pain followed the fear, a pain that seemed to be a living, breathing thing. He knew there was more to come, and he recoiled away from it, hungering, craving for the light.

It pulled at him—the light. Once again, he felt warm and cosy. He felt alive and well, but he wanted more of the light. He strived, with everything he had, toward it, but he couldn't move from where he was. He greatly longed for it. How could he get to the light?

Josiah couldn't describe the dull ache that threatened to snuff the very life out of him. He and Danny had been phoning and circling around in the police cruiser for about two hours, and they still hadn't heard from or seen Elise. A police bulletin had been put out with descriptions of her, Jack, and their vehicles.

He couldn't show up at the hospital without Elise; that would only alert her mother to further worry. However, he had contacted Alisha after finding out she had left the church and had gone to the hospital. Elise had not shown up there, nor had she called.

He slowly became aware of the words Danny was speaking into the car radio. Danny looked over at him.

"We're going two blocks. They found her car."

When they arrived at the scene, there were two other officers checking and searching Elise's gold-toned Corolla. Josiah exited the cruiser before Danny could finish instructing him not to touch anything.

The officers must have recognized him because they nodded respectfully and continued their work with gloved hands. Danny passed by him as he stood staring at the car. Even though it was Elise's car, he felt as if they were invading his personal space, yet they had a job to do.

Danny came back to him. "They're sealing the car. They haven't found anything to indicate any struggle or injury. Was this a usual route for her to travel, especially from her apartment to the hospital?"

Josiah pulled his gaze away from the car. "No, Dan. I don't see why she would have come this way." He rubbed at his forehead, kneading the skin intensely. He felt such a loss of control. Where was she? He was desperate to see her, hold her, and protect her.

"Are you sure, Jo?" Danny asked.

Josiah thought. "Wait a minute. She would have come this way to get to my old house, but…" His enthusiasm faded. "She wouldn't have had a reason. The house has been empty."

Danny looked around with restless eyes. He focused on Josiah. "We should check anyway. What else have we got to do?"

"Pray," Josiah breathed in a desperate tone. "Danny, I've never felt this helpless. The only thing that compares is when my mother lay dying of cancer, and I couldn't do a thing to stop it."

Danny reached out a strong hand and grabbed his shoulder. "Don't go there, Josiah. Elise isn't dying. You can't start thinking like that." He pulled at Josiah.

"Come on, let's go check the house."

*   *   *

Elise was halfway back through the bathroom when she heard the bedroom door swing opened. Seconds later, Jack was glaring across at her. His hair was wild and his heavy shirt hung loosely. His eyes darkened, and his face began to contort.

Elise felt her breath catch in her throat. *Jesus,* she thought and, immediately, a word dropped into her mind: *Toilet.* She quickly gestured toward the toilet, moaning elaborately as she did so. Jack shifted his gaze in that direction, and understanding initiated a softening of his features.

He walked over to her and worked the tape from her mouth. It stung her skin, but she welcomed its removal.

"I couldn't get back," he said in a curiously hushed voice. "They seemed to be everywhere, and I couldn't get back."

While he worked on her hands with the pocket knife, Elise asked, "Who was everywhere?" It felt good to be able to talk, even to a crazy man.

"The police," he answered, then backed away from her, looking almost embarrassed. "Come out when you're done." He shut the door, firmly.

After using the facilities, which she was grateful for, and washing her hands, Elise slowly exited the bathroom. She watched Jack pace back and forth in front of the indoor window, as she dried her hands on her slacks. He turned to look at her with desperate eyes.

"Are you sure he's not dead? I never even meant to shoot him. People make me to do terrible things—awful things."

Elise faced him, at a distance. "When I last saw him, he was alive, but he hasn't awakened from surgery yet."

Jack angrily grabbed at his head. "Why didn't he listen to me? All I wanted to do was trade you for my family. I thought if he could feel what I felt, losing my family, maybe he would understand better."

Elise remained still. She didn't want to upset the apple cart. Right now, he seemed more troubled than belligerent. She also took some comfort in knowing the police were probably looking for her. Josiah would have made sure of that after she failed to appear at the church. She just hoped they weren't too worried. She didn't want to think how her mother would deal with knowing her daughter had also been abducted.

"Why my father, Jack? Why did you choose my..." Suddenly, it dawned on her with frightening clarity. Jack Roper was the client. All along, he had been the one who caused her father no end of grief. She noticed he was watching her. She backed up and sat in her former place, her back supported by the wall.

He kept watching her intently, then he pulled his knife from his pocket. He paused to grab the duct tape from where he had thrown it on the floor, then proceeded to bind her again.

"Why did you look at me so funny?" he asked cautiously.

"You were my dad's patient, weren't you?" she asked softly. "Did you make the phone calls, Jack?"

He stumbled forward slightly, then straightened and stiffened as if trying to maintain some semblance of self-control.

"I wanted him to know how I felt. I needed him to understand what no one has ever understood. I needed to get my family back. It's not normal for a man to have to live without his family." He pivoted away from her and went to shove the knife and duct tape on the floor in one corner of the room, then he positioned himself beside them.

"Why did you call me?" she dared to ask. Somehow, she felt talking to him was more about him than her. He obviously needed help, yet her father had given up on him. She and her mother had encouraged him to.

"I–I don't know," he stuttered, not quite looking at her. "I wanted you, his daughter, to know my pain. How would you like it if your father was taken from you? My girls…" He grabbed his head, scraping his hands through his sandy hair. He looked at her with wounded eyes. "My girls have no daddy. Did you know I had no daddy? My–my mother hated me!" He jumped up and started pacing in front of the indoor window. "I didn't mean to scare you or your mother; I had no choice! I got your information from April's things. It was only fair for Dr. Everson and his family to suffer as me and my family have. You all needed to understand what I was going through."

"Jack," she called. When he didn't answer, she raised her voice. "Jack!"

"What!" he yelled, then jerked and looked around wildly. "Do you think they heard?"

"Who, the police?" she hazarded a guess.

"No," he said, as if she were crazy. "The voices. I don't know why I hear them. I never used to hear them before. They tell me to do bad things, but they're not speaking to me about you. They won't tell me what to do with you."

She shifted slightly to ease her discomfort. Her shoulders and back were sore, and her hands were starting to feel numb. She wasn't sure what she was feeling emotionally; everything seemed surreal, and she couldn't understand her lack of fear. Instead, she felt immense compassion for the man who stood with clenched fists before her.

"What are you going to do now, Jack?"

He looked at her as if wondering why she was there, then he sat back down. He leaned against the wall under the inner window and rolled his head back. His hands came up to his face and he started sobbing—great, heaving, gasping sobs.

"I–I don't k–now. It's too late. They've wrecked everything, and April won't want me back now. My mother never wanted me, but I hated where they put me. I hated every," he swore, "place they put me." Suddenly, he glared at her. "I never touched my girls." He looked up and laughed out loudly. "You hear that! No matter what, I never hurt my girls!"

Elise felt her heartache, because she remembered what Josiah had said about Jack's neglect of his daughters. He had completely cut himself off from them, probably out of fear of abusing them as his mother had abused him. Unfortunately, he had focused his violent energies on his wife.

Suddenly, Jack was completely still, listening. He gathered the duct tape and knife, then got up quickly and silently. He forced the tape into his pants pocket and pocketed the knife in the other before grabbing her arm tightly and dragging her to her feet. He pulled the handgun from under his shirt and indicated for her to be silent. They were listening to faint noises down below.

Josiah looked around in the dimness of the living room and dining room, then moved into the kitchen. Everything looked undisturbed on this floor. No one was there, but he still called her name before moving to the second floor.

"I checked upstairs," Danny said, when he met Josiah on the second floor. "Everything looks pretty quiet."

Josiah sighed deeply, dragging his hand across the back of his neck. He was tired and hungry, but couldn't think of resting or eating.

What if night came and they still had no knowledge of her whereabouts? How would he stay sane?

"Josiah," Danny called, looking at him strangely. "Come on, let's go. Let's check her place one more time."

They had made it to the bottom of the stairs when he saw it. He would have missed it if he hadn't been looking down, weighed down by growing despair.

"Danny, look," he said, stooping to pick up a silver chain with a cross pendant.

Danny turned to examine the piece of jewellery dangling from Josiah's hand. "Isn't that Elise's?" he asked, frowning with cop curiosity.

"Yeah," Josiah confirmed, "from the Sungs. I don't know what it's doing here."

"It's not broken at the clasp," Danny said. "It may have been poorly connected and fell off without her knowing."

Josiah started to put it in his pocket, but Danny held out his hand while pulling a small plastic bag from his pocket. "Here, Jo, let me have it. You'll get it back."

Josiah froze and eyed the bag with growing horror. Elise's necklace had become a piece of evidence.

When the movement throughout the house had died down, and it had been silent for a while, Jack finally let her go. He flew out of the closet, probably to check at the window. Her stomach ached where his shoulder had dug into her after he had flung her over himself to carry her through the bathroom to the closet. She could hear him going through the rest of the house. She couldn't help it; she started to cry silently. She was sure it had been Josiah she had heard, with someone else.

Had they seen the necklace she had covertly dropped while going upstairs? They had been so close, even in the room, but they hadn't searched the closet. She had wanted so badly to cause some diversion, but Jack had kept the gun pointed toward the doorway separating the closet from the bathroom. The first person appearing would most likely have been shot.

He came back, wild haired and wild eyed, to find her sitting on the closet floor weeping. He slid the gun inside the waist of his pants and covered it with his shirt. Then he sat down a few feet from her.

"I couldn't help it," he moaned. "I had to keep everyone safe. Look, I didn't have to hurt anyone. I hope your father will be okay. I didn't mean to shoot him, but we were struggling for the gun, and— and it happened. He was shot. It was his fault!"

"Jack, please, you have to let me go," she said between sobs. "My mother will be so worried when I don't show up at the hospital. She already has my father to worry about."

He plucked nervously at his clothes. "I know, I know," he said, irritated. "I'm trying to think of what to do."

"They're not going to trade your family for me, Jack. You've got to let me go."

"Stop telling me what to do!" he yelled, jumping up. He backed away from her. "I–I know all that. You're my h–hostage so I can get away. Far, far away." He said, waving his hand around the room.

There was silence, then she said gently, "Jack, please let me help you."

He directed his gaze on her. "How can you help me? Your father couldn't help me."

She reached for all the hope that was in her. "Jesus can help you, Jack. He loves you with a love that never ends. He wants to help you."

He started shaking right in front of her. He clenched his fists as if to control himself. "No, no one can help me. I'm eternally lost."

She pressed on. "Jesus never turns anyone away who comes to Him. Only accept that He took your punishment on the cross for all of your wrongs. Accept the new life He has for you, if you're willing."

He stumbled a few paces back. "No, no!"

She felt a strong urging within her to continue. "He can set you free, Jack, if you just ask."

Jack's entire body was heaving and trembling. Suddenly, he turned and ran from the closet.

Josiah gently stroked the glass covering Elise's smiling face in the picture. The photograph was of them both, but he only saw her face. Her big brown eyes laughed at him, and her beautiful, full lips begged to be kissed. He wanted to feel the ripples of her curly locks for real. He felt his hand shake as he replaced the photo on the bedside table. As if with a mind of its own, his shoulder heaved and his right fist came up and dove hard into the softness of the bed.

"Oh, God," he whispered fiercely, "Please, please, let us find her. Help us find her alive and well."

"Jo," Danny said, coming into the room. "The super is going to lock up now."

After Danny thanked the apartment superintendent, they made their way to the elevator.

Josiah didn't know why, but he felt a great desire to have something of Elise's. Why hadn't he taken something from the apartment?

"Danny, do you think I can hold the bag until we get to the station?" Danny had decided they should stop by the police station on the way from Elise's apartment.

At first, Danny looked puzzled, but then understanding dawned. "Sure," he said softly, and pulled the bag from his pocket.

Josiah accepted it just as the elevator doors drew opened. He stepped out and nearly bumped into Jake Morris.

"Whoa there, big fellow," Jake said with a chuckle. They almost knocked heads as they both bent to retrieve the bagged necklace that had fallen from Josiah's hand.

"Is that a gift for Elise?" Jake asked, eying the bag curiously. He looked up at Josiah through wide-rimmed glasses. "You look like you've seen better days, Josiah."

Josiah sighed and looked at Danny who was standing beside him.

"Officer?" Jake questioned anxiously. "What's wrong?"

Josiah answered. "The necklace is Elise's. She lost it. Jake, have you seen Elise at all today?"

"Lost it?" he asked, ignoring Josiah's question, but then answered it with his next statement. "I saw her with it on this morning."

"What?" Josiah and Danny asked at the same time.

"Is that the one her pastor's kids gave to her?" Jake asked.

"Yes," Josiah replied. "Are you sure she had it on this morning, Jake?" Josiah was feeling an unmistakable rush of adrenaline.

Jake smiled knowingly and tapped his glasses smartly. "As you can see, I have been wearing my glasses, as directed by your lovely fiancée. I had them on this morning, too. I saw the cross necklace on her, not the gold heart."

Danny seemed to lean into Jake. "Was there anything else, Mr. Morris? Did you see anything else unusual this morning after talking to Elise?"

Jake thought for a moment that seemed like an eternity to Josiah, but he could have kissed him after what he said next.

"You mean, like her getting into her car with some guy who wasn't—" He paused to look at him, "Josiah?"

"What guy?" Josiah asked eagerly.

"What did he look like?" Danny asked at the same time.

"One at a time," Jake entreated, frowning at them as if they were naughty boys.

Josiah put his hands on Jake's bowed shoulders. "Sorry, Jake, but this is really important. Elise is missing, and we need to find her."

Jake's expression changed dramatically. "Well, why didn't you say so?" Then he proceeded to give a full description of a man that sounded very much like Jack Roper.

Josiah heard Jake mutter, "Good thing I was wearing my glasses," as he and Danny rushed out of the building into a rainy autumn's early dusk. Before they had reached the police cruiser, Danny was already calling for back-up.

Elise stayed in the closet, praying for her release and praying for Jack. She had never thought she would ever have opportunity to literally follow the Bible's teaching to pray for her enemy. She could hear him, somewhere outside the bedroom, moaning and groaning. She couldn't fathom what was happening. Was he having some sort of psychotic episode? She felt weary and forlorn. She wanted to know how her dad was, how her mother was holding up. She wanted Josiah. She felt the tears threatening again and shook her head angrily.

"No more of that. You've got to get out of here," she told herself quietly. She listened for Jack. She couldn't hear anything. Instead of trying to stand up, she scooted toward the bathroom on her hands and bottom. The bathroom tiles felt cool under her hands, which were feeling very numb. She shoved across to the bedroom. Who would have thought Josiah's famous bachelor retreat would have become her prison?

She rested on the carpeted floor and looked out the open doorway to the space below. She still couldn't see or hear Jack. She shoved herself double-time until she was positioned just outside the bedroom on the top step which led down to the rest of the bachelor retreat. Just as she made a move to descend, she heard an earth shattering wail that filled her heart with fright.

Above the heavy thudding of her heart, she could hear a lot of commotion in the house below. She was on the third floor, but outside of the bedroom she could hear more clearly. She tensed when she heard footsteps thundering up the stairs. It sounded like more than one person. Was one of them Jack?

She nearly screamed when Jack burst into the room. Right on his tail was—Josiah! Jack was heading for her, when Josiah dived at him from behind and caught hold of him around the middle. They both landed with a thud. Jack was on his belly clawing to get out from under the weight that was pinning him down. Suddenly, Elise saw Jack's hand move downwards.

Danny burst upon the scene, seconds later, just as Elise cried, "He has a gun, Danny! He has a gun!"

Elise watched, heart in her throat, as Jack's hand whipped out and a deafening blast was heard.

Danny was shoved backwards instantly, and his drawn gun flew from his grasp as he hit the floor.

It took only seconds for Josiah to look at her, then at Danny, before she heard a roar burst from him as he clamped a strong hand over Jack's gun arm. She saw the extreme redness of Jack's face as he struggled to maintain control of the weapon. She could only see the top of Josiah's dark head bent over as he expended a concentrated effort. His arm muscles bulged greatly as he applied pressure to Jack's wrist.

The gun fell from Jack's hand, and he began wailing like a wounded animal. He started thrashing wildly, and it was all Josiah could do to keep hold of him. He managed to stare up at Elise as she struggled toward them. Suddenly, with Josiah's attention diverted to her, Jack thrashed free and scrambled on his hands and knees toward the stairs. Josiah made to go after him, then noticed Danny laying still. He stared at Elise.

"Let him go," she said, giving him permission. "Danny needs you."

"Sweetheart, are you okay?" Josiah asked as he scrambled on his hands and knees over to Danny. He checked the pulse at Danny's neck, then pulled his phone from his pocket.

"I'm okay," she assured him. "But, please, help Danny."

He nodded, then they both smiled in sweet relief when the sounds of touch dialling on Josiah's phone and the police sirens outside coincided with Danny's hoarse, "Please tell me you didn't let him go, Jo."

Thanks to Danny's earlier call, it was only a few minutes before Danny's fellow officers arrived, it seemed, in droves. Some were there to take over his care until the paramedics arrived, others were scouring the house, while others were on the chase after Jack.

It hadn't been forever, but to Elise it definitely seemed that long since she had felt so safe, cared for, and loved in Josiah's arms. They were sitting on the floor in a corner of the lounge area, listening to the gentle patter of rain on the third storey windows. Elise was propped up against Josiah, unbound, but encircled in his arms. She had given her statement again and again, but she didn't mind, not when she felt like she had just been born anew.

Josiah had wanted to get her out of there, but she had begged him to sit with her for a moment so that her last memories of this day would be of him holding her safe, not of her being held there unwillingly. This had, after all, been his old home, and was soon to be Rick's and Alisha's. No, she didn't want to just scurry out of there. This place had been in her past and would still very much be in her future.

"He was here, with me, in this house," she murmured against Josiah.

"Who?" he asked gently, stroking her hair, her shoulder, her arm. He couldn't seem to stop touching her.

"God. I mean, I know He's in me, but I felt He was also with me. I didn't have the fear you would expect."

He bent his head over her. "Really?"

"Yes. I was lonely and sorrowful. I missed you and worried about Mom and Dad, but I felt Him with me."

He sighed deeply. "Well, there were a lot of prayers going up for you."

"I know," she said simply. "And I'm grateful. I'm ready now. I should go see my parents."

He squeezed her shoulders and bent to kiss her gently, tenderly. His eyes were dark with hidden emotion. "Let's go," he said.

Chapter Twenty-Eight

Celia's watchful gaze was not on her husband, but on all of the contraptions in the ICU room, all the equipment that kept her husband monitored and alive. She resented them as much as she accepted his need for them. She had had many hard moments in her life, but none that challenged her philosophies like this.

What was life anyway? One could only control so much of it, and ultimately no one really had much say when it came to dying. David believed in the soul. Where would his go should he die tonight? Where would any of their souls go when they died? The idea of having no soul and death being nothingness held no appeal to Celia at this moment. The thought of being with loved ones in the afterlife gave a sense of hope and purpose. At least, that's what Elise had shared with her when she had eventually talked about her new walk in Christ.

Elise had found a personal relationship with the God of the universe. How could anyone compete with or challenge that? Her daughter had an assurance she and David did not have of where she would be after she died, of where she would spend eternity. Celia was beginning to feel an aching need for that assurance now.

"Mrs. Everson?"

Celia looked up to see Dr. Brant observing her. "Doctor," she acknowledged.

"Your daughter has not come yet?" The petite doctor stood beside her where she sat at her husband's bedside. Her brown eyes seemed filled with genuine rather than professional concern.

Celia shook her head slowly and frowned. "No, I'm not sure what has happened. Alisha has been trying to reach her and her fiancé for me."

Dr. Brant smiled. "Alisha is a good nurse and a good friend. She also believes highly in prayer."

Celia pulled her gaze from the still form of her husband to search the doctor's face. "What do you believe, Doctor? You've seen so much death, I'm sure. What do you believe of the Christian faith about life after death?"

Dr. Brant seemed uncomfortable. Her raven hair was bound at the nape of her neck, and her slightly tanned skin glowed with vitality. Celia guessed her age to be mid-forties, but she wore it well.

"I was raised in my people's way from a young child, but was introduced to Christianity as a young adult. I cannot say what I really believe, but I have seen many things not adequately explained by medicine or science."

Celia nodded, then focused back on her husband. No movement, no words from him. How she wished for one more sound of his voice, one more sight of his blue eyes looking at her. She felt her chest tighten and tears gather in her eyes.

"Would you like to speak with a minister?" Dr. Brant asked gently.

Celia shook her head wordlessly, then spoke in a strained voice. "My minister has been here." She coughed, wanting to dislodge the pressure in her throat. "He basically prepared me to accept my husband's impending death."

Dr. Brant was silent for a moment. "Perhaps he thought he was doing what was best," she commented carefully.

Celia felt her anger riled. "He could at least have offered me some hope while he was at it." She felt her insides quiver. Soon her hands began to follow suit as a wave of anxiety washed over her.

"Mrs. Everson?" Dr. Brant was leaning over her.

"Mom?"

Celia took a refreshing gulp of air that seemed to come out of nowhere. "Elise," she cried, reaching for her daughter as Dr. Brant stepped aside. Celia felt her world begin to right itself, if only for a moment.

Josiah paced nervously in the ICU waiting room after Elise had hurried off to be with her parents. Everything in him had wanted to keep her at his side and in his sight, but he had to abide by the number of visitors restriction.

The officer who had transported them was outside using his cell phone. Elise had insisted on being brought straight to the hospital. It was just as well. Elise had spoken to Alisha by phone and had been told that it was getting harder to keep Celia satisfied about their absence.

He paused his movements when the young officer entered the room. They were the only two present, as visiting hours was almost over.

"Do you want to come with me to get your vehicle while Miss Everson is with her folks?" the officer asked.

"Sure," Josiah responded, and followed him after taking one last look down the well-lit corridor where Elise had gone.

After leaving the hospital, Josiah was a silent companion in the police cruiser. His mind was filled with pictures and thoughts of his beloved and the events preceding her discovery. The knowledge that Jack had been responsible for crank calls, abductions, and shootings was bizarre. Yet why had they not seen it? All the signs had been there.

Josiah also felt hurt. He had taken Jack under his wing and given him a chance to turn his life around. He had been aware that Jack was receiving counselling for sociopathic disorders, but had been oblivious that David Everson had been the psychiatrist treating Jack.

He had counselled Jack himself, and had tried to befriend him. Jack had repaid him by committing crimes against his future wife and father-in-law. Already, deep down, he knew he had to forgive him. Yet every time he thought of him with Elise, taking her away and holding her captive, he felt a harsh bitterness rise up in him that begged for justice.

They were on a major road, leading from the hospital to Hope Alive Church, and were approaching a major intersection when the officer put his flashing lights on before pulling over. Josiah looked out at the wet conditions from the earlier rain, then his eyes were drawn to what looked like a vehicle accident ahead.

"Please, stay in the car, Mr. Alexander," the officer said before exiting the vehicle.

Josiah peered out of the windshield at the cluster of vehicles ahead. There were enough flashing lights, along with street lights, for him to make out a fire truck and an ambulance. Most of the other vehicles were police cars. He could also hear another siren approaching not far off. He remembered what the officer had said, but he felt an incredible urge to go. His curiosity got the better of him, and he left the cruiser.

He walked between the gathering rows of traffic to the scene of the accident. It didn't take him long to recognize the truck that was practically wrapped around a concrete light post. It belonged to Jack Roper. He felt sick in his gut. So this was the result of the police chase. While in his old house with Elise, he had overheard some police communications regarding the search for Jack. Apparently, Jack had left on foot to wherever he had stashed his truck, and had been lost to the police for a time. Josiah didn't know when they had picked up his trail again.

More people were gathering and the police were beginning to back them up, but Josiah managed to get close to his escort officer.

"Mr. Alexander—" the young man started to say.

"That's Jack Roper, isn't it?" Josiah cut in. The officer nodded solemnly, then watched as the paramedics worked on Jack, who had been rescued from the mangled vehicle. He was secured to a gurney and appeared to be very agitated. Josiah could hear him calling out what sounded like April's name.

"Let me go to him," Josiah said, then walked off without waiting for a reply.

"Mr. Alexander!" the officer called, and Josiah felt his arm being grabbed from behind just as Jack noticed him.

"Josiah," he croaked. "P–please, let me talk to him." Jack's eyes were firmly fixed in Josiah's direction, as if hungry for a familiar face. The paramedics looked up briefly.

"You know him, sir?" the one at Jack's head asked.

"Yes," Josiah responded as the officer released him. "I'm his employer."

"Josiah, please, I–I'm dying. Please, help me go over s–s–safely."
His head was bloody and so was his chest where the paramedics had
cut his shirt. He had a neck brace on and the start of an IV.

Josiah felt a heaviness in his heart, but in a split second he knew
what he had to do. He looked into Jack's terrified eyes. "Just call out to
Jesus, Jack. Ask Him to forgive you and to accept you."

Jack never took his eyes off Josiah, even as the paramedics worked
and talked back and forth to each other. They seemed frustrated with
Jack's agitation and kept trying to calm him. For one breathstopping
moment, Jack's eyes rolled back in his head, but his mouth continued
to work.

"J–Jesus, f–forgive me… a–accept me…" His words were slurred,
but they were surprisingly sweet to Josiah's ears.

The paramedics were looking grim. "Okay, let's go. We gotta go
now!" one of them said with urgency.

Josiah stepped back. As Jack was loaded into the back of the ambulance, Josiah heard a gurgling sound coming from him as he struggled to speak.

"April. T–tell April." Jack's voice was fading, but he had been
heard.

Josiah watched the ambulance gather speed and fly through the
night. The commotion around him took second place as his thoughts
dwelt on the man who lay, possibly dying. A man who, like the thief
on the cross, asked for a chance in paradise with the Son of God. He
felt extremely humbled, believing Jack would have his paradise, and if
God, who was perfectly holy, could forgive someone like Jack Roper,
then so could he.

*   *   *

As soon as she opened the door, Josiah stepped, like a breath of fresh air, into her parents' home. The slight coolness from his jacket penetrated her long-sleeved satin pyjamas as he wrapped his arms around her. He kissed her with such passionate abandon that she could scarcely breathe. Finally, he raised his head and searched her face with a new, possessive look she had not seen before.

"Are you sure you're okay?" he asked with intense seriousness.

"I'm sure," she assured him, leaning against his arms behind her.

"Are you sure you weren't hurt?"

"Josiah," she whispered fiercely, "I recall you and the police asking me that sufficiently last night. Please, I don't want you waking Mom." She moved out of his arms. "If you insist on coming over so early, then at least do it quietly."

She was smiling, and he was grinning from ear to ear. He brushed her cheek gently with one hand, then trailed it along the wild curls of her loose hair.

"You really are okay, aren't you?" His dark eyes had a tender look.

She reached up to touch his strong jaw line. "I'll be fine, I promise. The Lord has been good, and you need a shave."

She laughed lightly and evaded him as he reached for her once more. She led him into the dim kitchen, looking back at him as she went. He followed, looking like a hungry man, but not for the breakfast she was planning on making him and her mother.

She padded barefoot to the kitchen counter, then turned to face him. "I'll make something—" She didn't finish. He had her trapped at the counter, too close for comfort. He smelled wonderful and looked too handsome for his own good.

"Josiah," she pleaded, looking up at him. Her father was comatose, her mother was grieving, she had survived an abduction, but this man, just by his nearness, fuddled her thinking in ways she didn't understand.

"I thought, what if I had lost you?" he managed, his lips against her forehead. "What if I hadn't found you in time? I don't know how…" His voice shook, and he placed his hands on both sides of her head. He tilted her head back so he could look deeply into her eyes. There were tears in his.

His face appeared flushed, even through the brown of his skin. Her throat tightened and her eyes burned. He was crying for her. She had never seen him cry before, and the sight of his tears, now overflowing, washed her heart with an unfamiliar ache.

"Oh, Jose," she cried, and then it all poured out. She clung to him tightly as he held her close. She cried and cried, because what had happened in the last twenty-four hours now seemed more overwhelming than ever as the reality of it settled on her.

When she was able, she wiped his tears away with trembling hands while he kissed hers away. That's how Celia found them in her kitchen.

"*Mes enfants?*"

Elise turned her head to see her mother standing just inside the kitchen doorway, wrapped in her housecoat. She looked fragile and lonely. They both moved toward her.

Hours later, at Georgeton General Hospital, Elise and Josiah sat with David for a while, then left Celia there with Solomon. Celia had actually requested his presence and his prayers in her husband's ICU room.

Elise and Josiah went down to the floor where Danny Rowe was and walked hand in hand to his room. He was sitting up, looking at a magazine. His hair was standing on end, and he looked overtly bored with his inactivity.

His face lit up when he saw them. "Well, well, if it isn't the love birds. Hi, guys!"

Elise went over to him and gently hugged him, being mindful of his bandaged left shoulder. "Oh, Danny," she said, "I'm so glad you're going to be all right."

Josiah gently thumped him on his good shoulder from the other side of the bed. "It takes more than a bullet to put good old Dan out of commission." He also gave Danny a heartfelt hug.

"You two are a sight for sore eyes. I really hope I can get out of here soon. It's just a flesh wound, but they're worried about infection because I had a fever last night. Give me a break."

Elise scolded him. "It's for your own good, Danny. I, for one, want you whole. I was scared silly when I saw you go down. I never got to thank you, but thank you so much for rescuing me."

Danny seemed embarrassed. He pulled his hospital gown closer. "Elise, it was this big hunk of yours who did the rescuing. I just came along for the ride." He turned and glared at Josiah. "I told you to stay put. You could have gotten yourself killed."

Josiah looked down at him. "I'm not the one who was shot," he said mildly.

Danny frowned at him, then looked up at Elise. "You should have seen him go berserk when he saw Jack on the stairs. After that, he was deaf to anything I had to say." He looked back at Josiah. "If you ever tire of the world of buildings, consider police work."

Josiah joined Elise on her side of the bed. "Thanks, man. Seriously, I couldn't have done it without you. You're a great cop."

Danny nodded slowly, accepting the praise. "I'm just glad Elise is okay. I'm not so sure about Jack Roper."

Elise felt a mixture of emotions at the mention of Jack's name. She gently eased herself onto the side of Danny's bed. "Josiah told me what happened. Has anyone heard how he's doing?"

"Not good," Danny admitted. "I'm not even sure if he made it through the night."

"He had major internal bleeding," Josiah said from above her. His fingers were gently kneading the skin at the back of her neck.

"It's so sad," Elise declared. She looked at both men. Their eyes were averted. "What about April?"

Danny looked at her, his grey eyes filled with emotion. "She came to see me this morning and she was a mess." He winced from pain as he shifted slowly in the bed. "She blames herself some. She thinks she enabled him because she didn't always report his misdeeds."

Elise rose and moved toward the head of Danny's bed. "Are you okay, Danny? Can I do anything for you?" She knew his heart, as well as his body, was in pain.

Danny held up his good arm and smiled slightly. "No, Elise. Save all your ministrations for Josiah. If you try to fluff my pillows or anything like that, you'll cause me to black out from the pain."

Elise heard Josiah chuckle. She glared at Danny. "You watch too many movies. I wasn't going to fluff your pillows."

Danny threw a wise guy glance at Josiah. "Oh yeah? That's what April tried to do this morning. Nearly threw me into oblivion."

"I bet you didn't deny her, Dan," Josiah teased.

Danny laughed good-naturedly, then winced again. "Of course not. I didn't want to hurt her feelings."

Elise backed up against Josiah's solid form. "Men," she said in disgust. "Where is April now?"

Danny shook his head. "I'm not sure. She was upset about Dr. Everson, but she was downright frantic about you being kidnapped,

Elise. The investigator on the case had to question her, since the bullet from Dr. Everson was confirmed to have been from Jack's gun. Of course, now we all know that Jack, not Webster, was responsible."

Elise suddenly felt drained. "Poor April. Poor Webster," she breathed, but kept her thoughts about her father to herself. She still couldn't come to terms with his condition. She couldn't imagine letting go of him yet.

"Don't feel too sorry for Webster Myers," Danny said. "He had it coming by adding to the whole drama with his antics. He confused the whole investigation by stalking you. The first time you saw a pickup truck outside your new place, it was Jack. The second time, when Josiah came upon the other, it was Webster. And, of course, you know the peeping Tom was Webster."

Elise pushed her hands up to the sides of her face. "This is all too much for me. I just want to know where April is, then I'll go back and sit with my mother."

"I'm right here, Elise."

They all turned to look toward the doorway where April stood looking forlorn. Her eyes were red and her hands were clutching the straps of her handbag tightly. Her clothes were rumpled as if she had slept in them, but she seemed unaware of it.

"Jack died an hour ago," she informed them.

Even though Josiah and Danny had partially prepared Elise for the possibility of Jack's death, April's announcement still shocked her. She slowly walked toward April, even as she heard Danny's hoarse prompting.

"Go to her, Elise."

April's blue eyes were wide as she gazed into Elise's, then they filled with tears. Her lips trembled as Elise folded her into her arms, and she began to sob heartrendingly. Elise dared not move even when a nurse appeared at the doorway to check on Danny.

Chapter Twenty-Nine

Elise sat looking at her father. His hand felt cool and dry in hers. It was the end of visiting hours, and she had promised her mother she would stay until the end, if she would go home early and rest. Her mother did not look well, and she was not eating well. Elise desired so much to make it all better for them, but she was powerless. She could only support and pray.

"Daddy, as soon as you wake up, Josiah and I want you to help us furnish the house. It's going to be a huge job, and we definitely want your English sense of what's appropriate. Please don't let us do it on our own. Josiah's too ultra modern when it comes to this sort of thing, and I'm too flowery. As for Mom, she's too eccentric. She'd have the place full of antiques, and I can't abide antiques."

David remained silent and still with white sheets around him, tubes running to and from him, and machines blipping the only evidence of his continued life. The constant scent of antiseptic hung in the room as if knowing its rightful place. Her heart ached. She had prayed and prayed and willed him to awaken. God seemed silent on this front. Yet Solomon had said God's silence was not always His answer. Sometimes His answer was hidden in the silence, waiting to come out.

She sighed heavily and prepared to leave. She bent down to kiss her father's forehead. "I'll see you tomorrow, Dad. Sleep well. I'll be praying for you."

She turned to go, then paused. Had she seen his eyelids move? She held her breath and waited. Nothing. Perhaps it had been her imagination. She made her way out to the waiting room where she knew Josiah held vigil for her.

She didn't want him to go, but he would have to soon. Elise lay against Josiah, snug on her parents' family room couch. The lights were dim, and apart from them the house was silent. It was late and they had been talking for a while. It was as if they were trying to make up for lost and stolen time, trying to sort through the many recent events in order to focus on the future.

"How much longer are you off from school?" Josiah's voice rumbled in her ear. His fingers were threaded through hers and he held her securely with the other hand.

"It's another three weeks now. A whole month. My boss insisted that so much trauma needed so much time."

Josiah chuckled. "I wonder who tells people who work for themselves that they need so much time."

"Their wife or husband does," she whispered smartly. "If they're not married, maybe their secretary does."

"What about their fiancé?" he joked.

"That doesn't count. It's not permanent enough."

He puffed in disbelief. "A secretary is more permanent than a fiancé?"

She twisted her neck to look at him. "Fiancés come and go, but good secretaries are hard to find."

"You're being cruel, and if I had my way, we would elope."

She giggled, then accepted his kiss to silence her.

"I love you more than words can say," he declared. He moved the hand that was playing with her fingers to gently touch her cheek. "For me, you are it, now and always. You are my permanent permanence."

"That's so sweet," she said, smiling against his fingers, which now caressed her lips. "I promise you are also my permanent permanence."

"Will you go with me to Jack's funeral?" he asked hesitantly. His fingers were laced through hers again.

"Of course," she responded immediately. "Josiah, I hold no unforgiveness toward Jack. He gave himself over to something that held him captive. Something that wouldn't let him go. I'm so relieved he truly found freedom in the end."

"You believe that?"

"Yes. According to what you told me, yes."

Josiah sighed and shifted slightly. "Perhaps your time with him was for a greater purpose than we know. You said he ran from the hope you offered, but in the end he begged for that same hope."

Elise felt her eyes tear up. Wasn't it just like the Lord Jesus to take a wretched life and redeem it, even at the last moment? She sniffled.

"Are you crying?" Josiah asked, bending his head to see her face.

"No," she whispered.

"Liar," he countered. "It's okay, though. There are many people like Jack in the world, bound by their past, who need our prayers and our tears. Now, that peeping Tom Webster is another story."

"Josiah," she scolded, elbowing him slightly. "The Websters of this world also feel lonely and disenfranchised. They need our prayers and tears, too."

He was silent for a time, then couldn't seem to help it. "Sure, I'll pray for Webster Myers, but it will be a cold day in hell before I'll be able to drum up any tears for him."

"Josiah!" she exclaimed softly. He laughed out loud, and she struggled out of his arms. "Shh, you'll wake Mom," she gently scolded as she placed her hand firmly over his mouth. He grabbed hold of her wrist, then pulled her securely onto him.

"Baby, don't start what you can't finish," he challenged. His gaze held hers as strongly as his arms held her to him. Temptation pulled at her dangerously, and instinctively she knew it was the same for him. They remained motionless except for the intensity of their breathing. When his arms tightened around her, she knew he was losing the battle.

"Josiah," she spoke, trying to break the spell. "It's late. You should go now." For one breathtaking moment, she thought he wouldn't follow her lead, but then he let her go and eased her off himself before standing to his feet. He had his hands on his hips as he looked down at her standing before him. He smiled lopsidedly, then gently tapped her chin with one finger.

"To all our tomorrows," he declared lovingly.

"To all our tomorrows," she repeated. He took her hand and they walked out of the room and through the hall to the front door. There he gave her a bear hug and a brief kiss.

"I'm at the office tomorrow," he reminded her. "Will you come see me at lunch?"

"I will," she concurred gladly. "Solomon will sit with Mom then, so she won't be alone."

"I'm praying for your dad."

"I know," she said, looking down.

"Hey," he said, gently forcing her chin up with one hand. "Whatever happens, He'll get us through it. He'll get your mother through it. You've got to believe that nothing is outside His control."

"That He's not wringing His hands trying to figure out what to do," she said, smiling.

"Exactly," he affirmed strongly. "Before it happened, he knew it would. He allowed it for reasons we may never know. Ultimately, we have to trust Him."

After one last kiss, Elise waved him into the night. She stood in the semi-dark foyer, feeling lost. She looked toward the stairs and thought of her old room. How many more nights would she have to sleep there, wondering what news she would hear of her father? How many nights would she wonder about her mother, barely hanging on to living, seeming merely to survive?

"Please, God," she spoke into the empty foyer. "Please, will you show me what's to come, and prepare me for it? Please, Lord Jesus, prepare us for it."

She reached into the dark, knowing for whom she searched, but not knowing where to find him. Her hair hung in loose rivers down her front and back, and she wore a light, flowing, pale gown. Her feet were bare. The road she walked on was bumpy, but she felt a Presence guiding her around the ruts and bumps. Sometimes she stumbled a little, but then she felt the power of the Presence holding her up, sometimes lifting her up. Her thoughts were not just her own, for they were known to the One with her. She wasn't sure how, but she sensed Him with her as well as being part of her. She felt safe with Him. She didn't always know His thoughts, but sometimes she would have a deep understanding of His communion with her.

She yearned for that communion now to help her with her quest. There was so much fog, so many clouds. She couldn't see her way. Her heart and thoughts yearned for the way. She stood still, realizing that the Presence was showing her something.

She watched as the fog cleared away and the clouds parted above her head. She saw clearly. A tall man walked toward her from the distance. He appeared to have been on a journey because he had a sack flung over his back. He came closer, and she smiled as she recognized her father, the one she had been searching for. He had on tattered clothing and his feet were bare. When he reached her, he smiled gently, his eyes lighting up. Then he turned to the One beside her and laid his load at His feet. Her father got on his knees before the Presence. She did not know how long he stayed there, but when he rose, his face glowed with new life and vitality. He looked at her and held his hand out to her, smiling. She felt the strength of his love and care.

"I have been made whole," he declared in a hushed voice. "I have been made well in my body and my soul. I'll see you soon."

"But you're here with me. I can see you now," she responded, holding onto his hand.

"No," he said gently. "I'll see you soon."

Elise awoke slowly. It took a moment for her to sort through her dreams to reality. It had been so real, and she ached for her father. She sat up in bed and rested her back against the pillows. She couldn't shake the sense that she had been given a message. Did God speak to people through dreams as He had in ancient times? She looked over at her Bible on the bedside table. She reached for it and thumbed through the pages, then rested it on her lap. She picked up her watch, since her mother had left no electronics in her old room. It was 6:30 a.m., too early to call Solomon.

They all looked at her as if she had grown horns.

"God told you that your father would awaken?" Alisha asked gently.

"Yes," Elise insisted. She was having breakfast with Alisha, Keisha, April, and Bethany at the Sungs' house.

"Well, I believe that can happen," Keisha spoke up. She looked around Bethany's kitchen table at everyone. "My maternal grandmother used to dream all the time, and a lot of them came true."

April remained silent, but lowered the cup that had been poised under her mouth. She still appeared tired and frail. This gathering for encouragement was just as much for her as for Elise.

Alisha looked at Bethany, it seemed, for direction.

"Well, why don't you tell us about it?" Bethany suggested softly. Elise found encouragement in her soft brown eyes and gentle smile.

She took a deep breath and, without leaving out any details, relayed her dream to them. In the cozy warmth of Bethany's kitchen, the women listened with spellbound attention until she was finished.

"That's so beautiful." April was the first to speak. Elise looked at the rest, wondering if she should be feeling foolish. Somehow, she didn't. She felt a strength and boldness in her convictions.

"That's really out there," Keisha declared, then frowned. "Yet it sounds exactly like a God thing."

Alisha looked at Bethany, then at Elise. Doubt was etched on her face.

"Go ahead, Ali, I can take it," Elise said, trying to keep her tone light.

Instead, Bethany spoke up. "Elise, Keisha could be right. You, though, are the only one who knows what you sensed as you dreamed. You are the perfect one to know if you were given a spiritual insight or if you had just dreamed your heart's desire. God may not always give us what we want, but He promised to give us what we need."

The women remained silent for a moment, then Alisha spoke. "Okay, I'll withhold my verdict until the jury comes out—meaning, until your father wakes up."

Later, after breakfast was over, Elise stepped out of Bethany's powder room to find Alisha waiting for her outside the door. She cornered Elise, her green eyes full of concern.

"Lise, I didn't mean to make you feel bad about your dream. Heavens knows you have enough on your plate already. I just don't want you to get your hopes up only to have them dashed."

Elise touched her gently on the shoulder. "Ali, don't worry about it. If I've learned one thing in all of this, it's to not sweat the small stuff. I need all my friends to help keep me balanced and strong, and you've been very supportive, Ali. Thank you."

Alisha looked puzzled, as if she had not expected that answer, but before she could comment, Keisha appeared.

"I've got to go, Elise. Please take care, and I'll keep in touch so I know what's going on." She brushed past Alisha to give Elise a warm hug. "I really miss you at school, and those kids are going to drive me nuts with their daily concerns about you."

"Thanks, Keisha," Elise said as she returned the hug. She gently tugged at the length of freshly-done braids under her hand. "I really appreciate all you've done. The meals and everything."

Keisha's dark eyes flashed, and she waved off the praise. "Oh, don't even think of it. It's not every day I know people who get kidnapped and shot at. I just really hope and pray the best for you and your family."

"Thanks, Keisha."

"See you, Reds," Keisha said to Alisha as she hugged her goodbye.

"We'll see you around Keisha," Alisha promised.

"Wow," Elise said, looking at her watch. "I really have to get going, too. I promised Mom I would be back by ten. She insisted I didn't miss this breakfast with all of you, that she'd be fine with Solomon. She seems to take a lot of comfort in Solomon's visits. She doesn't seem very happy with her pastor right now."

"Are you leaving?" Bethany asked, joining them in the hall.

"Elise has to go back to the hospital," Alisha answered, "but I'll hang around for a while. I–I need some advice."

Elise laughed lightly. "She means she wants to have some counsel about her and Rick. She's afraid to go to Solomon, so she's coming to you. I told her Solomon likes Rick, and not to be—"

"Elise," Alisha cautioned. Her eyes looked unconvincingly fierce and her lips were set in a firm line.

"Well, it's true," Elise defended.

"What's wrong with Rick?" Bethany asked curiously.

"Nothing," both younger women answered at the same time. They laughed, then Alisha softened. She directed her concerns to Bethany.

"He's just, you know, a little rough around the edges. I don't want to go into a commitment with him blindly, so I thought to get some, well, advice."

Elise's heart went out to her friend. She seemed so vulnerable. She was most definitely in love with Rick Phillips.

Bethany chuckled softly and eased her arm around Alisha's shoulder. "It's good for you to be concerned," she began in her soft Scottish accent. "After Elise and April go, I'll tell you a few things about what Solomon and I think about your Rick. I promise you won't be disappointed."

Before Elise left, Bethany took her aside and said for her ears only, "Make sure and tell Solomon your dream."

Celia didn't understand why, but she always felt comforted when Solomon Sung came to see her husband. She suspected he was there for her more than anything else. Elise, Josiah, and Adam probably didn't know how much she was aware of their worry over her. She knew that at some point she would have to start living again, but the time of release had not yet arrived. She needed her vigils by her husband's bedside. She didn't know how much longer she would have with him.

Elise had returned from breakfast to stay with her. She had sensed a restlessness in her daughter, so when Solomon put in an appearance, she was only too happy to release her. When Elise asked to talk with him outside the room, Celia didn't question, before or after, what it had been about.

Now that Elise was off to see Josiah, she felt free to focus on David. It had taken much out of her to process the news of her daughter's abduction. Her upset, at the news being kept from her, had been short-lived when she saw the vulnerable look on Elise's face. Elise had been through so much, and the others had only been trying to spare her further grief. How could she remain perturbed with them? How could she not take time to offer her child the care she was reserving for her husband? She could do nothing for him right now, but when Elise was with her she tried her best to care for her.

Celia glanced at Solomon's big form by her husband's bedside, and knew he was silently communing with his Lord for them both. She was grateful.

"You look tired," Josiah commented as Elise toyed with her sandwich. She had brought lunch to his office, but was hardly eating her share. She raised her brown eyes to look at him. She sighed loudly.

"I just wish this was all over. I feel like I'm in limbo." She shoved her lunch aside on his desk. She was slouched in his leather chair, and it seemed to swallow her up. He could tell she was losing weight and that worried him; she didn't have much to lose in the first place.

He got up and went to her, swivelling the chair so she faced him.

"Come here," he directed and took hold of her arms to pull her up. Afterwards, he took her place and pulled her onto his lap. With the chair swivelled so its back was to the desk, they looked out the office window together.

"Tell me what I can do for you. You know I'll do anything." He spoke into the hair at the top of her head. The familiar fragrance of her wavy strands filled him with delight and wonder that she belonged to him. He had no doubt he would do as much as give his life for her.

She reached up to touch his cheek, briefly. "What else can I ask? You do so much already."

"I'll do more," he promised.

"No, Josiah," she said, gently shaking her head. "You have work. I'll feel even worse if you're strained."

He tightened his hold on her, not knowing what else to say. He noticed how the flow of her tan, tweed skirt covered his legs as well.

Such a simple sight held such great significance, a metaphor of two lives merging as one. Yes, he would do anything for her.

"May I tell you something?" she asked in a small voice.

"Anything," he responded, kissing her hair.

What she proceeded to tell him was not remotely close to anything he had anticipated. The dream she relayed was so vivid and intriguing, it gave him goose bumps.

"I think God gave me a message that Dad would be okay." She twisted slightly so she could see his face. "I feel it with every fibre of my being." She stared at him, waiting for his response. He felt inadequate, and chose his words carefully.

"I do believe God speaks to us in many ways, including dreams. The Bible speaks of it. I guess, if you're not sure because this sort of thing has never happened before, then you wait to see how it plays out. Then you'll know for next time."

She was silent, and he was feeling uncomfortable. He didn't want to let her down when she was already feeling so low. Her next words surprised him.

"Thanks, Jose. You're such a wise man." She turned to settle back against him. "The Bible does say a prophet is known by the prophecies that come true, so a dreamer must also be known by the dreams that come true."

His response was hindered by a soft knock on his office door. Elise immediately stood up. He chuckled at her obvious embarrassment and rose at a more leisurely pace.

"Ow!" he responded to the swat she directed to his upper arm. He noticed his father through the glass door, then turned to grin at her. "I hope my father didn't see his future daughter-in-law being abusive."

Adam opened the door and stepped in when he saw Josiah's approach. His face seemed to hold a cautious excitement.

"Elise. Josiah. David is showing signs of waking up!"

*   *   *

David struggled to get to the light, but couldn't seem to get there, no matter how hard he tried. Everything in him strained away from the darkness at his left, even as he felt its forceful pull as if it had all rights to him. He felt weary and lonely. He cried out to the light, desperate for a way to it, a way out of the no-place he was in. Slowly a difference eased its way into his senses. He felt a stronger presence from the light. He waited in hopeful anticipation. There were no words or sounds that he could hear, but yet the message was clear. The message of hope from the light—no, the Light—was clear. He yearned to go to the Light, but he felt hindered. Then he felt a sharp pain in his head that started to spread through him. He gasped, breathing heavily, before hearing voices.

David suddenly felt the weight of his body. His mouth felt full and his tongue trapped. He felt his eyelids twitch as he tried to open his eyes. He needed to see. Where was the Light? His eyes opened. There was a big man standing there. David peered at him, ignoring the sounds around him. David knew him, but couldn't remember his name. Something from the man drew him, pulled at him. Then he realized what it was. This man had a presence within him. It was the presence of the Light.

Chapter Thirty

Elise no longer played self-consciously. The beautiful music, flowing from the ivory keys under her fingers, filled Hope Alive Church and blended harmoniously with the voices of the choir. She led and carried the voices with her music. When Alisha stepped from the choir to do a solo, Elise wanted to weep from the beauty of it all.

All of those who were close to her were here. Only her father was absent as he lay, still recuperating, in Georgeton General Hospital. Two weeks had passed since her father had awakened, and Dr. Gaho Brant predicted that, miraculously, David Everson would have a full recovery.

During the rousing applause, Elise left the piano and went to join her mother and Josiah. She received her mother's glowing smile as she sat between them.

"That was so very beautiful," Celia stressed. "You make my heart so glad."

Elise squeezed her mother's hand, then found Josiah's. His palm was warm as his hand enveloped hers. She turned her head to catch his wink.

"Great job," he whispered. Elise smiled her thanks, then gave her attention to Solomon Sung as he opened the Word of God.

His sermon delved into the awesome knowledge of the presence of God in us. The presence of God to change us from the inside out was an amazing concept and an amazing truth!

Elise thought of all her family and friends, and the changes wrought over the last six months. In some ways, it seemed like six years. Next week, she would be back teaching. Life would continue on: she would celebrate the recovery of her father with her mother, she would see the house decorated and completely furnished, and she would see Josiah moved in. The list went on. But she knew a difference. She had been changed—an incredible, lasting change that would probably not have happened without all that had transpired, the good and the bad. She was thankful.

The late autumn air was cold and crisp as Elise held the door of *Ma Maison* opened for another guest. The guest was Rick.

"Where is he?" she asked him, mindful of the group of people in the kitchen behind her.

Rick grinned boyishly. "Now, don't worry your pretty little head, Elise. He'll be here."

"Is he here yet?" Celia asked, walking up to them from the kitchen. She had remembered to close the kitchen doors to keep everyone contained.

"No," Elise said, looking at Rick pointedly. Suddenly, they heard a sound from outside.

Rick clapped his hands together. "That's my boy now. All right, Elise, you go organize the masses."

Elise took hold of her mother's hand. "Remember, Rick, tell him I want him in the kitchen."

"Will do," Rick said, waving her and Celia away. "Now, get."

Elise giggled and moved quickly with her mother toward the kitchen doors. She felt like a kid about to win a prize. She and Celia stuffed into the kitchen with the rest who had come with them from church. Josiah had no idea.

Everyone seemed to hold their breath at the sounds beyond the kitchen doors. It was an overcast afternoon, and they had turned the lights off because of the French doors' translucency. Elise heard a snort that sounded like Alisha, then a shush from someone else. Her patience was about at an end when the kitchen doors were pulled opened.

"*Surprise!*"

Elise watched Josiah's eyes light up and his mouth fall open. He was still in his fall jacket.

"What the blazes—" he started.

"Happy birthday! Congratulations!"

Everyone clapped and cheered, then started singing Happy Birthday. Elise went to him and stood on tiptoes to throw her arms around him.

"We're celebrating your architectural license as well! It's been a long time coming!" she yelled into his ear. His arm encircled her waist and together they faced the group of about thirty people as they finished the song.

Josiah was smiling. "Well, I don't know what to say. I'm totally floored."

"Just don't stay on the floor too long. We want to party!" Danny called out. After that, everyone poured out into the hall congratulating Josiah. He suffered under their ministrations for a while, then held his hands up and bellowed.

"Okay, everyone! Just give me a moment. I need to bring something in."

Elise watched him quickly walk out the front door. She looked around, wondering where Rick was. For that matter, where was her mother? April came to stand beside her.

"He looked really surprised," she commented. Her skin was slightly flushed, and she seemed so much better. For a week after Jack's funeral, she had been a recluse. This was her first real outing since then.

"Yes, he was," Elise agreed, watching the door. It opened and she nearly lost her balance. Her hands flew up to her mouth.

"Daddy!" she half-squealed, half-sobbed. She looked from her father to Josiah. He stood behind her father's wheelchair. Her mother came in, followed by Rick.

"Surprise, sweetheart," Josiah said softly. His eyes held a warm, tender look.

April's gentle nudge finally set her in motion. With tears now overflowing, she rushed to her father, falling on her knees before him. He stroked her hair gently.

"Your mother and Josiah were determined I should be here for this," David murmured.

She looked up at him through the tears. He was smiling ever so gently, and his blue eyes shimmered with unshed tears. He looked well.

"Oh, Dad, I'm so glad to see you out. I–it means so much." Suddenly, she stood and leaned over him. "Will you be okay?"

"He's okay, Elise. Don't worry about him," Alisha said from behind her.

Elise turned to see the sparkle in Alisha's eyes.

"Besides, I'll have my eyes on him the whole time," she promised.

Even with Alisha's eyes on her father, Elise still watched him diligently the whole afternoon.

She noticed Solomon and Bethany spending a lot of time with him, too. Of course, her mother hardly left his side. She was glad to know that he had been discharged with homecare provisions. He still had some pain and stiffness in his left chest and shoulder areas, and his breathing was a little laboured at times. She remembered, after he had awoken in the hospital, how he had kept pointing at Solomon. When he had been free from the ventilator tubing, he had struggled to speak. "I want what he has. I want the Light." He had said it over and over until the staff had to pay attention. They had wanted Solomon to leave the room, but thought better of it after they had suggested it and her father grew frantic.

The Light. Her father had encountered Jesus Christ while in a coma, and had received Him while awake. God *had* spoken to her through a dream.

The party lasted well into the evening, but Alisha and Rick left early with Celia and David. Josiah felt grateful for so much. He had been truly surprised here, in his sparsely furnished house. Everyone had been in such a festive mood. They had all parked in the nearest neighbour's yard before hiking over to his property. Leave it to Elise to already know the neighbours well enough to ask such a favour. The food had been great and everyone had brought a dish to share.

He looked around the dining room, which opened up to the kitchen nook. Elise was doing a great job of adding more pieces to the house. It was just as well she had been off school. She had brought scores of furniture books and magazines into the hospital to her father. After getting suggestions from her father, she would come and accost him so they could make decisions together—and, of course, so he could pay for those decisions. They had managed just one argument throughout all the house decorating and furnishing decisions. Money. She was peeved that he didn't want her to spend any of hers. He hadn't understood until she had explained that it made her feel as if it wasn't really her house. He'd easily caved, and offered to let her purchase all bathroom decor and supplies. He had stayed clear from any mention of the kitchen. Alisha had a bridal shower planned with that theme in mind, and had threatened him with mental anguish if Elise so much as bought one piece of cutlery. One didn't argue with a redhead on a mission.

He went into the foyer to join Elise and April. They had been in deep conversation as April waited for Danny. Danny had brought her and was taking her home. Not surprisingly, after Jack's death, April had began softening toward Danny. No doubt, his injury at her deceased husband's hand also played a role.

"So, they're doing fine?" Elise was asking April.

"They really are, Elise. I think they didn't bond with him enough to miss him. They know he's dead, but it hasn't seemed to affect their day to day. I just decided on the counselling just to be sure." She paused and smiled at Josiah as he stood behind Elise.

"You're doing a great job with those girls, April."

"Thanks, Josiah. By the grace of God, I hope to continue."

336

"With maybe a little help," Josiah suggested, nodding toward Danny's approaching figure.

April turned to look. She looked back at them, blushing.

"Well, it looks like we're the last to go, April. Are you ready?" Danny asked, oblivious to all that had just transpired.

"Sure," she responded, avoiding Josiah's eye. She embraced Elise, then gave Josiah a quick hug.

"Thanks, Dan," Josiah said, giving him a hug. "How's the arm?"

Dan rotated his shoulder slowly. "Almost good as new. I decided I've had enough of paperwork. Time to get back into the action."

"You've got to make sure it's the right time, Danny," April reminded gently.

Danny winked at Josiah. "Don't you just love it when they fawn over you?"

The men laughed as they walked to the door; the women rolled their eyes.

After the door was shut, Josiah leaned heavily against it. He opened his arms for Elise to walk into his embrace. He squeezed her tightly.

"Thanks so much for everything. I had no idea."

She looked up at him with sleepy eyes. "*You* had no idea? What I did doesn't match what you did for me. Seeing my father out of that hospital was the best gift you could have given me."

He smiled, revelling in the warmth of her praise. "That wasn't a real biggy. He had to be discharged anyway. I just persuaded Dr. Brant to do it a little earlier. I do aim to please."

She laughed and rested her head against his chest. The feel of her against him reminded Josiah of coming home. He would move into their house just before Christmas, but it wouldn't truly be home for him until she joined him about five months after.

He suddenly remembered something. "You know your cross necklace?"

"Mm-hmm," she murmured. She was almost a dead weight against him.

"Do you know they can't find it at the station? I'm pretty sure it got there, but no one seems to know where it is."

That got her attention. "Really?"

"Yeah. It's odd." He ran his palms across her back, smoothing the heavy fabric of her blouse. He remembered something else.

"There's something I've been wanting to do," he said.

"Josiah," she complained as he moved, leaving her without support.

"One sec," he insisted, then reached into his pants pocket. He pulled out a small vial of oil.

"What's that?" she asked.

"I borrowed Solomon's anointing oil."

She looked at him and the vial, puzzled. She reached up to tighten the band holding her hair at the base of her neck, then gestured toward the vial.

"So what are you going to do with it?"

"Come on," he said, taking her hand. He pulled one of the double doors opened and went out, pulling her behind him.

"Josiah, it's cold and dark," she cried.

"This is important," he told her. "Now, look up at the top of the door post." When she did, he opened the vial and dabbed a generous amount on his fingers. He reached up and ran his fingers along the wood across the top of the door posts.

"I'm anointing the house," he explained. "The oil symbolizes the presence of the Holy Spirit in our house."

"God in our house?" she asked.

"Exactly."

"Don't you have to say something?" Elise asked.

He pondered for moment, then the words flowed, "I anoint our house—our home—in the name of the Father, Son, and Holy Spirit. This symbolizes our desire to have your Presence with us, always, oh Lord."

He closed the vial and slipped it back into his pocket. Elise took his oily fingers and wiped them with a tissue from her pocket.

"That's perfect," she declared. "With God in my body-house and my home-house, no matter what happens, it's perfect."

He laughed, feeling jubilant. He reached for Elise, marvelling at the smile lighting up her beautiful face. "I think we need to seal that with a kiss," he said. And they did.

Josiah stood waiting for his first glimpse of her. Lily and Mya Roper, who looked adorable in their frilly white dresses, were being held in one place by April who was dressed the same as Alisha and Keisha. He knew the women looked beautiful, but not much else had registered.

The Sung twins, Joshua and Jordan, stood quietly by Rick, Danny, and Gavin. Josiah had gotten to know Gavin quite well after he had immigrated to Canada four months ago, under Keisha's sworn statement that he would be a great architectural asset to Alexander's Contracting and Design. She had not lied.

Josiah caught his father's eye where he sat beside Celia and her cousin from Africa. Adam smiled and nodded his head encouragingly. Josiah glanced nervously at Solomon, who finally gave the signal to begin the music for the wedding march. The glass doors, which were covered by some type of white fabric, were opened. He held his breath at the vision of his glorious bride. He had never had a more surreal moment.

Elise heard the music and turned to cling to her father. He patted her veiled back gently.

"It's your moment now, my love." His eyes were smiling along with his mouth. He obviously had no doubts about giving his only child away.

Elise took a deep breath as the doors before her opened, and she saw, through her wispy veil, the long flower-strewn walk before her. Her father's steady arm and the beautiful music helped propel her along. She knew the sanctuary was full of guests, but found it hard to focus on any particular person. Spring flower bouquets, in the colour theme of white, green, and pale apricot, graced the shoulders of the aisle seats and the decorative posts where her beloved waited for her.

Everything paled now that she could see his face. His eyes were focused on her, and the smile that slowly etched his features were answered by her own smile. She gripped her father's arm and tried to keep in step under the layers of white satin and lace that seem to surround her from head to toe. Just before she reached Josiah, she saw her mother, who now shared her faith, standing before a front row seat. The glance they shared spoke volumes.

Elise felt the pressure of her father's hand upon her, reminding her to stop as Solomon asked the question, "Who gives this woman to be married?"

Her father answered firmly. "Her mother and I."

When her hand was taken by Josiah, she felt the pressure of tears behind her eyes. Her lips trembled, with a mind of their own, as she witnessed the look of love and tenderness in his gaze.

Throughout Solomon's admonitions, Elise struggled to focus, wanting only to be lost in Josiah's gaze. His eyes spoke many things to her. Finally the twins relinquished their guardianship of the wedding bands, and she became Mrs. Josiah David Alexander. Finally, she had come home.

The rows of trees along the sides of the driveway were mysteriously beautiful in the moonlight. When the sight of *Ma Maison* greeted them, Elise felt a wondrous thrill.

Josiah parked their new car in the driveway, and they sat gazing, aided by the ground lights, at the spring flowers that dotted the landscape. Josiah brought her hand to his lips; the hand he hadn't let go since they finally escaped from the wedding party still going full swing. They had only taken the trouble to say goodbye to their parents, and to Jake and Margaret, who had practically chased them down.

Elise sat contentedly with her gown surrounding her, practically filling the front seat of the car.

Alisha, her maid of honour, had removed her veil hours ago. The white sequined, flared sleeves at her wrist contrasted sharply with the black of Josiah's suit.

"Welcome home," Josiah said softly.

She smiled across at him, her handsome prince. She reached with her free hand to touch his face. "It was too beautiful."

"Yes," he agreed.

"It almost hurts," she continued. "I'm so grateful for all of God's gifts. I hope to carry the memories of the good to help me in the bad times."

Josiah chuckled and kissed her hand again before reaching into the glove compartment to pull something out. He held her silver necklace with the cross pendant for her to see. It glimmered in the moonlight.

"My necklace. Where did you get it?" Elise still couldn't explain how it had come undone during her drive with Jack, but, at the time, she had kept it hidden in her palm until its deliberate fall in the Alexanders' old house.

Josiah shook his head slowly. "You will not believe this."

"Try me," she said, leaning toward him.

"Webster Myers had it. He took it from the police station, right from under their noses. He was still being held there when Danny brought it in after the truth was found out. Webster was released and, I guess, took this with him."

Elise was horrified. "Josiah, you don't think he'll bother me again?"

"I don't think so. The very fact that he returned it says something. Apparently he had waited for Solomon outside the church after the ceremony and handed it to him."

Elise stared at her husband dumbly.

"He also gave Solomon a message for us. He was returning the necklace with the knowledge that one door was forever closed to him, but perhaps he would return to the message of the cross, which offered another door."

Elise blinked rapidly. She didn't know what to think. Josiah hung the chain from the rear-view mirror. The cross dangled gently. They both stared at it.

"Maybe we should leave it there to remind us of something," Elise remarked.

"Other than God's grace? What?"

"I don't know. I'll think of something."

Josiah laughed loudly. He pushed his door opened and came around to her side. "I don't think life with you will ever be dull, Mrs.

Alexander. Come on, we need to rest. We have a big trip ahead of us tomorrow."

Elise accepted his assistance from the car, then he bent to pull yards of white satin from the front seat.

"Is that all we're going to do tonight? Rest?"

He straightened and looked at her curiously, then searchingly. The longer he stared at her, the more nervous she felt. A slow smile spread across his lips.

"What do you think?" he finally asked, then went back around to the driver's side and got in. "Wait for me on the porch," he called to her as he drove the car toward the garages.

Elise bundled the length of her gown into her arms and made her way up to the porch. Suddenly, the front door opened and Josiah appeared from inside the house. He strode purposefully toward her, and before she could utter a word, held her face with both hands and kissed her breathless.

Afterwards, he picked her up, volumes of gown and all, and walked into the house. The door slammed shut behind them. Only they and God were in the house.